MALORY'S *MORTE DARTHUR*

THE NEW MIDDLE AGES

BONNIE WHEELER, *Series Editor*

The New Middle Ages presents transdisciplinary studies of medieval cultures. It includes both scholarly monographs and essay collections.

PUBLISHED BY PALGRAVE:

MALORY'S *MORTE DARTHUR*

REMAKING ARTHURIAN TRADITION

Catherine Batt

palgrave

First published 2002 by PALGRAVE™
175 Fifth Avenue, New York, N.Y.10010 and
Houndmills, Basingstoke, Hampshire RG21 6XS.
Companies and representatives throughout the world.

PALGRAVE is the new global publishing imprint of St. Martin's Press
LLC Scholarly and Reference Division and Palgrave Publishers Ltd.
(formerly Macmillan Press Ltd.).

ISBN 0-312-22998-4

Library of Congress Cataloging-in-Publication Data
Batt, Catherine.
Malory's Morte Darthur : remaking Arthurian tradition / Catherine Batt.
    p.   cm.—(The new Middle Ages series)
  Includes bibliographical references and index.
  ISBN 0–312–22998–4
  1. Malory, Thomas, Sir, 15th cent. Morte d'Arthur 2. Malory, Thomas,
Sir, 15th cent.—Technique.   3. Arthurian romances—History and
criticism.   4. Romances, English—History and criticism.   5. Knights
and knighthood in literature.   6. Kings and rulers in literature.
7. Narration (rhetoric) 8. Rhetoric, Medieval. I. Title: Morte
Darthur.   II. Title.   III. New Middle Ages.

PR 2045.B38   2002
823'.2—dc21

                                                    2001052308

A catalogue record for this book is available from the British Library.

Design by Letra Libre, Inc.

First edition: May 2002
10 9 8 7 6 5 4 3 2 1

Printed in the United States of America.

For my parents

CONTENTS

SERIES EDITOR'S FOREWORD

The New Middle Ages contributes to lively transdisciplinary conversations in medieval cultural studies through its scholarly monographs and essay collections. This series provides engaging work in a contemporary idiom about precise (if often diverse) practices, expressions, and ideologies in the Middle Ages. In this ground-breaking, theoretically informed study of the late-fifteenth-century *Le Morte Darthur,* Catherine Batt reconfigures our perception of Malory as an athletic and intellectually adroit reader of available English and French Arthurian materials and models. Batt is keenly sensitive to the historical contexts and cultural imbrications of late-medieval vernacular texts, and she grounds her analysis of Malory's reading practices in theoretical and material terms. As she says, Malory "tests literary conceptualizations of history, nationalism, gender, and selfhood, and considers the failures of social and legal institutionalizations of violence, in a critique of literary and of social order." Malory mediates literary traditions just as he meditates on the uses (and usefulness) of literature. Thus Malory's dismantling and remaking of history of King Arthur and his realm is a project fraught with tension and instability. Batt deftly details ways in which Malory recuperates the past without nostalgia but with profound emotional engagement. This remarkably cogent and challenging study establishes a new grid on which we can continue to build a richer understanding of the later Middle Ages.

Bonnie Wheeler
Southern Methodist University

ACKNOWLEDGMENTS

Critical works tend to replicate their subject of study, and this book has had its share of deferral, divagation, unhap Malory could not have imagined, and authorial cries for good deliverance. For helping me to bring the work to a good end after all, I should like to thank friends, among them former and current colleagues, who listened to ideas and read drafts of various chapters: Fiona Becket, Julia Boffey, David Fairer, Jennifer Goodman, Francis O'Gorman, and Elizabeth Maslen. I owe a special debt to Shirley Chew and to Brian Glover, wise critics and generous friends. Thanks to Bonnie Wheeler, general editor of the series, for her enthusiasm and support for the project, and to Meg Weaver, production editor at Palgrave, for patiently overseeing its progress from typescript to book.

I am grateful to staff at the British Library, at the Bibliothèque Nationale, Paris, and at the John Rylands University Library of Manchester, for allowing me to consult manuscripts, early printed books, and microfilms in their collections.

The jacket illustration of folio 435r of British Library MS Additional 59678 is reproduced by permission of the British Library. My thanks to the School of English, University of Leeds, for a grant to pay for the photographic and copyright costs involved, and for grants for various library visits. In several paragraphs in chapters two, three, and four, I draw on material published in my earlier article, "Malory and Rape," *Arthuriana* 7.3 (1997): 78–99, and I thank Bonnie Wheeler, as journal editor, for permission to do so.

PREFACE

For, lyke as wynter rasure dothe allway arace and deface grene summer, so
faryth hit by unstable love in man and woman, for in many persones there
ys no stabylité: for we may se all day, for a lytyll blaste of wyntres rasure,
anone we shall deface and lay aparte trew love, for lytyll or nowght, that
coste muche thynge. Thys ys no wysedome nother no stabylité, but hit ys
fyeblenes of nature and grete disworshyp, whosomever usyth thys [. . .] But
the olde love was nat so.[1]

The "May passage" (3:1119.1–3:1120.13) is one of the most famous of
Malory's apparently original interpolations in the last section of the *Morte
Darthur,* but critical tradition also finds it puzzling, a source of interpretive
confusion.[2] Yet, this passage is central to how the *Morte* configures the relation between narrator, subject matter, and imagined reader, and is therefore crucial to an understanding of Malory's method in general. In the
above extract, the narrator, discussing the nature of human love, invokes
the wisdom and stability of the past, of which Arthur's days are exemplary,
in order to contrast its self-restraint with present incontinence. In Arthur's
days, deference, mutual respect, and abstinence characterized relationships,
but now we precipitately destroy the once valuable commodity of "trew
love." Such behavior is the curse of modern sexual and social interaction,
"no wysedome nother no stabylité." It seems odd to have the narrator here
judge, and find wanting, modern human behavior against the mores of a
story that often owes its very existence to the declared necessity, sometimes
acknowledged, sometimes covert, of gratifying (usually male) desire. The
Morte presents a highly conventional self-justifying narrative of desire in
the account of the circumstances surrounding Arthur's conception, where
the impatient Uther, anxious for immediate satisfaction, literally falls ill
"for angre and for love of fayre Igrayne" (1:8.11–12).[3] But to recall this
episode from Arthur's days, as the May passage would seem to urge, only
makes us aware of the distance between textual event and the later apparently moralizing summary of it.

This is not the only disquieting aspect of the passage. In traditional rhetorical terms, a May topos invokes love and its renewal, and even if an author such as Chaucer deploys it playfully, or negatively, it usually reassures the reader, providing a site in and from which to place the action and interpret the text. To some extent, these lines fulfill this latter function, as the narrator encourages his audience to assess the significance of the tale from a historically aware perspective. Recent (serious) work on this passage has sought to explain its extraordinariness by pointing out how Vinaver, in his editing of the Winchester manuscript, has skewed our responses by making it introductory to the episode he calls "The Knight of the Cart," whereas in the manuscript, as in the concluding chapter to Book 18 of Caxton's edition, it functions as the ending to the previous sequence of adventures.[4] But this excavation of editorial structural dislocation only partially accounts for the passage's disjunctions and problems. My purpose here is to trace those problems and to examine their implications for the broader structure and concerns of the *Morte* proper.

In the first instance, the lines create a particular community of readers for the text and set up specific terms for the audience's reception of the material. It exhorts that community—in this case, those of us, men and women, who are "true lovers," those of us who are, by implication, prepared to engage with the story—to respond in an appropriately sympathetic way to the characters' emotions. Yet, the effect of the passage as a whole is ambiguous. On one level, the topos and the meditation the narrator develops from it constitute, for the reader, a point of contact with the narrative. We even appear to share a privileged viewpoint with the writer. But while the topos is a means of access to the nature of the story and of its values, contextually it is far from comforting. This is not simply because the explicit view of the past in this passage correlates uneasily with the instability, also evident elsewhere in the *Morte,* that marks both past event and its conceptualization.

By invoking "wisdom" and "stability," the narrator marks out these virtues as desirable, but in effect draws our attention to their absence, from the past as we have experienced it through the book and also from a disillusioned time present in which the author invites us to share. Yet, as a rhetorical "set piece," the May passage also exposes as complex the narrator's presentation of the tale, and our relation, as readers, to the narrative, to its central characters, and to the language that supposedly affords us access to its meaning. We have then to tease out the interpretive purpose of the May passage, to assess whether its disjunctions engage or alienate us. The narratorial voice exhorts readers to positive recollection, by means of a metaphor of cyclic renewal that illuminates human behavior and responsibility. But near-simultaneous with the process of recuperation is the

act of careless "negligence," a weak-willed response to adverse external circumstance—"wyntres rasure"—that serves to cancel out "trew love." The
narrator appeals to our sense of emotional engagement, only to implicate
us morally and culturally. We are not simply unmindful of true love; the
terms describing our destructive forgetfulness, "deface" and "lay aparte,"
invoke the erasure and disregarding of manuscript witness,[5] which is inca-
pable of partaking in nature's regenerative cycle. Material access to memory appears lost through "natural" processes and through human failures
alike, with little hope of recuperation, whether of cultural artifact or moral
integrity. For the narrator figuratively conflates betrayals at the level of individual personal intimacy with a collective failure to preserve the documentation of a manuscript culture, a failure in which, with his "loss" of the
"very mater of Shevalere de Charyot" (3:1154.12–13), the narrator participates (though, paradoxically, in disrupting and curtailing the French narrative, that particular instance of loss also preserves a particular chivalric
integrity for Launcelot). And both cultural and individual "betrayals" are,
we learn, concomitant on lack of "worship."

  This conflation raises questions about the relationship between literature
and life, to uncomfortable effect. As an inscribed readership, we are unhap-
pily positioned between an appeal to measure our own accountability in a
postlapsarian world and a denunciation of our instability, which latter failing, if accurate, would seem to obstruct any moral awareness and obviate
any such appeal. The violence and destructiveness attributed to both reader
and writer, simultaneous with the recuperation (and failure of recuperation)
of story and of emotional engagement, further displace moral agency onto
the reader at the same time as they occlude investigation of those manifestations of physical violence that form the greater part of the narrative
proper. In this way, the narrator projects onto the reader issues one might
want him more properly to address in the text itself. The vocabulary of
"worship" posits a conflation of readerly and chivalric integrity that becomes explicit as the narrator develops his theme. But the constitution of
the inscribed readership itself changes in the course of the May passage as
it partially accommodates the reader within the Morte's social vision. The
narrator writes of the nobility of love in the hearts of man and woman, later
qualified ethically and socially as "worshypfull man" and "worshypfull
woman."[6] But his amplification quickly re-casts the reader in a masculine
role within a hierarchical Arthurian society in which self-assertive, self-
justifying violence is natural to social interaction and to chivalric identity:
"But firste reserve the honoure to God, and secundely thy quarell muste
com of thy lady. And such love I calle vertuouse love" (3:1119.28–30). The
narratorial voice here reproduces uncritically the Morte's general tendency
to assume love as a motive for violence, and violence as a tender of love.

The argument even implies that acts of violence play an important role in the maintenance of sexual fidelity because they are part of the continued deferral of love's consummation, a consummation for which, warns the narrator, modern men and women are overeager. In then shifting attention from public masculine militaristic modes of defining and expressing love and "worship" to the instability and shame engendered by the instant gratification of sexual appetite, here the symptom of a modern degeneracy, the narrator bypasses the ethical and moral problems he himself introduces through his link between love and arms.

In the May passage we are, as "masculinized" readers, made answerable for questions of love and violence inherent but not resolved in Malory's work. Implicit in our positioning is not simply the burden of interpretation but a responsibility for the constitution of the text itself. So the text implies a connection between our supposed preference, over deferral of sexual activity and dilation of narrative, for the consummation of sexual love and the destruction of manuscripts and the stories they contain.[7] The narrator offers us an exemplary reading of the Arthurian world, and as he does so he takes us to task, both for his own, partial, investment in things Arthurian, and for the difficulties of translating that investment into lived experience. We are invited to endorse the exemplarity of Guinevere's character that here anticipates narrative closure—"whyle she lyved she was a trew lover, and therefor she had a good ende" (3:1120.12–13)—but the apparent lack of logic in this last line suggests a gap between the Arthurian world of the imagination and the Arthurian world of the text. The May passage's prescriptions for the culturally implicated reader exacerbate this gap, for, rather than "explain" the *Morte* to us, it instead offers, in its construction of the reader, a mirroring of its own hermeneutic difficulties. Later narrative appeals to the reader will make clear that in this, the May passage is not a textual aberration but paradigmatic of the *Morte's* method. I would argue then that this passage is important for the way in which it signals concerns integral to the *Morte;* the definition of the individual through sex and violence, violence as narrative impetus, the problematic relation between the sexes, the occasionally fluid nature of gender identification, and the reader's implicit role in and responsibility for the structuring of the narrative.

A contradictory representation of reader response and engagement emerges in the last books. Contradiction in representation does not of course confine itself in the text to the constructed readership, but addresses to and about readers are especially significant because of the central structural importance Malory's work explicitly accords reading. The reader reception mentioned above is also that of the *Morte* itself, for the narrator presents his writings to us largely as readings of sources taking place in intermittently defined and designated cultural, literary, and stylistic contexts.

The narrative can be partial and subjective, sometimes reproducing the story only haphazardly. The narrator comments several times on the declared physical problems of retrieving a complete Arthurian text, but the different narrative forms and emphases also contribute to the sense of fragmentation by suggesting that the mode of categorization and the forms of recollection appropriate to the wealth and nature of the material available remain unclear. While the *Morte* depends for its effects, and often for its very intelligibility, on a store of residual knowledge about its Arthurian subjects, full engagement with certain aspects of the legend may themselves demand forgetfulness of other, related, information. Yet, the choice of one mode of organizing Arthurian material brings into play, by association, others that have been put to one side, "laid apart," as the narrator says, although from the phrase it is unclear whether the "undesirable" material is dismissed for ever, or simply pushed further into the recesses of memory only to emerge again, as happens reiteratively in Malory's narrative, in another form or context.

In his allusiveness, and in his structuring of the story in part through reference to the practice of reading, which requires that a reader also supply the proclaimed and assumed deficiencies of the text, Malory makes prominent what I shall argue are elements central to English reworkings of Arthurian narrative: a stress on an extratextual "knowledge" of the subject and on pragmatic audience reception of each retelling of the tale. The French Arthurian writings Malory uses take a different path and instead suggest the interpretive difficulties of a text arise from the competitiveness of their inscribed diverse claims to a written authoritativeness. In medieval French Arthurian cyclic prose romance, access to a moral framework and a more straightforward pattern of narrative causation than Malory provides are corollaries of its stress on self-validating written authority as exemplified by the autonomy of "li contes," the story itself. Malory's fiction of the *Morte* as a series of readings often conflates the roles of reader, writer, and text, and this highlights the possibility of choice and responsibility at the formal level of narrative direction. The declarations of intent scattered throughout the *Morte*—"Now seyth the tale" (2:981.1), "Now leve we of this mater and speke we of sir Palomydes" (2:769.1), "And so I leve here of this tale" (3:1154.1)—intimate that the narratorial voice, the imagined readership and "the book" are all engaged in establishing narrative event, which becomes at the same time a search for meaning. Yet, the *Morte* does not have the assurance of textual authority and stability its French sources ostensibly promise. Instead, it articulates more urgently the importance of and desire for a community of understanding and response, while at the same time it does not guarantee the ultimate realization of such a community.

Malory does not, however, offer us a consistent sense of engagement and control through his pragmatic, "participatory" model. Insofar as I want to trace the tensions between the desire for a fully "recoverable" Arthurian narrative, and the *Morte's* inevitable contingency and fragmentation at the level of organization and articulation, my work corroborates research that places Malory's writings in the general context of the social uncertainties of the fifteenth century.[8] But within this context I want to argue especially that the paradox of Malory's enterprise draws on English literary traditions regarding the transmission of Arthurian legend as I distinguish them from the French, considered interactively with those French sources.[9] I also develop the implications of Malorian instability for the interaction of structure and theme in his Arthuriad. There is some agreement that Arthur and his world hold a specific historical importance for an English audience, even that the impulse to national identity can annex Arthur for its own purposes. Yet, in the historical narratives themselves, from Geoffrey of Monmouth's *Historia* onward, Arthur and Arthurian subject matter often focus problems of, or in other ways comment metatextually on, the methodology of the literary work in which they feature. English romances on Arthur, while they may carry a historically referential subtext, are experimental, inquiring, and in their execution often nonconfirmatory or otherwise exploratory of assumptions about the Arthurian milieu. Every English retelling questions the emphases of previous works and rewrites Arthur's relevance and significance for the needs of what it projects as its immediate audience.

The motive behind Malory's *Morte* may intermittently appear to be the desire to retrieve, and accord an unproblematic status to, the Arthurian, but in working through the legend's various narrative paradigms and the complexities of "our" engagement with them, the author implicitly expresses anxiety about the gap between an ideologically straightforward Arthurian world and the difficulties of realizing it textually. Instead, Malory continually brings the nature and function of Arthurian literature into question, prompting reconsiderations of how the material relates to issues of historical awareness, nationhood, the constitution of masculine heroic identity, and constructions of gender and social order and interaction. Where the French texts investigate the status of the written, and the issue of textual integrity in general, in the *Morte* there is a shift to tracing value through the vulnerable human body, specifically the body of Launcelot as hero. In this, Malory is in part taking his cue from the French texts in which, although the tendency is to refract textual interest through a female body, Lancelot himself may serve as a fantasy site of physical fragmentation. This study in part seeks to define the precise nature of Malory's construction of the inherent instability of (especially) the male physical body as locus of meaning and to show how this technique reflects the more experimental concerns of the text as a whole. We may investigate this treatment of the male body in terms of what Thomas Csordas calls "embodiment," by which he denotes the physical as "the existential ground" of culture and of the self.[10] Embodiment collapses the duality of mind and body that obtains in postmedieval constructions of selfhood, and emphasizes the body's role in perceptual experience and engagement in the world.[11] Csordas offers embodiment as a phenomenological paradigm, but it usefully alerts us to the textual complexity of the chivalric self as dynamic cultural agent in the *Morte,* and especially to the problematizing capacity of its narrative representation.

The *Morte* conveys the desire for stable reference points in an uncertain and subjective environment, reference points that pronouncements on the "worship" of particular knights, their arrangement into hierarchies, and the "honor" of Arthur's court, provide. At the same time, the text's organization and its narrative substance, so dependent on the operation of violence, suggest that such coordinates offer only a notional continuity, and that the nature of heroism, and the very tenets of social order, are critical issues open to a worrying dissolution and reformulation. Close analysis of specific aspects of the *Morte,* the foci of which my reading of the May passage determines, will demonstrate how Malory contextualizes an apparently stabilizing rhetoric to call into question the very possibility of achieving stability. As part of this investigation, I shall look at some of the consequences of his interweaving of different forms of identification with and alienation from the Arthurian legend on the part of the reader.

The May passage urges us to a remembrance of past Arthurian event, and chapter one examines the possibilities of retrieving, and distinguishing between, Continental and insular experiences of reading Arthurian literature, to gauge a historical and a literary reader response to these texts. I examine the narrative organization of the Vulgate Cycle of Arthurian romance, and of the later French prose works it engenders, especially the manuscript of Micheau Gonnot's Arthuriad (Paris, Bibliothèque Nationale, fonds français, 112), and suggest that the French and English narratives have different central emphases, on writing, and on reading and performance respectively, and that this distinction in presentation is paradigmatic for the development of Arthurian romance in the two vernaculars. Insular audiences would, I argue, regard English and French as distinct literary registers for the treatment of Arthurian material. I place the *Morte Darthur* in this context, to suggest that the contingency of Malory's Arthurian narrative is part of the author's structural deployment of an awareness of multiple perspectives on Arthur particular to Arthurian literature in Middle English. I will show how Malory also questions those "English" perspectives by refracting them through an awareness of the assumptions of the French narratives in his own composition. Thus, Malory locates his own text "between" French and English treatments of the subject, although it is also important that we recognize that this "betweenness" is not consistent throughout the *Morte*. The *Morte,* as locus of productivity and also of cultural questioning by virtue of cultural overlapping, occupies an "interstitial" position (to borrow a term from Homi Bhabha).[12] This awareness of plural contexts and sitings is Malory's point of departure for an Arthurian narrative that constantly interrogates other means of accounting for and controlling human existence even as it invokes them, whether those are institutions such as the law, or narrative paradigms that encourage a particular interpretation of the world.

Other chapters examine Malory's work divided according to narrative blocks largely suggested by the layout of the Winchester manuscript of the *Morte*[13] (although the *Tristram* section has a chapter to itself), because these divisions correspond well to differences one can trace on the level of inscribed reader response to, and participation with, textual event. Again, the preoccupations of the May passage underlie my choice of thematic areas of investigation, and there will be continual reference to Launcelot as exemplary of the troubled masculinity that is a central focus of anxiety in the *Morte*. Chapter two demonstrates how the structural reorganization of the Arthurian legend Malory undertakes in the early part of the *Morte* has repercussions for the text's epistemology. Caxton's preface to the *Morte* may seem out of sympathy with Malory in its apparent suggestion that for the reader the recuperation (or more exactly, the imposition) of a moral framework is relatively straightforward. But Caxton's elaborate historicizing moves to "authenticate" Arthur—when compared to the way he presents history in some of his other prologues—also suggest the high degree of selectivity requisite to recuperate an unproblematic Arthurian past.

Caxton interestingly ignores Merlin in his assessment of Arthurian historicity, but Merlin is particularly important to the early part of the *Morte* because of his continual association with authorial intention and textual authority, with social order, and with concepts of historical process, in English and Latin texts as well as in the French romances. To gain some understanding of fifteenth-century readers' expectations of this figure, the chapter looks at how, in the English Prose *Merlin,* Merlin functions especially as a counselor who affords the community a sense of historical awareness. This work, and the self-referential and moral framework of the *Suite du Merlin,* an important source for Malory, illuminates how Malory rewrites Merlin's function. Where these texts tend to use Merlin to synthesize experience, in the *Morte,* Merlin belongs to a multifarious Arthurian world, the plural nature of which we ourselves construct through the conflicting registers available to describe it. And partly through the representation of Merlin, the first portion of Malory's text sketches the complexities of Malory's Arthurian environment, its demonstrable lack of a providentialist frame, and the lack of an underpinning moral legitimization of violence. The ostensibly surer moral and generic coordinates of the sources compete with more pragmatically expressed concerns over the relation between human and divine law and the regulation of violence. From Ygrayne's experience onward, rape also features in the narrative as of central importance in focusing issues of desire, of gender relations, of physical integrity (more often masculine than feminine), and of power. Malory raises questions not only about how the Arthurian world functions but also about the nature of its social order, its possible relation to a fifteenth-century present, and the traditional ways in which it is interpreted and accounted for.

This exploration of relations between literary and social orders continues in the rest of the Arthuriad, by means of a series of stylistically different sections that themselves demand continuing revision of their own literary premises, that is, they make and then remake the very tradition they construct. Chapter three considers the modes of narrative organization and of masculine martial self-presentation and the assumptions underlying them, in what are apparently some of the most individuated stories of the *Morte*, the *Tale of Arthur and Lucius,* and the respective tales of Launcelot and of Gareth. All three *Tales* address issues of control and containment, in terms of the construction and interaction of physical integrity, masculine heroic identity, the feminine, social order, the channeling of violence, and narrative structure. Each account selectively presents a set of possibilities for Arthurian narrative, and the reader, written into the apparatus of the text's organization, is implicated in the interpretive frame for the material each narrative supplies. The *Tales* offer various facets of heroism. Arthur's foreign crusadelike campaign sets good knighthood within a nationalist context, but while this account draws heavily on the Alliterative *Morte Arthure,* it dislocates the action from the English tradition's Arthurian chronology, which uses the episode to unite tragedy and history. The near invulnerability of Malory's heroes becomes the physical correlative to the narrative's fantasy vision of history. The adventures of Launcelot, meanwhile, demonstrate the vulnerability of the hero as social construct, at the same time as they involve a regendering of the reader as inquiring subject, and the tale of Gareth concerns an initially autonomous individual who, in what one might term a remasculinized environment, becomes subject to different sets of social demands. The juxtaposition of these diverse recountings serves to compartmentalize rather than synthesize the different elements that have a purchase on the Arthurian legend. The retelling of the story of Arthur and Lucius ultimately shows how uncomplicated engagement with the triumphalist Arthur and his army is at the expense of an awareness of historical process, inside or outside the *Morte,* and Gareth's success story exists only within a particular, hermetically closed-off world. And where the person of Launcelot would seem to promise continuity, consistently brought to mind as he is, in his own tale and elsewhere, as the subject of others' discourse and the sum of their expectations and desires, the conflicting nature of those expectations, in part the consequence of the objectifying and sexualizing of Lancelot that is by tradition integral to his definition as hero, is made the site of some anxiety in the narrative, as in the rest of the *Morte.*

Chapter four investigates how the *Book of Sir Tristram,* while it appears to be the section of the *Morte* most in line with French narrative methodology, also registers important distinctions. The integrative, encyclopedic model the French Prose *Tristan* and Gonnot's compilation supply (an integration evident in, for example, the career of the *beste glatissant* in Gonnot's collection), contrasts with Malory's more searching model, as his elusive Questing Beast exemplifies. Launcelot and Tristram are focal points for narrative and for reader alike, but the narrative also displaces Tristram from his position as hero, and from the literary registers that distinguish him in the French prose texts, and the treatment of letters in general indicates something of the troubled relation between text and physical person that haunts the *Morte.* Tristram and Launcelot have different heroic functions. As the episodes of their respective madnesses demonstrate, Tristram operates within already established narrative parameters, whereas Launcelot's role expands the boundaries of the narrative's concerns. Launcelot is both a locus of desired stability, and the means by which the reader is made to confront the increasing complexity of the Arthurian world. Launcelot's breakdown, a failure to contain the diverse claims made on him as hero— but also part of his resistance to the terms of his definition—is simultaneously a temporary narrative failure to cope with the diverse elements in the story.

Chapter five looks at how, while the Grail "restores" Launcelot, and at the same time rescues and establishes a fresh focus for the narrative, *The Tale of the Sankgreal* proves more disorienting than the preceding books, for here the text itself appropriates the values and choices previously accorded the reader and/or narrator, while leaving in suspension its status and efficacy as a "devotional" text, only partially integrating within its structure elements familiar to fifteenth-century devotional practice. Although proclaimed a "holy" book, the tale appears to bar access to grace even as it promises objectivity, stability, fulfillment, and completion. Central to the exposition of the Divine is Perceval's Sister, whose role demonstrates the gap between Grail narrative and the potential for the social accommodation of religious meaning. Her narrative also returns us to the problems of the legitimization of violence, refracted through gender issues, we encounter with the adventures of Balin toward the beginning of the *Morte*. In the Grail story generally, the material world appears subject to a different, unexplained, hermeneutics, with the human physical redefined within a spiritual framework and partly dislocated from the pragmatically constituted values with which it is associated elsewhere in the text. Especially traumatic for Launcelot in this respect is the treatment of fatherhood as material fact and as spiritual metaphor. Where Thomas Hoccleve, over fifty years earlier, had confidently placed religious matters outside the reach of Arthurian romance, Malory's partial dismantling of the French Grail story's method and epistemology tests its relevance in the context of fifteenth-century anxieties about faith and community, but in this context I shall also discuss the later, non-*Sankgreal* episode of the "Healing of Sir Urry" as an ambivalent celebration of the redemptive by means of the ritual deployment of chivalric embodiment that simultaneously articulates the power and the limits of Malory's Arthurian vocabulary, and reflects on narratorial positioning and perspective.

In chapter six, I consider how, after the Grail story, Malory brings together reader, narrator, and narrative in a movement toward collective commemoration, the modes of which, however, mark a loss of community rather than its constitution. I look in further detail at the May passage, and trace its antecedents in Chaucer's writings, specifically the *Prologue* to the *Legend of Good Women,* to argue for its significance to Malory's conceptualization of Arthurian legend as the focus of an attempt to engage with the past. But Malory also recognizes the limitations of the conceptual framework, and especially of any metaphoric matrix, at our disposal fully to construct that past as, for example, the gap between Guinevere's ostensible ritual function and her narrative presence indicates. I explore the tensions and displacements inherent in the contextualization of various modes of representation, of commemoration and of mourning, rites associated with death drawn from fifteenth-century practice, and the "exemplary" readings the characters themselves, the narrator, and the text's editors, offer. Malory's renewal and reworking of French and English subject matter and models emerges as no idealized and nostalgic historical recreation. Rather, his project of incomplete recuperation, which incorporates both emotional engagement and a sense of loss, interrogates the uses of Arthurian legend but also meditates on the uses of literature in general, questioning, from a masculine perspective, the ontological and epistemological bases of fifteenth-century writing.

CHAPTER 1

STRUCTURES AND TRADITIONS

Cultural Backgrounds

Froissart recounts, in his *Chronicles,* how two enemy knights in the Hundred Years' War are astonished to find they bear identical heraldic devices, "une bleue dame ouvrée de broudure ou ray d'un soleil sus le senestre brach" [a blue lady worked in embroidery with a sunbeam to the left side]. The Frenchman Clermont accuses the Englishman: "Chandos, Chandos, ce sont bien des posnées de vos Englès qui ne scevent aviser riens de nouvel; mès quanqu'il / voient, leur est biel." [Chandos, Chandos, these are indeed the vaunts of you English, who know nothing about devising anything new, but whatever they see is fine for them (to take)].[1] Historically, the replication of arms proper among knights of the same country gives cause for concern, and there are procedures to decide on prior claims, as the dispute between Sir Richard le Scrope and Sir Robert Grosvenor, 1385–90, famously illustrates.[2] In the Chandos-Clermont dispute, the parties meet at a time of truce, just before the Battle of Poitiers, and the issue has no official settlement, although Froissart notes darkly that some think Clermont's verbal altercation with Chandos plays no small part in the former's subsequent death, slain on the battlefield with no quarter given.[3] The pragmatics of war, possibly combined with English vindictiveness, serve to silence the Frenchman rather than to prove his claim wrong. The incident invites interpretation as illustrating French assumptions about English cultural parasitism,[4] as the extant heraldic rolls record no historical association between this ambivalent image of religious or secular devotion and a Chandos or a Clermont.[5] The design is more reminiscent of the fanciful personal emblems chosen for tournaments or described in romance than of the inherited family charges knights used to identify themselves on the battlefield.[6] The sign is indeed associated with Arthur—whose shield, as some texts describe it, bears a Madonna—rather than with historical knights.[7]

That Froissart should signal this confrontation, primarily paradigmatic of cultural, and especially literary, relations between the two countries, by means of a possibly "Arthurian" device, is apposite for the late-medieval Franco-British literary scene. Continental writers might claim as great an interest in Arthur as do insular authors, and one whose loyalties were primarily to French culture could interpret as indicative of poverty of imagination both the popularity of French texts in England and the number of Arthurian works in English that translate or rework French originals. The duplication is an apt metaphor for prior claims to Arthurian romance. Yet, as a cultural parable, Froissart's story also raises other issues. The device, and the dialogue and subsequent narrative relating to it, misleadingly direct us to read English and French response to Arthurian legend as the same in kind. To use the image as cultural metaphor assumes writers in English have uniform objectives and intentions, and seek only to replicate, within a common framework, French material they find attractive. The opposition of the two knights obscures the tangled nature of their cultural situation, one at which the very names of the antagonists hint ("Messires Jehan de Chandos" and "Messires Jehans de Clermont"), and suggest a shared ancestry that makes it difficult to draw a sharp division between insular and Continental interests.

Malory's own work emerges as a literary analogue to this contest for cultural possession and legitimization. This study asks what the designation "French" or "English" might encompass in terms of Arthurian legend for the fourteenth and fifteenth centuries, and argues for a complex cultural legacy for Malory's art that makes poignant the *Morte's* narrative search for stability. The cyclic form of French Arthurian prose romance, along with its derivatives and continuations, offers the closest prose model for the *Morte,* but Malory evidently also draws on insular traditions and on other English reworkings of cyclic material. This chapter considers examples of the later medieval reception of Arthurian literature in England and in France, in the light of cultural conditions specific to the production of English and French vernacular writings, and argues for a particularly English refraction of French Arthurian literary concerns in Malory's work.

From the eleventh to the fifteenth centuries, administrative, legal, ecclesiastical, and cultural areas of British life draw on the resources of several languages—Anglo-Norman, French, English, and Latin, as well as the Celtic languages—and although there is some debate over how to establish with certainty which social and cultural groups knew which languages during which eras, English adaptations of French Arthurian texts are produced in an extraordinarily rich area of vernacular interaction. As a literary medium, the English vernacular serves diverse social groups[8] and interacts fluidly with other vernaculars, as also with Latin. This interaction shapes English literary awareness differently from romance vernacular writings' positioning of themselves in reaction to, but also in imitation of, Latin "authoritative" texts. Such English vernacular self-consciousness arguably underlies the experimental range of English Arthurian writings. Explicit English textual assertions of authorial responsibility and reader response also differ from the authorizing fictions of the French prose romances, most notably in their emphasis on reading and on performance rather than on the written, and this mode of self-presentation may in part account for why a large corpus of French, but not English, prose texts develops from the Vulgate Cycle, the most popular grouping of French Arthurian romances.

To designate Arthurian literatures as "French" or "English" may itself be to set up terms of convenience initially obstructive to understanding the cultural conditions that produce, and engage with, such writings. While a heightened awareness of Arthur's dynastic and immediate political importance and relevance is assumed for writers in English,[9] Michelle Warren argues powerfully that twelfth- and thirteenth-century Arthurian texts, from Geoffrey of Monmouth's Latin *Historia* (ca. 1138) and its adaptations by Wace of Jersey (*Le Roman de Brut*) and the English Laȝamon (*Brut*), to the (probably) Champenois Vulgate Cycle, speak from and to "border" interests, and across different constituencies, historiographical and political.[10] Geoffrey's *Historia,* together with its "Prophecies of Merlin," circulates widely on the continent (especially in Normandy and Champagne) with vaticinatory, legal, and historical material.[11] Merlin and his prophecies suggest a paradigm for reflection on the nature of history writing, and critical debate about the *Historia's* political bias testifies to Geoffrey's sharpened perceptions of nationhood and history making, manifest in his charting of disjunction, discontinuity, and interrupted genealogy, as much as of continuity.[12] Geoffrey leaves a double Arthurian legacy, which allows for self-reflexive historical analysis,[13] and creates space (in, for example, the laconic mention of a nine-year period of peace during Arthur's reign) for the material dilation of a fictive Arthurian world.[14] These interests converge with the emergence of romance as a literary mode, and the ambivalence of the Arthurian as historical subject—Wace says such stories are not all lies, nor yet all true[15]—is perhaps particularly attractive to writers in French, who are explicitly anxious to authorize a literary vernacular; this authorization is central to the evolution and dominance of Arthurian prose romance. The vernacular, romance, and the malleability of Arthur as literary subject are, then, all at issue.[16]

Twelfth-century vernacular literature in France, as Michel Zink demonstrates, defines itself against Latin literature, but also appropriates Latin's authorizing, book-centered, strategies.[17] The vernacular authors of some of the earliest romances, the *romans antiques*, claim to draw on Latin originals for their classical stories of love and dynasty, their backdrops the fall of Troy and the growth and consolidation of empire. These writers, however, privilege French as the literary medium for the prestigious cultural genealogy they are thereby consolidating, for their own literary enterprise as for their courtly patrons.[18] Stories of Troy have an immediate political relevance by virtue of the association of European royal families with the translation of power from East to West, in which the Trojan legend has a prominent role.[19] The twelfth-century Angevin-Plantagenet court and Anglo-Norman rule in general, meanwhile, has a vested interest in Arthurian as well as Trojan myth, and Francis Ingledew has noted how Geoffrey of Monmouth's *Historia* draws on the historiographical potential of both resources and offers, through Arthur, a model of secular history rulers can readily exploit.[20] In insular terms, the *Historia* is background to "Arthur"'s participation in a dynamic historical process, including Henry II's political program, through literature and such events as the "discovery" of the king's bones at Glastonbury in the late twelfth century.[21]

On the Continent, Arthurian material partakes in claims to literary authoritativeness that transcend assertions of veracity, in order to assert the autonomy of vernacular writing itself.[22] Latin Arthurian narratives anticipate a literary play with the function and uses of writing;[23] when writers in French adapt Latin models to vernacular purposes, however, they implicitly find the Arthurian condition reflects their own ambivalence—of anxiety or pleasure—about literary status, and so rework the effects of this particular self-consciousness to produce historiographically experimental and inquiring prose romance. This body of literature quickly evolves a spatial and chronological frame of reference for Arthurian adventure. The Vulgate Cycle (ca. 1215–35) takes inspiration from the prose version of "Robert de Boron"'s early-thirteenth-century cycle, which recounted the story of the Grail, from Joseph of Arimathea's day to the time of Arthur, Merlin, and Perceval.[24] The *Estoire del Saint Graal* and the Vulgate *Merlin,* chronologically the first texts in the series, establish, by means of the Grail and the eponymous prophet, a miraculous and sociopolitical background for Arthurian history. The last books of the Cycle, *La Queste del Saint Graal* and *La Mort le roi Artu,* chart the fulfillment of the Grail and Arthurian society's demise. These opening and closing volumes frame the career of Lancelot, whose adventures constitute the lengthy central section, the Prose *Lancelot*.[25]

The Vulgate romances' appropriation of ambivalent authorizing strategies for Arthurian writing make possible their reading as either conservative or iconoclastic in their implicit claim to historicity through their use of prose, and in their pressing of scriptural and religious reference into the service of an Arthurian story capable of containing diverse literary and historical paradigms.[26] Michelle Warren's fine account of Vulgate Cycle politics links the texts to the environment and concerns of the romances of Chrétien de Troyes, and aligns their deeply ambivalent projection of Arthurian history with aristocratic anxieties about centralized kingship.[27] Certainly the Vulgate form allows for the forceful expression of a political agenda; the Italian author of the late-thirteenth-century *Prophecies de Merlin* shares the Cycle's anxieties over the recuperation of text and meaning, and intercalates romance narrative with prophetic material to comment on contemporary political event.[28] At the same time, the Vulgate Cycle constructs a self-contained fictional world in which Arthur and his court are primarily the vehicle of its ambivalent self-authorizing and metatextual literary strategies. The Cycle proclaims itself definitive; the last lines of *La Mort le roi Artu* warn that any amplification of the material can only be a lie, echoing the Book of Deuteronomy's similar prescription against textual interference.[29] Its structure allows for later additions, however, which proclaim themselves part of the process of reclaiming the full Arthurian story.[30] The Post-Vulgate Cycle or *Roman du Graal* (ca. 1230–40), for example, incorporates versions of the *Estoire del Saint Graal,* a continuation of de Boron's *Merlin* known as the *Suite du Merlin,* extracts from the Vulgate *Lancelot,* the First Version of the Prose *Tristan,* the Post-Vulgate versions of the *Queste,* and the *Mort.* This reworking integrates the Grail more fully with other Arthurian adventures.[31] Later French prose narrative treatments of the Arthurian legend, such as *Guiron le Courtois* or the Second Version of the Prose *Tristan,* further amplify chivalric adventure by introducing new characters and expanding on the exploits of heroic individuals in what is by now a familiar Arthurian setting.[32] The great Arthurian compilation (now Paris, Bibliothèque Nationale, MS fonds français 112), finished in July 1470, for Jacques d'Armagnac, Duke of Nemours, by Micheau Gonnot, is the fullest example of the form of later French romances, and demands comparison with Malory's Arthuriad as a near-contemporaneous Continental production.[33]

I have suggested that the political and historical variousness of insular Arthurian associations, and a polyglot culture that conceptualizes Latin-vernacular relations differently from the continental, make for a broader literary self-reflexivity for Arthurian texts in English. Questions of textual access aside,[34] a combination of factors might account for English literary choices. Some features, such as a dynastic subtext for Arthur, or an apparent insular tradition of Gawain narratives, might not alone account for English attitudes to French texts, although the notion of a "Gawain tradition" might illuminate a formal preference among writers in English.[35] Felicity Riddy plausibly suggests, however, that English readers, with the historical background Geoffrey of Monmouth and chronicles such as the *Brut* provide, have a special interest in the material the Vulgate shares with the *Historia*.[36] Documentary evidence of the existence, provenance, ownership, and circulation of French cyclic romance in England, and of the knowledge of Anglo-Norman and French, incomplete though it might be, suggests this literature is itself part of the range of approaches to the Arthurian available to an insular culture. Yet, although English writers might draw on the Vulgate's historical and epistemological models, their tendency seems to be toward experimentation with both subject matter and presentational form, so they do not share the source texts' precise anxieties over authorizing the written, nor do they follow their homogenizing and encyclopedic literary program.

The earliest extant work in the Vulgate-derived English Arthurian corpus, *Of Arthour and of Merlin* (dating from 1250–1300), draws on the Vulgate *Merlin*. *Joseph of Arimathie* (ca. 1350, extant in a single manuscript ca. 1400) takes material from the Vulgate *Estoire del Saint Graal,* refracted, its latest editor notes, through a portion of the *Queste del Saint Graal,*[37] and the later-fourteenth-century Stanzaic *Le Morte Arthur* adapts the last book in the Vulgate sequence, *La Mort le roi Artu*. More reworkings survive from the fifteenth century: Henry Lovelich (writing for a London mercantile audience) translates both the *Estoire del Saint Graal* and *Merlin*. The (ca. 1450) English Prose *Merlin* closely translates the Vulgate *Merlin,* and the later-fifteenth-century Scottish *Lancelot of the Laik* is roughly contemporaneous with Malory.[38] Malory's *Morte Darthur,* which draws on both the *Suite du Merlin* and the Vulgate *Merlin,* on parts of the *Lancelot* and *Tristan,* and on *La Mort le roi Artu,* as well as on English texts, constitutes a synthesis of vernacular writings, unprecedented in English for length and comprehensiveness, but other English redactors' literary forms and choices also influence Malory's structural and narrative preoccupations.

Caxton's discussion of the Arthurian legend's viability, in the Prologue to his 1485 edition of the *Morte Darthur,* reflects the anxieties of the age over the problems of establishing authenticity. But Malory's text, especially as the Winchester manuscript presents it, belongs to what I would term an English tradition of writing about Arthur. Where the French texts are interested in the play with and control of a literary form that, once established, is a given, the *Morte's* very structure depends precisely on a concern over the forms the recovery of and engagement with the story should take. This treatment makes meaning continually open to negotiation. It is less a spirit of nostalgic nationalism that informs Malory's choice of subject than an anxiety about the subjectivity and instability of our narrative constructions of history, one all the more fraught because of the subtext of national identity that has come to inform English perceptions of Arthur. Even Cax-

ton will resolve the difficulties surrounding Arthur and his possible relation to an English historical past by reminding us that faith in what is written is a matter of personal choice (1:cxlvi.10–11). The multifarious
Arthurian world the English texts present is a suitable subject for Malory,
for whom the written does not necessarily encode stable and uniform response, and the ambivalent nature of the Arthurian is the more marked
when mediated through a fifteenth-century English self-conscious mode
of writing that simultaneously engages with, and is anxious about, particular rhetorical and literary forms as the means to the retrieval and ordering of knowledge.

Malory is not then trying to refract a sophisticated and modish Continental romance form through the lens of an incoherent English romance
"tradition" but draws on characteristics particular to each. While we need
to treat manuscript and other documentary evidence with some caution,
French Arthurian literature seems to have enjoyed a consistent popularity
among the French-speaking English. And if it is not the case that English-
and French-speaking audiences form distinct communities in Britain,[39] it
becomes less tenable to judge English romance as constrained by the vernacular's clumsy inadequacy, or by the need to make the subject matter
comprehensible in oral performance to an uncultured public.[40] The precise use and status of different vernaculars in Britain during the period is
of course open to debate; Michael Clanchy shows how surviving documentation does not necessarily accurately reflect which languages were
being spoken where, and in what circumstances.[41] From the thirteenth to
the fifteenth centuries, however, Anglo-Norman emerges as the language
of English legal record, and there is evidence it serves as a kind of insular
lingua franca, a useful means of communication in the face of the different dialect forms of English.[42] There is some indication, too, of bi- and
trilingualism, which led to fruitful literary cross-fertilization.[43]

Insular communities' polylingualism can sharpen appreciation of vernaculars operating as literary registers, which enriches an individual text's
interpretive possibilities. Thomas Bestul cites the example of Edmund
Rich's thirteenth-century devotional *Miroir de Sainte Eglise,* and the debate
as to whether the Anglo-Norman or the Latin version is the "original"
text, when he argues for a reciprocal interrelation of Latin and vernacular,
to replace a model of language relations dependent on perceived cultural
elitism and fixed hierarchies.[44] Deployment of a particular vernacular may
be as much the result of conscious choice as of necessity, and a literary
awareness of languages may be in evidence in (not specifically macaronic)
vernacular works.[45] The international prestige of French does not automatically relegate English to the cultural margins, for English may feature
in individual texts as a specific literary strategy. It can define an audience

and its relationship to the material as well as relay authorial intention. Robert Mannyng of Brunne, in his *Story of England* (1338), mentions "grete bokes" in French prose in praise of Arthur, as an accessible narrative resource.[46] As translation or adaptation, the English text functions less as a marginal glossing than as an active critical response to, and interaction with, its source.

Vernaculars may also work together as particular registers. *Of Arthour and Of Merlin* in the Auchinleck manuscript (the product of a London bookshop of the 1330s) intimates a range of language use in social and literary contexts. The introduction gives practical reasons for the use of English: "Mani noble ich haue yseiȝe / Þat no Freynsche couþe seye."[47] But English is also an appropriate vehicle for the Matter of Britain for an English-speaking audience, English audience's apparent ignorance of French apart: "Riȝt is þat Inglische vnderstond / Þat was born in Inglond" (21–22). While the poet acknowledges the prestige of knowing French and Latin (17–18), the narrative deploys them in social contexts. Gawain receives letters written in Latin (8560), which is the learned language Merlin speaks to the King's counselors who want him dead (1566–70). French is the language of courtly address; Merlin calls Ban and Bohors "Bieu sengours" [fair lords] (3607), and Gwenore uses French (6545–46) in courteous talk with Arthur.[48] The narrative is conscious of the decorum of language, and the occasional narratorial throwaway remark suggests a cast of mind that can think in French and English interchangeably.[49] English is not the only language of insular nationhood; Hugh the Despenser, in 1324, encourages his troops in Gascony by promising them, in French, that they will regain land lost to the enemy, to the honor of king, fighters, and "nostre lange" [our language].[50] By 1485, Caxton has, among other arguments, a chauvinistic justification for publishing a text in English on a national hero, but this does not preclude the audience's also reading in French.[51] *Of Arthour,* meanwhile, suggests a flexibility in language use, and a more fluid relation between languages as registers in a culturally diverse society than modern assumptions about uniformity of language and cohesion of nationhood might allow.[52]

Of Arthour does not translate the French text directly, but this does not mean that only an imperfect copy was available. The poem's casual references to Lancelot (8906) and the Grail (8902) assume audience knowledge of other branches of the legend, but material evidence for cyclical knowledge of romances is scant. On the Continent, detailed inventories of libraries, such as that of Charles V of France, bear witness to a lively and broad social interest in this literary form.[53] The lack of inventories from before 1535 makes it difficult to reconstruct early English royal libraries.[54] Yet, throughout the fourteenth century, English and French royal households seem to share literary tastes.[55] Isabella, Queen to Edward II and daughter of Philip IV of France, owned copies of several Arthurian works, and her large volume of "the acts of Arthur" was possibly a Vulgate Cycle.[56] Henry V certainly borrowed romances such as *Guiron le Courtois*.[57] With the influence of Burgundian court fashion on Edward IV and his circle, the royal library comes to be stocked with romances.[58] Aristocrats and clerics also enjoy romances throughout this period. In 1305, Guy de Beauchamp leaves a handsome collection of books to Bordesley Abbey, including romances of Lancelot, Joseph of Arimathea, the Grail, and Arthur.[59] Inventories of goods seized from Simon de Burley in 1388, and from Thomas, Duke of Gloucester, in 1397, reveal a similar interest in French romance. Simon de Burley's booklist includes a romance of Arthur, a book of the "Prophecies of Merlin," and a "bruyt" (although this last may be in English or French). Gloucester's French books include a *Merlin, a Lancelot,* and a book "about Arthur."[60] Clerics donate books of romance (among others) to religious foundations. In the late fourteenth century, Nicholas of Hereford, Prior of Evesham Abbey, Worcestershire, gives to the priory of Penwortham in Lancashire what seem to be a *Queste* and a *Mort le roi Artu,* and a fifteenth-century catalogue for St. Augustine's, Canterbury, mentions French books of Lancelot and of the Grail.[61]

Although no records unequivocally assign a complete copy of the Vulgate to an English family or individual of the period, this appears to be primarily a failing of documentation, which may indicate only vaguely a "French" or "romance" volume's contents. What Richard Roos's will, made in March 1482, calls "my grete booke called saint Grall" is in fact an imperfect copy of the *Estoire del Saint Graal,* the *Queste del Saint Graal,* and *La Mort le roi Artu* (now British Library, MS Royal 14.e.iii).[62] Information on manuscript production and dissemination, however, shows that England was part of the international market for the expensive editions of romance the French and Italian ateliers produced throughout the medieval period.[63] The Paris bookshop owner Reynault de Montet had French and English clients; in 1402, he supplied the Duke of Berry with a complete version of the Vulgate Cycle (now Paris, Bibliothèque Nationale MSS fonds français 117–120) for three hundred crowns. In 1414, he sold a copy of a Tristan to Richard Courtenay, Bishop of Norwich, for 151 crowns.[64]

The fifteenth century witnesses a huge increase in the production of manuscripts in English and available to a broad reading public, and a large proportion of the English romances written between 1100 and 1500 survives only in fifteenth-century manuscripts.[65] English romance does not seem to substitute for French romance. In Cambridge, University Library MS Additional 7071, for example, a fifteenth-century English scribe has replaced several (presumably damaged) leaves in a fourteenth-century manuscript of the *Estoire del Saint Graal* and the *Suite du Merlin*.[66] On both sides of the Channel, men and women owned manuscripts of romances that appear to have been read, rather than simply kept as valuable artifacts.[67] Carol Meale argues from the availability of French romance in England that the identification of the Morte's author as the Thomas Malory of Papworth St. Agnes is precarious if it rests primarily on the idea that Anthony Wydville, as Malory's patron, would have given him access to the French royal library inherited from John, Duke of Bedford.[68]

Late-medieval English culture knows French romance as part of the international literary scene. If, as Riddy suggests, Galfredian emphases largely dictate the choice of Arthurian material in English, these also correlate with the generic preoccupations others have traced for Middle English romance, such as a stress on social order and community, and the importance of political counsel.[69] The insular audience is not of course homogeneous, and issues of class, gender, education, and profession will witness to different kinds of knowledge and engagement with things Arthurian. Yet, if the physical evidence argues for little more than a general awareness of the Arthurian legend among the literate members of English society, and for some knowledge of the dominant French narrative of that legend, this is sufficient context against which English authors may define their own writings. Manuscript study reveals some correlation between the surviving manuscript contexts of English adaptations from the Vulgate, and the sense the English texts convey, not only of partiality and fragmentation (in comparison with the sources) but also of immediate engagement with, and of a localized response to, the material. The organization of a manuscript can direct a reader toward a particular response, whether moral or aesthetic. The early French prose romances are themselves dynamic, and might be subject to anthologizing and extrapolation.[70] But the Vulgate Cycle's form, and manuscript presentation of its individual romances, intimate the separate components exist within a larger frame, and encourage the production of narratives that aim to consolidate Arthurian material and accrete narrative detail within the particular epistemology the Vulgate provides.[71] Later English texts, meanwhile, regardless of whether their source is Continental or indigenous, present themselves as "readings" of Arthurian material within contexts (Arthurian or non-Arthurian), which often serve to complement or challenge the original texts' epistemology. The possibility of multiple readings of and narratives for Arthur is then part of a generalized interpretive background for the English texts in a way that does not obtain in the French Vulgate, in which ambivalence is differently encoded and there is a tighter control over the parameters of the Arthurian world.

Manuscripts of English works, however, show two general trends. Manuscript context can encourage a particular reading of a work: *Lancelot of the*

Laik, for example, is extant uniquely in a collection of religious and advice literature, although the language of good counsel is only one of its emergent registers. But manuscripts also evince an impulse toward diverse interpretations of Arthur. So Lincoln, Dean and Chapter Library MS 91—the "Lincoln Thornton" manuscript—contains Arthurian items as dissimilar as the Alliterative *Morte Arthure, Sir Perceval of Galles,* and *The Awntyrs Off Arthure.*[72] There is room in one compilation to discuss Arthur in terms of the making of history and historiography (in the *Morte*), of an imaginative world of romance (*Perceval*), of a localized historical relevance, and of the conjunction of his world with popular narrative concerning death and salvation (in the *Awntyrs*).[73] Where French continuations, such as BN MS f.fr. 112, seek to contain diverse material within formal structures, English texts make form and context part of their interrogation of the source texts.

Authorizing the Text: The Vulgate Cycle

The apparent homogeneity of the later Vulgate-based French prose depends on the system of authorship the Cycle establishes, and on the dominance of the "story" itself as authenticating strategy. Internal references to competing authors and to the narrative's autonomy construct an elaborate system, which ultimately bespeaks a deep unease and anxiety about the related issues of the intersection of divine and secular, and the literary status of the vernacular.[74] Later texts may ignore the Vulgate's paradoxes when they draw on the Cycle to establish their own literary genealogies. Reference to "li contes," that is, the story itself, rather than a narrating first-person voice, establishes a central narrative authority. "Li contes" may organize the narrative, direct our attention to a specific episode, or change the focus of the subject matter: "Mais ore ne parole li contes chi endroit plus de mon seignor Gauvain [. . .] anchois retourne a parler de Hector" [But now the story speaks no more of Sir Gawain [. . .] and returns to speak of Hector].[75] For Emmanuèle Baumgartner, reference to "li contes" is primarily structural in function; it signals the layout of the narrative material, without usurping the role of the narratorial voice that asserts the truth of what it proclaims, intervenes to pass comment on events, and (as indeed does "li contes") presents the material as if to a listening audience.[76] For Roberta Krueger, however, the voice of the "story" makes for "the fiction of the text as author, the self-generating text."[77] The text effectively grows out of the accretion of, and discrepancies between, its disparate voices, sometimes in agreement, sometimes in tension, one with another.

In the *Lancelot* account of the relationship between Ninienne and Merlin (Micha 7:38–43; Lacy 2:11–12), these different means of authorization interact, to show how, while prose is roomy enough to contain multiple voices, and serve various interests, local modifications highlight the competitiveness endemic to its authorization. This section describes Merlin as diabolical, and presents "le prophete as Englois" [the prophet of the English] (Micha 7:38; Lacy 2:11 translates as "the English prophet") in a more negative light than elsewhere in the cycle. Merlin's mother, in this version a beautiful proud young woman who refuses to take any husband she can see, attracts the attention of an incubus, who himself names the child he engenders. Merlin, malevolent, remains unbaptized: "Ii fu de la nature son peire dechevans et desloiaus et sot quanques cuers pooit savoir de toute perverse science" [He was of the same nature as his father, deceptive and disloyal, and he possessed all the false and perverted knowledge that an individual could have] (Micha 7:41; Lacy 2:12).

Merlin's history here diverges from the "orthodox" de Boron-derived Vulgate *Merlin* version (3–19; Lacy 1:167–76), but appropriates authorizing strategies to insist on its veracity. In *Lancelot,* both narrator and "story" tell the same tale: "De teus manieres de dyables fu estrais Merlins, che dist li contes des Estoires, et si vous dirai comment" [From such manner of devils, according to the story in the Chronicles, Merlin sprang, and I will tell you how] (Micha 7:39; Lacy 2:11).[78] The text demands reader collusion; "we" (the text tells us) know, from written accounts, about the sexual sin of Lucifer and his followers (traditionally, Lucifer's sin is one of pride) and their subsequent punishment (Micha 7:39; Lacy 2:11). The episode highlights the text's authenticating strategies; it stresses narratorial intervention, and both internal and extratextual documentary evidence. Not just the story but also the British Chronicles (Micha 7:38; Lacy 2:11) support the narratorial rationalization of the Lady of the Lake's fairy status as signifying she is skilled in magic (Micha 7:38; Lacy 2:11), and place Merlin historically as "Prophet of the English," while "we" collude to revise popular notions concerning the sin that cost the rebel angels heaven.

This concentration of authorization focuses narrative mediation at a crucial textual juncture. In the story, power is passing from Merlin (generator of narrative and guardian of speaking and writing) to the enchantress Ninienne,[79] and access to the story must continue in spite of Merlin's absence. The narrative disposes of Merlin and appropriates his paradigms of writing, making possible our continuing engagement with the tale. This method also demonstrates to what extent the text depends on the reader's good faith in its authorizing fictions. Some scribes, presumably loyal to narrative consistency over and above support for textual method, silently omit this account of Merlin.[80] Their action shows that to lose faith in the book completely would be to renounce all possibility of its continuation; the later romances are therefore material witness to a faith in what

Micheau Gonnot, in BN MS f.fr. 112, calls "la vraie histoire" [the true story], and in the possibility of its recovery. If internal factual inconsistencies trouble some copyists, the cluster of anxieties around who authors the text is the very basis of its production, and the prose romance continuators implicitly accept and exploit these tensions.

In addition to the interactive authority of "story" and individuated narrating voice, the romances, as they develop, identify a shifting genealogy of scribes and authors. These may be persons who feature as characters within the narrative (such as Merlin), or others, "outside" the story, such as "Walter Map." Moreover, the narrative builds audaciously on scriptural precedent. The first romance in the Vulgate sequence, the *Estoire del Saint Graal,* declares itself from the beginning to be an extraordinary piece of divine revelation. The narrator identifies himself as scribe, priest, hermit, and abject sinner, to whom Christ Himself vouchsafes a book of marvels, the very legibility of which depends on the reader's having first purified both body and soul, by fasting and confession.[81] This book as Christ's Word substitutes for, and is equated with, Christ as Word Incarnate, in an extraordinary sequence of events that uses scriptural reference to authenticate the book, and confirms romance landscape as the site of revelation. The scribe's adventures prior to his copying the text show how the eternal divine structures both temporal experience and the means of recording it. The *Estoire* thus appropriates divine language to sanction its material. Yet, the claim for this tale as divinely written appears to undo itself through its own argument on the foolhardiness of making such an assertion when even the incarnate Christ writes so rarely (1:258–59; Lacy 1:76), and so makes for a self-reflexive play on authorial and mediating modes, the preposterousness of which invites us to reexamine the means by which we authenticate the written.[82]

In the following book, *Merlin,* the ambivalent prophet, of semidiabolical parentage and yet redeemed, mediating between God and humankind, institutes writing as a commemorative medium. Blase the hermit faithfully records Merlin's words in a book from which the present romance derives (121; Lacy 1:223).[83] Merlin's interventions open the text to a different kind of narrative, one not bound by that of (ironically invoked) divine revelation but more inscrutably a mixture of human compulsion and divine volition. Merlin proposes the conjunction of texts that constitutes the Vulgate itself, a series the hermeneutical key of which is its own agglomeration, when he tells Blase that his book (which appears to cover most of the events of the *Estoire,* as well as the *Merlin*) will make sense only in terms of a supplementary "book of Joseph" the scribe must later find (20; Lacy 1:176). At the same time, the *Merlin* implicitly undermines the originary status of the prophet's book when it names the knight Nascien as the hermit-narrator of the *Estoire* (222; Lacy 1:289).[84] Merlin and Blase's practice of documenting recent events is taken over by others in the Vulgate. In *Merlin,* Guenièvre has scholars record what happens (321; Lacy 1:345), and in the *Lancelot,* four scribes record the deeds of prowess of Arthur's knights (Micha 8:488–89; Lacy 2:238). Wise men also disseminate knowledge independently of Merlin. Maistres Hélie de Toulouse cites Merlin as authority (Micha 1:54–55; Lacy 2:252–53), but also possesses a supplementary source of wisdom, a mysterious book (Micha 1:67; Lacy 2:255). Across the Cycle, a multitude of witnesses, clerks, priests, and knights appears as responsible both for the existence of "li contes" and its preservation. Sometimes different modes of recuperation challenge one other, while at a local level, as in the *Lancelot* passage about Merlin, the fiction's multiple authorization of an alternative version may occasion scribal anxiety. The variety of documentary media conveys a sense of an exhaustive retrieval of factual matter but simultaneously throws into relief the anomalies in narrative continuity. Warren notes that the slips in accuracy make ambivalent the text's claims to truth, and she identifies the Cycle's historical uncertainty with the ambivalent political desires of the French aristocracy with and for whom these texts originate.[85]

These historical illogicalities also work in narrative terms to sustain romance amplification and unaccountability. The secret love between Lancelot and Guenièvre, for example, should remain unknown to us, and Lancelot's later painting of the affair on the walls of a room in Morgain's castle (Micha 5:52–53; Lacy 3:218–19) only partially accounts for the information with which "li contes" provides us.[86] Such slippages, however, like the possibility of a gap between the vernacular texts and their declared sources, serve to generate further narrative, as well as to privilege certain elements beyond the text's normative parameters, particularly Lancelot and Guenièvre's love. The strata of copyists, translators, and compilers separating us from a declared "original" text ensure endless attempts at recovering the full "true" story, but make the filling of lacunae the work of the text rather than of the reader. The story balances between definitiveness and dilation. The *Estoire* claims to be what Christ wrote with his own hand, to which any addition could only be a lie (1:257; Lacy 1:76). The last lines of the *Queste del Saint Graal* announce as its author Walter Map, who has had recourse to the Grail quest depositions of Sir Bors, preserved in Latin in Salisbury library, and has translated them into French for Henry, his king.[87] The opening lines of *La Mort le roi Artu* claim the same patron's curiosity is responsible for Map's writing this last book (1; Lacy 4:91), but here there is no mention of translation, and the *Mort* ends by affirming, as we saw above, that the subject matter is now exhausted. The reference to Walter Map, historically a writer of Latin, is probably part of the romance writer's game with modes of authorization—and a joke at the expense of

Map's reputation, for this scholar is famously ambivalent about the value of vernacular writing.[88] The lines also suggest a comment on the political interests of Henry II, for whom it is expedient that Arthur should be good and dead. But the "historical" reference drawing the book's production into the world of an identifiable (if fictively constructed) medieval readership also serves here to bring the fiction to an end. Later writers endorse the romances' paradoxical fictions about their origins. Their amplifications continue the Vulgate's dual authorizing method of subsuming all into the proclamatory narrative of "li contes," while naming individual scribes and authors. The continuations adopt the Vulgate's self-referential histories to legitimize their own, and supply further genealogies, for Arthurian authors as for Arthurian heroes. Thus, the later French romances employ a historical (and often an English historical) specificity as part of a literary dialogue with the earlier texts. Rusticiano da Pisa, in the prologue to his late-thirteenth-century Compilation, claims his source is an Arthurian romance owned by Edward I of England, which Rusticiano himself translated at the time the king went on crusade.[89] Luces declares himself author of the Prose *Tristan,* an English knight and Lord of Gat near Salisbury.[90] He thus has topographical associations with both the Last Battle, and the written Grail testament Arthur commissions at the end of the *Queste del Saint Graal.* Luces's prologue to the *Tristan* stresses French as the apposite register for this material, which has been translated from a Latin source, "le grant livre del Latin" (Curtis 1:39). The factual basis of English authorship of Arthurian romance in French is far from certain, although R. Howard Bloch identifies as Anglo-Norman the legal processes of *La Mort le roi Artu.*[91] In terms of fictional linkage, however, prologues and epilogues refer the reader to a body of generically similar literature as a frame for the work s/he is reading. The French prose continuations produce a reassuring literary scheme, and the tensions of plural authorship and multiple sources belong to the network that sustains the subject matter. Later additions do not challenge, but replicate and strengthen, those authenticating strategies, facilitating further adventures and further books. Romance narrative, in its continual dilation, appropriates the Vulgate's "historicizing" mode as a stabilizing factor.

English Works: Experiments in Tradition

The English texts' deployment of historicizing procedures makes for more idiosyncratic and collectively less cohesive readings of the Arthurian world than the French historical fictions offer.[92] Correlative with a wider-ranging historical reference in the English texts is a different attitude to the status of the written word, the literary importance of the "story" as a physical entity.

Whereas the "true story" in the Vulgate is the site of literary play and anxiety, the English works scrutinize the very structure and constitution of the text. The narrating voice of the French prose romance has a spatial, bookish, as well as a temporal, oral, referent, as the phrase "ci dist li contes" [here the story says] intimates.[93] The narrating voices of those English adaptations that call on the resources of English romance forms concern themselves with a "time now" of performance, and frequently structure and comment on the subject. Internal emphasis is less on the written vernacular and more on the importance to the text of the politics of reception. English authors seem less concerned with recuperating a "whole text" than with the interpretive possibilities various Arthurian contexts afford the material with which they engage, and in this light I shall consider aspects of the thirteenth-century *Of Arthour and Of Merlin,* of the Stanzaic *Le Morte Arthur,* and of one of the later medieval adaptations from the Vulgate, *Lancelot of the Laik.*

The Auchinleck manuscript provides a context for *Of Arthour and Of Merlin,* one that highlights the adaptor's interest in both romance and lineage. As well as saints' lives and pious material, the collection contains *Amis and Amiloun, Guy of Warwick, Sir Tristrem, Kyng Alisaunder,* and *Sir Orfeo,* and more overtly historical and political material, such as *The Sayings of the Four Philosophers,* a roll of Norman barons, and a version of the *Liber Regum Anglie,* edited as the *Anonymous Short English Metrical Chronicle.*[94] The same scribe copies both *Of Arthour* and the *Chronicle,* and in the latter uses other material from the manuscript, such as *Richard Coeur de Lion,*[95] yet does not seek to correlate details in the *Chronicle* with those in *Of Arthour,* which suggests a pragmatic attitude to the recuperation and deployment of Arthurian material. The *Chronicle* account of Arthur, somewhat fragmented in form, demonstrates an eclectic knowledge of both continental and insular Arthurian narrative.[96] The young hero called from Wales to defeat the wicked King Fortiger belongs to historical tradition (1039–42). But the text resembles events in *La Mort le roi Artu* in its depiction of the civil war that threatens with Lancelot's abduction of Gwinore (1071–74). Lancelot, "curteys & hende" (1087), finally returns the queen to Arthur, but this narrative line is cut short with the story of Cradoc, who arrives at court with a cloak that has the magical property of exposing adulteresses (1103–06). The episode recalls the fabliau "Du Mantel mautaillié,"[97] although here the garment becomes material witness to Arthur's reign, for the curious may still go and view the cloak at Glastonbury (1107–08). Again, the story has no development; the entry for Arthur ends abruptly with a note that the king reigned for twenty-two years and is buried at Glastonbury. Material evidence, historical fact, romance, and fabliau narratives, together with an interest in chronology and lineage, are packed into a brief and disjunctive history of Arthur, under a general rubric "Hou Inglond first bigan," which refers us to the *Brut* for further information (fol. 304r). The discrepancy in detail between two accounts of Arthur's career in the same manuscript appears unimportant. Rather, *Of Arthour* and the *Chronicle* together attest to an insouciant awareness of the importance of form as key to Arthurian literature's placement and reception. The *Chronicle*'s haphazard account of Arthur threatens to break its formal boundaries, but its author contains it (if somewhat untidily) within the chronological structure of the line of kings of "Inglond." *Of Arthour* similarly directs information to a community receptive to tales of nationhood but signals the containment and manipulation of the story narratorially. The English redactor draws from the Vulgate *Merlin* an account of British history from the death of King Constans to the defeat of King Rion at the hands of Arthur, Constans's grandson.[98] In keeping with this emphasis, there is a sharp focus on the prophet's political importance. As in the *Chronicle, Of Arthour*'s narrating voice refers us to "Þe brut" for corroborative evidence (538; 3675),[99] and the linear structure contributes to the sense of a "historical" narrative. But the narrator also presents the story in such a way as to draw attention to the intervention of a mediating voice, not simply pacing the narrative after the fashion of "li contes" in the French original but also emphasizing authorial control, the sense of a relationship between taleteller and audience, and the interplay of oral and written in the sense of what constitutes a text. This is not to set a French concern with the authoritative value of the written absolutely against an English play on the fluctuating meanings of the oral, for the French texts "speak" to us in different voices, too, and extant English romances are of course written texts. I want rather to identify a difference in rhetorical emphasis: the *Of Arthour* poet, like other English redactors, stresses the spoken word, especially in the context of storytelling, to figure the selective refashioning of Arthurian legend for a specific community at every "performance," that is, for every rewriting and re-presentation of source material.

Of Arthour traces events of national historical significance, and comments on history's unfolding. Merlin and the narrator embody respectively the complexities of historical process and response to history in a narrative tailored to the English-speaking audience it addresses. The author "Englishes" the story on a broad thematic plane as in local detail. So, for example, when Merlin's mother stands accused of extramarital sexual relations, her trial follows not the source but a version of the English legal system, where an advisory jury of twelve individuals with some specialist knowledge is called on to give evidence (923–64).[100] Thorlac Turville-Petre, considering this poem in the context of an interest in a crusading theme he traces throughout the manuscript, regards as "astonishing" the author's easy equation of the "British" with the "English," and notes how conveniently Arthur's enemies the Saxons are translated into "Saracens," against whom the king wages a Holy War.[101] As with the legal detail, the invocation of crusade has the effect of registering fourteenth-century concerns, but it simultaneously draws attention to its particular representation of the Arthurian world. The poet's simplified version of Arthurian history requires audience collusion.

The poem's introduction acknowledges the prescriptive value of the written; it provides knowledge to keep us "Fram sinne and fram warldes care" (14). In the context of an immediate personal relation with the narrator ("Now ich ȝou telle þis romaunce" [31]), documentary evidence, "As we finde writen in bok" (486), provides the foundation for history and its understanding. The urgency of a "present-time" of storytelling, and the radical revision that makes this tale one of continuing national relevance, are mutually reinforcing. To make history intelligible, *Of Arthour* maintains a linear narrative that demonstrates the relation between volition and deed, and also reorganizes the material to establish more clearly the royal line of British/English kings. So, for example, the English author prunes and rearranges in order to recount in one episode the quadruple marriage, between Uther and Ygerne, and between Ygerne's daughters and the kings Nanters, Lot, and Vriens (2593–2626). Lineage emerges as central to stability. The story opens not (as in the source text) with an account of Merlin's birth but with the condition of the country's monarchy, and how Fortiger disrupts the legitimate line through his wickedness. Merlin's task is to help to restore the line; here he is a guardian of legitimacy, and ironically so, in view of his own dubious parentage. He declares his political function—"icham a ferly sond [extraordinary envoy]/ Born to gode to al þis lond" (1119–20)—and the poem foregrounds his "historical" role. The tale of Grisandole and the Emperor of Rome, for example, in the French source demonstrative of Merlin's unique ability to transcend time and place (281–92; Lacy 1:323–29), becomes an account of a woman in disguise in Fortiger's own household (1345–1436), an episode the resolution of which reflects on Merlin's ability to correct domestic and political disorder, as he makes clear when he tells Fortiger his sin will bring about the ruin of Britain (1634–80). Merlin promises that a "gret conseyle" (1674) of good men will hold with the legitimate heirs to the English throne. It is Merlin's own task to maintain this unanimity of agreement among the worthy by means of counsel and good advice.[102]

Merlin's good counsel suggests human agency is to some degree accountable for the course of events, and the narrator complements this with further moral observation. It is made clear that Fortiger has corrupted the nation by allowing the intermarriage of Christian with heathen (477–92), and that defeat at Uther's hands is the price he pays for his "unriȝt" (1902), although we are assured that, in the end, evil will pass ("Wrong wil wende," 1898). Recourse to proverbial wisdom further engages attention in a tale about "our folk" (341), "our men" (323), and "þis lond" (487). Whereas in the French text Merlin's prophecies relate to events in later texts, the English version uses Merlin to involve the reader in the same historical world as the narrative. Merlin's pronouncements serve to place the text itself historically. Of Merlin's prophecies we learn:

> Sum fel now late also
> And sum beþ nouȝt ȝete ago,
> For it is alle þester [obscure] þing
> Nil ich make þerof no telling
> Ac forþ ichil [I will] wiþ mi tale.(1703–07)

The narrator's suggestion that Merlin's prescience extends to the present time of the poem's telling and beyond departs from the source, where Merlin simply reports the successful completion of his task (*Merlin* 35; Lacy 1:185). But the poet is also careful to delimit the romance's political compass. There is a further vaticinatory link between "time then" and "time now" when Merlin tells Blase of "profecies and oþer þing / Þat sum beþ passed and sum coming" (8575–76).[103] This stress on historical effect, coupled with judgmental resumés of events such as Fortiger's fall, aligns the narrator with the advice-giving Merlin, insofar as the prophet guides the actions of the characters, while the narrator indicates to the audience an appropriate response to events. At the same time, as the reluctance to expound on prophecy demonstrates, and as the concept of Arthur as crusader reinforces, we are made aware that the text before us is selective. *Of Arthour* ostensibly promotes historical awareness of the story, but does not treat of it exhaustively. It hints instead at the possibilities for further engagement with the material, directing us, implicitly and explicitly, out toward other texts. Where the French prose romances are interested more in the interrelation of their amplified material and of their authorizing strategies, the English poet simultaneously indicates and exploits the value of the present tale in terms of historical parameters for Arthur, which seem highly flexible for the English-reading audience (certainly as far as the Auchinleck manuscript's composition implies). The author here rigorously harnesses historical reference to an uncontentious concern with "good counsel," rather than with specific contemporary politics.

The sense of audience engagement, and the narrator's ostensibly tapping into a community of interest in Arthur that exists outside the confines of the narrative proper, sets the English account apart from its French source. The writer also helps create that specific audience by recourse to the strategy of "minstrel address"—"Now ich you telle" (31)—typical of Middle English romance.[104] The romance motif gives the material a particular context, and is itself modified to comment on the Arthurian subject's potential. Other aspects of the text's poetic, notably its extraordinary imagery and other stylistic devices, testify, Burnley observes, to the English redactor's "coherent purpose."[105] *Of Arthour's* style demonstrates an ability to rework immediate source material, and to operate within poetic terms that recall Anglo-Norman, French, and English modes of battle description.[106] Furthermore, aspects of the style identify the poet as author of another romance, *Kyng Alisaunder,* comparison with which suggest the author may be aiming at a particular effect in *Of Arthour.*[107] Some of the imagery derives from *Merlin,* as when Arthur and his men strike on shields "like carpenters" (6043–44), where the French compares the sound of warriors dealing blows to that of carpenters at their work (147; Lacy 1:247). But the comparison of the chaotic detritus of battle to a crow's nest, with limbs strewn about like its component sticks (9171–74) imitates (whether consciously or not) the kind of transformational imagery Laȝamon famously employs in his *Brut* to celebrate Arthur's military strength. Thus, in the *Brut,* Arthur characterizes his enemy Colgrim as a helpless goat to his predatory wolf, and his vanquished enemies as "steel fish" in the river shallows, their scales gleaming like shields, their fins like spears.[108] Other collocations in *Of Arthour,* such as the battlefield running with blood (5757–58), find analogy in English romances, such as *Havelok,* where blood similarly floods the ground.[109] The use of quasi-formulaic language and motifs within English verse romances makes of them an identifiable contextualizing frame within which to read *Of Arthour.*

A stylistic device apparently particular to the *Of Arthour/ Kyng Alisaunder* author is the unusual and exaggerated use in both poems of what Macrae-Gibson calls "headpieces,"[110] topoi introductory to various sections. In *Kyng Alisaunder,* these draw on a range of lyric motifs, proverbs, and occupations; in *Of Arthour,* they invoke seasonal activities. Some of the latter headpieces have clear parallels in *Merlin:* so both texts describe Gawain and his brothers setting out in Maytime, evoked as a time of birdsong and verdant renewal (*Merlin,* 134; *Of Arthour,* 4675–80). Others are independent interpolations. Some of them are consonant in mood with the narrative, so lines on June as a time for love (8657–62) precede an account of the love between Arthur and Gwenore. But others stand in ironical relation to the action. The evocation of April as "mirie" (259–64) is at odds with Fortiger's taking over the land. This same apparent irony is incidentally in evidence in *Merlin,* in an episode where the Saxons are victims of a savage surprise attack by the Christians, one balmy clear April night

(166; Lacy 1:258).[111] *Of Arthour's* more frequent use of lyrical interludes, however, marks them out as a different register. But compared with *Kyng Alisaunder,* their deployment is aberrant. The interpolations in the former work draw on the collocations and topoi familiar to romance. So a few lines may typically combine pious utterance, sententia, and the "placings" of romance plot: "Jt fareþ wiþ man so dooþ wiþ floure [. . .] Fair is lefdy in boure, / And also kniȝth in armoure" (4313–18). Other asides are playful: "Good it were to ben kniȝth, / Nere tourneyment and dedly fiȝth" (7352–53). The headpieces here operate as grotesque marginalia, trying out a range of possibilities and contradictions around the central text.

Of Arthour does not convey this same sense of a space having been set aside for the articulation of disparate topoi but hints instead at registers only partially integrated with the work. It does so, significantly, at those transitional points that mark the textual disposition of the narrative, supplementing, for example, the French formula "but now the story turns":

> Lete we hem now at þis segeing [besieging]
> [. . .]Who so wille ȝiue lest [listen]
> Mai now here noble gest. [tale]
> Mirie it is in somers tide
> Foules [birds] singe in forest wide
> Swaines gin on iustinge ride [young men go jousting]
> Maidens tiffen hem [adorn themselves] in pride. (7614–22)

Just as the text signals the existence of Arthurian material—and of responses to it—that do not become part of the narrative proper, so here the author employs a narratorial design, the pattern of which gestures toward the encyclopedic while remaining puzzlingly anomalous in its inclusiveness. It both shows the author's control of the romance and leaves open the question of how one constitutes the Arthurian text; what does one leave out or include? What space is there for the string of associations mention of Arthur might bring to mind?

The "chapter heading" nature of the lyrical insertions stresses how the narrator organizes and directs our reading of the narrative, but also indicates what, once alluded to, remains unpursued or unresolved. The sense English Arthurian romance imparts of its own performance usefully reflects an element of contingency. To have a speaker delivering the story to a listening audience as part of the narrative process creates an impression of the tale being shaped even as we receive it. It is interesting, in the light of differences between English and French Arthurian narrative, that Coleman distinguishes between French and Burgundian public reading as "official" and dominated by a patron, and English reading as a more "communal" enterprise.[112] *Of Arthour*'s audience is of course also a group of readers, referred to other books for further information. But while the narrator of the Arthurian romance affirms that the story's veracity is anchored in written texts, the fiction of orality suggests the active engagement and interest of narrator and audience constitute the work in hand.

In the Stanzaic *Le Morte Arthur,* the importance of the spoken and pragmatic over the written word is evident both in the framing of the narrative, and in the way it adapts its source, *La Mort le roi Artu,* which latter text is more concerned, on both narrative and metatextual levels, with accurate documentation. Where the *Mort* works within the context of a definable body of Arthurian writings, the stanzaic poem is less stable in relation to other texts, and yet its sparse style and repeated collocations create internal logic and meaning. Where the French text investigates cause and effect, the English poem more starkly registers feeling and response. *La Mort le roi Artu* relates to the preceding *Queste del Saint Graal,* both through its declared authorship and in terms of narrative continuity. The stanzaic poem is seemingly independent, opening with an address to "Lordingis" to listen to one of the Arthurian "aunturis" (vaguely defined as very numerous) that took place in the time of "oure eldris;" Arthur is part of "our" history, but the weight of his historical importance is a matter of personal emphasis.[113] The Grail quest, abruptly and briefly invoked, is a brutal and apparently secular affair, marking an end to external threat through the killing of enemies; its adventures, all "Fynisshid and to ende brought" (12), are cut off from the events of this poem. Where the *Mort* documents the recent past, and the moral accountability of the quest's survivors,[114] the Stanzaic *Morte* charts a four-year period of inactivity before the action gets under way again.

Just as the poem begins through the imagined interaction of performer and audience, rather than as a fictional account of poet and literary patron, so it takes an oral exchange to begin the narrative proper. Arthur and Gaynour, lying abed, tell each other stories, and the queen, regretting that the knights, because inactive, are no longer spoken of, advises Arthur to hold a tournament, that they might reclaim their honor "And byspoke of on every syde" (34). Arthur and Gaynour speak, after the manner of romance narrators, of the Round Table knights, "that euyr so doughty were in dede" (28). At the end of the poem, the prayers offered for the souls of Gaynour and Arthur function also as the closing prayer conventional to romance: "Jhesu, that suffred woundes sore / Graunt us all the blysse of hevyn" (3968–70).[115] Such elision makes a formal connection between the pragmatic performance of romance storytelling and the way in which this particular narrative has unfolded. The Stanzaic *Morte* engages a particular romance rhetoric to shape both narrative and perception of event. Among the most striking stylistic features of the poem is the repetition of certain phrases that take on common currency for narrator and characters alike, and fulfill a variety of functions. The repeated assertion of the love between individuals, for example, can be a statement of fact, or the explanation of motive, but it most often stands as a mnemonic marker of what is of emotional significance in the tale. We learn that Lancelot determines not to go to the Winchester tournament because of his feeling for Gaynour, "for love þat was theym bytwene" (55). This economically states the most important factor in the story at this point, where the *Mort* instead presents Lancelot's situation discursively. In the French text, he has again fallen in love with the queen, in spite of his resolve to be chaste after his adventures on the Grail quest. Yet, Lancelot's motive for not attending the tournament at once is his desire to fight in disguise, not that which the ill-willed Agravain supplies, a wish to be alone with Arthur's wife (*Mort* 6; Lacy 4:92). In the *Mort,* Lancelot explains his plan to Guenièvre, and there is a formal leave-taking between queen and subject. In the English version, however, Gaynour at once expresses fear of discovery of the love "us by-twene" (72). The story, less cluttered than the French account, does not articulate what prompts Lancelot to act as he does, although the fact of the love-relationship remains prominent.

When Lancelot finally returns to court after Gawain has spread the rumor of his love of the Maid of Ascolot, Gaynour does not show the anger Guenièvre shows but tearfully laments to Lancelot that this should be the end of "The loue þat hathe be us bytwene" (742), and requests that he reveal this now former mutual love (752–55) to no one. Lancelot interprets this as rejection and disappears into the forest, leaving others to deplore "That evyr love was them bytwene" (799). The phrase registers, but cannot analyze, the intensity of Lancelot's love. In the *Mort,* conversely, the episode of the putative love affair leads the queen to denounce Lancelot, for which Bors in turn denounces her, in conventional antifeminist terms, as the latest in a line of women to shame noble men and to wreak the destruction of whole kingdoms by their actions (*Mort* 69–72; Lacy 4:109). This kind of extended analysis is alien to the Stanzaic *Morte,* which makes different connections between its constituent elements by means of repetition of collocation.[116] It highlights other instances of mutual love; so Gawain mentions "The love that has bene bytwene us twoo" (1701) when he takes Lancelot's side in the face of Agravain's wish to expose him as Gaynour's lover. Lancelot, on hearing of his accidental killing of Gaheries, exclaims on "The love that hathe betwexte us bene" (2024), and requests during his campaign against Arthur that his king should remember "The love that hathe be us bytwene" (2937). The poem does not avoid judgment, but its means of conveying emotional intensity asks that we mark and remember rather than evaluate. Awareness is retrospective, as when

Gaynour affirms "For we togedyr han loved us dere, / All thys sorowfull werre hathe be" (3640–41). Gaynour and Lancelot are of course not solely culpable; Gaynour's "confession" signals the change in her life, from queen to nun, more satisfactorily than it accounts for the course of events.

In the French text, both narrator and characters interpret the action in the light of earlier events, in the Cycle as in the *Mort* proper, and invoke both Fortune and the exigencies of a moral universe to examine the human condition and the nature of responsibility. Arthur's vision of Fortune before the Battle of Salisbury Plain is part of a series of warnings and explanations of the events to come, and follows a dream in which the dead Gawain warns him that confrontation with Mordred can only end in tragedy (*Mort* 225–26; Lacy 4:149). Lady Fortune carefully glosses for Arthur the significance of her wheel, and his own fate, for none can be so high that he will not fall from the highest earthly power (*Mort* 227; Lacy 4:149–50). Merlin has already signposted the site of battle, and the archbishop whose advice Arthur has sought affirms the truth of the prophetic writing (228–29; Lacy 4:150). In the English version, Arthur's dream is the more horrifying because it is impressionistic rather than explicit. The reader must supply, from a recognition of the motif, any moral commentary on the vision of the crowned king who finds himself, now atop a wheel, now plunged among dragons. The overall effect is of horror and helplessness. But the description also has resonance across the text. Arthur sits on the wheel adorned "With many a besaunte, broche, and be" (3179). After the last battle, the pillagers' treatment of the slain recalls this highest point of glory: "They refte theym besaunt, broche, and bee" (3419). The text substitutes allusiveness for commentary, and metonym for causation. The *Mort* gives a meticulous account of the end of Arthur's reign, and correlative with the scrupulousness of the text's production is the detailed self-interrogation, testimony, and record of the actants in the drama. Accordingly, the French text is more specific about the causes of tragedy. The Stanzaic *Morte,* with its greater stress on rumor, on the fact of emotional engagement, and on event rather than on its causes, offers fewer certainties.

The French prose texts lay claim to authoritative truth, but clerics, or wise men such as Merlin, control particular hermeneutic strategies, such as the imagery that offers pathways through the different narratives. The late-fifteenth-century Scottish *Lancelot of the Laik* transforms the *Lancelot* account of Galehaut's war against Arthur (Micha 7:434–8:128; Lacy 2:107–49), and focuses questions of romance identity and literary hermeneutics in ways that invite comparison both with the source's methodology and with Malory. The author makes the language of romance, including the interpretive clues particular to the *Lancelot,* part of the articulation of his individuated and controlling poetic voice. He co-opts the French Arthurian narrative and its claim to revealed truth into an adroit exposition of various rhetorical and poetic registers, both public and private, supplementing his source with material drawn from other genres, from complaint and advice literature, and so declares his own literary versatility and his authority as translator and reinventor of romance. *Lancelot of the Laik* owes much to recognizably Chaucerian modes of writing, especially, I would argue, the *Legend of Good Women*. The poet frames the Arthurian extract within a dream vision of which he as narrator is the central subject, and in the course of which he describes how he has come to write the tale that follows.

The prologue provides a synopsis for the poem, which survives only in incomplete form.[117] The pivotal series of Lancelot adventures that constitutes the poem's central narrative shows the young hero's political importance to Arthur and establishes him as Guenièvre's lover, for the sequence culminates in the first kiss between queen and knight. In the French, Arthur seeks interpretation of a dream in which he physically disintegrates, losing his hair and his fingers (Micha 7:434–35; Lacy 2:107–08). The counselors, finding in it premonitions of disaster, offer him instead only a mysterious warning they claim unable to explain; without the "watery lion," the "physician," and the advice of the "flower," he will lose all earthly honor (Micha 7:437; Lacy 2:108). Prince Galehaut and his forces threaten Arthur's kingdom: Lancelot, imprisoned by the Lady of Malehaut, obtains from her a temporary release to go and fight, in disguise, for his king, and so distinguishes himself that Galehaut, in admiration of Lancelot's chivalry, makes peace with Arthur. Critical attention has focused on the poem's amplification (1275–2144) of a long section in which a wise man reveals to Arthur that the strange signs he has seen are emblematic respectively of Jesus Christ, God, and the Virgin Mary. The wise man makes this explanation part of a sermon to Arthur on his responsibility to his people and his duty to God and to the Church (Micha 8:16–29; Lacy 2:120–24). Prologue apart, the section on good governance is the extant poem's longest addition to its source, and the poem's manuscript context of religious and moral subject matter further invites critical attention to this material.[118] The advice section has also excited interest for its possible extratextual historical referent—for example, as a warning to James III.[119] But the tenets of good rule also function within the ambitiously wide-ranging self-authorizing poetic the Scottish writer establishes.

The narrator-lover translates from source to target language, but he also "translates" in that he uses metaphor, playing on literal and figurative meanings to set up parallels between his role as poet-lover and the hero Lancelot; both the framed Arthurian narrative and Lancelot as lover are offered as tender of and as surrogate for the poet's own feeling. At the same time, the expansions of a generalizing and sententious political Arthurian discourse draw attention to the ambivalence at the heart of Arthurian narrative proper, which, especially in its French Vulgate manifestation, uneasily negotiates the overlapping claims of the personal and the political. In the Vulgate, the Lancelot-Guenièvre narrative is anomalous within the various terms the Vulgate encodes for authoritative witness to events. In inscribing himself as part of the love interest, the Scottish narrator turns the Vulgate inside out, and shifts the focus from that of internal textual authorization to a more general extratextual debate about the claims of, and relationships between, poetic authority, texts, and patrons. On May Day (12), when all is under Love's governance, the narrator, a distraught "thochtful" lover, finds himself in a trancelike state similar to that of his narrative's protagonist, except that his "exasy" (76), at the prompting of a little bird, the God of Love's emissary, will produce poetry, while his hero's (277) will spur the adventures constitutive of poetry's subject. The Maytime opening and the strictures of Love also suggest a prototype for our poet in the narrator of the *Prologue* to the *Legend of Good Women*. Unlike him in his personal relation to love, the later narrator shares the Chaucer persona's creativity and an interest in the interaction between literal and figurative. Told to banish melancholy, he tells of one who has conquered "the sorowful castell" (259) (a reference to Lancelot's Dolorous Garde adventure [Micha 7:311–33; Lacy 2:75–80]). Lancelot and the writer are both in love's bonds, and both suffer the "sword" of love's desire and pain (29, 699–701), but Lancelot is subject to and then transcends love's metaphors, literalizing them through chivalric action: on the battlefield, burning in the fire of love, he strikes his adversary "throuch and throuch the hart" (1091–93). Lancelot's deeds win him Guinevere and reaffirm his public status as a "good knight."

The juxtaposition of Lancelot's experience with the poet's declared situation aligns different manifestations of amorous solipsism—the fictitious character's and the self-fictionalizing poet's—that reflect on the poem's literary self-consciousness, for the central referent is literature itself rather than emotional sympathy, as is clear from the opening spring topos. Lancelot is one about whom scholars read in "diverss bukis" (204). At the end of the prologue, the narrator defers not to his desired lady but to the "Flour of poyetis" (320). The poet deploys floral metaphor to link the Virgin Mary and Lancelot (the flower of chivalry) as (each in her/his own compass) redemptive figures in the poem.[120] But this metaphoric patterning, as the beginning and ending of the prologue demonstrate, also involves the poet's own relation to literary precedent and literary decorum and production.

The sequence in which Amytans advises Arthur inscribes a further literariness. Where the French text emphasizes social obligation and clerical control, the later adaptation stresses social reciprocity, while the poet exercises control of literary register. The poet's Amytans borrows from advice literature his warning against flatterers (1918–98) and Alexander the Great as exemplum (1837–55), directing us to further literary, as well as ethical, contexts. The narrator carefully circumscribes his role; he refers us to "the holl romans" (1436) for Arthur's confession, for "I am no confessour" (1439). Instead, he interweaves the figure of Lancelot, acting out his public duties informed by his private feelings, with his poetic demonstration of his ability to manipulate registers, which constitutes the poem as a whole. Arthurian literature here synthesizes public and private, which the narrator turns to his own advantage. If Lancelot as lover is the poet's surrogate, acting out a story proleptic of the writer's own success in love, his military success matches the poet's presentation of advice literature as public poetry. *Lancelot of the Laik* is a public poem that speaks private desires, a "personal" poem open to a number of "public" readings and emphases, just as Lancelot's career can be read as primarily "public" or "private" service and devotion. The range of audiences and audience response the poem suggests reinforces this plurality of interpretation. Commissioned by the God of Love, the poem courts the lady for whom it is written. The poet defers to other lovers (who are also skillful poets) to correct his literary efforts (177–89), while the "mirror for princes" material testifies that it serves a broader, socially oriented, poetics. Through recourse to different registers, the author makes Arthurian narrative's tensions between public and private identity, and its problems of knowledge and authority, a question of rhetorical mastery. The poet lightly suggests himself aware of the source's epistemology and control of the physical and replaces its elite encodings of knowledge with a poetics he himself controls.

The poet, in identifying the anonymous wise counselor of his source as "Amytans," in an episode involving dreams and symbols, is alluding to another sequence, integral to the romance's interpretive strategies, in which an "Amustans" helps expose the False Guenièvre (Micha 1:159; Lacy 2:276). "Guenièvre" is Arthur's queen's half-sister, daughter of King Leodegan and Leodegan's seneschal's wife,[121] for whom Arthur has repudiated his true queen. The identical appearance of the two Guenièvres (Micha 1:95; Lacy 2:262) concentrates questions of identity and interpretation. The False Guenièvre highlights, and then displaces and defers, the political problem the True Guenièvre's desire poses in the broader Vulgate narrative. Arthur's adulterous liaison with the False Guenièvre draws sympathy for the true queen and for Lancelot, but also displaces onto this "other woman"'s surrogate body the question of the Lancelot-Guenièvre relation, through its implicit interrogation of the queen's function. Where Arthur only dreams of bodily departition, the impostor queen begins to rot from within and deliquesces (Micha 1:153–55; Lacy 2:275). Her own corrupt and corrupting body confirms both Amustans's denunciation of her and the justice of the Pope's indignant interdiction of Arthur's realm (Micha 1:153; Lacy 2:275). "Guenièvre"'s bizarrely doubled and destroyed body is the locus of a transgressive guilt; this locus absorbs and then dissolves the guilt of those who survive, and blurs the boundaries between the articulable and the unspeakable. It is, however, only one of the most spectacular of the Vulgate's conjunctions of somatic corruption and "misinterpretation" (which embraces treachery, misrepresentation, and ignorance). By this means, the text regulates the parameters and meanings of both body and narrative.

The *Lancelot* thus spectacularly draws attention to its determination of textual meaning and its arbitrariness of focus, which in turn makes prominent the lack of control of individual characters, who have to ask interpreters to reveal the narrative's secret knowledge. The story of the False Guenièvre graphically demonstrates how the text inscribes bodies (especially, though not uniquely, women's bodies) in the service of its epistemology. Mention of Amytans in the Scottish text signals the gulf between the poem and its source; in *Lancelot of the Laik,* revelation is not reserved for the elite, but translates into the reassuring proverbial encodings of advice literature. Instead of the *conte*'s (and its wise men's) nexus of interpretation, there is reassurance that as lovers or as rulers we can retrieve meaning through and in response to registers we already know, the courtly troping Chaucer has made familiar to us, or the comfortingly familiar encodings of advice literature. Whereas one might ultimately trace a particular political relevance for the poem, then, its focal point is the poet, in control of what Judith Ferster calls "the play of deference and challenge" endemic to advice literature.[122] The somatic is important for the Scottish poet, as for the Vulgate, but the narrator appropriates Lancelot's body in the interests of his own concerns with the relations between language, action, and literature. In part, the author builds his links between Arthurian story and fifteenth-century redaction through a Chaucerian poetic; Malory, as we shall see, co-opts Chaucer rather more disturbingly into his reflections on the literary means of making sense of Arthurian narrative and into his considerations of an individual writer's ability to resolve Arthurian legend's inherent tensions.

The Art of Compilation: Gonnot and Malory

The French prose romance narratives, the Vulgate Cycle and its literary dilations, locate themselves within a given framework, their parameters drawn as part of a specific literary enterprise. English treatments do not duplicate French concerns but are more individualistic, acknowledging a range of extratextual associations for Arthur. Historical, literary, and cultural conditions do not suggest we can measure the "originality" of English Arthurian texts only according to a traditional translation studies model of comparison between source and target languages. Malory's work needs, as contextualizing frame, a flexible cultural model that can both recognize Arthur's different roles for English audiences and appreciate the *Morte*'s achievement in the context of late-medieval England's (still) multilingual culture, one in which "Englishness" is increasingly at issue, but that is at the same time deeply imbricated with literature written in French.

Any attempt to determine the nature of the *Morte* must also account for the evident slippage between the cultural world of the Arthuriad, which privileges the authority of a "French book" both imaginary and real, and the historical world of Malory, in which Caxton reads Malory's "English" book in a nationalist context, and in which "France" is a place of dispossession, where the English have lost territories in 1453. Felicity Riddy invokes this historical situation to characterize Malory's work as "a post-imperial, or even post-colonial, text," in that it speaks to the concerns and anxieties of English gentry only recently dislodged from Continental lands.[123] Riddy's brief invocation of socioeconomic circumstances stylishly bridges a worrying gap between literary and historical worlds by allocating Malory's prose a compensatory function.[124] But such a formulation also takes for granted the nature of the literary territories at issue in the relation between French and English cultures that informs Malory's work. While, for example, the identification of the Arthurian realm as "all Englond" (1:7.2) rather than "Britain" supports a view that Malory (following other English redactors) rewrites the legend for the late-fifteenth-century English "gentleman," the inscribed deference to the "French book" as locus of authority leads us back to the Clermont/Chandos argument about cultural debts. Rather than see Malory's project as nationalist, yet somehow embarrassed or compromised by the literary past of its material, however, we could turn to literature on postcolonialism, and specifically to those postcolonial critical writings that emphasize the hermeneutic importance of the "siting" of literature arising from a multicultural situation, to account for Malory's mode of narrative authorization. Homi Bhabha's formulation of the culturally "interstitial," for example, as a space that relations between, and displacements of, different cultures can produce, has implications for understanding Malory's text, as does the work of Tejaswini Niranjana, who engages with translation as a "problematic."[125]

Where, in material terms, can we position the *Morte?* Culturally and historically, its bulk aligns it with a French tradition of Arthurian writing, but the construction of the "whole book" suggests Malory's method incorporates and interrogates both English and French constructions of, and literary responses to, the Arthurian world. The work of Micheau Gonnot,

Malory's French contemporary, exemplifies the French tradition of re-working Arthurian prose romance. Gonnot is primarily a compiler, one who, as Bonaventure would have it, puts together others' writings rather than his own.[126] On the last folio of BN MS f.fr. 112, he announces his name, his home, his profession of priest, and his having completed this work in July 1470.[127] Gonnot copied this text (and several others) for Jacques d'Armagnac, Duke of Nemours, who was executed in 1477 for plotting against Louis XI, and his books confiscated.[128] Malory inscribes his own Arthuriad as "drawyn by a knyght presoner" (1:180.21–22); he is both scribe and patron. These writers' historically verified professional standings align them with the clerical and secular writers and registers of Vulgate Arthuriana. To determine how Malory's declaration differs in kind from Gonnot's, we need establish how each text structurally deploys the relation between narrator, reader, and book.

Gonnot draws together material from the Vulgate and Post-Vulgate cycles, from the Prose *Tristan,* and later continuations of Arthurian legend such as *Guiron le Courtois.*[129] The first volume of the work is lost, and with it any initial statement of intention, but the prologues and epilogues in the remaining three volumes show how Gonnot keeps faith with textual authority. Those techniques familiar from French romance—the authority of "li contes," the named authors and patrons, the interest in the genealogies of the books as complement to the lineage of the heroes whose adventures they detail—organize BN f.fr. 112. Gonnot constructs a genealogy for his book. He incorporates colophons and incipits from texts such as *La Mort le roi Artu* and the *Queste del Saint Graal,* when he names Walter Map as translator and author at the appropriate points in his own compilation (4: fols. 182a-b; 233a). Some of his explanations of selection and organization conceal the text's possible originality behind references to traditional writers of Arthurian legend. The rubric at the beginning of the first extant volume credits "maistre Robert deborron," putative author of the earliest cyclic texts, and part of the network of Vulgate and Post-Vulgate authors, with translating tales of the young Lancelot, "en son temps le meilleur cheualier du monde" [in his time the best knight in the world], from Latin into French at the request of Henry of England (2:1a-b). The "de Boron" prologue that follows, however, appears unique to BN f.fr. 112. In it, the narrator cites the importance of finishing work begun—"car toute chose imparfaicte desire auenir a quelque utille et prouffitable perfection" [for every imperfect thing desires to attain to a certain useful and profitable perfection] (2: fol. 1a)—and aims to be inclusive: "touste la verite et la vraye histoire le racompteray le moins mal que je pourray" [I will tell the whole truth and the true story as best I can] (2: fol. 1b). The importance of "bonne chevalerie" will be evident in the actions of its exponents, the good knights Lancelot and Tristan, the compilation's principal protagonists (as in Malory). Good lineage guarantees good knighthood, and the text's own ancestry assures us of its truth. The prologue to Book Three (also original to BN f.fr. 112) links the compiler's enterprise more strongly with that of the knight errant. The writer justifies himself in chivalric language. Lancelot's deeds of arms must be chronicled: "trop seroye mauuais de le laisser" [it would be too wrong to abandon them] (3: fol. 1a), and Galahad later speaks in the same terms of his pursuit of the marvelous *beste glatissant:* "Or seroye je mauuais si je jamais laissoye ceste chasce a mon pouuoir deuant que je leusse menee affin" [Now I would be wrong were I ever to abandon this hunt, as much as it is in my power, before I had brought it to its conclusion] (4: fol. 147a). This recurring image of the compiler engaged in finishing what he has begun, complementary to that of the knight errant completing his quest, constitutes a lucid model of authorial and narrative process, and promises the recuperation and exposition of "bonne chevalerie" within the text.

The prologue at 4: fol. 1a–c prefaces material concerning the Grail, and invokes the Trinity and the Saints to help oversee the completion of this last part of the anthology. The text itself, the narrator assures us, contains nothing unauthorized, "et que je naye leu et visite en pluseurs liures anciens" [and which I have not read and encountered in several ancient books]. Gonnot's sources would have been physically present in the library of his patron, Jacques d'Armagnac, to authenticate his compilation.[130] The compiler again stresses the urgency of finishing what has been begun, adding a humble request for the forbearance of "bons et vrais hystoriens" [good and true historians]. The final justification for the text is similar to that in the introductions to other later French Arthurian prose works, as well as to Caxton's *Morte* prologue.[131] The prologue insists that this is above all a book of instruction:

> Car selon mon petit entendement les jeunes cheualiers et escuiers y pourront aprendre moult de beaux faitz darmes. et quant Ilz trouueront chose villaine ne de reprouche je leur conseille quilz ne le facent mye car les choses malfaictes sont escriptes aux liures pour les fouir et euiter Et les bonnes pour les ensuyure et les acomplir chaque homme de bon voloir. (4: fol. 1c)

> [For according to my small understanding, young knights and squires may learn a great deal from it about fine deeds of arms, and when they find anything ill-bred or reprehensible in it, I advise them not to imitate it, for bad things are written in books that they might be shunned and avoided, and good thing, that one every one might follow and attain them with a good will.]

Gonnot produces a definitive Arthuriad, and refers the reader to other texts for further corroborative information.[132] His work is not perhaps uniquely concerned with good governance, as Judson Boyce Allen has claimed,[133] but nor is Jacques d'Armagnac necessarily a conservative reader who, in Cedric Pickford's formulation, enthusiastically commissions copies of Arthurian narrative in a spirit of nostalgic escapism from "the reality of life."[134] The book's structure, however, meshes well with the Duke of Nemours' textbooks on knighthood that emphasize its system. For Gonnot, affirming the written Arthurian prose romance tradition is integral to the meaning and value of the chivalry he describes. This project may seem to do little more than expand Arthurian knights' adventures, while broadly maintaining the Vulgate structure, but locally the Vulgate suggests different modes of interpretation within the Cycle's broader eschatological and historiographical frames of reference. When Gonnot, however, anthologizes his material within the parameters of good knighthood and a by-now traditional authorizing romance form, he effectively reduces all Arthurian story to the same plane of understanding and mode of reception. Even the Grail story, in Gonnot an intercalation of the original *Queste del Saint Graal* with episodes from the versions in the Post-Vulgate and Tristan Cycles,[135] is set within the context of other events as yet another means for a knight to attain perfection; it conflates the values of earthly and heavenly "bonne chevalerie." And whereas juxtaposition of adventures might perhaps make room for a certain irony, the collection's compendiousness tends to emphasize similarity, monumentalizing a way of writing as much as the events the Arthuriad recounts.

In comparison with Gonnot's careful declarations of intent, Malory's organizing strategies are haphazard. BN f.fr. 112 is the crafted work of a practiced compiler. In the *Morte,* speculation about the author's life aside, references to the narrator as knight and prisoner suggest a more complex textual involvement. Malory-as-knight may echo Luces de Gat's authorizing strategy, but he also engages with the material on an individual level, while his being held captive frustrates his chivalric definition. In the *Morte,* a sense of displacement replaces a corroborative genealogy of authors and books, and requires continuing realignment of the relative importance of narrator, reader, and book. Malory, like Gonnot, traces the rise and fall of Arthurian society, but he is innovative in that he implicitly asks us intermittently to read against the grain of the "authorizing" reference points with which he provides us. Where Gonnot witnesses to a self-confirmatory "true story," the status of Malory's work appears less certain. References to a "French book" sometimes corroborate his text (1:286.13–14), and sometimes point out lacunae, as when he "overleaps" "grete bookis" on Launcelot (3:1154.1–2). Most famously, reference to a French antecedent signals a departure from the source, which bears comparison with the Chaucerian narrator's method in *Troilus and Criseyde;* as with invocation of Lollius, references to a French book call attention to potential interference with an originary text (real or imagined). Through "Lollius," Chaucer as writer playfully remakes the Troy legend's textual tradition. Malory, however, transcends recourse to a Latin source as a mode of authorizing vernacular writing, with a less stabilizing play between two vernaculars, a stratagem less tractable than Chaucer's ironies.

Troilus and Criseyde's Lollius fiction poses generally the question of authorial responsibility, as the disingenuous narratorial voice intermittently reminds us: "Disblameth me if any word be lame, / ffor as myn auctour seyde, so sey I."[136] Malory's invocation of textual precedent more specifically concerns the limits of control. In the *Tristram,* a note referring to a manuscript division in the source intrudes curiously into a dialogue between Tristram and Arthur concerning a shield's provenance. The *Morte* is a palimpsest, the "original" structure obtrusively visible:

> "Sir," [Tristram] seyde, "I had [a shield] of quene Morgan le Fay, suster to kynge Arthure."
>
> So here levith of this booke, for hit ys the firste booke of sir Trystram de Lyones. And the secunde boke begynnyth where sir Trystram smote downe kynge Arthure and sir Uwayne, bycause why he wolde nat telle hem wherefore that shylde was made. But to sey the soth, sir Trystram coude nat telle the cause, for he knew hit nat.
>
> "And yf hit be so ye can dyscryve what ye beare, ye are worthy to beare armys." (2:558.32–559.7)

This interpolation has the earlier literature leave unexpected material traces in the later text; the former structure appears more important than present narrative continuity.

The *Morte* shifts continually between its various components' claims to narrative control, as the dynamic of narrative implicitly depends on the varying responses and interactions of reader, writer, and texts. In some tales, the process of the story seems largely "our" choice, as with the reader's pursuit of the young hero in *The Noble Tale of Sir Launcelot du Lake,* so that, although the "Freynsh booke" (1:253.14) authorizes the hero's importance, reader and narrator together maintain the narrative focus, apparently without the French book's further mediation: "Now turne we to sir Launcelot that rode with the damesel" (1:269.17). At other times, the "story" controls its own telling, for example, in *The Tale of the Sankgreal,* although in the French text the autonomy of the "contes" is central to its self-authorization, whereas Malory's narrative so contextualizes this technique as to make us ponder our distance from, rather than our access to, revelation.

Variability as to what aspect of the literary process finally determines the text in front of us is then endemic in the *Morte,* as is variability in the precise nature of each of those constitutive aspects. Throughout, Malory depends heavily on our engagement with the physical. Harry Berger distinguishes between what he calls "the order of the body" and "the order of text" in human communication.[137] Technologies of the written, he suggests, increasingly "abstract" the text from the bodily performance of it that limits interpretive freedom, whether in Renaissance drama, or in the late-medieval oral delivery of written works. Malory may be said to appropriate for the written the trope of the communicating body, in that his fictive, "authorial body," that of the knight-prisoner, suggests a delimiting engagement with the text. This performative aspect is not, however, ultimately reassuring, partly because of the conflicted element in the authorial body's identification, and partly because it coexists with other modes of constructing the text. Launcelot's literary body similarly appears to offer a reassuring continuity but, through his presentation, the *Morte* suggests a certain recalcitrance attaches to the physical as ground of our engagement with the text on an epistemological level.

The *Morte* imagines the act of translation from the French book in a "time now" of active and inconsistently realized reception, although narrative event is generally recounted in the past tense rather than in the historic present. At the same time, Malory draws on "English" ways of writing about and understanding Arthur, as when he reworks the Alliterative *Morte,* although this latter text itself raises questions as to what constitutes "Englishness." Malory's narrative comes then to exist, and to be performed, in spaces "between" English and French Arthurian cultures and texts that already have some shared ground. This is where Homi Bhabha's writings help draw attention to the kind of space Malory's work occupies, and to what is at issue there.[138] Bhabha's concept of the interstitial arises from his examination of the relation, in terms of the postcolonial, between binary opposites of colonizer and colonized, difference and similarity. In the meeting between these binaries, he characterizes a space in which discourse is disrupted, a place productive of new and challenging meanings. Translation here has a special function as part of the emergent "new" culture that celebrates hybridity and destabilizes cultural identities. Bhabha's implicit suggestion that power structures collapse in the space between the polarities might seem a utopian and ahistorical view of cultural exchange and cross-influence.[139] But he also acknowledges the anxiety that can lurk at the borders between cultures.[140]

We might call Malory's text "interstitial" in its conflation of different cultural and literary figurings of Arthur, and also in the dynamic it sets up between modes of textual assertion and recuperation. The Vulgate makes interstitiality part of its structure; Lancelot and Guenièvre's liaison exists in its "gaps" in the documentation and retrieval of knowledge. Malory, meanwhile, presents the processes of the Arthuriad's construction as somewhat eccentric, and returns us to consider the impulses behind the *Morte*'s constituent elements, and our own responsibility for their interpretation and collation. Malory's enterprise is, furthermore, "anxious" in the sense of being caught between models. The "French" perspective on Arthurian legend as competitive writing makes it a site for considering modes of vernacular authorization, and it constructs the legitimacy and authentication of the Arthurian as part of that authorization, so that the Arthurian political domain is at the same time the domain of literary influence. The "English" stance views the literary articulation of Arthurian legend as performative, experimental, and inquiring, at the same time as Arthurian legend in England would appear more contentiously and contingently "political" than in France. In the *Morte,* each perspective reflects on the other by virtue of contiguity. The local level of textual engagement is "English" in its improvisatory and provisional nature. Although, for example, the text continues beyond Vinaver's *King Arthur* section, the colophon suggests that other interested readers (reading as men) can replace the present writer: "Who that woll make ony more lette hym seke other bookis of kynge Arthure or of sir Launcelot or sir Trystrams" (1:180.19–21). Yet, the idea of the "French book" as an authoritative work that exists outside this apparently haphazardly arrived-at English text and exercises intermittent influence on its constitution is similar to the implicit desire for, and frequent absence or problematization of, other forms of institutionalization and control one encounters in the *Morte*—for example, the rule of law, prescriptions of gender roles, and their interrelation. Notionally, an "authorized" version is available, but in the *Morte,* the very fact of "Englishness" may militate against its full recuperation. The only mention the *Morte* makes of "Englysshe bookes" is in the context of poetic unreliability, of the "favour of makers" (3:1260.5–7); in drawing largely on the Vulgate model for his own Arthuriad, Malory also recontextualizes the English literary encodings of Arthurian literature within which he presents his work as that of a pragmatic reader. This tests the historical perspectives possible for English retellings of Arthurian legend, and troubles our understanding of what constitutes history. Through the meeting of English and French traditions, Malory makes his Arthurian book the site for interrogating—rather than celebrating—ideas of identity, nation, narrative, and history.

CHAPTER 2

DESIRE, HISTORY, VIOLENCE:
MERLIN'S NARRATIVES

John Steinbeck observes of Malory's world that: "no moral law obtains."[1] Desire and violence drive the *Morte's* narrative and Merlin, as an "interstitial," culturally diverse character, brings their parameters into question, in an ostensibly ordered but locally unsettling text. In the *Morte,* the urge to order and historicize has to acknowledge the possibility that moral judgment, the legitimization of violence, and historical recuperation are contingent. This chapter traces some late-medieval ideas of the "historical" Arthurian world as context for Merlin's function in the *Morte.* In the *Suite du Merlin,* the prophet outlines the world's moral and textual boundaries, whereas in the English Prose *Merlin,* he mediates more immediate and practical concerns with the communication of counsel and good advice. For a fifteenth-century English audience, Arthur's potentially multiple significance inevitably provokes negotiation with the variety of extratextual associations he commands, from romance heroism to national dynastic pride. Merlin relates historiography and romance differently from Arthur, and is more complicatedly involved in questions of literary authorization and structure. Caxton's historicizing preface does not address Merlin's historical role, perhaps because Merlin's protean literary and political import demand even trickier negotiation of textual and cultural evidence than Arthur's case presents. Caxton leaves his readers to engage for themselves with the specificities of Malory's account, and instead elaborates a complex, arguably historically evasive, cultural background for Arthur. If the preface offers us an Arthurian history without Merlin, it also leaves us to speculate on this absence.

Caxton's Preface:
Historiography and the *Morte*'s Readership

After that I had accomplysshed and fynysshed dyvers hystoryes [. . .] many
noble and dyvers gentylmen of thys royame of Englond camen and de-
maunded me many and oftymes wherfore that I have not do made and en-
prynte the noble hystorye of the Saynt Greal and of the moost renomed
Crysten kyng, fyrst and chyef of the thre best Crysten, and worthy, kyng
Arthur, whyche ought moost to be remembred emonge us Englysshemen
tofore al other Crysten kynges. (1:cxliii.1–11)

Caxton's apparent skepticism regarding Arthur's historicity[2] constitutes,
in his 1485 preface, a subtle historical inquiry. Caxton tells us his printed
works range from the literature of private devotion to that of public action
and history. He had already elided the realms of the individual spiritual and
the social in *The Book of the Ordre of Chyualry* (ca. 1483–85), a translation
of Ramón Lull's *Libre de l'orde de cavalleria* that defines true knighthood as
inner integrity expressed in public service. In the epilogue, Caxton had
celebrated Arthur's times for their uncomplicated exercise of moral and
chivalric values.[3] The requests for stories of the Holy Grail and of Arthur
are the logical culmination of Caxton's interests in the personal and the
political, and are as much a publisher's advertisement as a plausible report
of customer demand. Before Caxton raises doubts as to Arthur's historicity, the register of nationalist interest in him already anticipates unanimity
of opinion between the publisher, the would-be readers, and those who
have access to the printed text, all cast as "us Englysshemen."[4] In the reported dialogue between potential eager readership and initially skeptical
publisher, Caxton exploits English historiographical and poetic traditions,
which allow for multiple perspectives on Arthur, and also shows himself
keenly aware of the mechanics of various interpretative strategies. As the
preface develops, we recognize how cultural contexts and apparently fixed
rhetorical procedures interact. Caxton constructs interlocking contextual
frames for Arthurian stories. The dialogue between publisher and readers
echoes the inscribed relation between minstrel-narrator and audience in
Middle English romance, where a narrative develops as a series of ques-
tionings of, and subjective engagements with, extant material. The preface,
rather than arguing through to a clear idea of what Arthur is, conveys the
difficulties of isolating what he means for a society familiar with him from
a range of cultural configurations.

For "us Englysshemen," the topos of Arthur as greatest of the Nine Worthies provides an appropriate focus for the demands of the market.[5] Yet this
apparently stable point of reference itself adumbrates nationalist, Christian,
and personal concerns. Documentary evidence, from "balade" and "prose" to

the Bible, supports the Worthies' existence as "known" fact (1:cxliii.12–25). As first of the Christian triad (1:cxliii.25–30), Arthur gains a context at once heroic, historical, literary, and rhetorical. The topos also shapes Caxton's own publishing venture: Arthur's history appears between that of *Godeffroy of Boloyne* (1480–81) and *Charles the Grete* (1485).[6] The prologues to these works create reader demand by matching their texts with familiar historical patterns. In its essence, the Nine Worthies topos exemplifies world history as the charting of exemplary men's heroic deeds. Caxton suggests, by means of the Worthies, that a chivalric Christian imperialism is the culmination of an ideologically grounded historical process that begins with the triads of Pagans and Jews, and his dedication of his book on the French crusader Godfrey to Edward IV suggests this model of history can override nationalist boundaries in the interests of religious cohesion. Caxton is here in tune with contemporary tastes and concerns. In 1472, the first printers in France had sent Edward a presentation copy of Cardinal Bessarion's *Orationes* (1471), which urged a Christian crusade against the Turks.[7] But the notion of pan-European crusade is not necessarily inimical to nationalism, and in the closing lines of the *Brut* or *Chronicles of England* (1480), Caxton has already linked Edward's claim to France, his "rightfull enheritaunce beyonde the see," with the Christian peace that is a precondition for a successful campaign against the Turk.[8] The anonymous "jantylmen" readers similarly reintroduce a nationalist inference for Arthur synchronous with his "universal" status as a great Christian leader; he deserves commemoration because he is a king of England born (1:cxliv.7–8). If Caxton makes room for a generalized view of Arthur as Christian hero, the nationalist emphasis also avoids any factional problems that might have arisen within the carefully constructed "English" community, had the editor named a patron for the Arthurian work.[9] Arthur thus becomes accessible to the broadest possible grouping of English-speaking readers, one united by national allegiance rather than local political loyalties.

Arthur-as-Worthy relates then in the readers' mind to both nationalism and pan-European Christianity, but the topos is not easily isolated from other Arthurian narratives. Consumer demand is for stories, in English, of Arthur's knights and the Holy Grail, and for the satisfaction of narrative closure, his "deth and endyng" (1:cxliv.4). Nationalist discourse appropriates English as linguistic medium. But Caxton is also identifying and filling a gap in the market: the invocation of a wide-ranging narrative, alongside Arthur's specific designation as Worthy, allows the "reluctant" publisher to focus on historiographical method, and the impulses to quantify and moralize Arthurian material. Caxton envisages history as directing the reader to particular moral response, possible because, in Hayden White's words, "he [*sic*] has been shown how the data conform to an icon

of a comprehensible finished process, a plot-structure with which he is familiar as part of his cultural endowment."[10] For one reader in the preface,
indeed, everything tends to a general proof of Arthur as national hero.
However, the material relics mentioned—the imprint of Arthur's seal at St.
Edward's shrine, Gawain's skull, Cradok's mantle (1:cxliv.30–36)—carry a
subtext of other stories, counterplots that allude to the whole sweep of
Arthur's reign, to his co-option as legitimate king into the English nationalist cause (through reference to Edward I, England's patron saint as well as
king), to the court as locus of chivalry, to the sexual scandal of the Cradok
story,[11] and to the internal dissent that leads to Gawain's death. The juxtaposition of diverse source material suggests that Arthurian narrative cannot escape the implications of its previous formulations and associations
but will always make us aware of the selective reading necessary to any uniform interpretation. If the preface establishes Arthur's historical reality with
a firm nationalist basis, it also foregrounds the artifice required to construct
such a reality. A last reference to Arthur as Worthy raises a question about
the transformational effect on the material of the language we use to accommodate it to a nexus of knowledge. Horst Schroeder reads Caxton's
prescriptive advice to the reader—"Doo after the good and leve the evyl,
and it shal brynge you to good fame and renommee" (1:cxlvi.7–8)—as
part of the progressive *embourgeoisement* of the Nine Worthies topos, which
shifts in the Middle Ages (as also to some extent in the course of Caxton's
preface) from the celebration of heroic deeds to the recommendation of
personal moral values.[12] This raises the question of how Arthur is best understood: in terms of a community's political position, or of personal moral
duty? And in what sense do these domains overlap?

The arguments about Arthur's historicity draw unsystematically on earlier historical opinion. The regret at the comparative dearth of English
Arthurian texts, and the idea that the legend is morally instructive, echo
Robert Mannyng.[13] Caxton's argument that some chroniclers' silence must
make us question Arthur's existence (1:cxliv.11–15) parallels Ranulph Higden's misgivings in the *Polychronicon*.[14] But the reader who sets out to change
Caxton's mind cites the *Polychronicon* as a Latin text that provides authoritative proof, along with Boccaccio's *De Casibus Virorum Illustrium* and Geoffrey
of Monmouth's *Historia*. The selectivity of the preface homogenizes into
complementary testimonies on biographical fact what extratextual knowledge reveals to be a series of conflicting accounts.[15] Here, Higden supplies
the detail of Arthur's tomb, Boccaccio places him within the "fall of princes"
framework, and Geoffrey "recounteth his lyf" (1:cxliv.21–27). This homogenizing extends to the catalogue of Arthurian artifacts, which reinforce other
tenders of Arthur's historicity: his position as Worthy, and the wealth of literature about him extant in other languages (1:cxlv.1–6).

Caxton's manipulation of historians runs counter to his formulation of history elsewhere, in the Proheme to his edition of Trevisa's translation of the *Polychronicon* (1482), as preferable to other written forms because it permanently stores past actions, and because it offers a consonance between event and language: "historye, representynge the thynges lyke unto the wordes, enbraceth al utylyte and prouffite." History imparts wisdom through the vicarious experience of the past; Caxton tells of how men can be disciplined, and learn responsibility, through hearing of "straunge mennes hurtes and scathes."[16] Louise Fradenburg and Carla Freccero have analyzed the implications for the homosocial of this idea of historical engagement.[17] Caxton's representation of relations between men's bodies effected through books suggests a plastic and pragmatic notion of history can inform one's response to the written word, and this offers a suggestive framework for exploring Malory's Arthuriad as a history of bodily encounters. The *Morte* preface clearly acknowledges the text's messy interpersonal uncontainability: "herein may be seen noble chyvalrye, curtosye, humanyté [. . .] murdre, hate, vertue, and synne" (1:cxlvi.4–6). Yet, rather than analyze Malory on these terms, Caxton takes refuge in a comfortable moral determinism: "al is wryton for our doctryne, and for to beware that we falle not to vyce ne synne" (1:cxlvi.11–13). The preface testifies to the power of current cultural appropriations of Arthur that might influence an interpretation of the *Morte,* while not pressing the case for the *Morte* itself as history; we are free to decide what is true (1:cxlvi.10–11). Caxton stops short of detailing precisely how, and also by whom, this difficult text is read. Robert Sturges suggests Caxton invokes an orderly society of royalty, aristocrats, and gentry (1:cxlvi.18–20) to contemplate "their own legendary national past."[18] Yet, the constitution of an idealized community to imitate the text's "actes" seems optimistically generalized,[19] as is the moral prescription for our reading. The troping of Arthur as historical involves an exposure, and a glossing-over, of the material's lack of homogeneity, and the difficulty involved in its management.

Caxton's rhetorical stratagems uncover some of the more troubling potentiality of Arthur as subject, and imitate in part Malory's own narrative tensions, even as they impose order on intractable material. To aid the reader, Caxton provides a summary of the chapters into which he has divided the book (1:cxlvi.29–31). Narrative coherence is consonant with moral understanding, Caxton suggests in his preface to *Charles the Grete,* in which he writes of reorganizing "hystoryes dysioyned wythoute ordre" to make the moral more graspable.[20] Caxton's synopses, like his editing method, tend to consistency in textual presentation so as to make the preface's prescriptive reading more easily applicable. This implies an instant decoding of the text, which obviates the need to look to the *Morte* itself for reading models to interpret its multifariousness. The ambivalent Merlin falls casualty to this reading, and in Caxton's synopsis his more troubling dimensions disappear, and his role at the inception of Arthurian society is straightforward. Some consideration of the tradition linking Merlin with textual creation, exposition, and generic appropriation will demonstrate how Malory rewrites the prophet and the issues associated with him; among these are historical process, counsel, gender, the direction and containment of violence, and the rule of law.

Narrative and Moral Order:
The English Prose *Merlin*

Fifteenth-century Continental and insular interpretations of Merlin stress his vaticinatory importance. Jehan de Waurin, writing his *Chroniques* for the Duke of Burgundy in the later fifteenth century, reappropriates the prophecies of Geoffrey's *Historia* as generalized condemnations of social ills for his own times.[21] In one fifteenth-century manuscript, the "Prophecies" circulate with political poems that mention Merlin to justify historical events.[22] Caroline D. Eckhardt observes that the Prose *Brut,* with its prophecies of the Six Last Kings of England, gives Merlin an immediate relevance for a British fifteenth-century audience.[23] This readership would be familiar with a Merlin who offered a political link between "time now" and Arthurian historiography, but Merlin's historical potentiality might also be read in the context of his conventional romance function as one who "poses generally the question of the relation between knowledge and power."[24] In French prose works—the Vulgate *Estoire de Merlin,* the Post-Vulgate *Suite*—this ambivalent figure, operating between historical, prophetic, and romance registers, is central to concerns about textual recuperation and continuity. In his Arthurian romance incarnation, integral to the text's audacious self-authorizing, Merlin may even appear to counter his "historical" role, by disrupting those issues of agency and genealogy at the heart of historical writing.

If romance claims Merlin for its own purposes, so that faith in the prophet is faith in the genre of romance, the Vulgate Cycle, by making him part of a network of competing and complementary authorities, also relativizes his significance within its overarching epistemology, and so goes some way to neutralize the more disturbing aspects of Merlin's influence. Merlin is an extraordinary overseer of Arthurian society, with privileged knowledge, and the end of the *Mort* recalls his power when Arthur discovers he has prewritten his destiny with a prophecy of the Last Battle (*Mort* 228; Lacy 4:150). Yet, this prophecy also shows the Cycle absorbing Merlin into a larger teleological plan, according to which the central characters seek to find a moral order in the world, as when Arthur declares that should he lose the battle against Mordred, it will be because of his sinfulness (*Mort* 229; Lacy 4:150).[25] In the *Lancelot,* when Merlin relinquishes his hold over knowledge and writing, "li contes" simultaneously confirms its authority, as we saw in chapter one. Set against the *Estoire,* with its testimony of divine revelation, the *Merlin* appears textually more ambivalent, and less prestigious, yet all these narratives belong to self-reflexive romance play on authoritativeness. When one reads *Merlin* in isolation, the Round Table the prophet institutes in Logres is a mystifying projection of political control and social order, which troublingly figures Merlin's own power. Merlin promises Uther honor to soul and to body with the institution of a table in imitation of Joseph's replication of the table of the Last Supper. These three tables will together figure the Trinity, and Merlin's Table thus has spiritual as well as secular significance (*Merlin* 54–55; Lacy 1:196–97). The Table is a place of election for which Merlin chooses only the worthiest, and a force for unity. Uther's men have no desire ever to leave him once they have taken a place there (55; Lacy 1:197). But the place Merlin leaves vacant for the future Grail knight also becomes the focus for those who seek to efface the prophet's political domination. A defiant transgressor of Merlin's prohibition against occupying the seat dies for his presumption, and Merlin returns to assert the "great meaning" of the Table and his control over it, but refuses to explain the transgressor's fate (57–58; Lacy 1:198–99). The Round Table functions as a largely inscrutable image of the origins and maintenance of political power through Merlin, and so marks the limits of romance's analysis of social control. In the context of the Vulgate, however, the incident reenacts the breaking of a similar prohibition regarding Joseph's table in the *Estoire* (*Estoire* 2:486–88; Lacy 1:138), and so suggests Merlin's table is primarily meaningful as the secular imitation of a spiritually informed precedent. The *Queste del Saint Graal,* meanwhile, reassigns the Round Table to a scheme of spiritual completion and wholeness; Perceval's aunt explains it replicates cosmic order (*Queste* 76; Lacy 4:26), and Galahad's claim to the Siege Perilous intersects Arthurian with salvation history. So the Vulgate frames and neutralizes the Round Table's unresolved political status.

Merlin's eponymous prophet demonstrates how romance may claim control of historical process but not necessarily engage with the responsibility of such knowledge. The mid-fifteenth-century English Prose *Merlin* closely translates the Vulgate *Merlin,* and forms a transition between French textual tradition and Malory's project. From a traditionalist perspective on translation, an adaptation might admit of no great originality, but John Johnston (building on Walter Benjamin's work) offers a conceptualization of translation as "simulacrum," more productive than the notion of "original" and "copy," whereby a translation, rather than being measured in terms of fidelity to its source, may propose itself as the "origin" of a new set of meanings.[26] At the same time, Paul de Man notes the potential for translation to expose the "mobility" and "instability" of the original.[27] The English Prose *Merlin*'s isolation and recontextualization of the Vulgate text writes large the paradoxes of Merlin's position, within an intensified concentration on those aspects of human organization seemingly under Merlin's control, the apprehension of history, legality, and social order. The English text is also particularly concerned with Merlin as paradigm of advice-giving and good counsel in the context of Arthur's rise to political power.

The English text follows the French in presenting Merlin within the moral absolutes of a dualistic universe, for the devils intend Merlin as an antichrist in retaliation against the triumph of the Divine.[28] Merlin and his pious mother disrupt this scheme, and the child's miraculous *enfances* imitate the narrative pattern of the apocryphal Infancy gospels.[29] But Merlin is also paradigmatic of human volition, for God has granted him free will: "he yaf hym fre choys to do what he wolde, for yef he wolde he myght yelde god his parte, en to the fende his also" (1:14). Merlin controls the past, in that Blase's book offers us narrative "knowinge" (1:143),[30] and foretells the future (1:53–54), the boundaries of his own knowledge circumscribed by God in despite of the Devil (1:32). Merlin transcends the antichrist framework and, throughout the text, re-presents literary and rhetorical structures of human knowledge. This he does both in his narrative formation of Arthurian history, and in self-contained episodes that demonstrate in condensed form the extraordinary control the prophet exercises, and the ease with which he appropriates others' power. In particular, the tale of Grisandole and the Emperor of Rome (2:420–37) reveals and corrects past fraud, while that of Flualis, Emperor of Jerusalem (2:631–34) depends on Merlin's prophetic knowledge.[31] Flualis has a violent and seemingly prophetic dream in which he and his family are torn apart by serpents, and his lands destroyed (2:633). Merlin mysteriously and abruptly intervenes to interpret the dream as prognosticatory of Flualis and his family's conversion to Christianity, a prophecy realized in the narrative (2:675–76), in which Flualis operates as a surrogate for Arthur and his Christian expansionism. Merlin's account images the Christianizing of the East as narrative complement to Arthur's crusades against the heathen Saxons in the West. Merlin's endeavor serves as narrative shorthand, ensuring dominance of the Arthurian worldview, while seeming to promise the eventual interpretability of other of his own obscure sayings.

The tale of the Emperor of Rome features Merlin in a more complex intervention. Merlin exposes the deception wrought by the empress, who is enjoying adulterous relations with a dozen young men disguised as women. He also reveals that the steward, Grisandole, is in fact a princess. Merlin punishes the wicked, and reestablishes the dynasty with the emperor and the newly identified princess at its head. Merlin also, however, reinvents himself as counselor, by consolidating, through narrative, the symbolic order he controls. Merlin first enters the Emperor of Rome's palace not as restorer of right order but in the guise of a chaos-wreaking hart that literally overturns civilized life: "and than he ran thourgh the tables a bandon and tombled mete and drynke all on an hepe, and be-gan ther-in a grete trouble of pottis and disshes" (2:422–23). In this bizarre disguise, he promises the Emperor that a wild man will explain his disturbing dream in which twelve young lions mount a crowned sow. The idea that wisdom is accessible from the margins of civilization replays Merlin's method elsewhere in the text; in his preliminary meetings with Pendragon, he similarly has recourse to disguise, appearing first as a beggar then as a herdsman, to make the ruler receptive to his advice (1:42–46). Merlin continually takes on the apparel of those outside society's jurisdiction, such as the wild man, or the apparently helpless, such as the blind (1:73), to signal his uncontainability within set terms. He is the channel through which the unknown becomes known and therefore usable.

When the disguised princess Grisandole goes into the forest to find this marvelous being, the hart reappears with advice on how to tame the wild man, and make him amenable to her will:

> "Purchese flessh newe and salt, and mylke and hony, and hoot breed newe bake, and bringe with the [. . .] a boy to turne the spite till it be I-nough rosted, and com in to this foreste by the moste vn-couthe weyes that thow canste fynde, and sette a table by the fier, and the breed, and the mylke, and the hony vpon the table [. . .] and doute the nought that the sauage man will come." (2:423–24)

This mixture of the raw and the cooked, of the trappings of civilization and wildness—tables set in forests—perfectly expresses Merlin's ambivalent location between nature and civilization.[32] But he is also the hart who shows Grisandole how to achieve her aim. He plots for himself his movement from forest to court, from the margin to center, where he will reveal truth.

On his way to court, Merlin-as-wild-man laughs at meaningless events (a group of beggars at an abbey gate, a squire's involuntary striking of his knight), and three times denounces the disguised Grisandole as unnatural and the cause of man's downfall (2:425–27). The text early on shows Merlin's laughter is marker of the power contingent on his privileged knowledge (1: 33–35), but only before the emperor does Merlin rewrite his history in such a way as sets him not between good and evil, but between the wild and the domestic (2:428). At court, he sets about a series of revelations and uncoverings He justifies the language used to Grisandole, while exonerating her from personal culpability: "by women ben many townes sonken and brent, and many a riche londe wasted and exiled, and moche peple slayn" (2:432).[33] His revelation that the empress is the insatiable sow of the emperor's dream who must be burned for her treasonable lust includes a denunciation of woman's tendency to lechery. The wild man also concedes, however, that some women are "full trewe" (2:433). Merlin's polarizing pronouncements on women locate his speech within, and endorse, a recognizable set of commonplaces, in particular the antifeminism on which the authority of the text is founded. They even suggest that he initiates this "wisdom," where the Vulgate context, by contrast, absorbs Merlin's experience into a recurrent misogynistic play on knowledge and power.[34]

Merlin's interpretation of the strange events, meanwhile, depends on special factual knowledge. The beggars are standing on the site of buried treasure, an echo of an earlier narrative episode (2:167–91), where a disguised Merlin reveals to Arthur the whereabouts of buried treasure. It is also a retelling, a new storymaking. Here Merlin's method recalls that of "moral tales" such as the *Gesta Romanorum,* where it is often the overlaying of one tale by another that constitutes the exemplary.[35] So he recasts the incident of the squire's beating of his knight in the language of Christian piety as a warning to those who oppress the poor, practice usury, or profit from abuse of the law (2:434). While others' disguises are unnatural, or morally reprehensible, Merlin's shape-changing complements his manipulation of linguistic registers: he alone can "speak other," rewrite allegorically. Merlin leaves at the door of the court (a significant location in view of Merlin's liminality), a message identifying himself as Merlin: "maister counseller to kynge Arthur of the grete Breteyne" (2:436), the words of which only a Greek messenger can decipher, at which point the letters disappear. The biblical echo suggests—but does not make explicit—divine approbation of Merlin, while the words themselves highlight his relation and service to King Arthur. The Grisandole episode crystallizes Merlin's nature and function, explicable partly by recourse to narrative precedents, and partly by Merlin's language, which bridges marvelous events and their explanation in culturally familiar registers (such as set pieces about women). Merlin's disguises are metaphors of his relation to society. The Grisandole episode even rehearses Merlin's eventual fate: tricked by a woman, he also organizes his own downfall (2:432). Most important, however, is what it makes explicit about Merlin as embodiment of counsel and advice: the sequence figures both the anomalousness and indefinability of counsel (in the person of Merlin), and yet assures us of the recuperability of wisdom. Counsel transforms knowledge into controlled action to a specific end, and a good society exercises it responsibly. In a fifteenth-century context, Merlin has formal and idiomatic ties with contemporary advice literature; but he also makes Arthurian society historically aware, and offers it a synthesizing model of its history.

The English text uses various historiographical procedures familiar to its readership. It stresses lineage and God's direction of events according to the moral behavior of human beings. Gabrielle Spiegel suggests that genealogy provides a model of social order and implicit causation to impart ideological meaning to historical narrative.[36] Merlin himself, as facilitator of generation, shares with the medieval chronicler this interest in lineage, and as continuity of regnal line links with continuity of narrative, Merlin is anxious that the Battle of Salisbury Plain will leave Britain "with-outen lorde, and with-outen heir" (2:579).[37] The English Prose *Merlin*'s proleptic account of British history shows how disruption of lineage initiates a period of chaos, of plague and slaughter (1:147), but also how this period of crisis is consequent on sin and must be viewed within the context of divine retribution. Elsewhere, within the historiographical tradition of the *Historia* and the *Brut,* the narrator observes that the Saxons overrun Britain "for synne and for mislyvinge" of its inhabitants, "as god hath ofte sithes chastysed diuerse remes" (2:191).[38] The text endorses a traditional, providentialist view of history, according to which, as John Capgrave has it in his *Abbreuiacion of Cronicles* (1462–63), human deeds are subject to "Goddis ordinauns."[39] The rebel King Ydier, for example, interprets his *vnhappe* as divine retribution: "ffor by the synne [. . .] that we have done a-gein (Arthur) falleth to vs all these myschaunces" (2:282).

Illicit sexual relations and illegitimacy, however, are not uniformally subject to moral censure. When Merlin explains his role as Arthur's guardian as the expiation of "synne" (1:87), Uther insouciantly ignores personal responsibility and displaces the moral issues onto Merlin: "Ye be so gode and so wise that ye can yow wele in this a-quyten." Other unions Merlin arranges—between Arthur and Lysanor (1:171), and between Ban and Agravadain's daughter (2:607–12)—are contingent less on the exercise of a divine foresight than on the gratification of present desire. The latter episode is poised uneasily between human volition and divine ordinance: explicitly a displacement of Merlin's own sexual desire for the girl (2:607), it is also glossed, before and after the event, as fated, for Ban has learned of his adultery in a dream (2:415), and Merlin knows Agravadain's daughter's child will prove a worthy knight (2:607). Only intermittently is sexual activity the object of moral scrutiny. The author reserves judgment on the story of Mordred's conception (1:179–81).

Similarly, no opprobrium attaches to Leodegan when he rapes Cleodalis's wife, which act leads to the birth of the false Gonnore (2:213–14), for whom Arthur repudiates his wife, although the narrator does observe how God allows events to unfold as they do because of the sinfulness of people in general (2:466). In the English Prose *Merlin,* the generation of children belongs rather more to the domain of romance narrative possibility than to moral and social controls. This lack of a consistent moral attitude in individual cases blurs the lines between human beings as responsible agents of their own destiny and as instruments of other powers, as well as suggesting a less than fully coherent role for Merlin. It is perhaps the mixture of familiar rationalization and a more random license on events that leads at least one fifteenth-century reader to note the text's odder sexual liaisons.[40] Merlin's participation in this ambivalence over sexual matters reinforces the claims of romance above historical pattern. The text leaves in suspension the nature and extent of human social control that historical narrative's interest in lineage might suggest, and draws us instead into a realm of romance necessitating reader collusion.

On the battlefield, moral issues might appear clearer. When he assures Arthur that, with God on his side, he will be victorious, Merlin endorses the equation between sin and mischance (2:578). But he also transcends such formulations when he creates, with the dragon banner, an image of historical process supplementary to written forms of knowledge and rich in connotation. A heavenly dragon first appears to Uther and his brother Pendragon to signal the propitious time for victory (1:56). After the battle, Merlin suggests a golden dragon emblem commemorate the dead Pendragon's bravery and acknowledge the hand of Providence (1:57).[41] Yet, when Merlin helps Arthur in his first great battle against the rebels, he gives him a dragon emblem of "grete significacion" and obscure origin: "no man cowde wit where Merlin it hadde" (1:115–16). That society has forgotten the earlier dragon image suggests each generation has to forge its historical awareness anew. Present at every encounter of Arthur's forces with the Saxons, the dragon becomes emblematic of Arthur's power (2:393).[42] It is also a prophetic sign, condensing history in foretelling the final catastrophe on Salisbury Plain (and, for the reader, outlining the plot of *La Mort le roi Artu*): "And the flame of fiere that com oute of the throte be-tokened the grete martire of peple that sholde be in his tyme, and the taile that was so tortuouse be-tokened the grete treson of the peple, be whom he was after be-traied" (2:393). This historical image is also a fire-breathing, dust-raising agent of destruction, a figuring of the kind of battle strategy Merlin employs, and a metonym for warfare in general. The enemy interprets it as a sign of divine anger and of misfortune in war

(2:406). Merlin's organizing presence on the battlefield, and his banner, makes him a reference point for martial procedure, at once the index of present power and, for the reader, historical awareness.

Against this historical model is King Rion's collection of the swords of those he conquers (2:620), and his beard-cloak, which at first mention carries the tribute of twenty kings, and for which he seeks trophies from ten more (1:115). (That Rion is later said to have nine kings subject to him [2:620] suggests the cloak is no accurate historical record.) Rion demands completion of his beard-cloak through Arthur to fulfill his ambitions. Partly in response to Rion, Merlin reinforces the power and significance of the dragon emblem through a sequence of disguises (2:614–15; 621–23). Arthur is at first baffled by the blind harper who asks to carry the banner into battle against Rion: Merlin as blind musician (seer, creator, commemorator, who harps "a lay of Breteigne" [2:615]), reminds Arthur's court both of his own function and of the importance of historical engagement. Only when Merlin reappears in the form of a child to repeat his request does Arthur, who has learned to read Merlin's codes, recognize him and grant his wish. The banner emblematizes Arthurian historical process; the society's sign of special election is an image of martial engagement that ironically also signifies the Arthurian world's inevitable downfall. The text supplies other historical images, however: Arthur's desire and struggle for Rion's sword Marmiadoise, for example, both exposes the similarities in personal ambition that Rion and Arthur share (that beard-cloak and dragon banner would seek to occlude), and more complexly relates the Arthurian world to Greek and Trojan mythography and history (1:340).[43]

Arthur acts independently of Merlin in his desire for the sword, and he also calls primarily not on Merlin's advice but on historical precedent when he refuses to pay tribute to Rome: "I owe to haue Rome by heritage as I haue Bretaigne" (2:642). Yet both sovereignty—Arthur wants Merlin to be "lorde of me and of all my londe" (2:567)—and historical process ultimately refer back to Merlin, who may also evade both. It is Merlin who foretells and explains Arthur's adventure with the Giant of Mont St. Michel (2: 644–45), and whose "conseile" realigns the war against Rome (2:638–64) with the exigencies of romance narrative when he tells Arthur to abandon a forward march and instead go to fight the Giant Cat of Lausanne (2:665). In the dragon banner, present pragmatic image of an historical role, Merlin provides the possibility of synoptic vision, but his own ultimately inscrutable alterity affirms such synthesis is not possible without him. He thus simultaneously represents the romance form's ability to encompass and appropriate the historical, and romance foreclosure of any radical investigation of history's forms and consequences.[44]

Away from the battlefield, Merlin consolidates the rules of social interaction through good counsel, and through Merlin the English text endorses contemporary advice strategies while also soliciting our good will and credence in Merlin. Merlin demonstrates control of wisdom and its sometimes surprising location. In the Grisandole episode, he moves explicitly from the margins of human experience to a central position, from which he elucidates what was hitherto confused and uninterpretable. In general, Merlin makes revelation and wisdom available in familiar conventional terms, and although he leaves the characters in the text to sort out for themselves the pragmatics of action, he also has a confirmatory role. In this, the romance bears a certain formal resemblance to advice literature such as Thomas Hoccleve's *Regiment of Princes* (ca. 1412), which similarly looks to familiar formulations of how to live well, and also encodes a more empirical tendency, evident in its identification of anomalous actants as channels of wisdom.[45] In the *Regiment,* Hoccleve shows counsel as a drama of social exchange. In its preface, a distressed and disorientated "Hoccleve" meets an Old Man, a character who at first appears to be only a marginal figure, inhabiting an indeterminate landscape, but who gradually takes on a central role as moral guide and dispenser of wisdom, and so facilitates Hoccleve's recovery of social function and literary purpose.[46] The English Prose *Merlin* does not encode advice forms as sophisticatedly as does the *Regiment,* but the poem illuminates the conventionality of the prose romance's endorsement of counsel as part of a network of social relations.

Advice literature in general proposes to accommodate social process and the written, and locates power within a social dynamic. Merlin apparently figures good advice, but frustrates efforts to determine the scope of human agency. He trains both the characters and the reader to appreciate his provisional hold on experience and on text alike. At the same time, he removes control from the human arena when he performs the movement from margin to center and relocates counsel in romance narrative. As a result, the English text deals with the bewildering unknowability of counsel by displacing the problem onto Merlin's physical person. It locates fixity of meaning in the ambivalent prophet. In the process, the proverbial, and social order, are not open to challenge or reformulation. Early on, the Prose *Merlin* underlines the need for "good counsel" to help the king determine the politically expedient. In this regard, Vortiger's career is exemplary. He has access to Merlin's wisdom only when it is too late, and so cannot read the significance of his continually crumbling tower as image of his transient power (1:27). The English text explicitly links credence in Merlin's organizational and cognitive skills and the stability of the realm.[47] But Merlin demands a deal of unconditional trust. His shape-changing links in disturbing fashion with his advice-giving properties: Uther is willing to believe his counsel, although "I can not sei what he is" (1:47).

Merlin uses disguise forcefully to remind the young Arthur of the contractual nature of advice. Merlin has earlier told the king of the whereabouts of buried treasure (1:150), but after the Battle of Bredigan, the spoils of war are divided and the treasure remains in the ground. Merlin returns in the guise of a "cherll," carrying two birds. Arthur asks if the hunter will sell or give him the birds, but Merlin rebukes him for his lack of generosity. He turns himself into a parable about the need to reward service before he reveals his identity (1:168). This translation of counsel into action generates narrative. Merlin's foreknowledge and political acumen recommend him to the British kings, but individuals also draw on his proverbial wisdom to regulate their conduct. When Utherpendragon suffers reversals in war, Merlin encourages him to read the experience as exemplary: "Now maist thow se that peple ne a-vaile not in bataile with-oute a gode lorde" (1:92). George Ashby's poem to rulers similarly notes that they will have more support "if ye go youre selfe to batail."[48] Others imitate Merlin's language when they attempt to rationalize or explain events. Aguysanx, when he observes of the threat of Saxon invasion that "Oure lorde that is so gracious, ne foryeteth neuer his seruaunt in what he be" (2:235), echoes Merlin's assurance to the disbelieving barons that the sword in the stone is God's grace made manifest, and his witness to Arthur's legitimacy: "I se well that god doth not foryete his seruaunte, thow he haue be a synner" (1:112).[49]

The text filters forms of advice through Merlin, whose presence is socially and structurally necessary; he helps to read the environment and social situations, as well as the written. Merlin articulates control through the merging of writing and landscape when he dictates to Blase prophetic "lettres" that he "sette by alle the weyes where the auentures were," to encourage questing knights (2:563). Merlin is of practical importance in battle (2:404–10), and he averts a dangerously violent combat that threatens at the tournament at Toraise (2:460). His absence then bodes ill for the tournament at Logres a little later (2:484–502), where Gawain fights wildly in a morally questionable encounter between the king's and the queen's forces at court, and the ritual of tournament soon cedes to "mortall werre" (2:488). Characters finally resolve the combat by imitating Merlin's conciliatory role and register. Nascien denounces the madness of the proceedings (2:492), Hervy comments on the sinfulness of such folly (2:497), and Gonnore finally calms the situation by appealing to Gawain's sense of "honour" and "profite" (2:500). In the written as in spoken wisdom, society imitates and incorporates Merlin's controls; Nimiane (2:312) and Morgan document in writing the skills they learn from Merlin, and Gonnore employs clerks to record knightly deeds (2:483). Merlin mediates between unwritten and written in the narrative, as well as between the accessible and the inaccessible written. But while the court attempts to attain stability through commemorative writing, textual strategies that center on the ambivalent Merlin make uncertain the very nature of the relation between writing and stability and, further, remind us that memory may exist independently of the written and that the written is not readily understood.

As if to emphasize Merlin's control over narrative development and interpretation, a dissolution of the narrative's encyclopedic impulse accompanies his disappearance. The young knight Segramor and nine companions go to seek the lost Merlin:

> [. . .] and in that quest be-fill many feire a-uentures wher-of this storie maketh no mencion, but [. . .] neuer cowde thei lerne no tidinges of that thei were meved for to seche; and at the yeres ende thei com a-gein and tolde theire a-uentures, and some ther were that tolde more theire shame than theire honoure, but trouthe moste thei sey by theire oth that thei hadden sworn; and in tho dayes gentilmen were so trewe, that thei wolde rather lese theire lif than be for-sworn.(2:687)

The fact that the Arthurian heroes maintain a sense of honesty testifies to the endurance of Merlin's influence, but the wholeness of the text and the documented integrity of those within it here part company. The extant copy of the English Prose *Merlin* breaks off just before the happy conclusion to an adventure in which Gawain learns the value of courtesy. Also missing are the French text's concluding episodes of Ban's political troubles and Lancelot's birth, which look forward to the *Lancelot*. Material accident reinforces the sense of the English text as a Merlin-narrative divorced from its explicatory context.

In the Vulgate context, the historiographical issues the text hints at can be left unresolved, in suspension like the prophet in his rock prison, while the narrative moves on to new adventures that place Merlin's activities in the context of broader Vulgate concerns. Lacking this context, the English works focus issues of power and social order. The paradigm of good counsel declares Merlin works for society's good; a "political" Merlin confirms the romance world as "relevant" to our own. But advice literature is also at the service of romance, for Merlin, in encoding traditional advice forms, delimits the Arthurian world and, rather than opening it up to fresh analysis, neutralizes its potential for examining the political arena. Merlin's presence does not solve the text's more intractable aspects, such as the question of the origins of wisdom, or why retribution is expected and exacted for some actions and not for others. The English Prose *Merlin* accentuates how the ambiguities surrounding both text and prophet serve the demands of a possibly perverse narrative, one that appears as historical mirror but is ultimately accountable only to the fictional world it constitutes.

Malory's *Morte Darthur*: Merlin and Pragmatism

The Winchester manuscript scribes conscientiously rubricate names, of persons (God excepted) and of places, and very occasionally of proper nouns. For Andrew Lynch, this underlines the *Morte*'s promotion of name as "index of power and prestige."[50] But rubrication can also highlight the inadequacy of name as expository system; knights, rather than ladies, are rescued from anonymity, for example. Merlin's name is, uniquely, abbreviated, which Helen Cooper interprets as operating narratively on a local level, and reflecting Merlin's extratextual power.[51] The inconsistent references to Merlin, using now his full name, now an abbreviation (for example, at fols. 17v–18r), also reflect an uncertainty about his status in a text that signals but does not investigate Merlin's distinct nature. Like the English Prose *Merlin,* the *Morte* notes Merlin's anomalous relation to and control of social order, but in the Prose *Merlin* the prophet, mysterious as he is, remains a central referent for the text's epistemology, whereas Merlin's control is less in evidence in the *Morte,* which suggests plurality rather than homogeneity in social organization. One consequence of this diversity is that society neither remembers nor processes the wise and prescient Merlin's advice. Merlin's occasional clarity marks this gap between his wisdom and the possibility of its promulgation. It denies us assurance of lasting equilibrium through Merlin's agency. In contrast to the function he performs in the English Prose *Merlin,* Malory's Merlin registers the desire for a stabilizing force that a more complex social network lacks.

The contrast between Malory's Merlin and the figure in another of his sources, the *Suite du Merlin* is even more startling. The *Suite* implicates Merlin in its establishment of a textual, social, and moral framework that serves as a basis for Arthurian narrative and epistemology, even though the text reserves to itself the revelation of full knowledge.[52] Malory's rewriting of an originally synthesizing character has implications for our apprehension of the moral principles on which the narrative rests. Caxton's synopses of the action obviate Merlin's more troubling dimensions; he emerges as the central advice giver and facilitator in Arthur's early reign, before he is finally imprisoned (1:5–6; 59–60; 123). This account realigns him sketchily with the prophet-enchanter of the French texts, and confirms that for Caxton, reading is a falling-in with established extratextual reading models. Certainly, in Malory's text, what Merlin signifies, textually and socially, depends on what we—and the characters—already know about him.[53] But Merlin is often more allusive than explicit, his role abbreviated and dislocated compared with the sources. In combining the unexpected with the conventional, Merlin belongs to the generic disparateness and plurality of direction that characterize the opening book of the *Morte Darthur.* The gaps in our knowledge about Merlin, and his structural displacement in the *Morte,* make him a disquieting and problematic focus of any attempt to form a theory of knowledge.

The responses to Merlin in the text show the difficulty of determining moral coordinates, and of relating violence and law, in a world in which event is open to plural explanation. Society defines Merlin according to its needs, and uses his advice pragmatically; but Merlin is here not the *Suite* codifier of knowledge. There is a lack of fit between Merlin's traditional function as social organizer and the narrative as it unfolds. So Arthur's marriage tacitly overrules the assurance, a few lines earlier, that the king took Merlin's advice (1:97.6–7). Merlin warns Arthur of Launcelot's and Guinevere's future love, yet acknowledges the force of desire: "thereas mannes herte is sette he woll be loth to returne" (1:97.26–27). The clarity of this warning demystifies the prophecy, where Malory's source tends to obfuscation, but its very transparency also highlights the question of why Arthur ignores the message. Part of the answer lies perhaps in Merlin's proverbial wisdom, unique to the *Morte,* which recognizes the pragmatics of human interaction,[54] where the *Suite* Merlin circumscribes human action. In the *Morte,* the search for meaning often depends more on the exigencies of the moment than on an all-encompassing moral prescription for human behavior. The *Morte* omits those authorizing strategies through which its sources link themselves with the records of Merlin's commemoration, disposition, and prognostication of material. So Blase, for example, has only one brief mention, as chronicler of Arthurian deeds, and there is no explicit link between his writings and the book we read (1:37.31–38.2). The *Suite* has narrator and prophet work together, after Balain's death, to map out an enchanted landscape for the story's future adventurous knights (1:193–97; Lacy 4:221–222). The author interrupts the account of Merlin's magical stage-management to explain the rationale behind the disposition of the narrative. Our experience of the text as organized by the author becomes consonant with the characters' experience of Merlin's shaping the narrative landscape. Malory, however, breaks the careful authenticating links between narrator, present "text," and extratextual narrative. He mentions the story of the Sankgreal as repository of information—concerning Perceval's Sister's blood-sacrifice, and Galahad's achievement of Balin's sword (1:82.9–14; 92.2–7)—but its relation to the text in front of us will be revealed only through the cumulative experience of our own reading.

The opening chapters of the *Morte* do not then link Merlin's creativity with the writer's task, nor does the "story" declare its orderly spatial and temporal organization. Malory's narrative is more random; rather than present us with a self-contained fictional world, the author often depends on our invoking extratextual referents to make sense of the narrative. The naming and name-withholding of Merlin is paradigmatic of this method. Examination of the episodes of the engendering of Arthur, Balin's experiences, Merlin's career, and the institution of the Pentecostal Oath will further illuminate the disruptions and problems of interpretation attendant on this narratorial procedure. By intermittently occluding an overarching frame of order, whether textual, legal, or world-historical, these episodes articulate an anxiety over authority and violence, especially with relation to the regulation of the gendered body, which is to become a pressing issue for the whole narrative.

The *in medias res* opening of the *Morte* assumes previous knowledge: "Hit befel in the dayes of Uther Pendragon, when he was kynge of all Englond and so regned" (1:7.1–2). Silent on the Vulgate / *Suite* history of Merlin as antichrist *manqué,* the *Morte* launches into the human physical world, and the issue of society's countenancing of excess. Against a background of uneasy peace, Uther's amoral love and anger "oute of measure," sets in motion the opening sequence of events.[55] Ygrayne's refusal to cede to Uther's desire ruptures the precarious reconciliation between the king and the Duke of Tintagel. Uther's privy council legitimizes the king's wrath, declaring the duke's disobedience reason enough for war (1:7.27). The result is a bloody stalemate, until Ulfin solves the problem by seeking out Merlin, an individual who seems to enjoy his full confidence, but of whose history or identity we learn nothing. Every act previous to this propitious encounter has resulted from a certain deliberation, but here it is not clear whether Merlin's volition, Ulfin's zeal, or pure happenstance is responsible for their meeting. Merlin's distinctive "begar's aray" sets him apart from those who seek his advice, but is neither the basis of further narrative development nor open to sententious comment.[56] In the *Morte,* Merlin at once defines the terms of his relation with Uther. He proposes to help satisfy Uther's frustrated desire, but initiates a schema of reciprocity for male social relations: "So ye wil be sworn unto me [. . .] to fulfille my desyre, ye shal have your desyre" (1:8.37–39). Malory's vocabulary here sits well with that of recent narratology, which finds desire a slippery but compelling term for the dynamic of narrative.[57] Merlin's extraordinary intervention makes possible the realization of sexual desire and so generates both Arthur and text. Merlin makes Uther's lack of measure the means to establishing the possibility of measure in Arthur, and in doing so he reads across the timescale as well as within the more immediate scheme of reciprocity.

This originary act is, however, exceptional in combining lack, satisfaction, social exchange, and Merlin's control in a morally uncertain sequence of events ultimately tending to the good of the realm. In the *Morte* as a whole, the term *desire* most frequently denotes volition, from a simple request to sexual or spiritual longing, usually defined within a network of social obligation. Yet, this network can entail unforeseen demands. Spiritual desire in the Grail quest is even more disconcerting, as its fulfillment is in God's gift, not contingent on the individual will. In the early part of the narrative, with the textual emphasis on desire rather than morality, Merlin's interventions suggest the social world's moral boundaries are unstably drawn: and, ultimately, Nineyve's exploitation of his own desire will leave him in narrative suspension. Merlin's fate marks the breakdown of his own scheme of reciprocity. In addition to identifying a system of reciprocity as the basis for social interaction, Merlin also sets himself up as a mouthpiece of God and a guardian of human law, an uneasy combination. As Nicholas Doe has shown, in fifteenth-century discussion, tensions may arise between the idea of a human law that, as the product of a voluntarist human will, bears little relation to abstract notions of right and wrong, and the notion that a divinely ordained natural law authorizes the human. In practice, one may have recourse to the claims of conscience or reason over the letter of the law in deciding a case, or one may overrule such considerations in favor of customary law.[58] Malory's text reflects this complex of attitudes to law by alternately obscuring and (through Merlin) invoking connections between divine ordinance, morality, and law. The provocative and morally questionable circumstances surrounding Arthur's conception relate to his status as legendary hero.[59] But the narrator and Merlin are equally anxious to assert the (in fifteenth-century English law) unquestionable legitimacy of an Arthur conceived after Gorlois's death and born in wedlock (1:9.26–29; 18.4–7).

John Fortescue, in his *In Praise of the Laws of England,* cites Continental civil law's retrospective legitimization of children as an encouragement to moral turpitude. He declares "chaste" the English law that recognizes as legitimate only those born in wedlock, for it discourages illicit sexuality.[60] However, Fortescue's claim for the superior moral force of English law does not squarely address the specific question of policing sexual activity before marriage. Malory's narrative betrays a similar shift between example and explication. Arthur may be technically legitimate, but his engendering still highlights the problem of Ygrayne's volition. The Prose *Brut* obviates this issue by having Ygerne reciprocate Uther's advances.[61] Malory's Ygrayne, however, is deceived, denied her child, and left without remedy in law, first, by virtue of her understanding of wifely obedience (1:10.22–26), and second, by reason of her womanhood. Accused of treason, she cannot fight on her own behalf (1:45.30–46.6). Through Ygrayne, these episodes assert the power of law and set it apart from questions of morality. It is important thematically and structurally to the *Morte* that rape is intrinsic to Arthur's conception. The sexual violence endemic to Arthurian narrative is here made visible, only to be occluded by women's relation to the legal institution.[62]

Merlin's interventions are, from the start of the *Morte,* more important as political maneuvers than as moral underpinnings for the narrative. The relation between Merlin and the Divine seems initially uncertain. The events leading up to Arthur's coronation do not assume Merlin is an instrument of destiny, nor do we know his motives; he simply has to engineer the ratification of Arthur's drawing the sword from the stone. There is no proof Merlin is doing other than invoking God's authority to validate his own when he promises he will make Uther name a successor (1:11.38). In contrast to the *Merlin,* where the prophet declares Arthur's succession, yet also produces written documentation from Uther to support Arthur's claim (90–91; Lacy 1:217), Uther verbally sanctions Arthur's kingship: "I gyve hym Gods blissyng and myne, and byd hym [. . .] clayme the croune" (1:12.5–7).[63] Other circumstances surrounding Arthur's election in Malory emphasize human agency's interaction with providence. As the "comyn peple," instrumental in Arthur's ascendancy, proclaim: "it is Goddes wille that he shalle be our kynge" (1:16.12–15). Where the sources give space to the claims of institutionalized religion, in the person of the archbishop, the *Morte* tacitly accords the Church secondary importance, stressing instead Merlin's "provydence" (1:15.40) and Arthur's allegiance to his people, his vow to be a good king, "to stand with true justyce fro thens forth the dayes of this lyf" (1:16.22–23).[64]

The *Morte* offers a retelling in which values are partly given and assumed, and partly emerge in the process of reporting. Merlin's interventions tend as much to introduce another perspective on the action as to demonstrate his autonomous power, and they also frequently intersect with other interests. At the battle against the eleven kings, for example, Merlin puts an end to the slaughter by warning Arthur of the consequences attendant on the loss of God's grace (1:36.26–32). This warning belongs to a corpus of prescriptive advice Arthur gratefully accepts (1:37.20–21), but although Merlin may invoke a moral framework, he subordinates it to the system of social reciprocity on which the process of battle is grounded. In the *Suite,* Merlin dispenses counsel within a providential framework, and gives shape to the narrative even as he explains its rationale: "Nus ne puet destorner que la volentés Nostre Signeur n'aviegne" [No one can prevent Our Lord's will from happening] (1:268; Lacy 4:242). Merlin in the *Morte* intermittently has a similar function as narrative guide illuminating moral obligation, as when he identifies as "adventure" the mystifying and disruptive sequence of events Arthur would rather ignore: "thes adventures muste be brought to an ende, othir ellis hit woll be disworshyp to you and to youre feste" (1:103.13–16). But Malory's characters see divine ordinance as operating more fluidly in relation to individual action than do their counterparts in the sources. Balin assumes (ironically in view of his own unhappy trajectory through life) a consonance between providence and chivalric system: "I shall take the aventure [. . .] that God woll ordayne for me" (1:64.12–13). But Pellinor, when Merlin tells him that future betrayal will be "penaunce" for his past deeds, dissociates God from what Merlin has identified as His intervention: "God may well fordo desteny" (1:120.9–10).

The *Morte's* lack of insistence on a scrupulous recording of origins (Arthur's case excepted), much less on their moral placing, in contrast to the *Suite's* interest in flawed beginnings and moral accountability, makes it more difficult to retrieve a providential patterning, and confuses the attribution of guilt and responsibility in a world in which boundaries—and therefore their transgression—are not always clear. We learn of Merlin only that he is "a devyls son" (1:126.20). Whether Lot or Arthur should die on the field of battle is not only something of which he has foreknowledge; it appears, sinisterly, to be in his gift (1:76.16–20). Although sin is not explicitly part of Merlin's own vocabulary, he defines certain acts as provocative of God's anger, and so censures Arthur's begetting of Mordred, "a childe that shal destroy you and all the knyghtes of youre realme" (1:44.16–19). But the young king responds as though from within a different dialogue: "I mervayle muche of thy wordis that I mon dye in batayle" (1:44.24–25). Merlin warns Arthur that God will punish him for his "fowle dedis" (1:44.26–27), yet simultaneously predicts for himself a "shamefull dethe," and for his king a "worshipfull dethe" (1:44.28–30). Merlin foretells future events in the context of factors significant to their interpretation but does not weigh moral judgment and social expediency. Furthermore, Malory's Mordred episode offers no moral commentary on Arthur's behavior, and Merlin does not restore order, but becomes the focus of displaced parental anger.[65] Arthur's attempt to root out future tragedy by casting children adrift fails, and the innocent drown, while Mordred survives (1:55.19–33). Of the bereaved parents, many blame Merlin: "So what for drede and for love, they helde their pece" (1:55.35–56.2). Peter Field suggests the anomalous picture of a "Herod" Arthur is residual of the Alliterative *Morte,* which in its surviving form has Arthur order the murder of (Mordred's) children in the interests of political stability;[66] yet the echoes of Herod, and the unfulfilled promise of an account of Mordred's *enfances* (1:55.33), also read as though the story, in the

absence of Merlin as established moral center, had not yet settled into a coherent or topically appropriate narrative or ethical pattern. An uneasily
maintained peace replaces the reconciliation of the source (*Suite* 1:65; Lacy
4:185). Malory's Merlin absorbs and contains moral complexity, a function
the *Suite* usually reserves for its female characters.

Balin

If Merlin exemplifies moral and narrative disjunction in the early part of
the *Morte,* Balin's career complementarily blurs coordinates for chivalric
hierarchy, destiny, and social order. The adventure of the Damsel's sword
(1:60.21–64.23) registers his worth, yet condemns him to fratricide. His
commitment to chivalric action leaves, seemingly in spite of himself, a trail
of devastation that culminates in his own violent end. For Jill Mann, Malory's version of the story obscures causation and moral discrimination
while reinforcing the knight's obligation to meet chivalric destiny.[67] In the
Suite, Balain, like Merlin, functions metatextually, for through him the
Suite arguably writes large its debts to, and ruptures with, the Grail history
of Chrétien's *Conte du Graal* and its *First Continuation.* In Chrétien's romance, the hapless innocent Perceval is cursed for his failure to ask the appropriate questions regarding the mysterious procession of lance, grail, and
dish he sees at the Grail castle, a failure mysteriously linked to the land's
desolation and his responsibility for his mother's death.[68] In the *First Continuation,* an invisible knight kills an unknown knight Gawain has taken
under his protection. Gawain takes on the knight's (unknown) quest and
finds himself, like Perceval before him, at the Grail castle, where he fails to
mend a broken sword, then learns the role of the bleeding lance at Christ's
Passion, but falls asleep before learning about the knight and his mysterious killer, waking to find he has only partially restored the land laid waste
by Perceval's earlier negligence.[69] The *Suite* reworks and combines the
episodes of the Grail castle and the theme of safe conduct, and in the
process inverts some of the Grail castle motifs, making it more immediately
a place of danger. It adumbrates the mystery of the bleeding lance, carried
in ritual process through the Fisher King's hall, with the lance the invisible knight Garlon wields as an anarchic weapon. Where Chrétien plays ur-
banely with questions of decorum, hospitality, ethics, and knightly courtesy
with regard to Perceval, Garlon as wayward perpetrator of violence is also
a server at the feast, and upbraids Balain for not eating or drinking (1:158;
Lacy 4:211). Balain, retracing Gawain's steps—but as angry adventurer—
precipitates a crisis through vigorous action, in contrast with his silent or
somnolent predecessors. The *Suite* rationalizes the Grail story and promises
to "bring to an end," by means of its fiction, what Chrétien's continuators

exploit as interminable romance; in doing so, it ingeniously alienates its own protagonist who, at the Grail castle, considers himself to have completed his quest in killing Garlon, when his part in the grander teleological scheme is only just under way (*Suite* 1:159; Lacy 4:211). Balain thinks himself protagonist of one narrative, only to find himself the lynchpin of another, the beginning of the adventure Galahad will complete.

In the *Morte* (as in the *Suite*), the breaking of safe conduct focuses issues of legal accountability and sovereign power, and of chivalric identity and responsibility. Balin is variously perpetrator and victim of breaches of safe conduct.[70] Balin's peremptory decapitation of the Lady of the Lake earns him his exile from Arthur's court because his action violates Arthur's implicit guarantee of protection for the Lady: "Therefore I shall never forgyff you that trespasse" (1:66.7–9).[71] Garlon, the Invisible Knight, later kills two knights, of whom, as in the *Suite,* one has delivered himself into Balin's safekeeping—"'Alas', seyde the knyght, 'I am slayne undir youre conduyte'" (1:80.12–13)—and the other has sworn to be Balin's companion when the latter has explained to him how he has taken up the dead man's quest (1:81.3–14). In the *Suite,* Merlin intervenes to identify the killer to Balain, and to reveal that in renouncing his quest he may avoid striking the Dolorous Stroke, to which Balain replies that to avenge one killed under his safe conduct takes precedence over other considerations (1:141; Lacy 4:206). Yet, shortly afterward, a hermit appears to mitigate Balain's actions by asserting that one has no choice but to endure adventures (1:143; Lacy 4:207). The *Suite* asks more pointedly than does Malory that we examine the relation between the specifics of chivalric ethical responsibility and the "destiny" underlying events.

Safe conduct, its transgression and punishment, belong to the problematic regulation of violence. In the *Suite,* breach of safe conduct explicitly shames Balain—his charge speaks of his "honte" and his own "damages" [harm] (1:132; Lacy 4:203). For Malory, the event is part of Balin's crisis, just as a later breach of safe conduct implicates Launcelot's chivalric identity, and Arthurian chivalric arbitration (1:284.15–286.18). Whereas in the *Suite* safe conduct exposes a tension between narratives ruled by different ethical imperatives, Malory's concern is with the divorce between narrative and the possibility of its ethical underpinning. The *Suite* author rewrites Grail material into a sequence of narratives that promises a "good end." In the *Morte,* Merlin's interventions are among the most curious in Balin's trajectory to the Dolorous Stroke. At the precipitate suicide of the Lady Colombe, Merlin tells Balin: "thou shalt stryke a stroke moste dolerous that ever man stroke, excepte the stroke of Oure Lorde Jesu Cryste" (1:72.26–27). With this causative link between grief-stricken death and kingdom-devastating stroke, Malory returns us to the mysteries of the

Grail narrative as Chrétien de Troyes conceives of them. In *Perceval,* a woman's death is key in a curious account of causation and accusation of moral responsibility. The *Suite* establishes the moral and textual parameters for the *Roman du Graal,* and Merlin offers narrative signposts through the chaos. Malory's Merlin isolates as crucial an accident, coded feminine, for which there is no readily performable restitution. His oblique rather than elucidatory reference to Christ here, and his peculiar linking of disparate acts, reinforce the seeming arbitrariness of experience, and recall Chrétien's literary world. At the same time, the prophet indicates an important aspect of the chivalric that the language of masculine engagement fails to address.

Balin denies his fate but, ignorant of the implications of his own actions, he fulfills the prophecy about him in the chaotic episode at the Grail castle, with its echoes, prolepses, and lack of fit between event and explanation. The paraphernalia of the Grail story—the wounded King Pellam's kinship to Joseph of Arimathea, Joseph's own presence in the castle, the identification as Longinus's of the "marvaylous spere" Balin snatches (1:84–86)—hardly explain the relationship between actions and consequences, whereas in the *Suite,* the Grail chamber is sacred, and a series of spoken prohibitions clearly marks Balain's actions as transgressive.[72] Balain's function in the text is to serve the *Suite's* revision of sacred history. The *Morte's* and the *Suite's* treatments serve as fictionalized manifestations of "mythical" and "divine" violence, as Walter Benjamin distinguishes them. Benjamin projects a mythical violence as part of the order of destiny, and opposes a "divine" violence to the "immediate violence" of myth: "If mythical violence is law-making, divine violence is law-destroying; if the former sets boundaries, the latter boundlessly destroys them; if mythical violence brings at once guilt and retribution, divine power only expiates."[73] This distinction suggests something of the *Suite's* (and the *Roman du Graal's*) appropriation of a messianic and apocalyptic element. The forms of violence the *Suite* institutionalizes by recourse to an apocryphal Grail history might be said to be mythical in action, although glossed as divine. Balin draws the retribution of the former for his unknowing infringement of unwritten rules and unmarked boundaries, whereas Balain is caught up in a series of events based on a fiction of "divine" violence, behind which is the promise of expiation. The *Suite* explains Balain's adventure in terms of providence. His sin is part of the *Roman's* recasting, in the Grail story, of the recognizable Christian pattern of fall, expiation, and redemption. Merlin tells Balain he is a new Eve, because, like her, he will break God's law and bring pain and misery to others: "tu trespasseras le commandement que nus ne doit trespasser" [you will break the commandment that no one should break] (1:86 Lacy 4:191). This interpretive hold on origins and process, and ritualized violence against Balain, is crucial to the historical and moral placing of human activity in the *Suite,* which evades the question of whether its deployment of the Divine and the trappings of institutionalized religion are ever more than subservient to the self-authorizing claims of a secular narrative.

Malory's version makes more urgent the relation of identity to violence in Balin's experiences. Balin encounters the extremes of what may constitute the "enemy" in violent engagement, from the foreign adversary on the battlefield, to the unknown quasi-supernatural forces at the Grail castle, to his similitude in the form of his own brother, Balan. Balin acts out the conflicted condition that constitutes chivalric identity.[74] The ambivalence of the knightly opponent as "same" or "other" also emerges in René Girard's conceptualization of violence, in *Violence and the Sacred,* a text that itself replicates some of the *Morte's* own elisions in this respect. For Girard, human violence is endemic and self-perpetuating; strife appears to be based not on difference but on similarity between antagonists.[75] Girard's evocation of masculine relationships based on reciprocal acts of violence could also describe the *Morte.* But as Sarah Kay powerfully observes, Girard's assertion of a violent reciprocity that both destroys and maintains differentiation makes for confusion, and for a depoliticization of violence.[76] Girard conceives of a violence that has to be "diverted" from the community in the form of a ritual sacrifice, which constitutes a "beneficial"—as opposed to an "impure"—violence. One might read the *Suite* Balain as (according to Post-Vulgate teleology) enacting this "beneficial" sacrifice, whereas Malory's Balin appears to be at a point of what Girard would call "sacrificial crisis," where the distinction between purifying and impure violence breaks down.[77] The "breakdown" is also inherent in Girard's schema, however, where the parameters of ritual violence are not clear. Balin's identity fails in a welter of violence; he loses the swords that define him, and, unwittingly transgressive, kills and is killed by his own brother.

Girard's analysis of male violence allows the female little space, but for mention of displacement in terms of a desire to blame forms of violence on women.[78] The *Morte* also has difficulty, although on a different plane, in correlating male-female relations with the exercise of violence. Several have noted how violence to women (inadvertent or otherwise) forms a leitmotif of Balin's career; for Deborah Ellis, it is a subcategory of the treachery that ineluctably pursues him.[79] Geraldine Heng suggests Balin is a "chronicle" knight, whose unhappy relation to the feminine charts his alienation from his chivalric self.[80] But this is perhaps less a failure for which the narrative indicts Balin than a narrative failure in itself. What Merlin's incongruous connection of Colombe's suicide and the Dolorous Stroke points out is a lack in social and judicial organization and recognition, both with regard to, and expressed in terms of, women's bodies, a failure that the Pentecostal Oath will later proclaim rather than remedy. While in the *Suite* Balain's misfortunes (partly brought on himself) serve to characterize him as "female," a "new Eve," necessary precursor to Galahad as redeemer, Balin does not have such an easily readable function in the *Morte,* which obscures the *Suite's* redemptive historical pattern and disrupts its teleological deployment of the feminine. Violence against women instead makes for confusion over the moral legitimization and the possibility of the divine underwriting of Arthurian violence and its social institutionalization. Balin's sword (in both *Morte* and *Suite*) is an ambivalent legacy, redemptive in function as the sword Galahad will draw from the stone, but also the instrument of death and a means of temporal social division (1:91.15–25). Yet, in the *Morte,* random physical injury negotiates chaos and redemption across the narrative. The unfortunate brothers Balin and Balan deal one another "seven grete woundes" in their fatal battle (1:89.31). Remarkably, Sir Urry, whom Launcelot heals, is the only other knight the *Morte* records as suffering seven wounds.[81] This retrospectively readable inscription of the somatic as redeemable through divine grace links Balin and Launcelot in a material matrix independent of Merlin.

Merlin oversees—rather than controls—Balin and Balan's romance landscape, and his social function seems more important than the assertion of his power. In the *Suite,* Pellinor and his damsel overhear a plot against Arthur's life. One speaker, persuaded of the folly of resistance to Arthur's rule, counsels prudence, but his interlocutor is confident of his plan (1:259–61; Lacy 4:240). Pellinor and the damsel assume Merlin will protect Arthur, and do not rush to alert the court. In the *Morte* (1:118.4–30), this event is narratively redundant, but it illuminates other areas of concern. The witnesses do not react to the scene, nor does Pellinor mention it at court (1:119.20–21). Where the *Suite* consolidates Merlin and Arthur's power, the spy in the *Morte* warns of Merlin's devil-granted knowledge (1:118.26), and declares Arthur's court a paragon of social cohesion: "there ys such a felyship that they may never be brokyn, and well-nyghe all the world holdith with Arthure" (1:118.13–18). His friend's reply troublingly intimates a social system of reciprocal relations inimical to Arthurian society:

> "I have brought a remedy with me that ys the grettist poysen that ever ye herde speke off [. . .] for we have a frende ryght nyghe the kynge, well cheryshed, that shall poysen kynge Arthur, for so hath he promysed our chyfftaynes, and receyved grete gyfftis for to do hit." (1:118.19–24)

There is a neat irony in the antithetical notion of poison as cure, and the very term "remedy" only occurs previously in the text in relation to Merlin.[82] The *Suite* assumes Arthur is protected against enemies within, but the English account does not resolve the question of how a tightly knit "felyship" may harbour a "well cheryshed" traitor. This political intrigue displaces Merlin's centrality to focus on the court as site of social interaction and potential dissent.

Women and Order

The *Morte* deploys social interchange as narrative dynamic, whereas the *Suite* delineates human relationships closely within a hierarchical power system, and so more rigorously defines women's roles, on legal, social, and literary levels. Women's importance is secondary to aggrandizing Merlin's role. Women also point out Merlin's ambivalence, and provide an exemplary gloss on events. When Merlin engineers the means to reveal Arthur's parentage to the recalcitrant barons, he is fulfilling his role in the French text as overseer of judicial procedure.[83] Ygerne, summoned to court, accused of murder and treason, in her defence proclaims the diabolical origins of the man who stole her unbaptized child (1:22; Lacy 4:173). Ygerne's imputing of evil motive to Merlin is an important safety valve for articulating his anomalousness, for credence in Merlin demands good faith as much as, if not more than, rational evidence: "Je sui Merlins, qui sai les obscures choses et les repostes, che savés vous bien, et pour chou me devés vous croire de chou que je vous dirai" [I'm Merlin, who know secrets and hidden things—you know that well—and therefore you must believe what I will tell you] (1:26; Lacy 4:174). Belief in the legitimacy of the often preposterous narrative requires a similar leap of faith; Merlin's authority and textual authority are mutually affirming. Denunciations of Merlin by the powerless simultaneously neutralize the threat of disbelief and remind us of the need for readerly faith in textual veracity. The *Morte,* however, shows more concern with the needs of the moment than with confirming Merlin's status, and, in Malory's version (1:44.31–46.15), Ygrayne's testimony carries more weight than in the source. The queen's dignified response to Ulfin's charge of treason for not revealing her son's identity acknowledges her lack of physical, and hence legal, autonomy (as noted above). But she also supplies important factual proof of Arthur's legitimacy. In the end, Merlin confirms Arthur's parentage, but Ulfin's charge to him, that he is more culpable than Ygrayne for not releasing this information sooner (1:46.4), does not celebrate Merlin's wisdom and power but raises an unresolved question about the apportioning of blame.

Women in the *Suite* also displace or contain the text's exemplary intentions. One instance is the episode of Tor's parentage, similar to Arthur's in that it demonstrates Merlin's omniscience. Merlin controls revelation of the true parentage of the supposedly lowborn Tor, who is anxious to be a knight. He anticipates Tor's mother's account of her rape by Pellinor

(1:252, 270–72; Lacy 4:237, 243). Pellinor as rapist receives no censure—
the "good knight" Tor would seem to vindicate both Pellinor's "noble" nature and his ugly behavior—and moral guilt attaches instead to the
violated countrywoman, who says Merlin is a devil unlike others because
he makes her confess, rather than conceal, her sin. She also, however, accuses Merlin of self-interest in displaying his knowledge rather than acting
for the love of God or herself (1:270; Lacy 4:243). The woman's witness
does not challenge Merlin but simply testifies to her honesty; she warns
her son not to be overproud at his sudden elevation in social class. The
treatment of Tor's mother exemplifies how the narrative's dispossessed
characters work within a moralistic framework, itself in the service of the
claims of chivalric lineage and story. Malory's drastically abbreviated account substitutes a confusing testimony on the part of the woman involved, which makes it impossible to establish either rape or consent:
"there mette with me a sterne knyght, and half be force he had my maydynhode" (1:101.13–14). The woman's puzzling witness is perhaps Malory's way of reconciling the fact of her motherhood with current medical
and legal assumptions that consider conception through rape as impossible, and so read Torre's very existence as proof of consent.[84] Furthermore,
Merlin's pragmatic advice to Torre in the face of the evidence reflects fifteenth-century legal practice: "youre fadir [. . .] may ryght well avaunce
you and youre modir both, for ye were begotyn or evir she was wedded"
(1:101.23–25).[85] Narrative interest has already moved on from a demonstration of Merlin's power, and settled on the temperamental difference between the chivalry-loving Torre and the rest of his family, to which nature
his physique bears further testimony (1:100.17–20). The *Suite* Merlin safe-
guards due forensic procedure; Malory's Merlin opportunistically exploits,
rather than makes, the law.

Since the Merlin of the *Suite* indisputably controls knowledge and its
written codification, Morgain and Niviene as would-be scientists depend
heavily on him for instruction. Merlin teaches both Morgain and Niviene
magic, and each barters the promise of sexual favors for knowledge. The
women reflect Merlin's own dual aspect; Morgain's lot is that of the devil,
and her increasing ugliness registers her carnal desire and search for illicit
knowledge (1:19–20; Lacy 4:172). The narrative carefully contextualizes the
potentially threatening female sexuality Niviene exercises when she imprisons Merlin. Merlin has told her the story of Diana and Faunus, whom
Diana kills to make way for another lover who, horrified, decapitates her
(1:282–87; Lacy 4:246–47). Niviene's declared fondness for the forest location of this tragedy hints synecdochally at a certain ruthlessness in her character, but when she later imprisons Merlin in the abode of two faithful
lovers, she says in her defense that she wished only to protect herself from

a diabolical sexual predator (2:335; Lacy 4:260). Extreme accounts of faithful and faithless female lovers cluster around Merlin's death-in-life, but
Niviene's sexuality is ultimately subsidiary to the familiar paradigm of the
wise man brought low by a woman (2:336; Lacy 4:261).

Just as the devil gives Merlin knowledge only of the past, so Morgain's
power is limited. In the *Suite,* Merlin gives Morgain a document telling
who will kill Arthur and Gawain, knowledge of which, Merlin warns her,
is fatal to women. When Morgain lodges the inscription in a tomb, it becomes an "evil custom" for which she is culpable, and it claims not women
but "good knights" as its victims (2:365–66; Lacy 4:269) Morgain figures
female disruption of a male-controlled text. After Merlin's mysterious disappearance, Morgain and Niviene, respectively the evil eminence and the
guardian angel of Arthurian society, bifurcate his nature and continue his
influence. The conventional representation of women—their disenfran-
chisement, or their positioning at the extremes of external influences for
the good, or to the detriment, of Arthurian society—itself emerges as a
reaccommodation and function of Merlin's power.

Such explicit control does not obtain in the *Morte,* where the sources
of women's knowledge are more diffuse. Malory has Morgan learn necromancy in a nunnery (1:10.8–10), independent of Merlin. Female power
emerges as more autonomous; Heng argues Arthurian society is incidental to the interests of those women familiar with magic and enchantment,
rather than (as in the *Suite*) defining of their function.[86] The *Morte* is also,
of course, sexist; Morgan's notorious defiance of her brother—for example, in the Arthur and Accolon episode (1:137–52)—assumes the spheres
of male and female power are oppositional and competitive. In addition,
a social decorum and the institution of law regulate women's behavior.
But the *Morte* does not share the *Suite's* consistent circumscription of female power. This makes for more various possibilities for male-female
narrative interaction. Indeed, Nineyve appears rather more skillful than
Merlin when she casts an infatuation-spell on Ettarde to punish her for
her bad treatment of Pelleas, to whom Nineyve gives both love and protection. In so doing, she elides enchantment, moral, social and poetic justice, and, above all, self-interest; moreover, she glosses the consequences of
her magic as "the ryghteuouse jugemente of God" (1:172.8), deploying,
like Merlin, a moral vocabulary to her own ends. In the *Suite,* Merlin's in-
carceration is contingent on the text's providential framework and its
contextualization of power and knowledge. The *Morte* substitutes a combination of practical exigency—Nineyve, nervous of Merlin, simply wants
to be rid of him (1:126.20–21)—and a somber determinism, the more
alarming because unexplained. As Merlin says, he cannot avoid his fate:
"hit woll not be" (1:125.22).

Merlin is not then the *Morte*'s ideological or structural core, although his very presence intimates a desire for just such a centralized function. The same impulse as he promotes toward accountability and rationalization, and the direction of human action, is in evidence in the Pentecostal Oath to which the knights swear each year (1:120.15–27), and just as the Malorian complexities of the narrative relativize Merlin's significance and power, so the Oath, which King Arthur institutes independently, is less a comprehensive set of laws than indicative of the sometimes oblique relation obtaining between the terms of knightly definition and control, some of them extra-textual, and the actualities of narrative experience. Representative of the impulse to manage human action, Merlin and the Pentecostal Oath also demonstrate the lack of contextualization that human beings have for action, whether in terms of powers higher than the human (as in Merlin's case), or outside an idealizing vision of the masculine Round Table Fellowship. Romance narrative, on which human action is also contingent, may run counter to the terms of the Oath, which exposes the narrative's tendency to disjunction between precept and action in that it seeks to locate stability in that aspect of the knight, his physical self expressed in violence, which is most susceptible to change and to plural interpretation.

The chivalric oath is as familiar to fifteenth-century historical experience as to fiction. The Pentecostal Oath has general analogues in romance, and in chivalric handbooks such as the account of Arthurian tournament Jacques d'Armagnac putatively authors, which includes an appendix of "Oaths and Ordinances of the Knights of the Round Table."[87] This text recreates a fictional milieu as a medium for aristocratic display through its rules for outer appearance and inner motivation, and takes for granted the relation between the morality of earthly chivalry, and divine imperatives. Richard Barber notes the Pentecostal Oath's similarity to the wording for the Investiture of Knights of the Bath.[88] The Pentecostal Oath, however, appears remarkably secular by contrast to these; even the timing of its enunciation draws attention to its appropriation, rather than observance, of religious festival. Arthur devises the Oath, but it also draws on regulations for good conduct arrived at empirically in the adventures of Gawain, Ywain, and Marhalt—prescriptions for knightly mercy, for example (1:106.23–35), or the rules of combat (1:160.33–35)—and so it optimistically intimates a consonance of individual and collective precept, volition and action.[89] Precepts may not always, however, translate straightforwardly into action. An injunction to defend ladies does not offer Pellinor the means to make the right choice about which of two women to help first (1:114.10–23). The male-centered domain the Oath describes, specifically the heightened awareness of the knight's body as unit of value and as instrument of violence to maintain the rule of law, its emphasis on reciprocal loyalty to the king, and its prescriptions for the protection of the disenfranchised (here specifically women) reflect conditions of fifteenth-century warfare more accurately than they describe either the functioning of the state, or the narrative circumstances of the *Morte* (while the injunction to "fle treson" suggests the possibility of its unwitting commission, as well as what Deborah Ellis calls its "contagious" nature[90]). In its attitude to rape, the Oath seems closest to the *Ordinances of War Made by King Henry V. at Mawnt* (July 1419), copied for John Paston in approximately 1469, which states that: "noman be so hardy to sle ne enforce no woman uppon (peyne of deth),"[91] where Round Table knights swear "to do ladyes, damesels, and jantilwomen and wydowes (socour:) strengthe hem in hir ryghtes, and never to enforce them, uppon payne of dethe" (1:120.20–23).

The martial oath emphasizes and justifies the knight's active social function under the king's jurisdiction, and delimits the knight's activity by providing for the safety of civilians and religious institutions alike. But in the Pentecostal Oath, the articulation of the law against rape in particular also isolates important aspects of Malory's narrative. The Oath's prescription and proscription regarding women redraws the nature of the feminine and asserts control over the female body by the king and his fellowship. Shocking as is the explicit acknowledgment that violence to women comes from the same quarter as their supposed protection, the proscription also suggests the Oath serves as a controlling countermove against the depredations of the unknown that are often emblematized in these early adventures as violence done to women's bodies, whether accidental or otherwise. The definition of woman as in need of defence and rapeable makes rape a founding aspect of social organization, a perspective Susan Brownmiller endorses when she identifies fear of rape as "probably the single causative factor in the original subjugation of woman by man," although rape is by no means endemic in human social structure.[92] Adventures preceding the Oath signal violence toward women as intrinsic to knightly adventure, but in puzzling ways, as when Merlin declares that Colombe's suicide is the "cause" of the Dolorous Stroke. Gawain, having accidentally killed a damsel, has already sworn always to help ladies (1:109.1–3). In the Prose *Merlin,* Nascien institutes an oath to help damsels, in chivalric response to Arthur's vow not to dine until he hears of some adventure: "yef any maiden [. . .] seche helpe or socour by so that it may be a-cheved by the body of oon knight a-gein a-nother, thei will [. . .] make alle the wronges to be redressed that to hir hath be don" (2:481). Woman, and what "to hir hath be don" are the impetus to adventure. Such oaths, with their emphasis on the maintenance of the rule of law through violence between men, occlude the narrative logic by means of which the focus on woman's sexual safety inevitably calls up her vulnerability, as in the ugly custom of Logres Chrétien de Troyes mentions, which has the action progress in a series of threats to and defenses of a woman's body, action on which Arthurian narrative is largely predicated.[93]

The Pentecostal Oath, with its prohibition of rape, addresses this oc-cluded issue directly, and draws attention to the cultural positioning of woman as physically and sexually vulnerable, even as it proclaims her "rights." That the threat to, and defenses of, woman's integrity potentially come from the same quarter, exemplifies the inherent tension in the oper-ation of violence in general in the *Morte,* and puts in question the status of the knight as law-enforcer, who agrees in this oath to be self-policing. Malory is institutionalizing the double aspect of rape in Arthurian legend, and rape also, in his wording, crosses the boundary between romance nar-rative and legal provision. The law both acknowledges masculine aggres-sion and seeks to contain and redirect it. Rape is central to the definition of the community and of its men in particular. In the context of the Oath, the preservation of women's wholeness can figure both an individual knight's integrity, and the consolidation of the rule of law. There is then a double appropriation of the female body, through physical rape as index of male chivalric integrity, and through an ethical reading of its significance, or even of its prevention. The rhetoric at the same time obscures the idea, present in the rest of the narrative, that men, too, may be exposed to sex-ual threat. The Oath's gendered reading of the male as "whole" and the fe-male as violable will itself, then, come under revision, particularly with regard to Launcelot.

Alain Chartier's Latin *Dialogue Familiaris Amici et Sodalis,* on the parlous state of the French nation, written in approximately 1425, translated in the second half of the fifteenth century as *A Familiar Dialogue of the Friend and the Fellow,* serves as appropriate gloss on Malory's Arthurian community, and its investments in the physical, beyond the markers Merlin sets down for understanding narrative process. The knights eventually learn painfully that: "the freele humanyte of the bodyes maketh not stable the kyngdomes but the celestyal vertu, whyche ys a yeft of God [. . .] stablyscheth ertheley thynges."[94] The Round Table collapses not through ungodliness but through a limited regnal and chivalric awareness, which the Pentecostal Oath, through its investment in particular cultural constructions of the body, institutionalizes at the same time as it seeks to legislate on intention and good will and yet leaves such pressing issues as treason undefined. Concomitantly, we as readers, together with the reader-narrator, encounter a vocabulary that offers only a fragmented knowledge of the Arthurian world; episodic chivalric narratives give no guarantee that the part will re-veal the nature of the whole. The means of regulating reading, like those of law-enforcing, are partial at best. At the end of the opening sequence of tales, "Malory" participates in this limited vision as "knyght presoner" and as writer. His injunction that we should "seke" other books on Arthur (1:180.19–20) blurs the reconstitutive processes of reading and writing, and makes the reader's independent response and further research the necessary adjunct to his own endeavors. Thus, the physically alienated knight declares his own work as incomplete, and yet suggests it may establish the possibility of a literary community that will "make [. . .] more." Derrida's notion of the *supplement* helpfully positions the reader/writer in relation to Malory's idiom. Derrida uses the term to signal writing's substitutive function and its simultaneous signaling of what is missing in the representation.[95] It thus illuminates the dynamic of translation, which simultaneously remedies and emphasizes lack.[96] In the French romances, a wealth of authorized voices and documents—inscribed in the text itself, or declared to assure completion beyond it, but still in terms of it—is what promises "more." Malory's narrator, however, invites the reader to mimic his procedures, and the reader's knowledge is now brought into play, now obscured, as the narratives, themselves the product of intra- and extratextual reading, unfold.

CHAPTER 3

NARRATIVE FORM AND HEROIC EXPECTATION: *THE TALE OF ARTHUR AND LUCIUS,* *THE NOBLE TALE OF SIR LAUNCELOT DU LAKE,* AND *THE TALE OF SIR GARETH OF ORKNEY*

The last chapter suggests that Malory's Arthuriad begins early on to dismantle a providentialist frame and the rule of law as perceivable means to the containment of violence. The Pentecostal Oath apparently sets the boundaries of chivalric life, for it brings violent action to social account, and under the control of the sovereign. Yet, in its specification of gender roles and its replication of terms of war as well as of romance, the Oath exposes both the tenuousness of our grounds of knowledge and a fissure between theoretical "knowledge" of chivalric control and the experiences both of the knights within the text and of our reading of that text. For the reader, generic expectations, the social worlds the text projects, and different literary registers harness and direct our responses to violence. This chapter looks at how Malory investigates and questions both the reader's and the writer's ability to establish and maintain the parameters of a self-contained fictional world. Violence works on the residual knowledge of reader and writer alike to point up the subjectivity and variability of our response to the Arthurian narrative as a whole. So the rhetorical constructions of violence, and the cultural assumptions implicit in the text, indicate a general slippage between action and interpretation, for the actants as for the readers. Elaine Scarry, in her seminal work on physical pain, writes of the body's "referential instability" in war, and of how cultural and political institutions yet make the body signify ideologically by virtue of juxtaposition.[1] Our accumulating memories of individual manifestations of Arthurian violence complicate our response to its generically various representation across the *Morte,* and the narrative works ideologically on bodies and our response to bodies' fragmentation. In complex relation to their sources, the three consecutive and formally discrete sets of stories sequential to Vinaver's *Tale of King Arthur* in the Winchester Manuscript (fols. 71r–148r) debate violence and its representations through a series of diverse Arthurian narratives that engage the differently constituted readerships inscribed in the text in continuing negotiations of what the Arthurian "means," deploying the male chivalric body as focus for celebration and for anxiety.

Our residual knowledge of an Arthurian world predicated on different narrative bases supplements our explicit positioning as readers within the separate texts. Each account articulates an interpretive position that demands intertextual consideration because, as with the rest of the *Morte,* the text appears to be refamiliarizing us, if in fragmented form, with what we already "know" and cannot easily "lay aparte"; we also accumulate particular associations and echoes as we work through the different narratives. While the Lucius episode refers us to "romance," and the other stories to "the French book," for narrative authentication, Malory in practice draws ostentatiously on the Alliterative *Morte* for his first tale, largely on the Vulgate (with some episodes from the *Perlesvaus*), for his account of Launcelot, and on a narrative with analogues in both French and English for his tale of Gareth. He displaces all three stories chronologically in the *Morte. The Tale of Arthur and Lucius,* with its at first sight unproblematic account of a successfully expansionist "historical" Arthurian empire, and *The Tale of Sir Gareth of Orkney,* envision a social stability achievable within, respectively, the sphere of military foreign engagement and the competitive domestic environment of court life and romance landscape. These relatively compact and self-contained accounts appear to compensate for the episodic and open-ended tales of Launcelot they enclose, and Launcelot appears as narratively the most flexible and the most vulnerable of heroes. In the framing stories themselves, he belongs to the general background of chivalry, but his positioning in his own set of adventures constitutes a critique of the French sources from which the *Noble Tale* largely derives, and also an expression of anxiety about how both to "read"—and at the same time keep intact—Launcelot as hero. For Malory's treatment of Launcelot bears analogy to the author's assimilation of French texts within the *Morte* proper, insofar as the cycles are confessedly incompletely represented within, yet intrinsic to, Malory's English version of Arthurian legend. Malory substitutes for the French concern and play with narrative pattern and literary authority an intensification of the French narratives' anxieties about the hero.

Recent criticism focuses on anxiety as a condition of the masculine—whether in social, literary, or historical contexts—and, with regard to the chivalric as a particularly conflicted area for male definition and enculturation, has drawn attention to Lancelot's fragile psyche, the constructedness of his masculinity, his vulnerability to "feminization," and the amenability of his selfhood to discussion in psychoanalytical, and especially Lacanian, terms.[2] Fragmentation and instability mark the psychic life of the hero as much in the sources as in the *Morte*. Malory's own reading of the protagonist, however, exemplifies in particular the anxieties Calvin Thomas traces in male attitudes toward representation within, and the practice of, writing.[3] Launcelot represents the variety, resilience, and contradictions of the Arthurian constructions of heroism at the same time as he embodies the tensions inherent in the fifteenth-century concern with recuperating stability through the vulnerable physical. Within this section of the *Morte,* the heroic male body and, correlatively, the female body, operate within and across different generic modes that complementarily explore the legacies of and possibilities for, Arthurian narrative. Malory's innovation in the *Noble Tale* is to implicate the readers in the play of masculine and feminine that forms an element in the crisis of representation Launcelot embodies in an Arthurian milieu that focuses the effects of different manifestations of masculine vulnerability and invulnerability in a fantasy of physical wholeness crucial to chivalric desire.[4]

The notion of embodiment, in Csordas's sense of the term, alerts us to the complexity of the chivalric self as dynamic cultural agent in the *Morte,* and especially to the problematizing narrative capacity of its representation. In the account of Arthur's campaign against Lucius, the cultural martial investment in the somatic, the relation between fighting bodies with which we are encouraged to identify, involves denial of bodily (biological) process, at the cost of an access to the narrative's historical and ethical dimensions. In his account of Launcelot, Malory dismantles some of the gender complexities of the sources, but the hero's (in some respects) unexamined male chivalric role—for example, Launcelot has no "beginning," in that his arrival at court and his knighting are not here recounted—engages the reader in the narrative's general strategy of disclosing the hero even as it seeks to protect him. In this account of the heroic Launcelot, it is primarily others' bodies, in particular the vulnerability of those bodies, that register his progress and define his own "worship," while his own body is subject to violation only in gruesome fantasy. In Gareth's tale, which invites reading as paradigmatic of a normative masculine romance heroism, the motif of physical vulnerability is again reformulated to suggest a fantasy in which violent male action is largely depoliticized. But the stress on narrative containment and on display in that tale will raise its own unresolved questions about enculturation and agency, as well as exposing the limits of chivalric narrative.

The Tale of Arthur and Lucius:
Containing Violence

Walter Benjamin observes of violence that as a means it lays claim to validity by being either law-making or law-preserving, but consequently "it cannot avoid being implicated in the problematic nature of law itself."[5] The *Tale of Arthur and Lucius*, however, occludes analysis of the legal foundation of Arthur's world by means of its mutually affirming assumptions, that of Arthur's status as legendary hero and of its nationalist perspective, assumptions into which we are drawn because they predicate our own activity as readers. *Arthur and Lucius* exemplifies, within formal limits, how violence serves to confirm Arthur's rule. Arthur's task is simply to answer disruptive violence with a violence demonstrative of the rule of law, and events appear neither to corrupt nor compromise him. Invocation of the rule of law is then part of the text's enclosing strategy, and violence to women figures as the displacement of masculine anxieties about integrity. Guinevere's emblematic association with nation and its defense in this section shores up ideologically the masculine martial role, but violence to women (as we saw in chapter two) exposes the problematics of the interrelation of violence and law at the same time as it apparently "contains" it, and Guinevere's role, in the context of the rest of the *Morte,* here occludes more troubling historical processes. As an evidently partisan text the *Tale* is also puzzling. It champions Arthur's cause, yet neutralizes Arthurian history, or reconfigures its features in disturbing ways, as when it invokes regnal continuity familiar from Geoffrey of Monmouth, and looks forward to its own closure, in having Constantine made a guardian of Britain when Arthur leaves on campaign (1:195.3–5; 3:1259.27–29).[6] The disjunction may seem a structural problem, arising from Malory's following the organization of the Vulgate, which also features a nontragic Roman campaign earlier in Arthur's reign. Malory has already signaled and deferred a Roman campaign (1:48.15–27), as though seeking an appropriate space for the episode in the Arthuriad, which deliberativeness further suggests the contingent, temporary, and fragile nature of the "historical" episode's containment.

In the Vulgate *Merlin,* the historical cedes peremptorily to the fabulous with the threat of the Cat of Lausanne at the end of the account of Arthur and Lucius (although the Roman threat resurfaces in the *Mort*). Malory's version, caught between marvel and chronicle, seems altogether more neurotic about historical process and its effects. Mention of Tristram indicates the story's chronological displacement. Malory's text, out of time in respect to its narrative placing, may appear politically irresponsible in divorcing the nationalistic element from the considerations of history integral to the Alliterative *Morte,*[7] for this source emphatically does not unconsideredly as-

sume or promote a nationalist perspective. The poem neither allows the
king to escape the consequences of his own behavior nor the reader to ignore her/his own moral position in the exposition of history that the text
provides.[8] But Malory is not extrapolating uncomplicated triumphalism
from a more searching original text. He introduces new complexities, for
example in his intermittent revision of the poem's representation of the
enemy as repellently other, which makes for different engagement with the
martial and the physical. Malory also marks his *Tale* stylistically, yet the import of the alliterative prose—with its echoes of the source-text and of re-
gional English literary register—is not clear. Is this a tactic calculated to
make us reconsider historiographic form and to critique this retelling? Or
is it simply that the narrator, in celebrating the actions of "our knights,"
uses a recognizably English register to implicate us in the text's nationalism through the very act of reading, and invites us as surrogate knights to
share in what amounts to little more than an exercise in wish-fulfillment?
What kind of "nationalism," indeed, is at stake? And how do the *Tale's* distinctive poetic register and the fantasies of physical wholeness in martial
encounter function as part of its historical vision?

   The campaign against Lucius is of course androcentric: women occupy
a domestic sphere that here has little active purchase on the narrative. Tristram's involvement with Isode (1:195.8–10) erases him from international
warfare. Guinevere, however, in the opening lines of the *Tale* (1:185.1–2), is
part of the consolidation of Arthur's power, and her person frames the
whole episode. Arthur makes her the tender of the trust with which he invests his regents, Baudwen and Constantine, when he leaves both her and
England in their care.[9] She is emblematic (as are other women who feature
in Arthur's campaign) of social stability or national security, the integrity of
which is threatened by the ravages of war or the malicious violence of such
as the Giant of St. Michael's Mount (which last figure subjects his retinue
of unhappy women to a gross parody of the domestic). Disruptions of social order figure as direct violations of, or implicit threats to, the female
body, in a deflection, if not outright substitution, of violence to the male,
while respect for female integrity will define the noble knight. The description of Guinevere's response to the men's departure figures her physical redundancy and also registers through her what is at stake. Her anguish
"that the kynge and all the lordys sholde so be departed" (1:195.11–12)
dramatizes and defuses the threat to the Fellowship. Her subsequent removal by the ladies of the court to her chamber recalls the traditional English romance motif of the "lady in the bower," which the *Kyng Alisaunder*
headpiece cites as image of romance decorum and that here also takes on
connotations of national security.[10] On Arthur's return to London, the welcome that Guinevere organizes, with "all other quenys and noble ladyes"

(1:246.24–25) constitutes an orthodox (if lightly sketched) royal entry. Late-medieval historical practice endorses Malory's implicit presentation of London as a "feminine," internal space (by metonymic association with the chamberbound Guinevere),[11] and the valorization of Arthur's rule by means of a public celebration in which the spouse is central object of the spectacle: "For there was never a solempner metyng in one cité togedyrs" (1:246.25–247.1).[12] The tale, poised between Guinevere's private grief and public joy, relates success in war, so the potential danger to "mery Inglond" itself does not materialize. Yet, between these manifestations, Guinevere also has a more disturbing figurative role, in a narrative in which the fantasy of masculine physical integrity tends toward ahistoricism rather than historical exemplarity.

The alliterative poem lays open to question the legitimacy of Arthur's exercise of power, especially with regard to his behavior on the journey to Rome, but Malory's text confirms Arthur's actions, by written historical witness from "the cronycles of this londe" (1:188.6),[13] as well as by militant Christian ideology. The text draws the boundaries of legitimate action and the rationale for violence. Medieval theory of war also justifies Arthur's refusal to pay tribute.[14] Moreover, Arthur has support from "the fayryst felyship of knyghtes [. . .] that durys on lyve, and thereto of wysedome and of fayre speche [. . .] they fayle of none" (1:192.13–16). The consonance of outward form and speech suggests to a reader of Caxton a chivalric embodiment of his straightforward characterization of historical writing, "representing the thynges lyke vnto the wordes,"[15] as we saw in chapter two. But the textual "body" that is *Arthur and Lucius* itself achieves an integral image of Arthur at the cost of the historical awareness that gives his actions meaning, and displaces violation anxieties onto Guinevere.

The Giant of St. Michael's Mount sets himself against Arthur, as perpetrator of the greatest atrocities. Rape is both his most heinous crime and the general metaphor for his violation of human and natural law, which here conveniently erases rape from its centrality to the internal tensions in the Arthurian social order to which other narratives testify.[16] In the Alliterative *Morte,* Arthur learns from an old woman of the Giant's ambition to gain his beard to complete the collection of beards that (after the manner of King Rion in *Merlin*) trims his garment. He is waiting "Till þe Bretouns kynge haue burneschte his lyppys / And sent his berde to that bolde" (1011–12). Malory mentions a beard-coat, but not this proposed humiliation of Arthur's manhood.[17] A horrifyingly intensified vision of violated womanhood substitutes for the threat to Arthur's physical integrity. In the poem, the grieving widow Arthur meets warns him that the giant has raped and murdered the Duchess of Brittany, and feasts on children, and will later rape and murder those who now prepare his food (1029–32).

Malory's prose version retains these details (1:200.16–202.3). In both versions, the giant devours boys and men, and consumes women sexually. Guinevere's physical person displaces her husband (and beard) as the supreme object of the Giant's desire. The old woman is emphatic that the Giant is lying in wait for the queen rather than the king: "But and thou have brought Arthurs wyff, dame Gwenyvere, he woll be more blyther of hir than thou haddyste geffyn hym halfendele Fraunce" (1:201.10–13).

Guinevere is then metonymically the ground of the conflict between Giant and Arthur; she emblematizes the integrity of both ruler and Arthurian community, and is the reason for the Giant's own dangerous continued presence in the region.[18] Arthur, meanwhile, retains his physical wholeness; he may suffer crushed ribs in the encounter (1:203.15–17), but only the Giant loses blood (1:203.11–14). The rubrication of the Winchester manuscript at this point corroborates Arthur's larger-than-life aspect: the red-inking of *Gesseraunte* and *Basnet* (fol. 76v) suggests that his armor is an extension, as well as protection, of self. The Giant crushes his *Coronal* (fol. 77v) down onto the earth with his club. As for the Giant's physical presence, the rubrication of his genitalia, in the passage where Arthur "swappis his *Genytrottys* in sondir" (fol. 77v), defines the instrument of transgressive behavior in the context of his uniquely monstrous nature rather than of his masculinity. The extraordinariness of the Giant's sexual violence discourages further speculation on the similarity between the imperialist expansionist plans of Arthur and those of the Giant.[19] With regard to rape, that Arthur, after a successful siege, has to prohibit his men from raping (1:243.11–14), simply acknowledges conditions of war; "not raping" is what distinguishes his troops from the enemy without, whether giants or the Roman forces. But the Arthurian subtext of rape troubles our reception here of rape as alien to the chivalric, just as there remains unresolved, in the poetry as in Malory (1:204.25–26), the question of whether the victorious Arthur's desire for the cloak of beards as a trophy denotes a fascination with exotic alterity or a commonality with the Giant.[20]

Arthur protects the threat to state and to his own person, both imaginatively figured as Guinevere, but if we read across the *Morte,* Malory's description in this earlier episode of how the Duchess of Brittany was abducted "as she rode [. . .] with her ryche knyghtes" (1:198.13–14), foreshadows the conditions in which Meleagaunt "rapes"—in the sense of abducting—Guinevere (3:1120.14–1122.7), and suggests that the parameters of Arthurian history are not always unproblematically containable. The similarities highlight retrospectively how the later narrative has to confront, as the earlier does not, the consequences of a historically actual as opposed to a figurally significant queen, in contexts in which the question of "legitimate possession" of Guinevere is less clear-cut.

Guinevere's placing in this *Tale* makes all the more disconcerting the effect of the later narrative's replaying of event and motif and anxious revisiting of locations, whereby, for example, Guinevere's chamber will become a site of contested political and ultimately (the narrator assures us) unknowable events. And it is perhaps in terms of the queen's constructed figural significance (quite apart from the difficulty of reconciling within one space her emblematic and historical functions), that Arthur notoriously laments, at the end of the *Morte,* that "quenys I myght have inow, but such a felyship of good knyghtes shall never be togydirs in no company" (3:1184.3–5). For the great bulk of this *Tale,* Guinevere's emblematic status is simply a given, and in narrative terms, it is Arthur's concern for the physical integrity of his Round Table knights that guarantees their wholeness as a community;[21] later in the *Morte,* it is the cultural relation between these physical bodies that Arthur cannot reconstitute, and over which he will lament.

An extraordinary alliterative English prose combines with "romaynes" authorization (1:245.6) to privilege this text as a site of cultural intersection, but it also requires careful analysis of its effects. The Winchester version of the text (or something similar to it) appears to have concerned commentators and editors alike.[22] The Caxton version makes for local changes in emphasis: it paraphrases and edits at points in the battle description where alliteration is most concentrated (as with, for example, the glossing of the account of Chastelayne's death and its avenging[23]). It modifies alliterative dialogue, or even omits it altogether, as when it loses Arthur's declaration of regal invulnerability: "there shall never harlot have happe [. . .] to kylle a crowned kynge that with creyme is anoynted" (1:227.21–23). Closer scrutiny of the alliteration may determine more precisely the ideology of this style, as of Caxton's revisions. Malory's alliterative technique is unusual primarily in its dense concentration, for, in the English Prose *Merlin,* alliterative collocation also intensifies descriptions of combat. An account of Ban and Bohors's battle against the Saxons, for example, uses what has been called the "decorum" of alliteration[24] to convey a panoramic view of the battlefield: "ther was many a grete growen spere frusshed a-sonder, and many a gome [man] to the grounde glode in a stounde." In the second attack, one can see "many a helme hurled on an hepe, and many a shafte and shelde frayen to-geder" (2:594). The English author has borrowed from the French *Merlin* the incremental "many a" [maint] to express the pace of battle,[25] but also exploits alliterative battle-rhetoric familiar from such poems as the *Morte Arthure,* and *The Siege of Jerusalem.*[26] Alliterative phrasing gives point to other descriptive passages, as when Brangore, rebel to Arthur, "wepte watir with his eyen" to see his men slaughtered in action (2:249),[27] or when the English text refines its source's

evocation of how the detritus of battle floats downstream to disrupt the
locus amoenus of King Carados's fertile gardens and alert him to Brangore's need of aid.[28] Chaucer, too, uses alliteration intensively and economically, to register heroic (and anonymous) endeavor, most famously in
the *Knight's Tale* tournament: [. . .] Ther shyveren shaftes upon sheeldes
thikke; [. . .] / The helmes they tohewen and toshrede; / Out brest the
blood with stierne stremes rede.[29]

Malory draws on both these techniques: while he does not limit alliteration to the Roman wars episode, its concentrated deployment there
(which writes large Chaucer's localized alliteration[30]), and its use to signal
aggression in Arthur's earlier rebuttal of the first set of messengers from
Rome—"on a fayre fylde I shall yelde [the Emperor] my trwage, that shall
be with a sherpe spere othir ellis with a sherpe swerde" (1:48.22–24)—
declares an intensified heroic vision that turns what in the English *Merlin*
is part of the repertoire of battle description into an ideological register.
Embedded reference to "oure noble knyghtes of mery Ingelonde"
(1:209.10) assumes the readers' unambiguous and collusive responses to the
story on the part of readers. But if the wider context suggests alliteration
here primarily promotes a specific nationalistic justification for warfare, in
passages descriptive of combat it also works self-reflexively to demonstrate
how its aesthetic channeling of perspective is part of this nationalist ideology. Alliteration invests the course of violence with a dynamic inevitability, as when Floridas defends himself against Feraunte's cousin:

> [. . .] to hym he flyngis with a swerde, that all the fleysshe of his flanke he
> flappys in sundir, that all the fylth of the freyke and many of his guttys fylle
> to the erthe.
>   Than lyghtly rydis a raynke for to rescowe that barowne [. . .] But the
> raynke Rycharde of the Rounde Table on a rede stede rode hym agaynste
> and threste hym thorow the shylde evyn to the herte. Than he rored full
> rudely, but rose he nevermore. (1:236.23–237.3)

The intermittent use of the historic present draws us into the action at
an immediate, local level;[31] the emphasis on the present moment engages
us in the narrowness of the worldview it endorses, on the side of the
Christian knight versus unbeliever and, in encouraging us to concentrate
on individual acts of heroism in local battle scenes, the text implicates its
readers in the very constitution of an unthinking partisanship that denies
us the detachment necessary to a more objective historicizing. The *Tale,*
concerned with the bodily integrity of Round Table knights, here offers
visceral descriptions of wounded opponents, removing the carnage of war
from "our knights."

Caxton (as we saw in chapter two) writes that through history, a man is "reformed by other and strange mennes hurtes," finely ambiguous as to whether otherness is a function of ideology as well as of time. The wounds detailed above assert Arthur's triumph rather than offer historical lessons. The Round Table certainly suffers losses (1:217.16–22, for example), but the knights are also to a degree invulnerable; moreover, while the enemy is intermittently exoticized, Round Table valor assimilates erstwhile opponents into the Arthurian community.[32] An intense interest in how Arthur relates to his knights overlays the fact of physical hurts. Arthur is a valiant fighter, but his first concern after battle is to heal his men: "And thus he let save many knyghtes that wente never to recover" (1:224.29–30). Malory contradicts the source (2177–2196) and has both Sir Kay and Sir Bedivere recover from their wounds. But he also includes a mock deathbed scene that stresses Arthur's compassion for Kay: "Than wepte kynge Arthure for routhe at his herte and seyde, 'Thou shalte lyve for ever, my herte thynkes'" (1:222.14–15). Arthur himself helps ascertain that Kay's wounds are not fatal, and then avenges his knight's injuries on the battlefield. This episode is not unique as a fantasy about the self-redemptive and salvific effects of war. *Arthur and Lucius* shows that the knight's integrity depends both metaphorically and somatically on the king and on personal valor. The battlefield can dramatize clashes of interest; so the impetuous Launcelot wins general approbation as a knight wishing to prove himself (1:213.31–35; 1:216.19–25) but his behavior also dismays his leader, who is concerned to save his men's lives (1:217:23–27). There is room in this partial text to debate the morality of these different emphases, on the wish to avoid "shame," and the prudent avoidance of fatality.[33] But the tale also denies the natural consequences of violence, reversing the effects of mutilation, suspending in the most obvious way the natural course of history by deferring death itself. The pull toward, and celebration of, "felyship," denies the possibility of the lessons of history.

The encounter between Priamus and Gawain marks a culmination of this fantasy of healing and valor, and asserts the spiritual election of the Round Table knights, as well as their military superiority, and makes candidature for the fellowship generously open. Gawain first meets Priamus when he has gone out on a mission the opening description of which locates his adventure both in romance experience and in soldierly undertaking. He is ostensibly on a foraging expedition, but he also leaves the British camp "wondyrs for to seke" (1:228.21; compare *Morte,* 2514). In the source, the bloody encounter with Priamus results in Gawain's victory, and the former promises to reveal to Gawain how he might staunch his poisoned wounds, on condition he be allowed to make a last confession, "for sake of thy Cryste" (2587).[34] Malory stresses the more positive syncretic aspects of the alliterative poem's account as he transforms the episode from implicit critique of crusading values and historical models to a celebration of martial fellowship and of paradoxically and fantastically regenerative properties of warfare.

Malory alters the source in having Priamus ask explicitly for baptism, in exchange for revealing to Gawain how he might staunch his wounds (1:230.24–231.4). Priamus appears here to be in no need of instruction in Christian doctrine. Gawain's valor (although uncompromisingly secular) has moved Priamus to desire conversion, and, reciprocally, his distillation of the waters of paradise (1:234.12–17) restores each to typically superlative physical health: "holer men than they were within an houres space was never lyvyng syn God the worlde made" (1:234.20–21). Priamus's assimilation into the company of Arthur's knights is simultaneously social and religious, and makes for positive continuity in confirming his worth even as it promises him future security within the fellowship: "Than the kynge in haste crystynde hym fayre and lette conferme hym Priamus, as he was afore, and lyghtly lete dubbe hym a deuke with his hondys, and made hym knyght of the Table Rounde" (1:241.8–11). Assurances of material support for Priamus form part of the *Tale's* triumphant conclusion (1:245.27–34). The Priamus-Gawain adventure and its outcome assert chivalric values and their automatic continuity, but the Arthuriad's later break of faith with Priamus is historically discontinuous. The text conflates him with that other virtuous heathen, Palomides, in the episode of the healing of Sir Urry, as "crystynde by the meanys of sir Trystram" (3:1149.18–19).[35] Priamus meets an ignominious and abrupt death in the chaos Launcelot unleashes when he rescues Guinevere (3.1177.23–30). His case poses the question of how one retrieves historical pattern in the face of revision of biographical fact.

Malory transforms the source's connection between militarism and religious conviction. Arthur envisages a further move east after becoming emperor, "to deme for His deth that for us all on the roode dyed" (1:245.2–3), and so echoes his counterpart in the English poem, who articulates this desire (3217) just before his portentous dream and news of Mordred's treachery send him home. The *Brut*, which finishes (in manuscript and print) with Edward IV's triumphant accession in 1461, invokes a pious faith in crusade as a form of narrative closure.[36] Caxton—although his version of Arthur's campaign, with its references to "unbelievers," reads more like a conventional crusade than does Winchester—omits Arthur's declaration,[37] perhaps because, where crusade in historiographical writing may occlude and so foreclose examination of current civil strife, Malory here puts it to radical use. The *Morte* elsewhere invokes crusade as a harmonizing of the religious and the martial that occurs outside the purview of the narrative, in an ultimately unrepresentable history; so we learn that

Arthur will return to "wynne the Holy Crosse," (3:1242.25), and
Launcelot's companions distinguish themselves against the "myscreantes, or
Turkes" (3:1260.14).[38] In the Alliterative *Morte*, the crusading element is
part of the investigation of historical responsibility.[39] But here, collective
heterosexual desire—"Sir kynge [. . .] reles us to sporte us with oure
wyffis" (1:246.6–9)—overturns state ideology. Arthur accedes, in a shift of
register that shifts the very terms of crusade, and wryly acknowledges the
gap between the will of God and the nature of human undertakings: "in-
owghe is as good as a feste, for to attemte God overmuche I holde hit not
wysedom" (1:246.11–13). The colonial design on Rome complete, the
emperorship achieved, Arthur is not subject to the historicizing context of,
for example, John Hardyng's Emperor Arthur, usurped in his absence by
Mordred, but simply returns home.[40] On one level, this is a lesson in mod-
eration: on another, it demands we reexamine the assumed relation between militarism, "spirituality," and nationalist enterprise.

Caxton (as we saw above) writes of history as a straightforward equation of things and words, but the curtailment of crusade is an example of
the strangely fragmented and inferential quality of historical event, and of
history's rhetorical paradigms. The prose hints at the complexities of the
Alliterative *Morte* Arthur's first dream, for example, when it intensifies the
destructiveness of the "dredfull dragon" that drowns Arthur's people
(1:196.10–11), and that is emblematic of Arthur himself, but it does not
explain its contradictions, and it omits the poem's further contextualizing
dream and Arthur's calling to account. This lack suspends the question of
the means to and limits of our historical understanding. Malory does not
replicate the Alliterative *Morte's* terms of inquiry but challenges us to connect allusively. We can, as one infers Caxton does, endorse the text's nationalistic militarism, or we can interpret its narrative siting and its lack of
historical consequence as an implicit critique of our processing of knowledge. The association of military campaigns with physical wholeness constitutes the ultimate war fantasy, and denies a historical position to both
war and to Arthur as Worthy. In this way, the text displaces Arthur's conventional characterization: "Fulfild of werre and of mortalite."[41]

The poem's dream of Fortune (3223–393) Malory omits will emerge at
the end of the *Morte* (3:1233.11–22), its nightmarish vagueness intimating
something known but long suppressed. If moral censure is not at issue on
Arthur's Roman campaign, in the *Morte* the king cannot ultimately avoid
confronting the process of history through the tropes traditionally invoked
for its understanding (and that will prove ultimately bewildering). But
what the Roman campaign suggests, in Malory's retelling, is a gap between
the kind of participation encouraged at the local level of reading, and the
possibility of broader historical understanding. Most prominent is an imag-

inative engagement with an idea of Arthurian community, as Malory implicates us in an uncritical reading of the Roman wars, one which extratextual knowledge overlays with darker traits. Such selectivity has its disadvantages; identification with the moment demands a general forgetfulness. If we attempt to maintain a triumphalism without historical process, we risk forgetting everything. The following tales also allude to our residual knowledge, in different ways: one exposes and also attempts to contain the untidy paradoxes of the romance world that trouble the formation of male chivalric identity, the other aims to foreclose anxiety by reasserting a familiar paradigm of knighthood.

The Noble Tale of Sir Launcelot du Lake:
Designs on Launcelot

The Vulgate Cycle details Lancelot's *enfances,* and early on indicates the parameters of his chivalric career. In his first major adventure, at the castle of the Dolorous Garde, the young knight simultaneously fulfills his destiny and wins the castle, and finds the site of his own grave (Micha 7:332; Lacy 2:80).[42] The *Morte* first mentions Launcelot, however, when Merlin institutes Colombe's grave as the site of "the grettist bateyle betwyxte two knyghtes that ever was or ever shall be, and the trewyst lovers; and yette none of hem shall slee other" (1:72.5–8).[43] Merlin then inscribes in gold, on the tomb, the names of Launcelot and Tristram. This intriguing contiguity of war, love, and (another's) death, and prophecy's appropriation of a commemorative medium, privileges Launcelot, but does not reveal how those elements—war, love, death denied or displaced—intersect to construct the hero. Aspects of the *Morte* (perhaps inevitably for its chivalric narrative) invest instead in keeping these elements apart. At the same time, Launcelot's person articulates a textual anxiety, over the overlapping versions that repeatedly revisit (in gendered terms) the paradoxes of his character's makeup,[44] and over the various mappings of the *Morte*'s narrative spaces, with their different claims. This gives him a split function, as the narrative assigns him a unitary value and role by insisting he is the paragon of knighthood; but his own fragmented history and his concomitantly alienated selfhood mirror the fractured nature of the *Morte*'s recuperations of the very terms of the Arthurian. Critical opinion, split between a view of Launcelot as "ideal," and another that sees primarily a troubled masculinity, reflects on one or other element of this double aspect.[45] Intensifying the gendered anxieties around pre-*Morte* versions of the hero, Malory makes Launcelot the site of a masculinity both "essential" and performative, which destabilizes rather than confirms the constitution of Launcelot's identity, especially as the *Noble Tale* attempts a Launcelot divorced from, but haunted by, the history the French prose texts assign him. Launcelot relates also to the conflicted nature of the active/passive "knight prisoner" (conceived narratorially, but not necessarily excluding the autobiographical) who writes him, and who may both project onto this character, and displace, his own anxieties about the masculine, its constitution, and its representation in writing when the social construction of masculinity demands repression of the male body, and writing, "as a corporeal and material process," emerges as "a scene of gender ambiguity" that disturbs such repression.[46]

Malory inherits from the French texts a male chivalric protagonist whose very name suggests the feminine:[47] but he arguably complicates an already complex model by further incorporating into his representation Chaucer's association of the Arthurian with female narrative. The *Nun's Priest's Tale's* mention of "the book of Launcelot de lake" elides both the fiction and its subject with a female audience's enthusiastic reception and "ful greet reverence" (VII, 3211–13). Chaucer's only Arthurian story is woman-voiced. In the *Squire's Tale,* Lancelot appears as the epitome of an endemically dissimulating (and also long-dead) courtesy.[48] Malory's hero too exists in the past and is fashioned by women, and intermittent struggles with Launcelot's unarticulated and unarticulable *courtois* relation to Guinevere form the *Morte's* subtext. Malory ostensibly presents a more compensatorily "masculine" Launcelot, where in the French texts women are more deeply involved in the construction of his chivalric identity (Guenièvre gives him a sword, the Lady of the Lake a shield[49]), and where the rhetoric of gender appears more fluidly deployed in relation to women as well as to men than it is in Malory.[50] In suppressing Launcelot's female-influenced history, Malory makes such occlusion a focus of interest. The reader of the *Noble Tale,* too, inevitably "knows" Launcelot as the Queen's lover, and the *Tale* implicates the reader when it represses mention of the hero's sexuality, only to have it reemerge as feminine curiosity. The female-constructed aspect of Launcelot, rather than being elided, becomes further entangled with the work of reader and writer, whereas in the Vulgate it is more clearly located as textual strategy.

The "noble talys" of Launcelot, although they follow a familiar romance structure of departure from the court, adventure, and return, are episodic and open-ended in comparison with their framing stories. The narrative derives largely from three episodes in the later part of the Prose *Lancelot,* and from an incident in the *Perlesvaus.*[51] As a sequence they can read either as self-contained or as intimately connected with the rest of the *Morte.*[52] The adventures also in part imitate, but are divorced from, those that locate Lancelot within the Vulgate's redemptive teleology. So Launcelot's trial at the Chapel Perilous, and his healing of the Round Table knight, Melyot de Logres (1:281.35–1:282.3) foreshadow later manifestations of grace and healing in the *Morte,* but do not introduce the Grail. Launcelot's fight against giants and the release of the silkworkers of Tintagel (1:272; compare the adventure of Terraguel in Micha 5:43–46; Lacy 3:216–217) stands in for the more chivalrically numinous Dolorous Garde adventure. Malory's episode celebrates Launcelot's care of "ladyes and damesels," and one of the ladies recounts a sanitized version of the castle's history, evidence of Arthur's ownership of Tintagel that proves vague both about Arthur's legitimacy and property rights (1:272.26–29), while it stresses Launcelot's unworldly search for honor rather than territorial gain. The episodes achieve their coherence not as part of a promised larger plan, but through their focus on Launcelot, who is as much a construction of others' perspectives and desires as he is an active agent. The greater number of actants in this text (in marked contrast to the source) declare they "know" Launcelot.[53] And as inscribed readers of this set of stories we pursue Launcelot uniquely. At several points the narrator exhorts us to refocus on the hero by "turning to" or "speaking of" him (1:269.17).[54] No less relentlessly do the women in the narrative determine his course of action and (as with the reader's role) reserve attention for him, to the extent that Malory even modifies the experiences of minor characters such as Lionel and Ector. In the source, young women give them information about which path to choose or which course to take (figuratively and literally), but here they learn directions from other knights or from male foresters.[55]

The question of who shows heroes their appropriate paths is integral to textual organization in the Vulgate Cycle. E. Jane Burns notes that the literally wayward directions of its unnamed damsels to the errant knights correspond to how the story itself directs the reader to the correct narrative route that is, more often than not, circuitous. Moreover, this feminine representation of the Vulgate's narrative aesthetics itself comes to dominate among the text's competing voices. Even the knights, in their male-voiced legalistic depositions of their experiences, submit to a process of feminization through the requirement that they tell good stories as well as accurate records.[56] The apparently rigorous documentary narratives that complement the Vulgate's declaredly masculine system of authorship have their own fictive equivocation, of course, as when Lancelot responds to Arthur's demands for accuracy with a selective witness that, to spare Guenièvre's feelings, omits details of his sexual encounter with Pelles's daughter (Micha 4:395; Lacy 3:206). The framing of Lancelot's story through oath-taking and recordkeeping reminds us forcefully how the sexual—most frequently and especially the Lancelot-Guenièvre relationship—does not find accommodation in the text's conventional documentary channels, even though the "contes" openly reveals it. The difference between love as "joy" or "harm" is secrecy, for revelation would shame the queen and make their love low and vile (Micha 8:116; Lacy 2:146). The gap between textual concealment and textual celebration of the Lancelot-Guenièvre affair makes of it a surplus that textual strategies do, however, control. This uncontainable, passionate liaison, excluded from official discourse, breaks its literary bounds and invites imitation (in literature and in life) of the kind in which Dante's Paolo and Francesca engage.[57] But the narrative also reclaims the text for its own program: the explicitly redemptive union between the "best knight" and the most beautiful and most noble maiden (Micha 4:209–210; Lacy 3:164), productive of the chaste Grail knight Galahad, depends on Lancelot's mistaking Pelles's daughter for the queen. So the narrator brings Lancelot's amours within a moral compass, pronounces them "pechié et [. . .] avoutire" [sin and adultery], but asserts that the intervention of a generous and loving God redirects and pardons carnal love (Micha 4:210; Lacy 3:164). The son's virginity compensates for the father's failings. The beginning of the redemptive phase of the Grail story appropriates the language of religious orthodoxy to relativize Lancelot's sexual activity, while the queen herself disappears from view.[58]

The Vulgate manipulates and recontextualizes the Lancelot-Guenièvre relationship as a structurally integral narrative component. By emphasizing the demands of propriety over knowledge, the "contes" focuses strongly on appearances, on the means by which Lancelot, in his individual encounters with women other than the queen, can acquit himself with honor and with courtesy. From this perspective, adventures function less to inscribe women's control as "directors" of chivalric action than to confirm Lancelot's chivalry. In the *Lancelot,* the hero famously comes to the aid of damsels, but he also often (directly or indirectly) causes their distress, for women who help him often find themselves subject to extreme violence as a result. Thus, the damsel who has earlier cured Lancelot of poisoning further enrages her angry abductor and would-be rapist simply by mentioning Lancelot's name, before the hero steps in to save her (Micha 4:215–19; Lacy 3:166–67). Lancelot saves Meleagant's sister from the stake; she stands accused of trying to kill her brother because she released Lancelot from his prison (Micha 2:219–22; Lacy 3:61–62).[59] The damsels are usually superlatively beautiful, which, with the repeated pattern of aid and rescue, reinforces their interchangeability; they allow Lancelot to assert his sexual fidelity and demonstrate his valor. The circularity of the women's experiences leads us back to Lancelot rather than to an examination of their own condition. Female desire is subsumed into Lancelot's sexual location between the jealous Morgain and the loving Guenièvre. The various damsels are a series of nonthreatening substitutions for the necessarily absent queen, and those who test his continence most severely are usually acting on the command of Morgain, as is, for example, the damsel who accompanies Lancelot to the Dolorous Tower (Micha 1:317–26; Lacy 2:315–18), and who tries in vain first to seduce him, and then to learn the name of the woman who already has his love. When Lancelot extricates himself from this difficult situation through the proper deployment of *courtois* speech, the lady praises his honor, and the test is over.

In the *Noble Tale,* feminine intervention has a narrower purpose. Malory targets Launcelot as the one knight female guides help.[60] Women's interest in him marks him out just as the alliterative style earlier marks out the particular nature of the Roman campaign. Even such an apparently "masculine" adventure as the episode in which Lancelot dons Kay's armor has a woman's hospitality as its starting point,[61] and women's motives (threatening or benign) primarily place the hero. From the queens, Morgan among them, who seek to constrain him to their love (1:256.24–258.12), to Bagdemagus's daughter, whose father is needs a champion at his tournament (1:258.27–34), women determine Launcelot's trajectory through the story. Malory thus projects what in the Vulgate pertains to narrative construction, or to the decorum of a relationship's disclosure, more precisely onto the person and definition of the hero. But in the *Tale,* the inscribed readers' (and writer's) interest in the literal path the hero takes locates "us" with women's material interventions and perspectives. "Our" "female" gaze guarantees the hero's currency as heterosexually desirable, but also sets up an interesting tension in relation to the narrative's play on masculinity. That the Vulgate's textual "surplus" becomes an "excess" of our own knowledge as romance readers further implicates us in the Launcelot-Guinevere relationship. Where the Vulgate guides, even dictates, response, "we" are party to an "open secret," the maintenance of which, in D. A. Miller's formulation, constructs our subjectivity as readers.[62] But while Miller suggests that in the Victorian novel the open secret registers the subject's resistance but also accommodation to a "totalizing system,"[63] our unsanctioned knowledge also effects our reading, for we inevitably construct the "missing" narrative.

At its inception, the *Tale* teasingly brings into play this technically unauthorized yet tantalizingly insistent extratextual knowledge, which disingenuously alludes to love as central to the traditional definition of the French-authored hero: "he loved the quene [. . .] above all other ladyes dayes of his lyff, and for hir he dud many dedys of armys and saved her frome the fyre thorow his noble chevalry" (1:253.17–19). This *occultatio* may promise a self-contained account of youthful endeavor, or warn implicitly that the story's premises are compromised from the beginning by what we know of the *Morte*'s conclusion.[64] Women's words to Launcelot similarly implicate us in his apprehension as sexualized hero—the connection with Guinevere is, for example, what Morgan "knows" about Launcelot (1:257.26–29).

At the center of the narrative, the Damsel of the White Palfrey articulates a general disappointment over Launcelot's apparent unavailability: "For I cowde never here sey that ever ye loved ony of no maner of degré, and that is grete pyté. But hit is noysed that ye love quene Gwenyvere"(1:270.20–23). Launcelot's evasive response—"I may nat warne peple to speke of me what hit pleasyth hem" (1:270.28–29)—links him in part with his *courtois* Vulgate self.[65] His generalizations about the problems of sexual entanglement—"And so who that usyth paramours shall be unhappy, and all thynge unhappy that is aboute them" (1:271.2–4)—echo the prescriptions of popular religion,[66] while one might link his observations on the restrictions of the married man's chivalric activities (1:270.29–32) to the narrative closure of Gareth's own later history. But this account offers not a psychologically realizable Launcelot or a gloss on chivalric biography as much as a register of anxiety about the relation between sexuality, violence, and textuality, which Launcelot imperfectly "solves" by invoking that commonplace of the romance plot, whether medieval or modern, which constantly defers the satisfaction of desire. In doing so, he anticipates of course the terms of the May passage, but he attempts also to displace the sexual interest in him the articulation of which guarantees his continued centrality even as it leaves him open to readings he claims he cannot control.

Such displacement, from the hero to "our" feminine reception of him, makes even more visible what Launcelot as character seeks to elide, and it identifies him as a site of resistance to, as much as confirmer of, his "known" selfhood. Conventionally, women's sexual inquiries in the text are seen as evidence of male anxiety about women, specifically the threat of female sexuality to the young Launcelot's sense of chivalric integrity.[67] But they link fundamentally with the representation of reading in a text that implicitly foregrounds the relationship between the knight and his queen but leaves readerly integrity to build any containing space for it. The text throws open the question of the affair's status and its relation to Arthurian adventure in general, and at the same time comments on the vulnerability of the masculine subject in a woman-mediated narrative. This gendered knowledge contextualizes problematically Kathleen Coyne Kelly's argument that Malory's prose "feminizes" the male body in battle to occlude the fact of violence against the male.[68] The text is further destabilizing when it connects gender with epistemology, and yet does not work through those gendered terms of our knowledge, nor ever quite resolve the play of male and female, masculine and feminine. The example of Belleus Coyne Kelly cites, where Belleus mistakes Launcelot for his lover (1:259.28–260.21), draws attention to how masculine identity, put in doubt, asserts itself through extreme violence.[69] Kelly notes how, in the aftermath, Launcelot staunches Belleus's blood (one of several scenes in which Launcelot is associated with healing): yet the resolution of the story also depends on Belleus's Lady, who negotiates for her lover a position at Arthur's court with Launcelot's sponsorship, in compensation for "the harmys that ye have done to me and to my lorde" (1:260.29). The feminizing relations of masculine combat do not also then automatically situate or prescribe the behavior of the text's women.

Gendered vocabulary for battle is also appropriated to men's uses in ways that extend beyond a function protective of male bodies (and may even have an intensifying opposite effect). Launcelot's violent acts range from the cartoonlike straightforward dispatch of a bridgekeeper—"Than sir Launcelot drew his swerde and put the stroke abacke, and clave his hede unto the pappys" (1:271.16–17)—who seeks to interrupt the linear progress of his narrative—"Why sholde I nat ryde this way? [. . .] I may not ryde besyde" (1:271.12–13)—to the more difficult strategems involved in fighting on behalf of one's peer. When Launcelot fights for Kay, for example, the narrator has Kay (in the register of passive sexuality) relinquish a masculinity to Launcelot that the hero will restore by making his prisoners yield to Kay: "Sir Kay for the plesure of that knyght suffyrd hym for to do his wylle and so stoode on syde" (1:273.25–26). A gendered language of power in fight scenes belongs to the narrative's ruthless processing of violence in terms of ethics and class; its absence can suggest an elision of ethical debate, as with giant-slaying or, more troublingly perhaps, with the killing of the rapist knight Perys, whose voice would perhaps question Launcelot's robust assertion that chivalry is against rape (1:269.22–36).

Jeffrey Cohen engagingly reads Lacan's imagery of enculturation, whereby the child moves from a perception of a fragmented self, a body in pieces, to "an illusory oneness," in the composition of the heroic warrior, whose literal armor suggests an integrity that proves to be fragile and violable.[70] Malory's intriguing figuration of Launcelot as precariously balanced between, or subject to, conflicting knowledges, plays further on this analogy with Lacan's anxious "body in pieces:" for Launcelot is sometimes more reassuringly known "in pieces" than as a "whole" that would have to reconcile the conflicted claims on him as hero, and so constitutes a threat. So, for example, Gawain's identification of Launcelot "by his rydyng" (1:278.14) expresses confidence in "knowing" a knight metonymically. Attempts to form a composite picture, as when the Damsel of the Palfrey notes his success against Terquyn and Perys, the one a destroyer of knights, the other of ladies, inevitably raise the question of his "open secret": "But one thyng [. . .] methynkes ye lak, ye that ar a knyght wyveles, that ye woll nat love som mayden" (1:270.18–20). Rather than confront a conflicted character, the narrative relays as a death fantasy the full objectification of an essentialized, controlled Launcelot, a fantasy that offers an analogue to modern writers' links of articulation and representation with death.[71]

The adventure concerning Gilberd the Bastard's corpse finally combines violence, death, and sex for Launcelot. Gilberd's body, which Launcelot first sees in the secular context of a great hall, initially constitutes a narrative impasse for Launcelot, helpless at the vision of the lifeless "knyght that was a semely man" (1:278.29–30). Julia Kristeva names the corpse the ultimate expression of the abject, of that which disturbs identity,[72] but the text seeks to retain a chivalric identity for the body even as it describes it. The brachet's confusion over whether the body is human or animal (Launcelot says she has traced "the feaute of blood" [1:278.35]),[73] and Gilberd's widow's distracted accusation of Launcelot, the only occasion where a woman temporarily misattributes actions to him, impart a sense of dislocation (1:278.33). The hero expresses sympathy, and moves on; but another damsel quickly enlists his aid, explaining (on the information of a sorceress) that Gilberd's adversary, Melyot, can only be healed by a piece of the former's bloody cloth and his sword. Launcelot recognizes Melyot as a Round Table knight and the adventure begins to cohere through the claims of "felyship": "to his helpe I woll do my power" (1.279:31–32). Launcelot's second encounter with the body is in the sinister atmosphere of the Chapel Perilous, where his successful completion of the adventure, and his refusal either to obey Hallewes's injunction to abandon the sword, or to kiss her, leads her to uncover a different set of significances for his actions.

In Hallewes's rereading, appearances belie meaning; Launcelot's encounters with and defiance of death are, she declares, a test of his sexual fidelity, and the chapel itself the expression of her desire for control of him: "I ordeyned this chapell for thy sake and for sir Gawayne" (1:281.9–10). Mention of past conquest qualifies Launcelot's status as sole object of desire; Hallewes even proposes further to commodify Launcelot, to use his violated body as a trophy with which to taunt Guinevere, in her explicit desire for his preserved corpse in preference, it seems, to his integral and living self:

> "[. . .] sytthen I myght nat rejoyse the nother thy body on lyve, I had kepte no more joy in this worlde but to have thy body dede. Than wolde I have bawmed hit and sered hit, and so to have kepte hit my lyve dayes; and dayly I sholde have clypped the and kyssed the, dispyte of quene Gwenyvere." (1:281.16–20)

The life-threatening, sexually rapacious witch is a commonplace of Western mythology. Western culture traditionally associates the feminine with the materiality of death, as well as with its representation and its allegorical significance.[74] Hallewes's fantasy, however, makes Launcelot simultaneously abject/object and relic, horribly sacralized through erotic desire. Yet Hallewes, although her language transgresses the *Morte's* sexual decorum, is simply extending the romance notion of the hero as concretized and fantastically "preserved" object, as fully known literary hero, defined in relation to Guinevere, in the eyes of other characters as of the readers. Launcelot's chivalric instincts deliver him from Hallewes. Her pronouncements have no more substantial reality than do the ghoulish knights who protect the marvelous chapel, and the threat of her obsessive desire absolutely to define and possess him soon dissolves: "And as the booke seyth [. . .] she toke suche sorow that she deyde within a fourtenyte" (1:281.24–25).[75] The fantasy-threat to Launcelot becomes a matter of life and death for Hallewes, and through her death the episode reaffirms normative male hegemonic values.[76] Launcelot reclaims the adventure with the healing of Melyot: "and anone an holer man in his lyff was he never" (1:282.2–3). "Felyship" redefines the parameters of violence and death and displaces Hallewes's claims. But fellowship's redemptive aspect depends on enchantment as much as on defying magic. The Hallewes episode thus raises the question of agency and control with regard to Launcelot's adventure at the same time as it involves us as readers in his objectification.[77] Death, real and imagined, brings into focus the narrative's confusions over the knight's autonomy, his status as hero, the possibility of wholeness, and the ends of violence. The strangest adventure is also the most serious assault on Launcelot's identity and integrity, yet it is resolved through a mystification of chivalry as a saving grace. Launcelot himself is the site of contest between the "givens" of chivalry and "our" narrative apprehension of it.

Launcelot's escape from Hallewes marks the beginning of the ascendency of male characters and their control over the female, with adventures that convey more strongly Launcelot's gradual anchoring within specific social bounds, with a concomitant concentration on questions of arbitration that unsettle the possibility of straightforward judgment. Physical vulnerability transfers from Launcelot to the women he encounters, such as the unnamed wives of Phelot and Pedyvere, who suffer violence at their husbands' hands. The Pedyvere episode at the end of the *Tale* has been read as a failure for Launcelot;[78] but comparison with the analogous adventure in the Vulgate, together with the way in which Malory's characters approach the question of judgment, suggest that the slighting of Launcelot's honor is secondary to the failure in the reach of Arthurian legislation and romance narrative that the problems of adjudication intimate. The French account (Micha 4:317–25, 339–45; Lacy 3:189–90, 193–94) is brutal in the extreme, and writes large violence to another as threat to

Lancelot's integrity. Lancelot, abandoning the young woman he is already accompanying, follows the sound of screaming to discover a knight abusing a beautiful woman he accuses of infidelity. In response to Lancelot's entreaties and threats that he desist, the knight decapitates the woman and defiantly throws her head in Lancelot's face. Overcome with shame, Lancelot pursues his antagonist to a castle, where the portcullis slices his horse in two (another assault on Lancelot's chivalric integrity) before he finally has the knight in his power. As Lancelot is about to kill him, the defeated man cries for mercy. Lancelot therefore devises for him a penance fitting to his crimes. The knight must trace a path to Arthur's court, where he must throw himself on the queen's mercy, and thence, if he is spared, to the courts of Bademagu and of the King of Norgales in turn, where he must ask the ladies for forgiveness. This reiterates Lancelot's recent chivalric trajectory, so imitates in part the hero's narrative. The murderer's journey is made grotesque by the accompaniment of the damsel's body, the stench of which threatens to prove fatal to him before he can complete his itinerary. The corpse's putrefaction is the material witness to his disregard of female honor, but when Arthur, to whose judgment the queen has deferentially delivered him, forgives the knight out of respect for Lancelot, he also arrests the process of putrefaction, and sweetly perfumes the body. The newly embalmed body signals the knight's rehabilitation. He expiates his crime by means of this secular pilgrimage, forgiven at each of his stopping points, and he finally buries the body at a hermit's chapel at the entrance to a forest, a place appropriate both to piety and romance (Micha 4:345; Lacy 3:194). The *Lancelot* accommodates its hero's humiliation, articulating a faith not only in his nobility, which makes possible the forgiveness of the felon, and in the judgments of the noble courts, whose arbitration is not called into question, but also in the very space of romance narrative.

Malory's version demonstrates a greater interest in the legal aspects of the case—the accused damsel, for example, has a voice, and both explains the grounds for her husband's suspicion and stoutly declares her innocence (1:284.30–34)—and Launcelot can cope neither with verbal equivocation nor sudden violence. Pedyvere has promised not to kill his wife in Launcelot's sight, by which oath he justifies her execution while he directs the hero's gaze elsewhere. Like his French counterpart, he begs for mercy, but Malory stresses Launcelot's increasing frustration rather than any confident adjudication. Launcelot refers the "shamefull" problem of the corpse-encumbered knight[79] to Guinevere, who in turn defers not to her husband but to a higher and spiritual authority. The penitential journey to the Pope in Rome does not retrace a trajectory so as to redeem both narrative and actant, as in the French, but takes Pedyvere into a different set of references altogether: "And after thys knyght sir Pedyvere fell to grete goodnesse and was an holy man and an hermyte" (1:286.17–18).[80] The normative Arthurian milieu of the *Noble Tale* lacks the French narrative's mechanism for the judgment and expiation of crime. Chivalry, law, and redemptive effect do not here coalesce. The difficulties of adjudication register the English romance's self-limitation, where the Vulgate asserts the self-authorizing procedures of its romance world.

Launcelot offers no verbal witness at the end of his adventures (1:286.19–287.27), whereas in the Prose *Lancelot* the hero's own testimony is carefully documented in writings that will be found among Arthur's possessions after the last battle, and that, we assume, constitute our book (Micha 4:396–97; Lacy 3:206). After the female placings of the hero, the official testifiers to Launcelot's prowess are, with the exception of Belleus's Lady, male. In the source, the hero's actions cause deep resentment, even a fatal hatred, among the rest of the Round Table, because of Arthur's fulsome praise of his best knight. Indirectly, his deeds and their recording set in train the events that will lead to his downfall (Micha 4:398–99; Lacy 3:206). Malory ironically shifts episodes from the end of the *Lancelot* to the earlier portion of his "whole book," and assures us that they consolidate the hero's reputation: "And so at that tyme sir Launcelot had the grettyste name of ony knyght of the worlde, and moste he was honoured of hyghe and lowe" (1:287.24–26). This optimistic conclusion attempts to arrest an image of Launcelot as exemplary, and points to the wish for stability, even as it recognizes the temporal nature of Launcelot's achievement. If Launcelot can transcend and represent a complex world of conflicting interests, the text has also inscribed us as readers whose response is not limited to identification with what is explicitly stated, and we help to construct the unspoken terms of Launcelot's identity, in a gendered reading that we must also police ourselves. Launcelot's confrontation with a fantasized death may be an attempt to exorcise the threat of representation, but Hallewes's end also seeks to demonize and disempower our inevitable sexualization of the hero. The narration, and our reading, create the tensions that make Malory's characters, and Launcelot in particular, appear more vulnerable than their Vulgate romance counterparts, in a fictive world that recognizes its limitations while at the same time demanding the reader collude in its imperfect strategies. Toward the end of the *Morte,* Launcelot is involved in issues of death and commemoration in ways that will further challenge our powers of retrieving meaning in and for the Arthurian world.

The Tale of Sir Gareth of Orkney: Chivalric Control

If we inevitably overread Launcelot because of our knowledge of him, the inscribed "we" take a more relaxed attitude to Gareth as narrative focus,[81]

and consequently appear less implicated and assume less control, in a story
that seemingly offers, on a formal as well as on a narrative plane, a reassuringly normative masculine fantasy of heroic action and reward. From un-
rooted unknown to happily married knight, the protagonist directs his
adventurous trajectory.[82] The reader of Launcelot's adventures implicitly
takes up a female-gendered perspective, and is guardian/repressor of a secret s/he helps construct, but the deployment of Gareth's names suggests
"we" know him from the perspective of the privileged male warrior, as well
as engaging in the broader perspective of narrative performance. Early on,
we learn with Launcelot the true identity of this Fair Unknown, whom
Kay has nicknamed Bewmaynes (1:299.27), but we also help maintain this
unthreatening secret, for the narrative does not generally call him Gareth
until his dwarf reveals his origins to Lyonesse and her family (1:329.25–29).
This gives the *Tale* the reassuring sense of a masquerade, a play in which
identity is not at stake so much as continually revealed and confirmed. The
latter part of the *Tale* revels in tournaments, but Gareth's first set of adventures, with Lynet as spectating "antiherald," and a supporting cast of brightly
colored knights, also imitates tournament's maturation narratives, in which,
as Louise Fradenburg describes, Youth's lawlessness is brought within the
orbit of a sanctioned economy of violence.[83] The difference for Gareth is
that his already "civilized" comportment obviates the need for education,
"naturalizes" violence, and more vigorously asserts his noble identity as beyond question. Gareth's indubitable identity sets him up as a model of secular chivalry, which his partial anticipation of the terms of Galahad's arrival
at court reinforces. Gareth appears at a time when Arthur holds the Round
Table "moste plenoure" (1:293.3–4). The description of imprisonment or
death as the pragmatic obstacles to the Table's being "fully complysshed" in
its knights (1:293.21–26) signals room for Gareth's assimilation while ig-
noring that (strictly speaking) only Galahad can fulfill the Round Table circle (2:855.12–14). Like Galahad, Gareth organizes his own knighting, at
Launcelot's hands, away from the court (1:299.19–34; cf. 2:854.9–33).[84] But
just as Galahad is inimitable, so the terms of Gareth's chivalric exemplarity
do not correspond to the narrative problematic of the rest of the *Morte*.

The *Tale of Sir Gareth of Orkney* works hard to contain and to formalize
the action, on narrative as on social levels, in such a way as obscures or
erases, rather than confronts and resolves, the paradoxes of chivalric representation and the history of which Gareth will inevitably be a part. This
sense of integrity and self-containedness responds well to critical analyses
that link the tale with bounded systems, whether those be the reassuring
narrative patterns of folktale, or social or epistemological frameworks, such
as those of alchemy, as Bonnie Wheeler delightfully traces, or the forms of
courtesy, as Felicity Riddy has elegantly pointed out as the means to link

the fifteenth-century aspirational reader with a chivalric narrative of social advancement.[85] This section looks at some of the internal interrelated attempts at containment—in terms of narrative, a downplaying of the threats of secrecy and the unknown, an "unproblematic" presentation of chivalric manhood,[86] the working through of gender relations, and the deployment of imagery—and at what its ruptures and elisions reveal of this text as wish-fulfillment. The story is laid out in a formal diptych structure in which elements organize themselves around the definition of the hero;[87] juxtaposition with the previous *Tale* suggests that the structure functions as a defense mechanism against romance surprise such as Launcelot experiences. Where Launcelot's tale accords a privileged central position to the interrogation of the hero's sexuality and motivation, together with the assumption that his sexual relations are intrinsic to his identity, the midpoint of Gareth's text is a formal marker, the "brode watir" (1:327.36), the sea at which the hero arrives at the end of the first phase of his adventures, when he has proved himself for Lyonesse, and from which he will turn to engage with events in the second half of his story, where his "honour is gradually relocated in a web of sexual, familial, and societal relationships."[88] Gareth's observance of physical boundaries here seems to indicate the romance hero's unproblematic accommodation within the limits (whether literal, literary, or social) of his environment (a little like the containing space of the tournament field). But the thematic stopping point of Gareth's narrative, just a few lines earlier, is his frustrated attempt to enter Lyonesse's castle: "and whan he com to the gate he founde there men armed, and pulled up the drawbrygge and drew the portcolyse" (1:327.1–3). This is the first time that he has been refused,[89] and for no good reason, as far as he can understand from his awareness of his own body as a unit of value with currency within the chivalric economy: "I have nat deserved that ye sholde shew me this straungenesse [. . .] I am sure I have bought your love with parte of the beste bloode within my body" (1:327.12–17). Lyonesse does not deny this easy link between the exercise of arms and the satisfaction of erotic desire, but addressing him as a "curteyse knyght" (1:327.18), she sends him away until such time as he will have proved himself worthy: "and loke that ye be of good comforte, for all shall be for your worshyp and for the best" (1:327.23–24).

The diptych structure sharpens other containing effects, such as the nature of Gareth's selfhood, as Davis points out. Jane Gallop would identify as classic Gareth's estimation of his body as currency: "men have their masculine identity to gain by being estranged from their bodies and dominating the bodies of others."[90] Gareth's agency is intensified in that he "embodies" what is already a literalizing metaphor in the *Morte*, in the nickname "Beaumains" [Fair hands]. "Hands" in Malory denote a knight's self-determined exercise of strength, his independent volition in feats of arms.[91] This "natural" aristocracy, and the "social magic" (to use Bourdieu's term) that is the institution of knighthood Launcelot confers on him, are mutually validatory.[92] And the body count in the first part of the tale assumes that Bewmaynes's valor is quantifiable in terms of the number of men he has defeated and killed. But the narrative is also careful to plot the social constructedness of his masculinity, and the wounds of violent engagement come to inscribe the social demands made of the initially quasi-autonomous knight. There is also a concern to map out the masculine externally, in terms of space, a concern that links with the balance of masculine and feminine in the context of the known and the unknown, and works in counterpoint to the action in the *Launcelot* section.

Gareth's attempt to enter Lyonesse's castle is his first venture into a space that has not been defined, or appropriated, by men, although, typically, this refusal is not a threat to masculinity but a structural marker, an impetus to a further series of adventures that will culminate in Gareth's reaccommodation at Arthur's court. Gareth as "Bewmaynes" (even Kay's strictly speaking ungrammatical nickname for him asserts the primacy of his maleness), setting himself against the declared expectations and judgments of his female companion Lynet, exists in a world carefully defined as masculine, as the enclosed spaces he inhabits in his first phase of adventures emphasize. At Arthur's court, he "sette hym downe amonge boyes and laddys" (1:295.26–27). He accepts lodging from knights he has defeated, and at Sir Persaunt's castle he refuses his host's offer of his daughter by way of hospitality, explicitly in terms of bonds between men: "'God deffende me,' seyde he, 'than that ever I sholde defoyle you to do sir Persaunte suche a shame!'" (1:315.9–10). When he arrives at his destination, before and after defending the Lady Lyonesse from the Red Knight, Bewmaynes occupies a series of marginal (although still masculine) spaces; in a hermit's cell, he eats the feast Lyonesse has sent him (1:318.33–35). His opponent defeated, Bewmaynes recuperates, with the help of the resourceful Lynet, not at Lyonesse's home but in a tent nearby (1:326.6–7). Lyonesse's castle is locked and defended against him, and it is at her brother Gryngamoure's castle that the lovers will meet and make their frustrated trysts. And while Launcelot always finds lodging with women, at the beginning of the second half of his tale, Gareth finds shelter at a "pore mannys house" (1:327.32). Gareth's masculine success is also registered in a male professionalization of domestic space at the conclusion to the *Tale*, where the defeated knights in turn request roles of butler, carver, and chamberlain at Gareth's wedding feast (1:361.12–362.9) in a taxonomy of service that bespeaks an orderly court.

The actants in violent encounters are also male. Although Gareth's rep-utation is of course founded on conflict, episodes of violence toward women, whether deliberate or accidental, which focus points of narrative or ethical crisis elsewhere in the *Morte* (and especially in regard to Launcelot), seem to have been excised from whatever sources Malory was working with. One episode in the *Lancelot* Vinaver identifies as a source has been rewritten so that Gareth, fairly early in his adventurous trajectory, having been alerted by a servant, saves one knight from six thieves (1:300.25–301.6). In the original tale, Gaheriet saves sir Brandeliz and his lady from knights avenging their kinsman, but the lady later dies of the beating she receives.[93] Only toward the end of his tale (complementing the increase in the incidence of male figures in Launcelot's latter adventures), does Gareth encounter a broader female population. A lady offers him lodging at Rouse's castle (1:355), for example, and he saves thirty ladies from the Brown Knight Without Pity (1:355). Adventures in the first half of the tale correlate with the general privileging of Gareth's masculine per-spective on "worship" as achievable through repeated feats of arms. In the tale of *Arthur and Lucius,* masculine martial valor defines itself in relation to and in defense of a domestic space, although its exercise is necessarily apart from it. In the *Launcelot* section, space is more fluid in significance, and women control the hero in the "open" spaces of forest paths and nar-rative possibility, as in the enclosed spaces of halls, dungeons, and castles. Read against Launcelot's experience, these instances of a masculine con-trol of space in Bewmaynes's story would seem to suggest a reclaimable and "demystified" universe in which action and meaning are, for the knight, accordingly more straightforward. But this sense of masculine space exists concomitantly (and worryingly) in a fantasy world that wipes out detailed analysis of causation for male-male violence, by having recourse to the feminine as the default. So the Red Knight, laying siege to Ly-onesse's castle, explains, as his motive for killing, and exposing to public shame the corpses of, some forty knights, a hatred of Round Table knights that arose from a former lover's report to him that "sir Launcelot du Lake othir ellys sir Gawayne" (1:325.2–3) killed her brothers, and the request that he promise to kill one of them in revenge. Gareth's easy forgiveness of the Red Knight—"insomuche all that he dud was at a ladyes requeste I blame hym the lesse" (1:325.24–25)—and the Red Knight's own testi-mony in extenuation of his career as "man-murtherer" (1:337.21), when he gives account of himself at Arthur's court—"for all the shamefull cus-toms that I used I ded hit at the requeste of a lady that I loved" (1:337.23–25)—work to disavow responsibility in the exercise of mascu-line violence, and expose the limits of a fantasy of male control through violence, and the inadequacy of violence as forensic tool.

The *Tale's* generic echoes also indicate a bypassing of opportunities for the greater moral complexity that the story might produce by working through some of the issues in gender relations the source-material confronts. The simplifications isolate and protect Gareth's masculinity from any traumatic division of loyalty, or from too deep a scrutiny. A tournament Olivier de La Marche describes, for example, held in 1470 before Margaret of York, has as its premise the journey from the beautiful kingdom of Childhood to the wasteland ("pays gasté") of Youth, through which the protagonist arrives at the Plain of Delight [Plaisance], and his adventures dramatize the pains of enculturation and sexual maturity—a knight of Dame Sauvaige, called Look [Regard] so wounds the young man that she has to nurse him back to health; the ensuing *pas d'armes* is to demonstrate his nobility and win her favor.[94] Lynet, retrospectively identified as a "Damesell Saveaige," accompanies Gareth, but she rewrites the terms of a pageant "wild woman" in that she is not sexually threatening, her gaze does not wound him, and Gareth himself rewrites her negative language as incitement to further feats of arms.[95] The gap between her dismissive accounts of his triumphs as a kitchen-boy's "hap"—"howsomever hit happenyth I ascape and they lye on the grounde" (1:304.35–36) responds Gareth—makes feminine judgment appear comic and exasperating; but, as she intimates later, her scornful behavior was a performance: "forgyff me all that I have mysseseyde" (1:313.13–14).[96]

The Fair Unknown type of romance, whereby the young aristocrat actively proves himself worthy of inclusion in a class to which he (wittingly or not) already belongs, similarly dramatizes an entry into civilization, and offers the opportunity to examine the relationship between love and social responsibility, and between modes of individual and social self-expression and identity. Gareth, as a "knowing" Fair Unknown, controls access to knowledge more often than he is kept in ignorance: rather than "prove" *himself*, as does the young Launcelot, he has set out to test his environment, to, as he puts it, "preve my frendys" (1:313.8). But the sexual aspect of the Fair Unknown narrative is not as straightforward as is its exercise of violence. In the fourteenth-century English *Lybeaus Desconus,* as in Renaut de Beaujeu's twelfth-century French *Le Bel Inconnu,* sex and magic are closely related as the hero enjoys a period of sexual license before a return to the Arthurian world, with its social values and hierarchies, and a "legitimate" bride. In *Lybeaus,* the solution to the hero Guinglain's divided loyalty is the denigration of the enchantress who claims his love. The narrator regrets Lybeaus's incontinence—"Alas he ne hadde y-be chast!"—but notes, too, the lady's power to dull his moral perception with her magic.[97] In *Le Bel Inconnu,* meanwhile, a narratorial intervention complicates the values of the text, and Renaud, in an epilogue, offers to effect the return of the hero, from the arms of Esmerée, the woman he has both rescued and married, into the embrace of his seductive fairy, if the lady the author loves looks kindly on him. Sexual and emotional values, as well as the power-play inherent in sexual relations, the ending to the poem intimates, transgress the social system the poem has just described, while the site of moral deliberation over desire and its reciprocation is itself located outside the poem.[98] Gareth's story acknowledges the possibility of divided sexual loyalties safely and comedically, in the hero's ignorance that the lady he encounters at Gringamoure's castle is the same as the lady he has already defended against the Red Knight: "And sir Gareth thought many tymes: 'Jesu, wolde that the lady of this Castell Perelus were so fayre as she is!'" (1:331.19–20). Gareth is happily disabused of his error before nightfall.

But where in the analogues the morally and socially fraught aspects of sexuality, the need to temper lust to social constraint, are issues for audience debate, or expressed in terms of conflicting sexual engagements, this text famously marks such issues on Gareth's body. Lyonesse and Gareth set a tryst "to abate their lustys secretly" (1:332.37–333.1). Miller writes of secrecy as a point of entry for subjectivity, and one that reinforces binarisms, for through it "the oppositions of private/public, inside/outside, subject/object are established, and the sanctity of their first term kept inviolate."[99] But Gareth and Lyonesse are too young and guileless to keep counsel, and Lynet collapses public and private to ensure that the notion of sexual desire and consummation as private space yields to social control. No sooner are Lyonesse and her lover locked in embrace, than an anonymous, ax-wielding knight attacks Gareth who, dealt a painful thigh wound by his opponent, decapitates him. Lynet quickly enters on the scene, and reconstitutes both the intruder's body and, she tells him, Gareth's—and the community's—honor: "all that I have done I woll avowe hit, and all shall be for your worshyp and us all" (1:334.32–34). A few days later the would-be lovers make a second tryst, the scene is reenacted, and Gareth's wound reopens, although he also chops his opponent's head into a hundred pieces, disposing of the fragments through the window. On this, as on the previous occasion, Gareth seems to come close to his own mortality: "he felle in a dedly sowne in the floure" (1:335.24–25). Lynet again enters on the scene, calmly gathers up the gobbets and reassembles the knight, and repeats that she works in the interests of honor (1:336.1–3). But Gareth's wound will not heal until the time of the Assumption Day tournament that will mark his reassimilation into the world of the Round Table knighthood. Recent readings note the sociopsychological implications of Gareth's wounding. For Andrew Lynch, the thigh wound "speaks of a deep patriarchal fear as well as its reassurance."[100] Laurie Finke and Martin Shichtman see the "out of control" violence of Gareth's and the knight's fight as a displacement of castration anxieties, and Lynet's ministrations as a legitimizing restoration of heterosexual masculinity.[101] Kathleen Coyne Kelly wittily interprets the knight's fragmentation as a projection of Gareth's own anxieties, in Lacanian mode, about "his own dissolution [. . .] in sexual intercourse."[102] Certainly these associations raise deep anxieties about masculine order, but the reiterated scenes also pose questions about the (im)possibilities of chivalric self-awareness. Although, by the end of his story, Gareth fully submits to the strictures of an institutionalized morality in his explicit desire for a wife rather than a mistress (1:360.3–5), he interprets his wound—which we eagerly read metaphorically—only as "unhappynesse" (1:342.12–13).[103] If Gareth's openness, his lack of secrecy, makes for the disappearance of the "subject" as we might understand it, the eruption of violence may be said to constitute a trauma as much narrative as psychological, a failure to make room for the "kyndely," natural, sexual, within a narrative of violence, a failure that demonstrates the narrative's inability to incorporate the sexual, other than in terms of deferral or closure,[104] and that instead returns us to Gareth's chivalric body as troubled open locus of signification, caught in a tension between autonomous agency and social inscribability.

The physical imagery in the *Tale* attempts to counter this hermeneutically baffling aspect of the body with a specificity of reference for the somatic. Gareth's hands are then evident markers of chivalric capability and volition, as we have seen. Blood, which is viscous, material, boundary-transgressing, and capable, Lynch notes, of "double and dangerous meanings"[105] across the *Morte,* in the *Tale* also seems "contained" temporarily by its deployment as synonym for lineage, as when others speculate on Gareth's origins as one of "full noble blood" (1: 307.22).[106] The many descriptions of violent physical encounter are economical in their specific mention of blood. Its absence may convey a sense of various opponents as so many obstacles in Bewmaynes's path, rather than as sentient beings; this seems the case with the two knights at the ford whom Bewmaynes dispatches (1:301.36–302.11). Blood is associated with "worthy" adversaries, and so literal blood and metaphoric blood complementarily link knights, as in the description of the encounter with the Red Knight (1:309.32–35). Apart from Gareth's bedside wounding, the greatest effusion of blood is the result of the meeting between Gawain and Gareth: "and than they [. . .] drewe there swerdys and gaff grete strokys, that the bloode trayled downe to the grounde; and so they fought two owres" (1:357.2–4). In a "happy" rewriting of mistaken identity between brothers (for which Balin and Balan's fight to the death is the evident countermodel),[107] Lynet intervenes to prevent loss of life, and has been on hand throughout to staunch blood and mend wounds. If Lynet's art can stop loss of blood, "blood" as kinship-awareness emerges as a less reliable mode of containment: Gawain has shown kindness to the young unknown at court because of his blood (1:295.33–34), but shared lineage has not made for intuitive brotherly recognition, nor prevented Gareth from attacking Gawain at the Assumption Day tournament when his identity is discovered (1:351.21–25). It is also Gawain who represents the eruption of history into this self-contained text, for we learn Gareth prefers the claims of noble community to brotherly ties: "Gareth [. . .] wythdrewe hymself fro his brother sir Gawaynes felyshyp, for he was evir vengeable, and where he hated he wolde be avenged with murther: and that hated sir Gareth" (1:360.32–36). The impulse to establish a symbolic narrative for Gareth, then, to read him metaphorically, inevitably involves a more sinister undertow that cannot divorce Gareth from the rest of Arthurian history, however nostalgic a final image of Gareth's wedding-feast and tournament the narrator conjures up.

That the narrative only once mentions Gareth as "Bewmaynes" outside of this *Tale*[108] suggests it cannot repeat the special conditions of this chivalric performance. If Launcelot's body is at times worryingly aside from containing forms of jurisdiction, by virtue of an intermittently invoked readerly textual subconscious, Gareth's body is part of a socially and materially realized public matrix that nevertheless exists only in a configuration that stands outside the Arthurian world's historical trajectory. Finke and Shichtman argue that by the end of his *Tale,* Gareth has attained a "symbolic" chivalric status that necessarily removes him from the exchanges of violence that have defined him.[109] The symbolic effect is achieved only at this point, however, in a vision of an Arthurian court of "tho dayes" (1:362.21) that cannot provide a foundational narrative for the rest of the *Morte,* nor a set of coordinates against which one may read and measure its troubling configurations of chivalry.

CHAPTER 4

SETTING LIMITS: TEXTUAL PARAMETERS
AND SITES OF RESISTANCE IN
THE BOOK OF SIR TRISTRAM

The relatively few sidenotes glossing the *Tristram* section of the Winchester Malory inscribe an intriguingly haphazard reader-response.[1] They do not uniquely underline narrative climaxes, but accord the same status to a fall from a horse at a tournament (the fate of Palomides, Dynadan, and Gareth at fol. 330v), as to the fatal consequence of Tristram's first great victory, over Marhalt (fol. 154v). Notes draw attention to the Princess of France's love-gift of a dog to Tristram (fol. 152r), and to the animal's role in the later recognition scene between Tristam and Isode (2:501.27–502.4) (fol. 205v). There is no comment on the crucial episode in which the lovers share the potion that seals their fate. Yet, there is a method of kinds in this selectivity, an interest in the recurrence of motif (the little dog represents devotion and recognition): the records of tournament procedure, the commemoration of who slew whom. Scattered associations and events play at the edges of this manuscript, and suggest random expressions of cultural and generic detritus as potential ordering and categorizing processes.

Recent work argues for the broader structural importance to the *Morte* of such cultural reference points; Karen Cherewatuk valuably extrapolates interests from the contents of compendious books available to later fifteenth-century gentry households that might prompt Malory's choices of theme and its treatment across his text, with "a catalogue of chivalric exercise" dominating the *Tristram* section.[2] Although this contextual rationale for the *Morte's* constitution is attractive, however, the marginalia themselves are highly apposite to a *Tristram* that Elizabeth Edwards, in an insightful reading of memory in the *Morte,* defines as "a long series of local reading sites with little total coherence." Edwards suggests that here, recognition is more important than local consistency. Forgetful in narration, the *Tristram* demands a certain good will on the part of the reader to accept its sometimes erratic storyline.[3] Edwards argues for Arthurian literature's "relentless metonymy," which reveals as pretense the recuperation of a fully comprehensive Arthurian "master text," and exposes the textual as itself "a negation of memory."[4] Malory's book is, then, a further "reiteration" of an ultimately nonexistent Arthurian text. Edwards offers an ingenious means to understanding not only this narrative's procedures, but the very condition of the textual. One might also ask, however, whether the same processes of recall operate, and whether the opportunities for cultural recognition are the same, and do the same work, in the *Tristan* as in the *Tristram*. As there are differences as well as similarities to uncover across the French prose compilations as well as between Malory and his sources, I want here to refine that sense of what and how the French and English works reiterate and remember. What reading criteria guide Malory's own redaction? And is the reader encouraged to deploy a categorizing knowledge allusively, like the sidenote writer, in ways that recognize and register the messiness of art as of life, or more formally, in order to give shape to the work?

In the *Morte,* the *Book of Sir Tristram* is closest in form to the compilatory structure of later medieval French prose Arthurian redactions, from which it takes its subject matter, and with which it shares lengthiness, intricacy of storyline, redundancy of narrative event, and a bewildering accretion of incident. The *Tristram* appears disorderly, in every sense of the word. Announcing itself as an orthodox chivalric biography—"Here begynnyth the fyrste boke of Trystrams de Lyones, and who was his fadir and hys modyr" (1:371.1)—it nevertheless leaves aside full biographies and defers endings so as to prolong displays of the masculine chivalric prowess it celebrates.[5] It confuses the chronological order of the whole, which makes it difficult to locate the *Tristram* adventures in relation to the episodes that precede them textually. For example, before Tristram's birth, Arthur already has under his governance "all the lordshyppis unto Roome" (1:371.19), yet Tristram is of an age to fight when the Roman campaign is chronicled earlier in the *Morte* (1:195.8–10), and he has already featured in Gareth's story (1:349–350).[6] This chronological disturbance, and the change of focus from Logres to Cornwall, mirrors the way Malory's main source, the Prose *Tristan,*[7] frays the ordering thematic strands of the Vulgate Cycle (the general chronology of which Malory follows) by extending and secularizing its chivalric narrative. Thematically, too, the *Tristram* is disturbing, and although Malory omits or underplays some of the source's episodes of violence to female integrity,[8] in his work, violence remains a meeting-place of love and enmity. Motivations of jealousy and fellowship alike are combat's preconditions, in a tale riven by conflict. The polarization of Arthur's and Mark's courts as "good" and "bad" respectively does not prescribe the morality of knights' deeds within those loci. The line between moral and social is indistinct; it is because their courts differ in "honor" rather than in mores, for example, that Lamerok would rather the magic horn exposed the ladies of Cornwall than of Camelot (1:443.31–34). Social and institutional structures show up dissent as much as unity. Inter- and intrafamily feuding is a feature of Arthurian life, while violence transgresses the bounds of the tournament field, which may focus aggression but can neither adequately control nor contain it.[9]

This chapter looks at some examples of how the *Tristram* departs from as well as imitates its French antecedents (which are themselves not necessarily homogeneous). The *Tristan* employs particular rhetorical strategies for narratorial self-presentation and for the construction of chivalric selfhood, and deploys letters and lyrics in complex exposition of literary forms and modes of communication. Malory elides and reworks lyrics and letters, so displacing Tristram from his particular heroic frame in the *Tristan*. In particular, the adaptation diminishes the *Tristan*'s private, affective space. Malory's adaptation thus becomes a site of narrative trauma, but the narrative also demonstrates a resistance to Launcelot's trajectory as hero. Exploration of the heroes' madnesses will expose how textual and structural parameters "contain" Tristram, while Launcelot comes to figure narrative and epistemological breakdown. The chapter concludes with a focus on the Questing Beast/*beste glatissant,* briefly to compare Malory's work with that of Micheau Gonnot, who is, like Malory, interweaving Vulgate, Post-Vulgate and *Tristan* material, but who is anxious to supply us with a "good end," where Malory structurally deploys deferral. Gonnot provides a model of synthesis and exemplarity against which to read Malory's treatment. Each writer registers opposing responses to the protean *Tristan*'s fluctuations between the allusive and the exhaustively explicatory.

Aspects of the Prose *Tristan* challenge, in material and rhetorical terms, later Continental prose romances' commemorative rhetoric, and promises of closure, where the English texts demand awareness of engagement as process. The manuscript tradition of Malory's source material itself suggests an intricate interplay with, and highly self-conscious response to, textuality, and to the Vulgate Cycle's model in particular. Growing out of established narrative forms, the versions of the thirteenth-century Prose *Tristan* are typically medieval literary enterprises.[10] They intercalate the Tristan legend with that of Arthur by opening up, and then supplying, gaps in Arthurian history and narrative, diachronic and synchronic, while formally and thematically the *Tristan* also counterbalances the Vulgate Cycle of which it is in part a redaction. The eighty or so *Tristan* manuscripts attest to its survival in several (similar) versions, and although it is possible to form some idea of which were most widely disseminated—Baumgartner identifies two dominant versions, composites of a lost, pre-1240 original[11]—the work's complex manuscript history poses difficult problems of literary retrieval and critical interpretation.

The Prose *Tristan* places the hero's ultimately tragic love for Iseut and his rivalry with his uncle King Mark in the context of Arthurian adventure. An account of Tristan's ancestors precedes the narrative of the hero's career proper, and Tristan's first major act of valor—which the *Tristan* places soon after Arthur's accession (Curtis 1:147) and which Micheau Gonnot correlates with the young Lancelot's conquest of the Dolorous Garde (2: fol. 65a)—is the defeat of the Round Table knight Le Morholt. Episodes of chivalric prowess interweave with the story of the relationship between Tristan and Iseut, recounted in part by means of letters and lyrics. The lovers find refuge outside Marc's jurisdiction, at the castle of Joyous Garde, and Tristan becomes a valued knight of the Round Table, and participates in the Grail quest (where the author incorporates episodes from the Vulgate and Post-Vulgate versions of the *Queste del Saint Graal*), but returns to see Iseut, only to be killed by Marc as he plays his harp for her, an event to which the *Morte* narrator and Launcelot allude (3:1149.28–35; 3:1173.12–20). Löseth's summary of the narratives and their variants shows how the *Tristan* versions extend narrative strands and complete stories of individual characters. The "fragmentary" nature of the *Tristan* manuscripts witnesses materially to the metonymic effect Edwards analyzes—although this sense of fragmentation exists in tandem with the late-medieval impulse toward Arthurian compendiousness. Colette-Anne Van Coolput suggests the *Tristan* is a concrete example of medieval reader response, and also a critique of cyclic organization, in that its selectivity secularizes its heroes (even Galahad) and so qualifies the teleological and eschatological strain of the Vulgate Cycle.[12] Certainly the *Tristan* aggressively appropriates aspects of the Grail story for a greatly expanded chivalric narrative. It presents itself as an individual reading of the material, although its author, Luces, still claims to be translating from a Latin book that gives the full Grail story (Curtis 1:39). Although "the story" features as organizing element, the narratorial voice, which suggests an immediate engagement between the knowing narrator and the audience, gives a provisional sense of authorial control.[13] The narrator makes clear his structuring of the story, his address to us, "je vos devise" (I tell you) competing with the Vulgate Cycle's play between and on written authorities.[14] The voice may even invite us to read the "book" for ourselves.[15] The narrator also intervenes directly at pivotal moments, most strikingly to mourn the couple's accidental drinking of the love-potion:

"Ha! Diex, quel boivre! Com il lor fu puis anious! Or ont beü; [. . .] Diex, quel duel! Il on beü lor destruction et lor mort." (Curtis 2:65) [Ah! God, what a drink! How harmful it proved to them! Now they have drunk; God, what sorrow! They have drunk their destruction and their death.][16] This interjection invokes the language of an earlier version, Thomas's famous poetic account of Tristan, which conflates the potion, love, and death.[17] It also anticipates the lyrics that will focus the characters' passions in such a way as structurally to complement, and to stand in counterpoint to, the narrative. The lyrics in effect construct a particular reading of narrative event, and provide a recall-system for charting the narrative's affective map.[18]

While the *Tristan* clears space for a subjective narrator, Malory inscribes a community of reception and engagement by readers and narrator. So he may present his text as an ambivalent encoding of narrative choice or material exigency, as when we learn there will be no "rehersall" (2:845.31) of the third part of the book. Direction might seem a collaborative decision, or the result of an exhortation: "Now leve we of this mater" (2:769.1). It might be dictated by textual autonomy: "Now levith of thys tale and spekith of sir Trystramys" (2:488.7); or again by fidelity to the subject matter of which "the Freynshe booke makith mension" (2:493.7).[19] At a local level, the pursuit of diverse subjects of interest (of Tristram and Launcelot as heroes, for example) is sometimes imagined as competition on the part of the different constituencies, with the reader and narrator together, or the text itself, claiming the initiative in narrative direction.[20] The explicitly selective organization intimates the existence of other stories and the established perspectives and prejudices behind the narrative we have to hand, which recalls the narrator's earlier injunction to us to "supplement" the text (1:180.19–23). The inscribed fiction of the "turning" audience doesn't assume readers' autonomy, but does raise the question (as does the *Launcelot* section) of what one might already "know." As we saw in chapter one, the point where the physical bounds of the source copy bisect a dialogue in Malory (2:558.34–35) forcefully reminds us, through the claims of antecedent material witness, of the unexpected influences of divisions already in place, and of the traces of our previous knowledge. In that sequence, the intrusion emphasizes Tristram's innocence; he is ignorant of his shield's significance. The note also signals the double focus of Malory's redaction of Tristram's story. Morgan has explained that the shield about which Arthur questions the hero "signyfieth kynge Arthure and quene Gwenyver, and a knyght that holdith them bothe in bondage and in servage" (2:554.30–32). The fissure, both in the manuscript and in the reported conversation between king and knight, is the point of entry for the reader's knowledge, in the face of the hero's ignorance of the shield's significance. As elsewhere in the Arthuriad, we are aware of the Launcelot-Guinevere relation, here given public yet coded articulation. The narrative attributes revelation to the mean-spirited, the treacherous, and, as in the *Noble Tale,* the female, here in the person of the malevolent Morgan, who behaves (like Hallewes) in "dispite" of Guinevere (2:558.7–9). The text thus makes a moral judgment on our uses of knowledge, at the same time as it draws attention, through the gap in the text, to the fact of that knowledge and the need to control it.

Other knowledge, held by the narrator, or by the "book," a site of privileged information, is selectively granted us. The specifically "French" book emerges (although not exclusively) as the repository of accurate information about sexual relations, from Isode le Blanche Maynes's virginity (1:434.33–435.4) to Keyhydyns's doomed love for Isode (2:493.7–10), Morgan's continuing desire for Launcelot (2:555.1–5) and the fact that Tristram and Isode are still lovers after Isode has been married to Mark (1:419.20–21). The narrator also has recourse to the inexpressible, as when he describes the lovers' reunion:

> And to telle the joyes that were betwyxte La Beall Isode and sir Trystramys, there ys no maker can make hit, nothir no harte can thynke hit, nother no penne can wryte hit, nother no mowth can speke hit. (2:493.2–6)

But whereas in the source this would have the effect of hyperbole, the feeling behind which the lyrical and epistolary articulations of love supply, in a narrative that largely excises the lyric mode it suggests more the limits of literary articulation and the subsequent displacement of the affective onto the (deficient) imagination of the reader, without supplying a framework for the processing of emotion. Similarly, the narrator does not keep a promise to tell the full story of Keyhydyns's unrequited love (2:493.10–11). The "boke" has knowledge to which we have no access. The French romances themselves offer no guarantee of promised narratives, but these omissions have different effects. For the complex lyric and prose interaction of the Prose *Tristan* invites the reader to engage with the chronological and emotional aspects of a fictional world within the parameters it constructs. Malory, however, substitutes for this engagement the uncertain processes of literary retrieval, whether those are conceived as material accident, acknowledgment of bookish authority, narratorial forgetfulness, or a narrative competition for the attentions of narrator and readers. As a consequence, these aspects of the text's "forgetfulness" make us confront the fact that the very processes of recall that constitute the text in front of us also constitute a site of loss.

Moves to compensate for this loss include the narrator's connections between and communities for, narrative, character, and reader, through strategies such as incidental topographical identification, which makes Logres, to which Tristram plans his escape with Isode, "this londe" (2:680.17–18), or through a character's sharing in the narrator's descriptive rhetoric of violence, as when Arthur, at a tournament, "lykened sir Trystram [. . .] unto a wood lyon; and he lykened sir Palomydes [. . .] unto a wood lybarde, and sir Gareth and sir Dynadan unto egir wolvis" (2:734.22–24). There is also regular appeal to the proverbial to contextualize event. Thus, Tristram asserts: "manhode is nat worthe but yf hit be medled with wysdome" (2:700.19–20), and narratorial comment observes that Segwarydes does not act on his resentment of Tristram: "for he that hath a prevy hurte is loth to have a shame outewarde" (1:396.15–16). The proverbial gives shape to the narrative's pragmatism and assumes agreement of moral and cultural perspective.[21] Most famously, the public celebration and language of Tristram's hunting skills cuts across fictional and historical worlds. If these lines have no direct source, hunting skills are part of Tristram's literary tradition.[22] Tristram excels at the hunt: "never jantylman more that ever we herde rede of" (1:375.17). "We" already participate in the narrator's literary social scene; "the booke seyth" (1:375.17–18) Tristram establishes the finer practices of hunting and their specialized vocabulary. The hunting locutions the narrator says we still employ find documentation in Tristram's "booke" (1:375.22). Hunting language reinforces class hierarchy and is permanent; its "goodly tearmys" will endure until "the Day of Dome" (1:375.24–26).

The narrator later reiterates the eulogy of Tristram and the courtly hunt, proclaiming himself a member of the elite through his own familiarity with its terms:

> For, as bookis reporte, of sir Trystram cam all the good termys of venery [. . .] and all the blastis that longed to all maner of game: fyrste to the uncoupelynge, to the sekynge, to the fyndynge, to the rechace, to the flyght, to the deth, and to the strake. (2:682.28–683.1)

A historicizing specificity accompanies this display; Tristram is the best hunter of "that tyme" (2:682.26), and the injunction that all "gentlemen" should praise Tristram and pray for his soul again expresses faith in the recuperability and continuity of Tristram's inheritance. The intervention in the Winchester MS (which Caxton omits) roundly corroborates this assertion: "Amen, sayde sir Thomas Malleorré" (2:683.4). This social world is fully consonant with that of King Arthur, who also welcomes Tristram to his court as the originator of hunting terms (2:571.29–34). The seamless accord between commemorative strategy, character, reader, and writer reflects (if primarily fictionally) a courtly and leisured society.[23]

However, this community of engagement, one joined through a specific form of textual encoding, may link only tangentially with narrative event.

Hunting per se defines Tristram and courtly activity, but as Isode warns, the hunter is in danger of becoming the prey, and on her advice Tristram takes the precaution of arming himself when he hunts (2:683.6–13), just as the alleged historical experience of the Newbold Revel Malory suggests more complex and sinister narratives might attach themselves to the business of hunting than this institutionalized and institutionalizing rhetoric allows.[24] And outside the *Tristram* section, the fact that technical hunting vocabulary is most marked in the episode of the woman hunter who accidentally shoots Launcelot (3:1104.3–1105.5) comments ironically on a faith in the hierarchizing potential of registers. The deployment of hunting terms as taxonomy, as a public register of class, and as self-contained and uncomplicated narrative trajectory, anticipates the spring topos in the May passage, where we have to work through the disjunction between the history we have read and both the interpretation we are offered of it, and our ideological positioning in relation to that interpretation. The narrator invokes a particular register, slightly divergent from that of the narrative, in order to translate its meaning. In the *Tristram,* furthermore, the hunt is part of the public language and display that substitutes for the *Tristan's* lyrically conveyed sense of the hero's interiority.

One can read the *Tristan's* interconnection of lyric and prose narrative, meanwhile, in relation to the increased literary interest (to which medieval French manuscripts attest) in grounding the "eternal present" of the lyric moment within a set of narrative data.[25] MS Vienna 2542 provides accompanying music for some of the lais, which facilitates their performance by the romance's audience.[26] Tristan is the first to sing a "lai" proper, although the riddles the Forest Giant poses and has posed to him in the pre-Tristan part of the romance suggest something of the power and alterity of poetry in relation to prose. Most of the Giant's riddles are horrifying metaphorized narratives of the crimes he has perpetrated, among them incest, cannibalism, and the slaughter of his mother, daughter, and brother (Curtis 1: 76; 79; 80; 90) and their guessing is a matter of life or death to the unfortunate travelers through the forest who encounter him. Their solution does not always lead to freedom, as Sador, nephew of Joseph of Arimathea, learns, but Sador is able to bargain his own knowledge for freedom when King Pelias of Leonois tells the Giant his love story—significantly, Pelias wants the wife of his knight, Sador (Curtis 1:82)—in a riddle the latter can't guess, and Apollo, son of Sador, finally defeats the Giant with a riddle that is an occluded telling of the latter's own confusion and downfall at Apollo's own hands (Curtis 1:91). The creative riddles, featuring as they do within the long genealogical introduction the *Tristan* affords its hero's tale, mark out beginnings and relationships as sites for "decoding" (and that provide the key to us as readers), as particular spaces for the interpretation of story, and as such anticipate the intensified emotional language of the lyrics. Standing in for genealogy and the beginnings of love-discourse as translatable and participatory code in Malory's version, are the immediate physical pain ("grymly throwys" [1:372.3]) of Tristram's mother's fatal labor, and her explicit linking of love and death, for her husband as for her son: "I muste dye here for (Melyodas's) sake [. . .] A, my lytyll son, thou haste murtherd thy modir!" (1:372.14; 19–20). Where the sad birth of Tristan is occasion for the narratorial aside that this is the beginning of a tale that all gentlemen who are lovers ("qui aiment por amors" [Curtis 1:126]) should hear, Malory offers no exegesis.

In the *Tristan,* lyrics provide lovers with a private language, and offer a site for them to express emotion, although lyrics also circulate independently of those who originated them, so they may also highlight complex issues of interpretation surrounding the specifics of a lyric's performance and reception, issues that become even more pressing when lyrics are sent as letters. Among the lyrics, thematic lais may muse in general terms on the nature of love (as with the laments of Lamorat [Ménard 4:77–80] and Palamède [Ménard 6:99–100]) while other songs are more specifically embedded in the narrative process of the story. If lyrics have a private function, they can also have a public purpose, as when Dinadan's *Lai voir disant* disseminates news of King Marc's perfidy (Ménard 4:344–45). The lyrics may be divorced from the context of their historical composition, and only feature later in the text, where they serve as points of remembrance and meditation on the lovers' experiences. Maureen Boulton notes how the lais function also as the mirror image of the plot.[27] So when Tristan flees in distress to the forest, thinking Iseut has forsaken him for Keyhydyns, he is followed by Palamède's damsel, a musician who performs for him lais that recount his affective history up to that point, recalling his involvement with Iseut and their brief happiness (Curtis 3:168).[28] Tristan then performs the *Lai mortel* (Curtis 3:170–73; *Tristan 1489* n.vi.b–n.vii.a), which foreshadows the end of the narrative, and the death attendant on love, while it is toward the end of the story that Tristan performs the *Lai du boire pesant,* about the pleasure and pain the potion has brought him.

The structural importance implicitly accorded lais, their circulation in a cultural mainstream, separate from Tristan's performance, makes for a sophisticated interplay of communication, especially when lais are sent as letters, and are performed. The Pentecost at which, in the Vulgate Cycle, the Grail adventures are to begin is, in the *Tristan* adaptation, the occasion for the appearance of an anonymous knight (Ménard 6:247–51). Arthur reads privately the letter he gives him; it is a lai that presages the loss of Arthur's supremacy and the beginning of sorrow. The knight sings a love song to the assembled court ("Amours, en mortel voie / M'aves mis" [Love, you have set me on a fatal path]) and, on the arrival of another knight, kills himself. The minstrel-knight's anonymity has several possible resonances, among them the presaging of Tristan's own death,[29] but the episode brings together the range of possibilities for the lai in the *Tristan,* as political missive, as expression of personal emotion, as secret or public declaration, and as point of transition between one narrative framework and another.

Malory mentions or summarizes lais and laments rather than reproduce them in full; Baumgartner suggests that, in the *Tristan,* lai and prose are part of a tension between love and arms, which the romance resolves in favor of the prose of masculine chivalric narrative.[30] From this perspective, Malory, excising lyric forms, rewrites more fully a central tendency of the *Tristan.* But the *Tristan* lyrics complexly negotiate social and literary spaces as well as the psychological spaces for Tristan and those other protagonists who muse on the nature of love. Malory's characters can declare their love movingly, but rather than explicitly connect declarations of love by means of formal register, Malory conflates the language of male chivalric prowess and heterosexual love. Elaine's promise of "service," to Launcelot, and her wish always to be with him (2:825.34–826.5), finds echo in the young Lavayne's desire never to leave Launcelot (2:1091.12–14). Palomides's melancholy self-reflection on the frustrations of love (2:779.25–780.2) then appears extraordinary rather than normative.[31] And the few lines reported of Lamerok's "dolefullyst complaynte of love that ever man herde" (2:579.19–20), are estranged from an interior love-language in their social identification of the object of desire:

> "O, thou fayre quene of Orkeney, kynge Lottys wyff and modir unto sir Gawayne and to sir Gaherys, and modir to many other, for thy love I am in grete paynys!" (2:579.23–25)

Where the French text supplies an alternating tension and complementarity of lyric and prose, a vocabulary of heroic social selfhood, on a single narrative plane, substitutes for different levels of understanding the self. Tristram's original register, and with it the affective life, is alienated. If the language of love is largely missing, one might call the *Tristram* a traumatic narrative, to the extent that it conforms to Cathy Caruth's definition of trauma history as "referential precisely to the extent that it is not fully perceived as it occurs," which she refines to suggest that such a history "can be grasped only in the very inaccessibility of its occurrence."[32] Writing of the repetition compulsion, Freud argues that the patient, wishing to guard against remembering, engages instead in transference that creates an intermediate region between illness and real life.[33] Malory's own translation operates perhaps as such a site of transference, trying to project the energies of the love narrative onto the ostensibly safer (but also troubled) terrain of the "public" and the masculine chivalric. This site of transference is not, in Freud's terms, "worked through," but the method establishes the distance between the French and English versions, and sets particular limits on Malory's narrative. Where the lyric expression of desire, for example, sublimates both sex and death, Malory's rather less formal accommodations of chivalry, sex, violence, and death, expose their interrelation more starkly and uncompromisingly. Repeated returns to the chivalric body, and the exercise of violence, in the *Tristram,* thus do service for a range of registers.

Letters also feature differently in the *Tristram* than in the source, where written exchanges between protagonists—especially between Iseut and Guenièvre, Tristan and Lancelot—establish private spaces in counterpoint to the public social arena, spaces for narrative comment, the cementing of relationships, meditations on love and its discourse. Addressees and writers use letters as surrogates for loved and loving bodies. Iseut, separated from Tristan, sends him a letter "en leu de mon cors" [in place of my body], of which her tears blur the text, and Tristan weeps over and kisses its seal (Curtis 3:89–90). Lancelot envies the very letter he sends to Tristan, its ability to "speak to" and be held by, the greatest knight in the world (Curtis 3:16). The fifteenth-century Middle English *Disce Mori* endorses this attitude when it identifies as a sign of carnal love, "þat þat oon lovere sendeth to þat oþer lettres of love, tokenes and yiftes, which be worshipped, kissed, used and kept as reliques."[34] The *Tristram* appropriates the epistolary's materiality and its affective spaces to different uses. For Malory, writing appears primarily a medium of public communication,[35] and the bias is toward the reiteration of narrative coordinates, reminders of allegiances and events, at the expense of the letter as material evidence and as interiorizing mode. So Mark's news to Palomides that Tristram went mad because of "a lettir that he founde" (2:498.1) leaves us wondering how Mark came by such knowledge. An original link recounts how Tristram and Isode are kept up-to-date with events toward the end of the *Book* with a letter from Guinevere explaining what happened to Launcelot (2:839.15–19). Malory's summary of letters further erodes the *Tristan's* vocabulary of interiority, and deprives Guenièvre and Iseut of the socially marked language that in the *Tristan* confirms their status as worthy lovers.[36] Instead, the female lovers' affective situations and perspectives fall casualty to a concern to address issues on a masculine social plane. This erases the sexual vocabulary, and so makes Isode sound faintly comic when, in conclusion to her "pyteuous lettirs" (the equivalent of Curtis 3:89–90), she proposes a pseudoménage with the rival Tristan has just married—"if hit pleased sir Trystram, to com to hir courte and brynge with hym Isode le Blaunche Maynys; and they shulde be kepte als well as herselff"

(2:481.3–9). Similarly, Guenièvre, addressed as an intimate of Love, in the French writes feelingly about love's pain and offers Iseut the consolation that sorrow will not endure (Curtis 2:173), but Malory's Guinevere's assurance to Isode that Tristram is subject to temporarily efficacious "craftes of sorsery" (1:436.5) substitutes for love discourse a (to the *Morte*) normative masculine formulation, and dismissal, of female sexual power.

That Malory sometimes substitutes letters for the *Tristan's* oral messages might suggest a pragmatic trust in the written above the spoken.[37] Letters appear almost less important for their content than for the bonds they forge between individuals by means of their expedition, and for their value as signals to the reader of how to configure social relations and understand event. In the *Tristan,* narrator and characters are particularly sensitive to the nature of letters, who might read them, and how they might interpret them. Malory's editing and elisions, meanwhile, sometimes make even the identification of particular letters and of their addressees unclear, as with the confusing circulation that begins with Fergus's arrival with letters from Cornwall (2:615–18). At this point in the text, "goodly lettirs" make their way between Tristram, and Arthur and Launcelot, who send him responses, but elision and some carelessly disposed pronouns make it difficult to trace exactly who receives what. We learn of Tristram's gratitude for Launcelot's support of him against Mark (2:615.29–32) but not of how he comes to receive the letters voicing such support; instead, it appears that the damsel messenger returns to Isode with letters especially for her from Arthur and Launcelot. The damsel goes on to give Mark threatening letters from Arthur and Launcelot, and Mark, not trusting the damsel as messenger, sends letters "pryvayly and secretely" (2:616.35) to Arthur and Guinevere, making both veiled and direct reference to Launcelot. Reference to the *Tristan* (Ménard 4:252–75) clarifies the issue of who writes to whom, and why. The *Tristan* describes in detail the letter as artifact and as literary oeuvre, and indicates precisely what is read privately and what publicly, and the sequence of the writing of and replying to missives. Marc sends Guenièvre a lai, and its form makes her anxious about its audience: "ele quidast q'il le feist canter apertement" [she feared he would have it sung openly] (Ménard 4:271). Guenièvre fears death should the letter be discovered, and shuts it up in a box (Ménard 4:274). When she forwards the lai to Lancelot, he reads it, and Lancelot's companion, Dinadan, reads its contents secretly, when his friend is asleep, before Lancelot tears it into a hundred pieces (Ménard 4:275). Dinadan decides independently to compose a reciprocal lai to shame Marc (Ménard 4:277).

Dinadan's lai is in keeping with his function as a paradoxically protean control for the *Tristan* narrative(s) in general.[38] Dinadan famously points out the follies and excesses of chivalric love as of knightly arms, yet is himself,

ultimately, prey to the lack of *mesure* he ridicules in others.[39] The lai Dinadan writes typically transgresses the form's established decorum, for we
learn that his song to Marc is composed to expose his dishonor, whereas
traditionally, lais celebrate goodness and courtesy (Ménard 4:277–78). He-
liot the harper sings Dinadan's *Lai voir disant* before Marc, and escapes physical violence only by pleading madness; he is prompted, he claims, by "la
folie ki est en moi" [the madness within me] (Ménard 4:346). Marc, be-
lieving Tristan to have written the song, directs his anger against him (Ménard 4:347). In the *Tristan,* then, this public exposure both confirms Marc's
villainous nature and crystallizes the ill will between uncle and nephew.

   In Malory's account, we do not learn what happens to the letter
Launcelot has received, and although Dynadan has furtively read its contents, in addition he has Launcelot reveal it to him orally on account of the
"grete truste" (2:618:5) he has in him. The plot to shame Mark and the
dissemination of the lai by many musicians is then devised and carried out
"by the wyll of kynge Arthure and of sir Launcelot" (2:618.15–16), details
unique to Malory, although Dynadan himself is credited with writing "the
worste lay that ever harper songe with harpe or with ony other instrument" (2:618.18–19). The *Morte* seems anxious to stress the lay's political
and public context. When, a little later (and near the midpoint of the
Book), Elyas the Harper explains his behavior to the enraged Mark, he does
not plead insanity like his French counterpart, but instead declares the
constraints of patronage: "I muste do as I am commaunded of thos lordis
that I beare the armys of" (2:627.4–5). Letters and lays thus function primarily in a social arena, and the nature of letters as surrogates and as con-
duits for human bodies and private emotions appears rather less important,
in this part of the *Tristram,* than in the source. Letters help to establish two
factions, Mark ranged against Arthur, Launcelot, and Tristram, and they assert homosocial loyalties through the behavior of Dynadan, whose shaming of Mark is part of a concerted and continuing campaign.

   The *Tristram's* treatment of the private reading of letters, for some, signals an anxiety over the "dangers of over-privatized behavior," specifically
the adulterous relations of the two couples.[40] But it is perhaps a troubling
lack of controlling coordinates and boundaries for the personal life that here
gives an impression of authorial moral judgment. Whereas Malory is both
strangely careless of letters, and ruptures the metaphorical equivalence between physical person and written word, in contrast to the French text's
sensitivity to their materiality and metaphoricity, he maintains a specific
focus on isolated incidents involving epistolary corporeality. The letter most
fully (and twice) described in the *Tristram* section is in the hands of King
Harmaunce's dead chivalric body (2:701:15–23; 713.10–21).[41] A physical
body registers a particular concern to reinforce the truth of a message

when, as J. Hillis Miller formulates it, writing "dispossesses both the writer and the receiver of themselves."[42] Harmaunce's case, however, seems to guarantee what we might term an ideological "repossession" of chivalric integrity. The contiguity of the mortally wounded chivalric self underscores the intensity of the letter that addresses itself to all knights, but implores the aid of one to avenge his death at the hands of lowborn ingrates. Palomides takes up the challenge; that Tristram has read the letter first and violated the sailors' warning that to take up the letter is to promise to avenge the king's death seems only to reinforce the interchangeability of good chivalric bodies, for "som of us may revenge his dethe as well as another" (2:701.9–10). As Donavin has noted, Palomides's adventures at the Red City anticipate in secular mode Galahad's experiences at Corbenic.[43] But Palomides refuses the inheritance promised Harmaunce's avenger, because the claims of knight errantry are more pressing (2:719.23–25). The episode confirms, through the unchristened but undoubtedly knightly Palomides, chivalric fellowship's ideological power.

Later in the *Morte,* other death-authorized letters, further underwritten by their conjunction with the physical, more variously involve Launcelot, expanding the reach of the narrative in terms of affective engagement and self-reflection. Perceval's Sister's body effects Launcelot's vicarious engagement with her adventures by means of the testimonial letter her brother places in her hand (2:1004.8–10). Elaine of Ascolat's beautiful corpse guarantees the emotional import of her letter, which requires that Launcelot finalize the commemorative process the Maid herself has put in train, by acting as her chief mourner (2:1096.31–35).[44] Gawain's own blood in signature of his reconciliatory letter to Launcelot, original with Malory (3:1231.7–1232.10), is tender of his sincerity and literalizes the relation between blood and the written at the point of death, although it requests action of Launcelot that circumstances will not allow him to undertake. These later, extraordinary, somatically authorized letters, retrospectively foreground the straightforwardness of the *Tristram*'s Harmaunce adventure. By means of this episode, the text appropriates for the reinforcement of chivalric power and fellowship those concerns with writing, composition, and death that are crucial to the *Tristan* characters' articulation of love. Because Malory has excised and reappropriated so drastically those elements usually associated with Tristan, the episode of Tristan's madness, integral to the portrayal of his emotional state, becomes for Tristram primarily a narrative problem of structural realignment.

Madness

Commentators have correlated social and moral issues when considering medieval instances of insanity.[45] Yet, Malory only lightly alludes to a relation between madness and moral guilt in episodes that alienate the Arthurian hero from social normality, and his protagonists' dilemmas are not fully comparable. John Trevisa's translation of Bartholomæus Anglicus's *De Proprietatibus* prefaces a discussion of frenzy with Deuteronomy's verse on madness as punishment for transgression of God's law—"Oure lord schal smyte þee wiþ woodnes"—but goes on to discuss insanity as physiological, rather than moral, in cause.[46] In the *Tristram,* the fact of madness relates less to moral gloss than to the nature of particular chivalric constructions of the self in relation to narrative and the irreconcilability of conflicting claims made on that self (especially when the notion of public and private is vexed), which leads to a temporary dissolution of both social hierarchic identity and the rational faculties. A social legitimization that simultaneously covers over Tristram's alienation from his traditional portrayal as lover contextualizes his madness, while Launcelot's insanity is part of a breakdown in a narrative both partially divorced from its sources' epistemology, and lacking the means to interrogate interiority. The story instead returns continually to celebrate, and also to worry at, the chivalric subject as site of masculine affirmation. Tristram's madness is contingent on the collapse of conceptual difference between social and sexual identities, evident in his use of the language of "treason" to articulate his feelings of "betrayal" by Isode. Launcelot's insanity is in the first instance a result of conflicting, and apparently equally valid, "kyndely" claims two women make on his person. While Tristram's experience relates to the social channeling of human emotion, Launcelot's madness becomes the occasion of the Grail's manifestation as transcendental divine mercy, and concerns the hero's place in the broader spiritual scheme. If the Grail "rescues" Launcelot from his narrative impasse, however, the episode also reenvisions Launcelot's role, and his madness forms part of the *Morte*'s complex of tensions between the necessary remaking of chivalric identity, and narrative explication.

Immediately prior to his period of insanity, Tristram is already socially displaced. A fugitive from Cornish justice (1:431.1–432.10), he is in clandestine residence at court, his presence known only to Isode and Keyhydyns. If love, like Launcelot's later experience of the Grail (2:1017.11–12), is beyond narrative expression, it is the articulating of the emotional in social terms that serves (as in the *Tristan*) to jolt the lovers' experience back into narrative event, and madness serves as the circumlocutory means to reestablishing Tristram in the chivalric economy. When Keyhydyns's love of Isode disrupts the secret world (2:493.12–34), the fact that Tristram has access to the whole story, the "lettirs and baladis," written "for very pure love," and the reciprocal letters sent by a compassionate Isode (where Tristan simply misconstrues Iseut's letters [Curtis 3:140]), writes large the English character's alienation from a poetic self in control of love's rhetoric.

Tristram's charge to Isode of being a "traytouras unto me" and to Keyhydyns of "falshed and treson" (2:494.4–5) is part of a pattern of characterizing sexual betrayal as treason,[47] and recalls the accusation Andret has
brought against Tristram (1:431.23–24). The social premise of treason offers several possibilities for narrative development, which are then blocked,
to disorientating and disjunctive effect. Keyhydyns's escape from Tristram's
wrath involves him in a ludicrous tableau with King Mark, who is incon-
gruously positioned with his chess game just beneath the window of the
room in which Tristram is supposedly in hiding from him (2:494.9–18).
Mark's complacent acceptance of Keyhydyns's poor excuse that he has
fallen out of the window in his sleep, together with the unexpected dissolution of any external threat to the person of Tristram, who has armed
himself in anticipation of attack from the king's forces, but then "rode forth
oute of the castell opynly" (2:484.26), figure a narrative at odds with itself.
Tristram himself now suffers a loss of integrity evident in the debasement
of his nature and his subsequent inability to act in social terms.

Tristram's madness manifests itself in his loss of memory, to which the
narrator draws our attention as the hero passes by the locus of his fight
with Palomides (1:495.30–32). His adventures in the wilderness oscillate
between an unknowing self, abased, alone, and without social definition,
and attempts at social and narrative rehabilitation. The action reestablishes
his social integration by degrees. In the episode in which the damsel plays
music to Tristram, Malory seems to have adapted the *Tristan* narrative with
Bartholomæus Anglicus's general observation in mind, on music as beneficial to the insane, who "schal be gladed wiþ instrumentis of musik and
somdel be occupied;"[48] but where in the French there is an explicit relation of lai to mental state, when Tristan at first declares himself unfit for
music—"Puis que mon cuer ne s'i acorde, coment le porroie je faire?" [As
my heart is not willing, how could I do it?] (Curtis 3:168)—and Tristan
sings what he says will be his last song, the "Lai mortel," before finally running mad at not finding the means for suicide (Curtis 3:173), in Malory,
music is an attractant (the lady can draw Tristram to her with music), but
also registers, not access to a poetic register, but inarticulacy: "whan he
founde the harpe [. . .] than wolde (Tristram) harpe and play thereuppon
and wepe togydirs" (2:496.10–12).

The herdsmen and shepherds, at the bottom of the social scale, and with
whom Tristram associates, treat him as a fool (2:496.23–24), but his subsequent violent defence of the men who both feed and ill-treat him marks
his reawakening to a sense of duty, although his instinctive ability to wield
a weapon does not immediately restore his sense of control, as, with
Dagonet's sword in his hand, he continues to behave like a madman
(2:498.21). The hermit who then finds Tristram substitutes food for the

sword (2:499.27–29), but this encounter with a man of God is not the turning point for Tristram's awareness. Nor does the hermit offer a moral perspective on his condition. And the text explicitly bypasses the opportunity to expostulate on madness as divine retribution. Tristram simply returns to the obscurity of the forest. Tristram's renewed contact with the court, after his killing of Tauleas the giant, finally returns him to sanity; washed, and fed on "hote suppyngis," he is brought to "remembraunce" (2:501.7–10). His identity finally revealed, the narrative recalls the earlier episode of Tristram's capture with Mark's demand that the hero be judged "to the dethe" (2:502.35). It is as if the story has come full circle primarily in order to relocate Tristram in legitimate relation to the Cornish court, and to correct the previous legal irregularity. Tristram now suffers due process of law, and a ten-year exile (2:503.1–4). The parallel with the hero's earlier dilemma is explicit in his catalogue of feats of valor, uttered at his banishment, in which, in his ironic play on the "reward" he has received for his deeds, he reminds the court of its bad faith toward him (1:431.14–22; 2:503.25–504.8). The period of madness thus foregrounds as a structural problem the legitimization and validation of Tristram's position. Tristram's recovery may lead Isode to reaffirm her love and loyalty, but leads neither to reappraisal nor transformation (although it incidentally removes the problem of Keyhydyns's love, as he is mentioned only once more after Isode banishes him [2:498.7–8]). As love is ineffable in narrative terms, Tristram's public definition, embedded within certain forms of social arbitration and evaluation, is primary. Tristram's madness ultimately makes possible his social realignment. The episode of Launcelot's insanity, meanwhile, relates more complexly to textual values, to conflicting claims of desire, to the hero's control, and to uncertainty, where the source promises fulfillment and cohesion.

Near the climactic point in the narrative, the trajectory of the "best" knight, Sir Launcelot, who in disguise kills and maims Arthurian knights, and slanders their king and queen (2:565–66) "bycause," he later tells Tristram, I wolde nat be knowyn" (2:571.17), is indistinguishable from that of the "worst," sir Brewnys sans Pité.[49] These events immediately precede the combat with Tristram, which leads to the latter's integration into the Round Table fellowship, and Riddy observes that Launcelot is here "enacting" violence's paradoxical combination of fellowship and hatred, which is at the heart of the *Tristram*.[50] Another aspect of violence's inherently paradoxical nature operative in the *Morte* (as chapter three has considered) is the tension contingent on the alternation of the wish to depoliticize, and even to "denarrativize," violence, to strip it of its consequences (as happens with Launcelot here), and the concern to legitimize and justify the autonomous heroic body. Launcelot's "enacting" of an alienation from his heroic self in this episode problematizes our knowledge. This uncharacteristic presentation compounds the unnerving quality of the anonymous fight with Tristram, which constitutes the heroes' long-prophesied meeting at the perron (2:568.21–570.2), a meeting that Gonnot, in his compilation, also prepares for and privileges as extraordinary (3: fols. 114a–115d). The marked troubling of Launcelot's identity immediately prior to an event that will confirm his "true" knighthood, registers a perverse (and unsuccessful) resistance to narrative inevitability, and by extension to the interrelation of determinism and volition in the construction of his heroic self. Later in the narrative, Launcelot will consciously affirm resistance to his role in Galahad's conception, and I want to consider the episode of Launcelot's madness in the context of this tacit discontent with the very terms of his heroic definition.

The Lancelot of the French tradition experiences several episodes of madness, which anxiously associate the chivalric male subject's instability with sexuality, but while the *Lancelot* has the hero's loss of control, after Guenièvre's discovery of him in her rival's bed, demonstrate the intensity of his love for the queen (Micha 6:176; Lacy 3:321), it assures us also of his larger teleological role as father of Galahad. Malory leaves vatic knowledge to Pelles and his daughter rather than offer narratorial explanation. When Elaine invites Launcelot to her bed, she does so in full knowledge of past and future event, while Launcelot has hardly responded to the written notice of his destiny on the dragon's tomb at Corbenic, with its coded inscription that a leopard will engender a lion, "whyche [. . .] shall passe all other knyghtes." (2:793.5–6).[51] Elaine, however, engages with equanimity in scarcely fathomable processes, and her announcement to Launcelot that she has sacrificed the "fayrest floure [. . .] that is my maydynhode that I shall never have agayne," that she might conceive the "nobelyste knyght of the worlde" (2:795.33–796.23), substitutes for what in the French text is a lengthy authorial discourse to the reader, on the necessary erasure of one woman's virginity to produce the "flower" of knights, Galahad (Micha 4:209–11; Lacy 3:164–65). Launcelot thus has knowledge of a role of which his French counterpart is at this stage ignorant, although the French text is far more explicit about the necessity of Lancelot's sin to salvation history. In the *Lancelot,* madness is the narrative means to refocus on the lovers after this conception, to accommodate and affirm Lancelot's inordinate passion for Guenièvre. From the beginning of his exile, he remembers the joy of his love for the queen, and suffers such sorrow on its account that he wants only death (Micha 6:176; Lacy 3:321). While he needs the regenerative grace of the Grail to heal him and bring him back into the narrative, once more "sane," his love is both unbearable and sustaining, simultaneously his greatest pain and his greatest comfort (Micha 6:232; Lacy 3:335).

Malory's retelling is far less explicit on both secular and spiritual planes, and so delineates less clearly the paradox of Launcelot's situation, by which his act of "synne" is necessary to the temporal realization of spiritual perfection in the person of Galahad. And rather than situate the hero between sexual fidelity to the queen and spiritual claims, the narrative robustly envisages other possible lines of development, as when Elaine declares her own rights to Launcelot and blames the queen's exile of the hero as socially and morally reprehensible (2:806.16). The English text makes Launcelot's madness a point of narrative breakdown because events now demand a remaking of Launcelot's identity, with insistence on that "knowledge"—his relation to Guinevere, his sexual activity—that has until now been a question of readerly decorum, so this transitional section, in which the Grail becomes manifest in the secular world, offers a more troubled heroic narrative than does the source. In addition to this redirection of knowledge, the narrative unsettlingly invokes and departs from earlier models in the *Morte,* as well as the source. The episode of Tristram's madness, for example, has some motifs and circumstances in common with Launcelot's "hartely sorow" (2:805.31). Launcelot leaves court, like Keyhydyns, via a window (2:806.3–4). In the forest, driven insane, he suffers abasement. As is the case for Gareth, the thigh wound he suffers, here from the boar he hunts (2:821.17–19), suggests, but does not make explicit, sexual sin.[52] The hermit who encounters Launcelot heals him, but cannot provide him with bodily nourishment, let alone spiritual sustenance, and only sends him "more wooder" (2:822.17). This leaves in suspension the question of Launcelot's possible culpability, but also foregrounds his later healing by the Grail as an act of grace. His adventures intimate a gradual rehabilitation to the courtly life.

As with Tristram, the prelude to Launcelot's reassimilation is his discovery, asleep in a garden, by the woman who loves him. But the similarities also effectively foreground the differences. Unlike Tristram, Launcelot is ashamed of his madness, but the exact nature of the guilt he feels is not clear. In Tristram's case, the restoration of his outward form suffices to give him back his rational faculties. But when Launcelot recovers his normal physical aspect at Blyaunte's home, he is not restored to "hys wytte" (2:819.27–28). Recovery comes only after a grave relapse and "by myracle and by vertu of" the Holy Grail (2:824.20–27). Launcelot's shame on coming to his senses is not spiritual or moral but social (2:825.10). Madness is not educative—"I have be myssefortuned" (2:825.15)—and Launcelot's concern is not with the deeper significance of the Grail but with his social rehabilitation, which he largely engineers. Like Tristram, Launcelot reclaims his identity through action, but he plays a more active role in setting up events that will prove his worth. He emphasizes his divorce from his proper milieu with a public declaration of his fault, but at the same time, the three-day tournament he organizes serves to reassert his knighthood. Integrity and integration, however, ultimately depend on Launcelot's return to Arthur's court. The Joyus Ile on which he establishes himself and where he seeks to regain his identity is also a locus of exclusion from his chivalric milieu, and Malory's Launcelot is as regretful of his distance from Arthur as from Guinevere: "he wolde onys every day loke towarde the realme of Logrys, where kynge Arthure and quene Gwenyver was, and than wolde he falle uppon a wepyng as hys harte shulde to-braste" (2:827.11–14).

Bound up with the issue of Launcelot's sanity and volition is the fact of his sexual betrayal, on which he insists vigorously. Prior to his breakdown, he tells Guinevere that he "was made to lye by" Elaine (2:802.20). He has recourse to the idiom of rape to mark the abuse done to his body, and denies consent in the fathering of Galahad, when he tells Elaine: "ye and dame Brusen made me for to lye by you magry myne hede" (2:825.26–27). Malory here registers Launcelot's distress in equal measure with the fact that deception is necessary to the conception of Galahad. Arthur Brittan has suggested that central to hegemonic masculinity is the way "men collectively appropriate women's reproductive labour in the family and in the public domain."[53] Where the French text exploits Lancelot's sinful desire to spiritually redemptive ends, Launcelot asserts his lack of volition and so throws into question, not only his specific traditional heroic definition, but also a fundamental means of defining and understanding masculinity. The appropriation of Launcelot's reproductive power in the interests of the perpetuation and fulfillment of the chivalric ethos and of the Arthurian narrative leads to a crisis in the *Morte* Launcelot's sense of identity. Launcelot's disavowal reverses the normative gender definitions of the Pentecostal Oath, where it is women who are sexually violable, and also offers an unusual perspective on masculine volition, for the resistant Launcelot is then in the same position as historical raped women who became mothers and had to face legal and medical authorities who considered the consent of both parties requisite for conception to take place.[54]

Launcelot's voiced resistance at the level of the physical highlights the issue of secrecy and its maintenance. He successfully reconstitutes his identity after the "trespass" to which he lays claim but that he does not define: "My name ys Le Shyvalere Ill Mafeete, that ys to sey 'the knyght that hath trespassed'" (2:826.22–23). Launcelot's black shield depicts a queen in silver, with an armed knight before her (2:827.8–10). In Morgan's hands, a proclamatory shield is malicious; in the *Lancelot,* the emblem, with the labored note that few know its import, assures us both of the hero's loyalty to the queen, and of its continuing concealment in "official" discourse (Micha

6:233; Lacy 3:335–36). In Malory, this unglossed shield is where readers' and (some) characters' "knowledges" tacitly converge. Karma Lochrie, building on D. A. Miller's work, invokes the example of the U.S. armed services' attempts to "contain" gay and lesbian sexuality by means of a silence that must, however, be broken if an individual is "accused," as part of a discussion of the roles secrecy plays in paradoxical political constructions of gender and sexuality across time and space. Homosexuals, in her modern example, become "open secrets whose telling is forbidden, even as the knowledge of their sexuality is not."[55] This complex of secrecy around sexuality, what Lochrie terms a (heterosexual) "privileged unknowing" that can inter alia maintain a gap between acts and identities, extends interestingly to the condition of Launcelot's sexual activity and its effects in the *Morte,* and strains against Launcelot's chivalric definition and his fathering of Galahad. What was readerly is now part of the court's social text. Arthur sees Galahad as "evidence" of a love for Elaine worth the forfeit of one's rational faculties (2:832.30–35). Launcelot's kin, meanwhile, "knew for whom he wente oute of hys mynde" (2:833.4–5). Launcelot's response carefully avoids social or moral explicitness: "yf I ded ony foly I have that I sought" (2:833:1–2). The court celebrates a nostalgic wholeness with the "joy" of Launcelot's return, but the sexual now openly belongs to Launcelot's "unspoken" identity. The latter part of the *Book of Sir Tristram* reasserts the importance of lineage and kinship, in ways that seek to valorize Launcelot's role as the father of Galahad and to accommodate this within the assurances of continuity that normative secular chivalric lineage provides. Thus for Arthur, Perceval's bloodline proves his knightliness (2:815.9–11), and the parentage of Bors's young son, Helyn, guarantees him a place at the Round Table (2:831.8–11). Elaine's last words to Launcelot about their son fix his identity in relation to his father in such a way as to establish, if only temporarily, the latter's superiority: "he shall preve the beste man of hys kynne excepte one" (2:832.12–13). But the characters' faith in genealogy as index of moral as of secular election sits less happily, both with Launcelot's resistance, and with Bors's vision of the Grail in this section, which intimates a differently constituted hierarchy whereby Launcelot will be surpassed in spiritual matters (2:801.16–33).

Shoshana Felman notes of writing on madness that as a genre with no metatext, it is a meeting place of "speaking madness and speaking of it." She argues further that the "mad" text resists interpretation, that it recounts above all "the specificity of its resistance to our reading."[56] The *Lancelot* has recourse to madness to keep in equal play, rather than to interrogate, the opposing claims on the protagonist, and his own desires. But the *Morte* appears to be resisting precisely this "traditional" delineation and positioning of Launcelot, and in the episode of his madness and his recovery from it, the narrative partially dismantles the rhetoric established for understanding his role, further displaces the burden of secrecy and knowledge, and registers an ambivalent relation to paternity, an ambivalence that the *Sankgreal* narrative inherits and to some extent uncomfortably deploys within its epistemology, as the next chapter will explore.

The *Beste Glatissant* and the Questing Beast

The *beste glatissant*/Questing Beast forms a suitable concluding focus to this section because it demonstrates how Malory's project differs from a dominant aspect of the French tradition Micheau Gonnot's manuscript exemplifies. Gonnot's compilation intercalates its sources so as to make the careers of the two central heroes, Tristan and Lancelot, parallel and complementary, extends the definition of chivalric prowess and focuses on chivalric biography in an exposition of the chivalric ethos. Gonnot's affirmed central project is to collate authoritative Arthurian material and to bring his story of positive chivalric action to a definitive "good end." This demands from the reader a particular good will and a faith in the written as authoritative, but the extension of chivalric action and adventure (in, for example, the events of the Post-Vulgate Grail material Gonnot includes), raises questions about the status of these self-declaredly authoritative writings. The Post-Vulgate Grail story, for example, includes the character of Arthur the Less, another illegitimate son of Arthur's, the product of a violent exogamous union, and a complement, Richard Trachsler notes, to the incestuous liaison that produces Mordred.[57] Whereas rape in Malory serves, inter alia, to concentrate tensions in the Arthurian social order, and to problematize the relation between life and literature (and in Launcelot's case, to mark a resistance to the hero's literary inheritance), the account of Arthur the Less's conception here signals a lack of resolution between recognizable feudal order and narrative event. Furthermore, rape is at once a premise of, and a source of anxiety for, French Arthurian narrative. Arthur the Less is conceived when the king, out hunting, finds and opportunistically rapes a beautiful and aristocratic girl whom he thinks (because she is alone) may be a fay (Bogdanow 2:472–473; Lacy 5:215). Her father, Tanas, arrives on the scene, and the subsequent debate over how to proceed invokes the vocabulary of feudal allegiance (the knight cannot kill the king because he is his lord), of "dishonor" done by one man to another, and of royal prerogative (Arthur wishes to keep the girl, and marry her off to one of his knights). That the father wishes to wait until he can determine whether his daughter is pregnant before he makes a decision about her future (2:474; Lacy 5:215) suggests heroic genealogies transcend social and moral considerations. Subsequent to the rape, however (and perhaps, for the narrative, in relativizing mitigation of Arthur's offense), Tanas annihilates his own family. Sexual jealousy leads him to kill his son, rape his daughter-in-law, kill his daughter, newly a mother, who has threatened to expose him, and abandon his grandson to wild animals. For all Gonnot's interest in conclusions, the tale does not recount what happens to Tanas, who, knowing the penalty for his crimes, plans to go into exile (2:476; Lacy 5:215). Arthur acknowledges, and associates the social expediency of concealing, his own "folie" and "pechié" [offense and sin] (2:479; Lacy 5:216), but is never called to account.

This curious contextualization of the king's act of rape draws attention to the problems of Arthurian legitimation even as it celebrates chivalric genealogy.[58] The female body is here the instrument of masculine transgression and the means to the brutal realization of chivalric desire and continuity, and the willful destruction of family sits disturbingly alongside the simultaneous endorsement of knightly continuity, and knightly class as guarantor of noble conduct. The violently generated narrative raises a question about Arthurian legitimization it seems unwilling to resolve. The replaying of motif—rape, another illegitimate "good knight"—confirms the self-justification of a circular Arthurian narrative, continually revisiting and reenacting familiar adventures.

An accusation of rape is central to the origin of the *beste glatissant* the Post-Vulgate *Queste* supplies. This composite and complex creature, as it emerges across a range of texts, itself emblematizes a developing French Arthurian narrative methodology. In the *Estoire del Saint Graal,* a mixed creature—"quant plus le regardoie et mains pooie savoir quele beste c'estoit" [the longer I looked at it, the less I knew what kind of animal it was] (1:13; Lacy 1:6)—a black and white beast with a sheep's head, dog's feet and legs, a fox's body, and a lion's tail, guides the priest-scribe across the romance landscape to retrieve his holy book (1:13; Lacy 1:6).[59] The *beste glatissant* "proper," that is, with continually baying hounds within it, that (in early manifestations) erupt from its body and attempt to destroy it and one another, appears first to trot into view in the *Perlesvaus,* and in Gerbert's *Continuation* of Chrétien's *Graal.* These texts respectively explain that the creature allegorically represents the relation between God and the twelve tribes of Israel, or the Church and the disruption caused by those who do not pay proper attention during mass.[60] The *beste,* then, belongs to romance's daring appropriation, even creation, of religious imagery and its exposition. The animal in *Perlesvaus* is small and snow-white, whereas in Gerbert's poem it is huge. Janina Traxler argues that the *Tristan* has a key role in consolidating the beast's extraordinary physical appearance, familiar in its parts but alien in its grotesque compositeness, with, for example, its serpent's head and lion's tail and leopard's body and deer's hooves, and the

noise of twenty hounds clamoring within it (Ménard 6:389).[61] The creature invites intertextual interpretation; Traxler suggests the *Tristan* audience
would appreciate the *beste's* earlier literary associations with a Grail quest,
and so read the hero Palamède's failure (in the *Tristan*) to achieve the quest
of the *beste*, as a moral comment on the simultaneous failure of his quest
for Iseut's love, and also as a sententious aside on the general moral condition of the questing knight.[62]

Gonnot's compendium conflates a version of the *Tristan* material that
links the beast with Palamède, and the Post-Vulgate *Suite* and *Queste's* exhaustive teleological and moral account. BN 112's first volume possibly
contained the *Suite* material concerning the *beste*, for its last book recounts
how Galahad catches sight of the variegated creature, the "beste diverse,"
King Arthur saw while at the fountain, when King Pellinor was hunting it
(Bogdanow 2:111; Lacy 5:136). The reference is to the *Suite* episode that
defines the marvel as an adventure for the individual knight errant, where
Pellinor tells Arthur he seeks to know "the truth about myself" by means
of the beast, for it must die at the hands of the worthiest of his line (*Suite*
1:5; Lacy 4:168). But genealogy also makes this a Grail adventure, for Merlin foretells that Pellinor's son Perceval will find out the "truth" of it (*Suite*
1:14; Lacy 4:171). For King Arthur, the *beste* crashes through the narrative
as one of a sequence of "marvels," which begins with his troubling dream
of the destruction of Logres and culminates in the revelation of his parentage, and of the news that he has committed incest with his sister and engendered one who will destroy the land (*Suite* 1:7–14; Lacy 4:169–70). The
Post-Vulgate deploys the animal as a complex emblem of narrative process.
Genealogy is crucial to the creature's spiritual and chivalric import
throughout. In volume two of BN 112, Palamède is linked with the mon-
ster, motivated by the desire to avenge his family whose death it has
caused. Palemède meets the beast by chance, when he is looking for Tristan, and BN 112's description of it at this point is lengthier and more fully
realized than in other *Tristan* narratives:

> Si voit quelle a teste et col de serpent barbellee et renfraigne les yeulx luisans
> comme charboncle la bouche ardant quil semble que feu en saille les oreilles
> droites comme un leurier corps et queue de lyon sur le dos aupres des es-
> paules auoit unes voilles reflambissans comme rayz de souleil et sur le faiz
> de la crouppe pareillent. Jambes auoit et pies de cerf le pomel estoit de di-
> uerses manieres tache car toutes les couleurs du monde y estoient. Le regart
> de ses yeulx estoit quil semblast que ce feussent ii torches. Ces dens estoient
> plus grans que dun grant sengler. (2: fol. 175b)

> [He saw that it had the barbed and sinister head and neck of a snake, its eyes
> glowing like carbuncles, a flaming mouth that seemed to shoot fire, ears up-

right like a greyhound's, the body and tail of a lion. On its back, near its
shoulders, was a pair of wings shimmering like sunbeams, as also on the top
of its rump. It had the legs and feet of a deer. Its forelegs were stained in various ways, for all the colors in the world were there. The glare of its eyes was
like that of two torches. Its teeth were bigger than those of a large boar.]

The "diverse" beast vividly embodies Gonnot's own compilation,
which contains diverse "branches" of adventure within one physical book.
In volume two, which uses *Tristan* material, the animal is a means to locating Palamède, who, when he first glimpses it, finds himself in an adventure that confirms his status as a "good knight" (2: fol. 58c),[63] and who
adopts the *beste* as his emblem. Volume two also has Palamède reveal his
quest is one of revenge, for his eleven brothers met their deaths at a burning lake where they were trying to destroy the animal (2: fol. 176c). This
event is paralleled later, when a knight-turned-hermit relates that his sons
were killed in similar circumstances (Bogdanow 2:128–29; Lacy 5:139).
These incidents anticipate the conditions in which the creature is finally
killed. Reiteration of motif highlights the widening terms of reference as
the *beste*'s broader significance is revealed, and more knights are implicated
in the adventure, which ceases to be uniquely Palamède's quest.

Ultimately, this becomes a story of chivalric integration. If the Saracen
Palamède, in the *Tristan,* does not achieve his quest, the Post-Vulgate
Queste spectacularly deploys the beast to chart origins and endings;
Palamède, destined to kill the creature, plunges his sword into it, with Galahad and Perceval as his companions (BN 112, 4:fol. 147c; Lacy 5:278). This
end consolidates the traditions surrounding the creature. Palamède does
not survive long after this triumph, for he is killed "sanz reson," without
cause, by Agravain and Gawain (4: fol. 149c; Lacy 5:282). Before he com-
mits suicide in grief at his son's death, his father Esclabor commands that
Palamède's epitaph be written in his own blood (4: fol. 150b; Lacy 5:283).
This gruesome act of commemoration "translates" lineage from the human
flesh to written remembrance, and ratifies the romance author's own activity. Meanwhile, the killing of the *beste* is retrospectively assimilated to
Galahad's mission, for King Pellehan tells him of the supernatural circumstances of its birth. King Ypomenes's daughter, a learned young woman
skilled in necromancy, desires her saintly brother, who repulses her, and she
falls prey to a devil who seduces her with the promise to help her achieve
her ends, and sleeps with her "tout ainsi comme fist le pere merlin a la
mere merlin" [just as Merlin's father lay with his mother] (4: fol. 151c-d;
Lacy 5:284). Pregnant, the girl accuses her brother of rape, and the prince
is thrown to starving dogs, but his last words warn that the child is the
devil's, and the devil will emerge incarnate in the form of a marvelous

beast. The beast will bear witness to the prince's innocence, for the dogs in its body will memorialize the death of the innocent man, and it will survive until such time as the "good knight" called Galahad joins in its quest. At its birth, the horrible creature runs off, the truth is uncovered, and the perjurer suffers a death even more horrible than that of her brother, in punishment for her crime.[64]

This account of the beast's origins is a culmination of a narrative concerned with right lineage and election, which nonetheless incorporates a troubling undercurrent of sexual violence. Gonnot accords the *beste* a particular narrative role; it allows the questing knight to attain the "perfection" of a completed adventure. By finally aligning the *beste*'s history with Galahad, Gonnot endorses a narrative in which a particular teleology gives apparent meaning to a world of marvelous adventures. The composite beast intriguingly embodies the contradictions of the Arthurian romances, with their multiple claims on the spiritual, social, historical, and biographical alike, and the internal competitiveness of their diverse authorities. The conflation of quarry and hunter in the hounds' occupation of the creature's belly serves as an intriguing image of the curiously circular narrative trajectory that makes Arthurian adventure, especially as the Post-Vulgate *Roman du Graal* recounts it, something of a textual act of faith. In Malory, as I have argued elsewhere, the Questing Beast is, by contrast, metonymic rather than metaphorical.[65] It signals less a point of narrative elucidation than a locus of mystery. By naming the animal the "Questing" Beast, Malory reinforces the sense of the creature's circularity, punning on its significance with regard to "knightly enterprise" and to the "searching after game" and the "baying of hounds."[66] Malory does not, however, reveal the Beast's "grete sygnyfycasion" (2:717.16), which cannot, it seems, translate into the *Morte* narrative, just as the "straunge sygnes and tokyns" (2:528.34) of the love-ravings of Palomides, who is linked with the Beast, here as in the *Tristan,* cannot find full representation. Where Gonnot combines the allusive and definitive traditions of the *beste,* Malory's Beast signals discontinuity.

The *beste,* for the anthologizing French texts, is paradigmatic of their mode of composition, their ready assimilation of diverse material, and their appropriation of material that claims a pious authority; Malory's noisy beast signals the lack of explanatory threads, a series of signifiers without the ultimate satisfaction of recovering an intelligible meaning. The Questing beast first appears in the early material Malory adapts from the *Suite du Merlin,* but he leaves it alien and perplexing in its allusiveness (even if Pellinor is certain of its status as confirmatory of his own worth [1:42.29–43.1]), rather than explicate its possible relation to Merlin's revelations to Arthur of family relations past and future. The Beast's future appearances seem irrelevant to the project as a whole, and signal the redundancy of romance narrative, and even of romance motivation. Palomides, who swears he will be baptized only when he has "enchyeved" his quest of the "beste glatysaunte" (2:717.14–15), is finally baptized as part of his social reconciliation with Tristram. The last line of the *Morte*'s *Tristram* section, with its image of Palomides pursuing the Questing Beast, suggests the whole operates as a story of omission and lack of completion. Malory's text emerges as different in kind from the French compilations, because it does not reassure us that a "full" text is retrievable, that, for example, the Beast has a recuperable and "readable" history. Gonnot attains a partial closure by means of the Post-Vulgate version of the Grail that finally conflates spiritual and social aspects of good knighthood. Malory's method more disturbingly exposes the fragility of our constitution of Arthurian narrative. By moving to the Vulgate version of the quest of the Holy Grail, rather than the more accommodating (if differently problematic) Post-Vulgate story, in spite of having already drawn on the Post-Vulgate *Suite,* Malory makes a different statement, one about the uncomfortable disjunctions of Arthurian narratives, whether in the sources or across the *Morte* itself.

CHAPTER 5

SPIRITUAL COMMUNITY,
GENDER, AND FATHERHOOD IN
THE TALE OF THE SANKGREAL

Bewar Oldcastel and for Crystes sake
Clymbe no more in holy writ so hie!
Rede the storie of Lancelot de lake,
Or Vegece of the aart of Chiualrie,
The seege of Troie or Thebes thee applie
To thyng þat may to thordre of knyght longe![1]

Is Hoccleve idiosyncratic, or even satirical when, reproaching the Lollard addressee of his "To Sir John Oldcastle" for the heresies which, he says, "un-man" him,[2] he recommends that, instead of troubling over the gospels, John Oldcastle remake himself as a masculine knightly subject (especially as one who expresses his Christian faith in violent and martial terms) fortified by reading the historical and chivalric books of the Old Testament (ll. 201–08), Vegetius's famous text on war strategy, and accounts of Lancelot and of Thebes and Troy?[3] Hoccleve goes on to assure Oldcastle that to question the validity of the sacrament of the Eucharist when the officiating priest is in mortal sin is to express a transgressive curiosity: "to deepe yee ransake" (l. 328). The term "ransack," denoting the exercise of an overcurious intellect in the context of a debate over "mak(ing) Crystes body" (ll. 326–27), also describes the medieval physician's searching, or "ransacking," of wounds, and figures Oldcastle's inquisitiveness as interference with Christ's own physical wholeness.[4] Oldcastle had, furthermore, appropriated religious emblem; his battle standard displayed the eucharistic chalice and its contents.[5] In his poem, Hoccleve genders feminine a lay curiosity about the divine, denounces those ignorant foolish women, "lewde calates" (l. 147) who seek knowledge of scripture, tells them to keep out of trouble, to sit at home and spin, and recommends literature other than the gospels as remedy for a probing into God's mysteries, which latter inquiry can only be injurious to spiritual and—as Oldcastle's heterodoxy is a political act—physical integrity.[6]

In this densely referenced poem, however, Hoccleve invokes as conservative and apolitical a range of literature, the classification of which can hardly have been straightforward and the political ramifications of which were surely at issue. One might readily question the neutrality of the Troy story in Lancastrian times, or the ingenuousness of associating Lancelot romances with "manliness" in the light of the Nun's Priest's aside on their popularity with female audiences, or indeed the poem's own later vigorous denunciation of (admittedly specifically heretical, not chivalric) adulterers, "yee þat rekken nat whos wyf yee take & holde" (ll. 371–72).[7] To invoke books of the Old Testament enacts the very blurring of boundaries between lay and clerical custodianship of religious knowledge against which Hoccleve's poem protests.[8] Writing in 1415, over fifty years before Malory, Hoccleve positions "masculine" romance in a context of conservative politics and proclaimed religious orthodoxy in opposition to a heterodoxy gendered female and to the unlawful appropriation of theological issues and Christian imagery properly the preserve of the Church. But Hoccleve's rhetorical method exposes how all writing, sacred or secular, is open to political manipulation, and how context can shape its meaning and reception. The scheme of gendered reading and the attack on Oldcastle's religious waywardness, ostensibly calculated to concentrate attention on the knight's transgression, draw attention to the hermeneutic force politics exercises.

If the poem's literary categories and their contents unravel even as Hoccleve proposes to knit them into coherent strategies for living, what space would he have made in his reading program for Arthurian Grail narrative, with its exacerbative conflation of religious and romance motif and its singular claims on Christ's body for its own purposes? It arguably fits categories of "cristenly prowesse" (l. 12) and of "errour" (l. 6). Hoccleve's disturbing rather than reassuring taxonomy, with its ranging of works of romance against selectively forbidden religious texts, intimates a particularly rich fifteenth-century interpretive context for Malory's translation of the *Queste del Saint Graal*. Caxton's preface treats straightforwardly of the "Saynt Greal," though the prayer in Wynkyn de Worde's 1498 edition, which introduces Book 13, endorses a pious reception for the narrative: "Therfore on all synfull soules blessid lord haue thou mercy that by the vertue of thy bytter passyon oure synnes may be forgeuen us And at the last daye of our Jugement we may come to thy kyngdome in heuen."[9] But several politicized sixteenth-century responses to Malory demonstrate the

intensely contingent nature of Grail narrative interpretations. So Roger
Ascham cautiously traces chivalric narrative's origins in an *acedia* endemic
in the representatives of a corrupt institutionalized religion, ascribing to
"idle Monkes" the production of books of chivalry such as the *Morte,*
which encourages delight in "open mans slaughter, and bold bawdrye."[10]
But Ascham's claim that the accessibility of chivalric romance simultaneously denies wholesome and spiritually uplifting literature to readers of the
vernacular suggests a mistrustful and defensive relation between explicitly
religious and didactic works and those later medieval romances for which
compilers and editors such as Gonnot and Caxton claim a specifically
moral focus.

Malory's remarkable thirteenth-century French source is itself no "trans-
parent" text, but encourages conflicting interpretations of its ostensibly allegorical method. It has been read as a Cistercian (or Cistercian-inspired)
corrective to the "earthly chivalry" and the worldly interests of the other
cyclic narratives, and also as a daring secular play on religious orthodoxies
and scriptural language.[11] Jon Whitman suggests the *Queste's* element of
"bodily presence" is at odds with its ostensible "spiritual program."[12] This
tension is, however, endemic in a hermeneutically aware work of "metaliterature," as Laurence de Looze describes it, engaged in rewriting the chivalric in terms of a religious semiotic on which it invites the reader to
elaborate.[13] If Malory's project situates itself in the "in-between" culturally,
and requires continuing negotiation of its different elements, the *Queste* is
already narratively and ethically interstitial. It draws on established literary
themes and methodologies,[14] and these it intercalates with the trends in
thirteenth-century spirituality it appropriates and reworks. So the *Queste* reflects changes to confession the fourth Lateran Council of 1215 prescribes
in a move from "interiorized" to "exteriorized" forms of religious practice,
and the narrative foci on confession and Grail quest trap the knights between divergent models of self-representation.[15] The *Queste's* daring lies in
its interweaving of the language of chivalry and of spiritual referents, its
confident rhetorical and typological play.

Malory's reworking of the *Queste* is ostensibly his most "faithful" redaction (if also a radically abbreviating one), but pressures from both the
Arthuriad context and from aspects of fifteenth-century attitudes to religious belief, with which the narrative intermittently intersects, make the
Sankgreal very different from his source. Although Felicity Riddy expertly
correlates aspects of the narrative with fifteenth-century lay belief,[16] there
are problems with extrapolating a theological position for Malory by re-
constructing his religious environment, especially as historians of fifteenth-
century gentry piety do not agree on mapping its parameters. Whereas
Colin Richmond argues for gentry religion as an increasingly individual

and privatized experience, with this class taking ever less interest in parish affairs, Eamon Duffy sees an actively and publicly pious laity much involved in the work of the Church.[17] The evidence suggests the gentry might carve out for themselves religious experiences of greater or lesser intensity and engagement, so one cannot make a priori assumptions about Malory's religion on the basis of social placing. Certainly, Malory does not seem particularly radical in his religion; his abbreviations suggest little interest in interpreting scripture, or in other areas in lay spirituality's development, such as an emphasis on private prayer, Marian devotion, and Christ's Passion,[18] and he does not use the *Sankgreal* to explore contemporary religious issues. He does, however, deploy the idioms of a fifteenth-century religious vernacular register, and the *Sankgreal,* if it does not confront, certainly dramatizes, some of the transitional aspects of fifteenth-century figurations of social organization and spiritual responsibility.

Mervyn James's survey of English society, from the later medieval to the post-Reformation period, traces the changing relation between state, religious ideology, and the role of violence in ways that illuminate some of the *Sankgreal's* concerns. James notes how pre-Reformation "honor" society resolves conflict through violence and legitimizes such action in moral terms, a legitimization accompanied by what he calls a "compartmentalization of religious culture," a division between sacred and secular, clergy and laity. One aspect of this division, James ventures, is that moral and religious problems find expression and resolution in institutionalized legal, rather than personal, terms.[19] The knight belongs to a corporate code of honor that exists to impose order and rule within the bounds civil and canon law dictate. At the same time, there is space for autonomous moral responsibility in an honor society, at least in the political arena, in the weighing up of various obligations, primarily to blood ties, but also to what Malory would call "felyship," as well as to the claims of the crown. An honor system views history as governed by fate, and so praises the maintenance of steadfastness in the face of its machinations. Consonant with this philosophy is a tendency not to see the person as morally condemned by events that befall him or her. But medieval England also witnesses a transition in the concept of "honor," as a consequence of a gradual fusing of perceptions formerly seen as the preserve of either Church or state, that is, as the country enters a "civil" society that abrogates to itself both honor and violence. Politics become "moralized" and history is increasingly viewed as providentialist, with the individual required to obey the strictures of laws human and divine, in a context where events themselves come to be seen as "vehicles of divine judgement."[20] Clearly the *Sankgreal* is intriguingly relevant to fifteenth-century concerns with responsibility, the rule of law, divine and human, and the reach of a determining fate. If James's polarization of "honor" and "civil" societies is a little schematic, it nonetheless offers a framework for understanding how the various experiences and responses of the Round Table knights, from the elect such as Galahad to the hapless, such as the worldly Gawain, whose view of chivalry is wholly secular, with Launcelot torn between the two worlds, and partially valorized by each, might intersect with shifting historical conceptualizations of knighthood and its place within a divinely appointed scheme of human law.

I want further to investigate some aspects of the *Sankgreal* as paradigmatic of a tendency to interrogate and revise categories of knowledge and access, to the divine as to the narrative's logic, even as those means of access are put into play. The narrative veers between the familiar and the unfamiliar, an effect the intermittent and not always explicated deployment of religious associations intensifies. The tale itself is predicated on an apparent textual stability that estranges us from our inscribed readerly function elsewhere in the *Morte*. Malory's heightened awareness of a connection between Grail and Eucharist brings into literary play the complex of social, political and religious issues that makes of Christ's body in the later Middle Ages a site of contention even as (or perhaps because) it promises unity.[21] This overlay of contemporary spiritual concerns contributes to the slipperiness of Malory's telling, for while it enlarges the text's terms of reference, as the religious references in the *Queste* specifically intend, the narrative accretes a bewildering range of possible meanings, but without the directional metaphorical support system the *Queste* offers. Perceval's Sister's interventions and especially her ultimate fate, her *imitatio Christi,* partake in a rewriting of Grail narrative that signals distance from—as much as access to—the spiritual. Several have noted the *Sankgreal*'s loss of cohesion in terms of hermeneutics, the fissures in its sign systems, and the difficulty the quest participants have in recognizing the exemplary as a system.[22] The *Queste* invites a certain readerly collusion to complete or supply allegorical interpretations, and to follow particular signposting. Malory's text dislocates us from a sense of black and white morality by refusing consistently to identify what works metaphorically, and so disrupts a clear sense of the literal and historical.

Launcelot is famously caught between different registers of earthly and divine chivalry, his own confusion and uncertainty mirroring the text's vagaries.[23] But his chivalric selfhood's displacements and reaccommodations belong to a broader project involving reader and author in the Grail story's destabilizing alienation of familiar terms, making us confront central epistemological questions. Launcelot refashions his identity after having resisted his function in Arthurian narrative as father to Galahad, the "good knight," and on his quest he actively seeks recognition as a "son" of God. Late-medieval vernacular devotional texts often discuss spiritual community and individual relations between the human and the Divine in terms of a parent-child relation. Malory reworks this idiom, an image of inclusiveness for the *Queste* and contemporary religious writings alike, and writes large Launcelot's distress by making the parent-child relation exclusive, reserving to the elect Grail knights the nomenclature of "sons." I shall consider how the spiritual language of fatherhood reflects on Launcelot's spiritual and historical condition, and consider what awareness of this motif brings to the episode of the healing of Sir Urry, which sets an unexpected manifestation of redemptive grace, and its human apprehension, outside the formal structures and proscriptions of the Grail narrative. The Urry episode reassesses Launcelot's Grail-quest relation to the Divine at the same time as it reconceptualizes the Vulgate narrative's values and remakes the relation between worldly event and divine grace.

Formally, the *Sankgreal* proclaims its singular integrity (and so highlights the instability that defines the rest of the Arthuriad and its values). Instead of relying on the intermittent authority of the "French book," or the vagaries of narratorial choice and the co-opting of the reader's volition in deciding narrative direction, the book of the Grail tells its own story. In this tale—with Perceval's Sister's account of the Ship of Faith an important exception—Malory closely follows the French technique in presenting the book as the organizing voice: "Now seyth the tale that whan sir Launcelot was ryddyn aftir sir Galahad [. . .] sir Percivale turned agayne unto the recluse" (2:905.1–3).[24] The reader is passive recipient of an integral body of knowledge, rather than its co-organizer. The only occasion of recourse to the (elsewhere familiar) formula, "Now turn we," involving both reader and narrator, articulates, on behalf of the reader, an agreement with the book's orientation, providing an apparent assurance of continuity with a focus on the two principal Grail knights, in the midst of the frightening near-apocalyptic aftermath of Perceval's Sister's death, and Bors's disappearance to help a wounded knight: "Now turne we to the two felowis. Now saith the tale that sir Galahad and sir Percivall were in a chapell all nyght in hir prayers" (2:1005: 1–3).[25]

While the formal level of Malory's text promises cohesion, however, its framing colophons, particularly in the Winchester Manuscript, draw attention to other claims on and involvement with, the telling and reception of the material. At the end of the *Tristram* the redactor promises:

[. . .] here folowyth the noble tale off the Sankegreall, whyche called ys the holy vessell and the sygnyfycacion of blyssed bloode off Oure Lorde Jesu Cryste, whyche was brought into thys londe by Joseph off Aramathye.

Therefore on all synfull, blyssed Lorde, have on thy knyght mercy. Amen. (2:845.32–846.5)

The colophon allows for conflicting perspectives on Malory's retelling. The Grail account may here compensate for the gaps and fissures of the incomplete Tristram story, or one may read the integrity of the Tristram story as the price of this alternative envisioning of wholeness.[26] Where the *Queste* playfully ascribes to Walter Map authorship of fictions the historical Map condemns, Malory's framing is rather more serious; (heterodox) mention of the Sankgreal as repository of Christ's blood, and the story's link with the conversion of "this londe" through Britain's legendary proto-evangelist Joseph of Arimathea, suggest to the fifteenth-century audience a political, religious, and historical relevance more immediate and inclusive than the *Queste*'s mention of a royal patron from the (admittedly not distant) past.[27] But the historical aspect that here seem so urgent is not straightforwardly retrievable in the narrative proper. And to emphasize "this land"'s Josephian link with the Grail exacerbates the loss felt with its removal at the end of the tale.[28] The rare word "signification" also hints that the epistemological will not be easily recuperable, for just as the "signification" of the Questing Beast proclaims and defers its meaning, so here the term invokes but does not explain the numinous.[29] The author instead appeals to God's mercy and, as one of a community of sinners on whose behalf he requests Christ's intercession, draws us into the story on religious terms and anticipates Launcelot's own humility.

Only at the end of the story does the "French book" identify the *Sankgreal* as a translation and clarify Malory's authorial role: "Thus endith the tale of the Sankgreal that was breffly drawyn oute of Freynshe—which ys a tale cronycled for one of the trewyst and of the holyest that ys in thys worlde—by sir Thomas Maleorré, knyght" (2:1037.8–12).[30] This ending makes explicit what the form of the telling resists, that human agency inevitably mediates the text, while the syntax makes ambiguous whether the text is "trewyst and holiest" by its nature, or because human subjectivity has "chronicled" it as such. Winchester also provides evidence of scribal confusion over the status of the Divine and its affiliates. The rubrisshing of proper names characteristic of the manuscript as a whole is inconsistently deployed here in mentions of God, the Virgin Mary, and the Sankgreal. The contradictions in the Winchester manuscript that blur certainties, yet declare the wholeness of the story, materially reflect the *Sankgreal*'s conflicting signals about its incorporation of spiritual registers. The omission of explicatory material, and a lack of spiritual development of some of the more immediately recognizable of Malory's emphases—such as an interest in the physical—makes for a fine tension between access to and blocking of religious knowledge and experience, both in the fifteenth-century context and in the narrative terms the text has established. Perceval's Sister partakes in that "partial accessing" of knowledge, and she leads us back to the confusion over the moral justification of human violence.

Perceval's Sister and Access to the Divine

Hoccleve's poem to Oldcastle displaces onto the feminine its anxieties about promulgating forbidden knowledge, but Perceval's Sister's actions and insights arguably provoke anxiety about how and what we "know" to begin with. In general, Malory retains the *Queste*'s apparent polarization of the feminine, as the occasion to sin (metaphorized in the Devil's disguises to tempt the Grail knights) or as the means to facilitate male spiritual journeys, although he also mutes this effect, especially with regard to Salvation history. At the same time, both *Queste* and *Morte* may deploy the feminine in more subtle ways. Although we hardly turn to Malory for a sustained investigation of late-medieval female spirituality, Perceval's Sister's gender is important to her function within the Grail narrative's epistemology and teleology, and she helps alienate the *Sankgreal* from the other Arthurian narratives. The name "Perceval's Sister" individuates the protagonist only relationally, and in her semianonymity she shares in the anomalousness of religious figures, for the Winchester scribe rubrisshes "Perceval's," but not "sister." The orthography thus intimates a spiritual status for her in the context of the Grail quest. But Perceval's Sister appears anomalous also in a narrative that excludes women as romance accessories; Grail adventurers learn of Nascien that the presence of ladies is inappropriate to the enterprise (2:868.15–869.19). This assumed sexualization of women makes for a tension in the representation of Perceval's Sister herself. For some, her representation does not transcend the implicitly eroticized terms that describe her relations, especially with Galahad.[31] Critical opinion divides on whether Perceval's Sister, in the *Queste* or in the *Sankgreal,* is a "subject" in her own right, or whether she is primarily an object facilitating access to the Divine for (male) others.[32] Certainly she serves as an aide to the elect Grail knights, Perceval, Bors, and Galahad, and initiates them into the mysteries of the Ship of Faith before she dies in order to heal the Leprous Lady, and so leaves the fellowship to complete the Grail adventures. Yet, she has, through sacrifice, a singular relation to the Divine that both "fulfills" and troubles the *Morte.* Furthermore, her account of the Dolorous Stroke as part of the Ship of Faith's history disrupts narrative linearity, and her actions, in part consonant with extratextual configurations of holy women's power, suggest a distance between her imitation of Christ and His inimitability for the Grail knights.[33] Her sacrifice also reminds us of the confusions in the *Morte* surrounding gendered violence and its justification, and the gaps between Malory's Arthurian chivalric history and the ideological rationale for violence the Vulgate cycle claims in imitation of Salvation history.

Perceval's Sister first appears as an unnamed woman who rouses Galahad from a night's rest at a hermitage, promises him "the hyghest adventure that ever ony knyght saw" (2:983.3–4), and takes him as far as, and then beyond, the sea that (we saw in chapter three) delimits the heroic trajectory of Gareth, the archetype of the secular "good knight." Malory makes her more mysterious than her *Queste* counterpart, for he does not identify her as the lady of the castle at which she and Galahad rest before continuing their journey to find Perceval, Bors, and the Ship of Faith.[34] Perceval's Sister is central to one of the most important narrative sequences: she guides the Grail knights onto the Ship, where she reveals her identity, explains the history and significance of the Sword of the Strange Girdles they find there, and the importance of the other artifacts, such as the miraculous spindles formed from the wood of the Tree of Life, and identifies herself as the virgin who can provide the girdle to complete the sword. A fifteenth-century translation of Aldhelm's treatise on virginity observes: "A mayde remembrith tho thinges that ben of God."[35] In a logical and striking signal of her election, Perceval's Sister, in the *Sankgreal,* knows the sacred history of the Ship of Faith in full. Yet, aspects of her historical account are as alienating as they are illuminating, as her part in the interrelated adventures of Ship and swords demonstrates.

The sword destined for Galahad lies on a bed in the Ship of Faith, which carries other strange cargo. The *Queste* offers, in a clearly signaled digression firmly authorized by the "contes" itself, the history of the Ship itself and of the three posts, white, green, and red, that form part of the bed:

> Et por ce que maintes genz le porroient oïr qui a mençonge le tendroient, se len ne lor faisoit entendant coment ce poroit avenir, si s'en destorne un poi li contes de sa droite voie et de sa matiere [. . .]

> [But since many listeners might find this tale hard to believe if they were not told just how this could have happened, the story here veers away from its straight path and its rightful subject]. (*Queste* 210; Lacy 4:67)

The divagations of romance, coded feminine, find privileged space in a self-justificatory episode in which romance meets with and explains Salvation history. In the *Queste,* Solomon, learning of the nobility of the last of his line, wishes to convey his own divinely revealed proleptic knowledge to his descendant (*Queste* 221; Lacy 4:70). Solomon's wife's craftiness, her *subtilité,* matched with his wisdom, his *sens* (*Queste* 222: Lacy 4:70), helps him in this scheme, for it is she who builds the Ship of Faith, and she suggests further that he ought to recognize his descendant's greatness with a gift. The rich sword of King David, placed in the Ship, will confirm the valor of the "best knight," while a virgin will provide the girdle to complete the sword's magnificence, and replace the poor trash that Solomon's

wife, with a keen sense of the limits of her role, has supplied. This marvel
is contextualized within Salvation history, to which the slips of wood from
the Tree of Life and its offshoots bear material witness, for the white, green,
and red hues recall, respectively, the erstwhile virginity of Adam and Eve,
the fertility of their sexual union after the Fall, and the first homicide,
when Cain kills Abel (*Queste* 212–19; Lacy 4:67–69). Solomon notes that
he and others (and even the crafter herself) need divine help to interpret
his wife's carefully wrought *merveilles;* indeed, the self-declaration of Ship
and Sword, and the little purse in which the Grail knights find documentation of the Ship's meaning and history, exist by divine intervention.
Solomon's wife's response is that all will be clear in the fullness of time
(*Queste* 225: Lacy 4:71).

A remarkable metatextually resonant and artful construct, the Ship is susceptible to diverse readings. For Robert Hanning, the episode particularizes
romance as literary project, demonstrating vernacular prose narrative's ability to combine doctrine, history and interpretation. Where Solomon represents the moral wisdom of thirteenth-century prose romance, his wife stands
for its "ingenuity." The author synthesizes both in a vehicle for Salvation history, the Ship, for which Perceval's Sister is historical and interpretive guide.[36]
Stephen Nichols sees a greater conflict between the rational and the emotive here. Romance desire and intuition, such as Solomon's wife exemplifies,
must be controlled by narratives based on a Solomon-like rationality, and in-
stituted by men.[37] Apart from her metaphoric association with romance
waywardness, woman (and her spiritual lot) is open to different interpretations. For Susan Aronstein, the text is a masculine appropriation of historically female religious discourse, which stifles woman's power through its
invocation of fallen Eve as model, while Jennifer Looper's interpretation of
the spindles cut from the Tree of Life as emblematic of an alternative female-
authored history, resistant to the *Queste's* general misogyny, accords the feminine a positive role.[38] Certainly, the *Queste* ambivalently rewrites for
Solomon the familiar Vulgate trope of women's perfidy as part of redemptive history, for it leaves open whether the revelation that Mary redeems
women's "wickedness" (220–21; Lacy 4:70) gives them as individuals a new
spiritual agency, or simply confirms their predetermined passive function.
The ambiguity of the word *fuissel* ("little piece of wood") leaves to the
reader's choice its specific translation as "spindle," and with it the fore-
grounding of an instrument richly figurative of women's work and sexuality.[39] Within an apparently typological text, anchored to the imperatives and
promises of Salvation history, the possibility of an "alternative" history
women oversee is, by virtue of the range of response its presentation elicits,
part of the ambiguity romance allows itself in constructing its own authority; we may read its deployment of the spiritual as iconoclastic or orthodox.

Malory's version of the Ship's history is the more striking because Perceval's Sister, and not the "story," tells the tale, as part of her dialogue with the Grail knights. This makes for a potentially more subjective recounting, one interpretively more open, because Malory radically abbreviates the *Queste*'s intercalations with Salvation history. Where the *Queste* Ship of Faith abrogates the tenets of religious faith to demand credence in the romance construct's narrative authority, Malory's text appears more involved with local effects than with cohesive narrative strategies. When Perceval's Sister reveals her identity to her brother, she invokes human affection—"I am thy syster [. . .] and therefore wete you welle ye ar the man that I moste love" (2:985.5–7)—where her French counterpart explains that her identity should give her words credence (*Queste* 201; Lacy 4:64). Malory also rewrites the *Queste*'s textual culture, so that Solomon's notion of women's evil nature is idiosyncratic rather than culturally supported; indeed, "olde bookis" (and divine revelation) themselves disabuse Solomon of his misogyny (2:991.27). Rather than muse on the transmission of knowledge, as in the *Queste,* Malory's Solomon puzzles over the promised good knight's identity, "who that sholde be, and what hys name myght be" (2:992.5), and his wife's shipbuilding ruse seems a curious answer to her husband's problem. Where the *Queste* assures narrative history will provide full understanding, Malory's modifications draw us into the narrative at certain points, but at others they signal the difficulty of recuperating continuity.

If Perceval's Sister has a historian's role, the story of the spindles suggests female history making. In the context of Hoccleve's proposed remedy for women's involvement in theology, the spindles are challenging and witty recraftings of scriptural events' miraculous recording. Malory, however, abbreviates the history of the Tree of Life to situate these events less clearly in an exegetical tradition. In the *Queste,* the trees, and human response to them, constitute God's covenant with His creation. Looper's positive reading of the *Queste* spindles suggests that in their charting of postlapsarian human history they promise society a reintegrative model of salvation, an alternative means of understanding the Fall, and this model competes with the text's dominant paradigm of spiritual elitism.[40] In Malory's synopsis, the tree's colors (for it is not clear, in the *Sankgreal,* when the one parent tree becomes several) refer primarily to historical events. It is because the virgin Eve planted it that the first tree is white (where the *Queste* here supplies a discourse on virginity and maidenhood). The tree turns green when Eve conceives Abel beneath it, and it turns red "in tokenyng of blood" (2:991.7) when Cain murders Abel. The reader has to supply narrative connection, with conventional biblical lore as with the Grail context, as Dean does when he sees an explicit mirroring of Arthurian history in scriptural history.[41] Yet, without readerly supplement, this starkly commemorative history does not readily translate into Arthurian time, nor is it straightforwardly apprehendable in broader narrative terms. The gendering of the "spindles" as female increases the effect of alienation in the context of the normatively masculine Grail narrative, but other artifacts convey a similar sense of discontinuity and confusion.

When it introduces the spindles, the *Sankgreal* adds to the paraphernalia of the Bed of the Ship of Faith two suspended swords (2:990.17). These unexplained swords' contiguity with the spindles invites speculation on masculine emblematic claims to historical control. Chivalric equipment clutters the *Sankgreal;* interestingly, the *Morte's* editorial commentary usually ascribes its proliferation to "misreading," and this masculine supplementarity may as often muddle, as facilitate, understanding. Launcelot straightforwardly regains his sword, helmet, and horse in metaphoric restoration of his chivalric selfhood after his confession (2:925.2–3), but Galahad gains an extra shield on the way to the Ship of Faith (2:983.20–22), and the restored Broken Sword at Corbenic takes on an unexplained numinous function (2:1027.30–33). The *Queste,* as Williams and Warren demonstrate, is careful to position swords and their histories in relation to its heroes. Galahad comes across several swords; at the beginning of the adventure, Lancelot knights his son, but Galahad, apparently rejecting the father, arrives at court without a sword, and claims the sword he draws from the floating stone as symbol of his election, while the Sword with the Strange Girdles images historically transcendent spirituality. As prelude to the climax of the narrative, Galahad, at Corbenic, mends the sword that wounded Joseph in the thigh (266; Lacy 4: 83–84). The final apportioning of swords is thematically appropriate; Galahad retains the Sword with the Strange Girdles, while Perceval gains the Sword in the Stone, and Bors (a chaste knight who has sinned carnally only once) the Broken Sword made whole.[42] Malory's version, however, disrupts the swords' historical and semantic continuity. Although, for example, Malory omits the *Queste* mention of how Perceval inherits the Sword in the Stone, it is not clear how Launcelot comes to possess this same sword that Merlin, in the Balin episode, destines for both him and Galahad.[43] There is no clear trajectory for Launcelot's sword. In a text intermittently careful about chivalric trappings (2:983.30–31; 1011.6), it seems as difficult for us to keep full track of swords as it is for Balin, in his adventure, to keep track of his.

The *Sankgreal* Sword with the Strange Girdles partakes of this disruption of event and artifact. It sinisterly incorporates in its fabric a rib from "the serpente of the fynde" (2:985.28–29), yet it signals the potential for wholeness where the *Queste* offers an instrument of divine proscription and justice, for the serpent-rib guarantees that whoever handles the sword will neither tire nor be hurt (2:985.30–31), whereas in the source it leaves the wielder immune to heat (202; Lacy 4:64). The bone of an exotic fish further promises the sword's wielder "so muche wyll that he shall never be wery" (2:985.34–986.1), whereas the French text asserts the warrior will forget everything but the task in hand (203; Lacy 4:64). In the *Queste,* the scabbard declares it must enter no vile or sinful place, or its bearer will regret it; but the wearer will receive no hurt in battle, on condition he carry it "nettement" (205; Lacy 4:65 translates "purely," Malory, "truly," 2:983.27). As Williams points out, the *Queste* explanation glosses the subsequent carnage at Carcelois, where Galahad takes bloody vengeance on the three brothers who violate and murder their sister (230; Lacy 4:73).[44] The *Sankgreal* account makes the sword less narratively referential in having it confirm the integrity of the destined Grail Knight. The gloss on its accoutrements also conflates social and moral in the promise that "the body of hym which I ought to hange by, he shall nat be shamed in no place whyle he ys gurde with the gurdyll" (2:987.28–30). In both *Sankgreal* and *Queste,* however, it is unclear to what extent the virtues of the hempen girdle will translate to the girdle that must replace it, and Perceval's Sister's girdle is ambivalent.

Several have noted the interrelation of male and female in both accounts of how Perceval's Sister completes Galahad's sword with her belt of hair,[45] but the French account is more ambiguous about divine appropriation of courtly imagery in this feminine encircling of the knightly. In the *Queste,* the woman's part in the girding of Galahad recalls the queen's sponsoring of Lancelot's sword (Micha 7:298; Lacy 2:71), and the scabbard's inscription blurs sexual and religious signs and values when it implicitly invites the virgin to fetishize that which she must deny in order to be fully spiritual, by asking that she make a girdle from "la riens de sus li que ele plus amera" [the thing on her person that she values most] (206; Lacy 4:65), her hair—although her sexuality ("riens") is surely also punningly at issue here, as the inscription puts the highest earthly price, her life, on the maintenance of her virginity. Malory's account does not insist on the girdle as doubly fetish and relic, but does give greater prominence to Perceval's Sister as explicator. It is perhaps coincidence that the Lollard author of the early fifteenth-century *Lanterne of Liȝt* comments on the figural significance of the girdle the faithful put around their loins, in St. Paul's list of "arms for the soul," in Ephesians 6.13: "þe first is a girdil of chastite. & þerbi mai we knowe þat Paul vsiþ þe witte of þe soule. & leeueþ bodili armour."[46] Yet, this aptly reflects Perceval's Sister's control of the bewildering sign system operative in the *Sankgreal.* Her completion of the marvel of the Sword of the Strange Girdles that replaces the sword Galahad drew from the stone assures us of the possibilities of interpretation, of a divinely inspired and underwritten hermeneutic. But New Testament

gloss and romance character part company where Perceval's Sister's readings of artifacts block access to, rather than facilitate, narrative understanding. The *Queste* Perceval's Sister names the scabbard "memory of blood,"
because it contains wood of the tree that memorializes Cain's slaying of
Abel (227; Lacy 4:72); her *Sankgreal* counterpart accords it the strange
nomenclature "mover of blood," which evokes continuing violence rather
than sacred history, and the strange explanation that "no man that hath
blood in hym ne shal never see that one party of the sheth whych was
made of the tree of lyffe" (2:995.16–18), suggests a distance between hu-
manity and the apprehension of sacred history.

Perceval's Sister's full account of the Sword with the Strange Girdles
also confuses the *Morte's* linear history. Integral to the Sword's violent history is another Dolorous Stroke, separate from the Stroke of Balin (who
has dealt *his* blow with what has become the Sword in the Floating Stone).
With the sword, King Hurlaine kills King Labor, father of the Maimed
King, and so makes Logres (which the *Morte* specifies as a liminal area, "the
londys of the two marchys" [2:987.11]) a Waste Land. Hurlaine is killed for
his presumption in returning to the Ship to fetch the scabbard. In the
Queste, Parlan, father to Pelles and therefore great-grandfather to Galahad,
is called the Maimed King, because of his own later Ship adventure, where
a lance wounds him as he attempts to draw the sword (209; Lacy 4:66). But
when Perceval's Sister tells this story, she identifies this character to Galahad as Pelles/Pelleaus, "youre grauntesyre" (2:990.14–15). Galahad, on
drawing the sword in the stone at the beginning of his quest, has declared
it his destiny to heal King Pelles; he identifies the weapon as the instrument of fratricide, for Balin slew Balan as a result of the "dolerous stroke"
Balin earlier gave Pelles (2:863.3–9). But in the *Sankgreal,* it is indeed Pellam, as the *Morte's* Balin episode itself asserts (1:82–86), and not the apparently sound Pelles, whom Balin wounds and whom Galahad later heals
(2:1030:33–1031.15).[47] Scribal error or authorial carelessness may explain
the entangling of father-son history,[48] but this does not solve the problem
of incompatible double founding moments of desolation. That the virgin
elect, Galahad and Perceval's Sister, should articulate versions of the historical level of the text different from, and ultimately disruptive of, the narrative we have already read, discourages reader understanding of historical
paradigms. Do we now follow this new history and "lay apart" the earlier
story? The alternative account of initiatory violence and redemptive patterning compounds confusion at the level of our grasp of narrative event
and explication; Perceval's Sister's death will raise further questions about
narrative disruption and completion.

The companions, after adventures that confirm them as the Grail elect,
arrive at a castle where the custom is that every young woman who passes

by must donate a dishful of her blood, in the hope of curing its leprous owner. In spite of resistance from the Grail knights, Perceval's sister sacrifices herself to heal this lady. The next day, divine intervention destroys the castle and its inhabitants. The *Queste* foregrounds the redundancy, both of Perceval's Sister's death, and of the custom of the castle, initiated in spite of a wise man's naming of Perceval's sister as the only woman capable of healing the sufferer (239; Lacy 4:75). The text both privileges and obscures Perceval's Sister's achievement; her death is extraordinary as a sacrificial episode divorced from the textual model of the sacramental, which latter promotes the Grail as repository of the Eucharist. It is perhaps, as Beckerling suggests, because the text is misogynistic that Perceval's Sister sacrifices herself to no apparent purpose, and so is denied the potential to figure redeemed womanhood fully, and attain the Grail.[49] The elements of *imitatio Christi,* however, combined with this character's eroticization, and the rehearsal of a gendered Salvation history that metatextually considers the nature and authorization of romance, suggest the *Queste,* through Perceval's Sister, registers daring claims to the transcendent power of romance's signifying systems. It then disingenuously occludes such claims by (no less misogynistically) embodying them in a female, narratively ill-accommodated character.

The *Sankgreal's* context for Perceval's Sister introduces a slippage between the sacrificial and the sacramental to reformulate what the Balin story has not resolved. Perceval's Sister's sacrifice fulfills the episode preceding Balin's Dolorous Stroke (in which Balin's damsel bleeds for, but cannot help, the Leprous Lady) as antecedent to Galahad's lifting of the curse on the Waste Land. Perceval's Sister dies to "gete me grete worship and soule helthe, and worship to my lynayge" (2:1002.30–32), and confirms the *Morte's* linear narrative prolepsis, which promises, in Balin's story, that Perceval's Sister will die to cure the lady (1:82.9–14). In chapter two, I suggested that the *Suite du Merlin,* recounting the history of the Dolorous Stroke, appropriates a model of divine retributive violence that Malory's Balin episode then undoes. The *Morte* severs the connections by which we can read Balin's depredations on the model of Salvation history, although it keeps in place the designation of Galahad as redeemer. Perceval's Sister's words (her account of the Dolorous Stroke) and actions (her sacrifice) respectively make redundant, and confirm, the Balin narrative, and her story, of violence to women, returns us urgently to the questions about the moral legitimization of violence the Balin episode generates.

If this Grail story is obfuscatory, a fifteenth-century devotional context can more easily accommodate Perceval's Sister's gendered model of sanctity. Her bleeding allies her with women saints and holy individuals whose blood is credited with miraculous powers.[50] Richard Kieckhefer sees fifteenth-century male hagiography, meanwhile, as having little investment in a vocabulary of engagement with the terms of Christ's physical body, reserving interest instead for miracles—that can themselves involve Christ-as-man or Christ-as-child—of the consecration of the host at mass,[51] manifestations the *Sankgreal* reflects in its Grail scenes. An extratextual religious context supplies some of the disjunctions of the account of Perceval's Sister's career; for example, the earthquake and the destruction of the castle attendant on her death (2:1004.14–1005.10), find analogues in the New Testament narrative of Christ's Passion, or the Old Testament destruction of wicked cities.[52] For Hoffman, the female protagonist's *imitatio* exposes Galahad's own failure at emulation of the Divine,[53] but Perceval's Sister, by embodying recognizable forms of spiritual emulation that then do not translate into sustained Arthurian narrative, perhaps rather more disturbingly draws general attention to the gaps between Grail narrative and orthodox spiritual paradigms. Her revision of history also brings the nature and purpose of Arthurian narrative into question. In the context of the *Morte*'s heightened awareness of the masculine physical, the later Urry episode reads in part as if to compensate for the way Perceval's Sister's sacrifice demarcates the limits of male chivalric Arthurian epistemology.

Perceval's Sister organizes her postmortem trajectory, asking that she be put in a mysterious ship, which will take her body to Sarras, where the knights will achieve the Grail, and where they must bury her (2:1003.21–29). Narrative echo reformulates the certainties of the masculine world. Her watery dispatch and the handheld written account of her adventures recall Harmaunce's provision for his corpse in the *Tristram,* and so mark the distance between the commemorative aspect of the Grail story and chivalric "felyship" 's ability to translate text and generate narrative in that earlier episode. Perceval's Sister's body, and the access to the Divine she represents, thus detach themselves from the rest of the Grail story. But on its way to Sarras, Perceval's Sister's body contiguously figures limitation and grace for Launcelot, who enters the ship. Through the letter he learns of the narrative denied him, and the ship marks the next stage of Launcelot's attempt at reintegration with the Divine, for it is here that figural and literal are conjoined, in his first address to Christ as "Swete Fadir" (2:1011.17),[54] and in his emotional reunion with his son (2:1012.16–23).

Spirituality and Paternal Anxiety

Chapter four addressed Launcelot's denial of volition in engendering Galahad as part of how the *Morte* constructs the hero in resistance to his French counterpart, whose trajectory he must follow. The reader then has to keep in play a complex range of "knowledges" about Launcelot. The *Sankgreal* co-opts Launcelot's parenthood into a nexus of secrecy and revelation that involves both spiritual and social knowledge and practices, and relates un-easily to Launcelot's attempts to cast himself spiritually as a "child" of God. Malory's motifs and metaphors of fatherhood in the *Sankgreal* intersect with fifteenth-century accounts of God the Father, but I want also to set the complexity of such imagery against the occlusions one meets in the work of Lacan, who defines the child's relation to the symbolic Father as the necessary means to enculturation. Lacan and Malory compare inter-estingly in that each appears to be working simultaneously in conformity with and against already available paradigms, whether literary or psycho-analytical. Lacan's occlusion of the biological father in his account of en-culturation offers an interesting counternarrative for Malory's treatment of biological fatherhood. The Grail itself invites psychoanalytical interpreta-tion as the object desire for which is constituted by its very absence,[55] al-though the association of the Grail with the Eucharist complicates this interpretation, for Aquinas explores the importance of the faithful's consti-tutive desire, in relation to the sacrament of the Eucharist, as a two-way process.[56] Attention to Lacan's assumption of a particularly masculinist en-culturation model may, however, also uncover something of the anxieties surrounding the *Sankgreal*'s investment in the literal.

Lacan bases his work on Freud's Oedipus complex, but where Freud grounds his view of the symbolic in human social order,[57] the Father for Lacan has (ostensibly) a symbolic function only. According to Lacan, the developing child finds that it is not loved for itself, and so desires to be the other's desire, but the mother desires the phallus, which the child cannot provide. The child then learns that it has to desire to be something that it is not in order to satisfy the desire of the mother. At the same time, the mother is exposed as "lacking," in that she herself has no phallus. The phal-lus (the Name of the Father) denotes the linguistic and cultural structures that constitute us as subjects. Entry into this symbolic order can only take place if the bond between mother and child is broken by the intervention of the taboo against incest, the Law of the Father, from outside this rela-tion. The Law of the Father is seen as the founding act of culture, and the incest taboo, reinforced by the threat of castration, forces the child into ex-istence as a cultured and gendered subject.[58] Jane Flax suggests that Lacan is disingenuous, and that Freud, in his originary idea of competition be-tween men in *Totem and Taboo,* which lies at the heart of a patriarchal psy-choanalytic explanation of the constructed self, is being more honest than the later thinker who claims there is no relation between the order of the symbolic and the historical, biological, father, for the "phallus" clearly "de-pends for its rhetorical effect" on its equivalence with "penis."[59] Lacan ar-gues that gender identity is a purely cultural construct, but he also employs masculine terms that place the father and his position always beyond the reach in inquiry: "Hence, male dominance becomes unanalyzable in theory and inescapable in practice."[60] Gilbert Chaitin's account, conversely, reads the phallus as operative at the level of impossibility, as displacement and fantasy.[61] Yet, Lacan's language returns us inevitably to the physical. The interest for Malory's text lies precisely in the continuing slippages between literal and figurative, and the implications of a deconstructionist phallic enterprise for a paradigm of the dynamics of power.

The *Sankgreal* may appear to occupy a more straightforwardly Freudian than Lacanian space in its simultaneous presentation of fathers divine and human. But rather than inscribe a human anxiety about the gap between the powers of the historical father and those of the divine (as might Freud), Malory, like Lacan, deploys a masculinist paradigm that functions on an uncritical and unconsidered (or even denied) dimension that has implications for our interpretation of the rest of the plot. Robert Con Davis has argued that Western culture seeks to privilege the father as discourse, but that it is in the narrativizing of the symbolic father that tensions emerge: the desire for stasis, for God as embodiment of justice and law, for example, conflicts with His "performative function in Christian narratives."[62] If Lacan leaves his language of the symbolic unexamined, Malory's narrative in part acts out the problem of situating the father that Lacan's master text does not want to address, and in doing so it registers a distress with human relations and their broader significance. Malory's account highlights the paradoxical status of Launcelot's fatherhood as sign of election and ground of sin. Stacey Hahn charts a progressively sinful and accountable Vulgate lineage for Lancelot, which the New Law of the *Queste* (and the Vulgate Cycle surrounding it) redeems.[63] Malory, in displacing narrative and teleology, partially dismantles this appropriative imitation of Salvation history. He famously "rescues" Launcelot from some of the *Queste* hermits' more humiliating castigations, but this also contributes to the ambiguity of Launcelot's position, as does the hero's attempt to write himself as a child of God.

In the *Queste,* the whole court speculates on a paternity the body and features of Galahad declare through their similarity to Lancelot's. Malory's version preserves some of the mystery of his origins for the Round Table knights, who "wyst nat frome whens he com but all only be God" (2:861.9–10).[64] Launcelot, meanwhile, appears to recognize his son (2:861.13–14), and Galahad responds to Guinevere that his father "shall be knowyn opynly and all betymys" (2:870.3–4). Later, a "good man" urges Launcelot to make his fatherhood of Galahad "knowyn opynly" (2:930.25).[65] In the *Sankgreal,* the knowledge of Galahad's paternity shares a vocabulary of revelation with Galahad in his role as "good knight," whom Evelake wishes to see "opynly" before he dies (2:908.25–34), and with the

Grail, which Gawain wants to see "more opynly" (2:866.10–11).[66] The presentation of Launcelot-as-father as privileged information enhances his "earthly" status. The *Queste* plays on literal and metaphoric levels of understanding, where Malory's text, allusive and metonymic, charts human sympathies and spiritual desires obliquely, because it fashions them within an emphasis on the literal that, confusingly for some of the quest participants, is intermittently co-opted for allegorical usage. For all the positive recognition of Launcelot's position as father, the father-son relation (in contrast to the idiom of the *Queste* as of fifteenth-century spirituality[67]) also marks the terms of Launcelot's exclusion from the full mysteries of the Grail; yet the episode of the healing of Sir Urry later crystallizes the ambivalence of Launcelot's treatment.

Boethius's Lady Philosophy informs her pupil that we create our God within the limits of our knowledge: "alle thing that is iwist nis nat knowen by his nature propre, but by the nature of hem that comprehenden it."[68] Romans 8.16 affirms: "For the Spirit himself giveth testimony to our spirit that we are the sons of God." The masculinist *Queste* deploys the name of God-the-Father within a scripturally approved metaphor of spiritual family for the Grail seekers. The faithful are all Children of a sustaining God-the-Father, and are also, as a hermit reminds Perceval, children of the Church (102; Lacy 4:34). The motif of father-son hatred describes the sinful state of the world at the time of the Incarnation, which is why the Heavenly Father sends to earth His own Son, whom Galahad imitates (37–38; Lacy 4:14), and the text characterizes a troubled society in similar terms, contrasting Perceval's piety with the violent mores of Wales, where sons kill their sick fathers rather than suffer the "dishonor" of having them die in their beds (95; Lacy 4:32). The father-son metaphor of religious language figures a compensatory, ideal, spiritual relation, in historical times of strife. So Perceval asks God to help him as a father might nurture his son (95; Lacy 4:32), and Bors invokes the same relation when he seeks counsel from a priest, in lieu of Christ as spiritual father (164; Lacy 4:53). Lancelot has a vision in which God appears to denounce him as not his true son, but to welcome Galahad as a beloved son (131; Lacy 4:43). The *Queste* makes explicit to Lancelot the nature of his exclusion. It also stresses individual moral responsibility, and so overturns the Prose *Lancelot* claim that Lancelot is unworthy to complete the adventures his son will perform because he is being punished for his own father's sin,[69] and stresses that Lancelot's own prayers are of more profit to him than are Galahad's (138–39; compare *Morte*, 2:931:1–6).[70] In its reworking of human relations to envisage the Divine, the *Queste* makes all the faithful the children of God, and distinguishes the elect as God's chivalric "servants," an appellation Lancelot finally receives just prior to his reunion with his son on the

Ship of Faith (249: Lacy 4:78). Lancelot and Galahad's parting words to each other invoke filial relations human and divine—they address each other as "sires" and "filz," and call God "Nostre Sires" (which can translate as both "Lord" and "Father")—but also transcend these relations with the pious wish that each may do well in God's knightly service (252; Lacy 4:79). Galahad's final words, that no prayer is more efficacious than one's own, emphasizes individual agency above the claims of genealogy.

Aquinas points out that no name or form of address is adequate to describe God, for while there is scriptural precedent for naming God as Father, He is beyond our knowledge, so we can only very loosely apprehend God and our relation to him.[71] Fifteenth-century vernacular devotional literature, however, vigorously deploys the parent-child relation as analogue for relations between the human and the Divine, most commonly (and unsurprisingly) in commentary on the fourth commandment and on the "Our Father." *Dives and Pauper,* like the *Queste,* makes a theological point by contrasting earthly and heavenly parenthood; thus we learn that the gospel injunction to hate one's parents and follow Christ obtained at a time "whan nyh3 al þe fadris & moodrys wern in fals belue & in dedly synne."[72] *Dives* also makes filial obedience the model for social conformity and the prerequisite for peace, the "principal cause of sauacion of londys, rewmys, & comountes," and urges us to understand that God is both father and mother to us, "& þerfor we arn boundyn to louyn hym & to worchepyn hym abouyn alle þinge."[73]

When Malory dismantles much of the *Queste*'s parent-child exegetical apparatus, and many of its minor characters' references to God as parent, the remaining gloomy troping of historical father-son relations emerges as the more negative. Mention of intergenerational strife, when "the fadir loved nat the sonne, nother the sonne loved nat the fadir" (2:882.32–33), comes to share more with chronicle than with Salvation history and pious commentary.[74] At the same time, a selective invocation of the Father is especially freighted, in a text that also stresses the importance of Launcelot's fatherhood, and has Launcelot address God as Father—and Galahad addresses Launcelot, "swete fadir," as Launcelot addresses God [2:1013.23; 1011.17]—but does not have God reciprocally call Launcelot His Son. This vocabulary of parenthood makes Launcelot's exclusion more poignant. The address "my trew chyldren," is uniquely reserved for the Grail knights, to whom Christ explains that they are to bear the Grail to Sarras, for all others are unworthy, "and therefore I shall disherite them of the honoure whych I have done them" (2:1030.28–29).[75] Even the Grail knights' status is later qualified—they are "My sunnes, and nat my chyeff sunnes" (2:1031.18).[76] In the *Sankgreal,* the naming of God as Father intensifies in the events leading to Launcelot's limited vision of the Grail.

Launcelot transgresses the prohibition to enter on the Grail scene at Corbenic in order to act on his impulse to help an aged priest, apparently laboring under his eucharistic burden, and cries out: "Fayre Fadir, Jesu Cryste, ne take hit for no synne if I helpe the good man whych hath grete nede of helpe." (2:1016.5–6). His subsequent punishment seems both privilege and rebuke, of a piece with the argument of the late-medieval devotional work, *The Chastising of God's Children,* that God's withdrawal of love may be token of His affection, just as a mother plays with her child by hiding from him, only to reappear and console him.[77] Launcelot certainly interprets his Grail experience as a divine gift (2:1017.6–9). If Launcelot's spiritual impulses cannot transcend the physical, the text at the last withholds the fulfillment of the model for spiritual community it has invoked, and a gap remains between biological and spiritual fatherhood.

John Lydgate's "Exposition of the Pater Noster" describes the faithful as "goostly children," to whom the word *father* gives courage to petition Him, in all obedience, for help, that we might come to share in His inheritance.[78] Lydgate presents his pious poem as a translation open to correction by all who hear it, but his aureate diction also co-opts literary paternity into the spiritual exercise, in his closing image of himself as a rhetorical "glenere on a large lond Among shokkys plentyvous of auctours," eager to gather flowers, only to find "the grene was repen."[79] This nod to the imagery of Chaucer's *Legend of Good Women*[80] suggests a consonance of literary and spiritual authorizations and imitations. The shared language of source and *Sankgreal,* meanwhile, emphasizes the distance between the texts. Grace Armstrong Savage claims for father-son relations (and specifically the Lancelot-Galahad connection) in the *Queste,* a reassuring continuity between chivalric valor and Christian heroism.[81] The emphasis in the *Sankgreal* on the father-son tie, conjoined with the problematizing of its metaphoric power, figures the text's uncertain inheritance of the *Queste*'s form and ideology. The paternal as metaphor for the Divine does not elucidate the numinous as much as split the historical world from the spiritual world.

The gulf between the narrative's engagement with Launcelot as father, and the intimation that spiritually he is a rejected son, is of a piece with a narrative methodology that, perhaps because it does not make straightforward equivalences between narrative levels, intimates an interior spiritual identity for Launcelot that remains inexplicit. In both versions of the Grail narrative, for example, when the hero recovers from his vision at Corbenic, he worries that he is no longer wearing his hair shirt (*Queste* 258–59 [Lacy 4:81]; *Morte* 2:1017.16–1018.9). In the *Queste,* Lancelot has received this shirt as part of his penance, and it emblematizes his spiritual quest, as those of the castle of Corbenic recognize. Its removal recalls the experience of its earlier owner, a hermit found dead, and without his hair shirt (and so feared to be an apostate), but a raised devil explains that his family's enemies despoiled him. The lack of the shirt is not then the sign of the hermit's spiritual failing but his enemies' doing. In the tradition of the Saint's Life, the hermit's body has remained inviolable to sword or fire (*Queste* 118–22; Lacy 4:39–40). A labored exposition of the relation between inner and outer becomes part of Lancelot's education, in a sermon that reads him as an exemplary figure; like the dead hermit, his circumstances are reread, for he now learns that where he was a model of rectitude, he is now a warning against lechery. Guenièvre as romance heroine is recast as evil seductress.[82] The lecherous Lancelot joins the long line of eminent men brought low by women, from Adam and Solomon to Samson and Absalom (125; Lacy 4:41). Romance and clerical misogyny retell man's history to reaffirm the text's metaphorics and to show how the extraordinary adventure is, after all, an all-too familiar story. Yet, Lancelot's counselor gives him the hermit's shirt, an outward sign of inward grace that is also talismanic, for as long as he wears it he will not commit a mortal sin (*Queste* has "ne pecheroiz mortelment," 129; Lacy 4:42 translates as "you will commit no further sin"). This (in orthodox religious terms) preposterous story interweaves antithetical and complementary readings. The dead hermit exemplifies the virtues of both the active and the contemplative life; Lancelot is condemned, but has the means to redemption, and the hair shirt also marks him out as one whom God chastises because He loves him most.

The *Morte* version removes most of the episode's interpretive apparatus, which makes more curious the account of the dead hermit, and imparts a greater sense of an interior spiritual life for Launcelot. In the *Sankgreal,* the old man's virtue appears the more potent, because it is not exhaustively explained and used as the point of departure to castigate the hero. The vindication of the old man's righteousness centers on his body rather than on readings of what he might signify, and the saintly man's inviolate body is the ultimate proof that he has not, as his fellow religious had feared, transgressed his rule (2:925.1–927.6). Similarly, Launcelot's behavior is not here read off against a series of exemplifications of vice and virtue. Instead, the emphasis is on human sympathy, on penitence and remorse rather than on condemnation, the denunciation of the sinner, and the superstitious magic accredited a saint's relics. Malory's spiritual counselor to Launcelot treats him with a certain indulgence; he tells him he would be "more abeler than ony man lyvynge" (2:927.15–16), were it not for his sin. His promise that the man's hair shirt "shall prevayle the gretly" (2:927.27) maintains a delicate balance between the material object's efficacy and the individual's own responsibility to avoid sin. The lack of explicit relation between the episode of the holy man and Launcelot's spiritual progress adds to the privacy and dignity of the sequence, hinting at the possibility of a spiritual development that the narrative does not openly articulate, just as the narrative is silent on the subject of any public response to Launcelot's donning his hair shirt again after the events at Corbenic (2:1017.27–1018.9). The Urry episode, which in some respects registers and compensates for the *Sankgreal's* suspension of divine response to Launcelot, revisits this earlier narrative's method.

The Healing of Sir Urry

As the *Sankgreal* denies Launcelot the Grail in its plenitude, the episode of the "Healing of Sir Urry" (3:1145–54), a coda to the "Knight of the Cart" episode and immediately before the inception of Agravain and Mordred's plot against the hero, compensates for Launcelot's relative failure on the Grail quest by extending divine grace to earthly values. The "Healing of Urry" demonstrates Launcelot's status as "best knight" and God's instrument. The Urry story is related prior to Launcelot's sustained control of his reputation—the summary substitutive of the declared loss of the "Shyvalere de Charyot" adventures explains that for a year he rides in an execution cart in defiance of those who seek to shame him (3:1154.3–8)—and immediately before those events that will lose him his good name. The Urry episode imparts a ritualistic power to the accretion of narrative event, in the famous roll call of knights who attempt to heal their fellow, and makes the chivalric, and Launcelot as its representative, the recipient of God's grace. Nothing in the French texts matches the story exactly; the germ of the episode, however, lies in a witty disquisition on the difficulty of locating both Lancelot and his chivalric selfhood's power, in a Prose *Lancelot* adventure that intercalates with Lancelot's apprehension of Galahad's preeminence, as the narrative prepares for the Grail adventures and their transcendent values. The Urry episode implicitly revisits the terms of the French hero's definition in that sequence, and reconceptualizes chivalric violence. In the famous image of Launcelot's weeping in response to the healing of Urry, the event also calls on the *Sankgreal's* complex of religious imagery in which God figures for Launcelot as (absent) parent, imagery that now, implicitly, and outside the space of the Grail quest, recognizes Launcelot as a "son of God." At the same time, for modern readers, psychoanalysis may supplement the religious frame of reference to elucidate this dense and difficult image of Launcelot as beaten child, to comment on what it reveals of the *Morte's* narration.

Urry's career and healing occupy the spatial coordinates of the continental European chivalric world, although its exact chronological placing is more difficult to determine. Having killed Sir Alpheus at a Spanish tournament, the Hungarian Urry falls victim to Alpheus's mother's magic arts, whereby his "seven grete woundis" (3:1145.13) will not heal "untyll the beste knyght of the worlde had serched" them (3:1145.19–20), and his own mother takes her son on a seven-year quest to find the cure. Urry painfully embodies the effects of violence, but his siting between powerful maternal wills offers an obfuscatory chivalric fantasy of violence as an impersonal event, rather than the enthusiastic male performance of a masculine ideology. Launcelot, as channel of healing, remakes Urry as figure of chivalric cohesion and wholeness, and simultaneously remakes the integrity of the Arthurian court:

> Than sir Launcelot kneled downe by the wounded knyghte [. . .] And than he hylde up hys hondys and loked unto the este, saiynge secretely unto hymselff, "Now, Blyssed Fadir and Son and Holy Goste, I beseche The [. . .] yeff me power to hele thys syke knyght by the grete vertu and grace of The, but, Good Lorde, never of myselff." [. . .] and forthwithall the woundis fayre heled [. . .]. And than the laste of all he serched hys honde, and anone it fayre healed [. . .] Than kynge Arthur and all the kynges and knyghtes kneled downe and gave thankynges and lovynge unto God and unto Hys Blyssed Modir. And ever sir Launcelote wepte, as he had bene a chylde that had bene beatyn." (3:1152.16–36; Vinaver's apostrophe omitted)

The healing of secular wounds through grace dignifies the effects of violence and partakes in that same strategy of disavowal as does the feminine framing and control of Urry's body. Urry emerges implicitly as a fantasy figure, in his embodiment of divine grace extended to earthly structures and values.

In using the female to obviate male agency, Malory limits Urry's narrative function in comparison with his source prototype; he has displaced onto Launcelot the more complex negotiations of wholeness and gender that involve the "knight in the litter" of the Vulgate. Launcelot, like the knight in the litter, is earlier wounded by a woman, although in different circumstances (3:1104.3–1105.6).[83] In the *Lancelot,* a knight recounts to the hero how a maiden has wounded him in the thigh, in surprising defense of an opponent he is pursuing, and another lady has said that only the best knight in the world can remove the arrow. The knight refuses to allow Lancelot to touch him, because he is not the best knight (Micha 5:66–69; Lacy 3:226). Learning of his error from King Bademagu, the hapless invalid spends some time following Lancelot through adventures that variously pose and answer the question of who deserves the title of "best knight." On his travels, Lancelot, chosen and found lacking, learns the limits of his ability as "good knight." His grandfather, in a vision, directs him to the Perilous Forest, but when he finds his grandfather's tomb there, Lancelot learns that although he is now the best knight, another will surpass him (Micha 5:130–31; Lacy 3:240). When the knight finally catches up with Lancelot, at the edge of the forest, on the margin of secular adventures, he lifts his hands to him in supplication "just as if Lancelot were God Himself" (Micha 5:181; Lacy 3:252). Lancelot heals him peremptorily, modest but not surprised at his ability to act as vehicle of God's grace, and tells the recovered knight to thank God, for "ce est plus par sa volente er par vos merites que par bonte que je aie en moi" [it is more through His will and your own merits than through any goodness I have in me] (Micha 5:181; Lacy 3:252). This power is of a piece with the Vulgate's occasional appropriations of the hagiographic to celebrate the chivalric.[84] With Galahad's advent, however, the French text must reaccommodate Lancelot's "good knighthood" to the next stage of the story. Nothing in Lancelot's appearance, for example, has at first sight inspired the wounded knight with confidence that this the knight he seeks. And if the romance is trying to find an appropriate space for Lancelot, it appears here to endorse the narrative trajectory itself as the surest location for knightly identity, and the retracing of the hero's steps as the efficacious means to physical and chivalric integrity and wholeness, as in the episode of Pedivere, which Malory makes part of his early Launcelot narratives, as we saw in chapter three.

Urry's healing, by contrast, takes place in public, and Urry's body's explicitly recognizes Launcelot's power: "my harte gyvith me more unto hym than to all thes that hath serched me" (3:1151.15–16). Urry's wounds sparely invoke the *Morte*'s somatic imagery, as we noted in chapter two with regard to Balin and Balan's hurts. While Urry's great wounds recall and by implication redeem the brothers' injuries, his hand wound (given the economy with which such a wound features in the *Morte*) is particularly associated with Launcelot's own sense of chivalric integrity. The nature of Urry's wounds draws together issues of social integration, moral integrity and the numinous; their healing signals reintegration for Launcelot after his own wounding at the bars of Guinevere's window at Meleagaunt's castle has called his integrity into question.[85] Yet, Urry's wounds also have extratextual religious resonance. While devotion to the five wounds of Christ is widespread, there are Christological associations, too, for the number seven. Thomas Brinton's late-fourteenth-century Good Friday sermon notes Christ sheds blood seven times, and Old Testament typology prefigures these episodes of bleeding.[86] Latin and vernacular traditions also associate the suffering Christ's left hand with human altruism and with divine grace. A Middle English prayer to Christ's wounds has the petitioner pray the wound on the left hand will preserve one from the sin of envy, and make one mindful of the "profit bodely & gostely" of others.[87] St. Gertrude, in *Legatus Divinae Pietatis*, specifically associates devotion to Christ's left hand with the third verse of Psalm 102, which praises the curative powers of the Lord, who "healeth all thy diseases," an apt association for the Urry episode.[88] Prayers link the left hand with God as "well of grace" or "well of mercy."[89] Launcelot prays to God that He might heal him through His "vertu and grace" (3:1152.24). The wound to Urry's left hand, then, which Launcelot heals last, both relates to the integrity of Launcelot himself, for whose body Urry's is here surrogate, and sacramentalizes the ideology of "felyship" operative in the *Morte* and dependent, as Andrew Lynch has imaginatively explored it, on good will.[90] Mutually reenforcing religious and textual imagery projects a chivalric wholeness. But while the French romance ultimately justifies Lancelot through its own narrative procedures, Malory's list of knights and their related adventures, invoked in the roll call of those summoned to heal Urry, accords a ritualistic status to textual event, yet emphasizes a divide between that narrative event (which, as we saw with the confusion of Palomides and Priamus, is also prey to inaccuracy) and the grace the Divine here offers the Arthurian world through Launcelot.[91]

The image of Launcelot weeping like a beaten child carries a highly complex range of associations for our interpretation of this episode. The Prose *Lancelot* provides a subtextual historical resonance for comparing Launcelot to a beaten child, in an event that establishes a particular relation between violence and nobility. The precocious and (the narration pointedly tells us) extremely well-mannered child Lancelot, after a hunting expedition has led him into unexpected adventures in the forest, is unjustly punished by his tutor, who strikes him, but it is in outrage at the latter's bad treatment of a greyhound that Lancelot beats him in his turn. When called to account for himself, the young Lancelot threatens further extreme violence against his tutor. The Lady of the Lake tolerates his aggressive behavior and so justifies the aristocratic regulation and exercise of violence as confirmation of his nobility; the event registers Lancelot's entry into manhood and his chivalric autonomy (Micha 7:81–86; Lacy 2:20–22). The Vulgate sanctions the child's violent behavior but the *Morte* figures Launcelot in an episode that exposes chivalry's violent agency, only to disavow its effects.

The only other character who weeps like a child in the *Morte* is Arthur, joyful at Gareth's return to his court after his adventures (1:358.19–20). The idiom occupies an analogous position in the narrative apparatus of the happy ending of Gareth's story, which the Urry episode imitates in that it effects and celebrates social integration with a tournament and a wedding (3:1153.7–24). Whiting lists only one other incidence of a simile of a *beaten* child for Middle English literature, the evocation of the childish petulance of the thwarted and deeply humiliated Absolon in Chaucer's *Miller's Tale*.[92] The Chaucerian example contrasts with Malory, for Absolon's tears suggest lack of awareness, rather than an inner life (and the ironic resonance of his name requires rather different investigation in terms of father-son relations). Recourse to the fifteenth-century language of human-divine relations, however, interestingly illuminates Launcelot's condition as a special child whom God chastises. The literature of parenthood, following biblical prescription, makes much of chastisement as an act of love; *The Chastising of God's Children* tells us that the more mothers love their children, the more they beat them, and that God strikes His chosen children "bittirli": "For as oure lord seieþ himself, he chastiseþ whom he loueþ."[93] The simile suggests Launcelot is just such a "chosen" child, and that his experience is redemptive. A fifteenth-century reader might well supply from devotional treatises an interpretation of Launcelot's response as tears of contrition and of compunction in the face of God's love. The *Contemplations of the Dread and Love of God* explains how the abject sinner regrets behavior that alienates her/him from God: "Compunccion is a gret lowenes of þe soule, spiringe out from þin herte wiþ teres of þin eynen, whan þou biþenkest þe uppon þi sinnes and uppon þe dredful dom of God."[94] One may read Launcelot as channel of God's grace, and interpret his role as compensatory of his *Sankgreal* experience. If the terms of Launcelot's paternity of Galahad do not quite square with a divine symbolic fatherhood, the image of Launcelot as castigated child at least brings him back into metaphoric spiritual relation with the Divine. The inarticulacy of Launcelot's response, however, urges us to supplement the narrative with a recreation of Launcelot's spiritual feeling.

The medieval idiom of the beaten child also recalls, for the modern reader, Freud's essay, "A Child is Being Beaten," with its extended discussion of masochistic fantasy, which to some extent revisits the ambivalence of pain and love with regard to one's relation to a figure in authority that the imagery of fifteenth-century devotional literature already addresses. Freud considers boys' and girls' fantasies of injury to others within the context of the Oedipus complex. Remarkable about his analysis is the way he "supplies" narrative for his analysands necessary to the logical development of his psychoanalytical exposition of fantasies of substitution, sexual jealousy, and humiliation.[95] Jeffrey Cohen introduces his study of the lovers in masochistic contract in Chrétien de Troyes's *Lancelot* with the contention that "Masochism and the creation of narratives which embody something extra, some necessary *surplus,* are always intertwined."[96] The need to "supply" something is integral also to our understanding of Malory's dense simile for Launcelot's response to healing Urry, and makes the simile paradigmatic of the reader's work in the *Morte,* while the Vulgate narrative already overtly polices and accommodates sexual and emotional *surplus.* It makes possible, too, the wide range of critical responses to the phrase, from an indictment of Launcelot to interpretation of his tears as nostalgic.[97] Issues of surrogacy and displacement, essential to Freud's investigation of beating fantasies, are also crucial to our access to the simile (which is also a narratorial evaluation). Kaja Silverman rigorously exposes the slippages in Freud's treatment of male and female participation in such fantasies, and the problems it raises with regard to female sexuality, and reminds us that the observing of the children being beaten, in female fantasy, is primarily the story of the person who is looking on, and whose relation to the action— that of controlling onlooker, or identifier with the beaten—in Freud's account, remains "irresolute."[98] This psychoanalytical narrative of engagement and spectatorship offers an oblique but telling illumination of Malory's simile, which functions on one level as authorial fantasy. This is not to suggest that the relation between Launcelot and the narrator is masochistic, but that perhaps this condensed, fantasized, exteriorized effect of violence, removed from the chivalric context, yet suggestive of Launcelot's "control" by a higher authority, together with its lack of explicit glossing, startlingly reconfigures for us the question of our relation to Launcelot's body and offers writer and reader a stark image of our complex and partial apprehension of the narrative and our participation with it.

To make sense of the simile, we turn to the interpretive contexts of our own reading. The description of Launcelot's weeping response to the act of grace that obscures the relation between violence and agency is also the signal of, and means to, authorial and reader creativity—it is we who have to "explain" why Launcelot should cry like a child. If the episode of the healing of Urry is a "pageant of unwholeness," as Catherine La Farge calls it, as much as an assertion of chivalric integrity,[99] it is partly because this narratorial aside on Launcelot, a subjective view on him which is also our means of access to him, holds in suspension for us the relations between the constitutive elements of Arthurian legend. A straightforward teleology for the Grail is seemingly not recoverable, yet the members of this Arthurian court are recipients of grace. Rather than rewriting the religious in terms of the chivalric, or reworking the *Queste* methodically in terms of late-medieval lay spiritual interests, Malory questions epistemologies, poised between the desire for assimilation of, and resistance to, the terms available for the constitution of Arthurian narrative, and the Urry episode, as a postscript to the *Sankgreal* material, exemplifies this tension. It reaffirms an ideological faith in the somatic, and in the affective, with the image of the beaten child as the point of supplementarity, for narrator as for reader. Urry's body and Launcelot's inscrutable reaction crystallize for us the hermeneutic difficulties of the *Morte* in general, and Launcelot's role especially indicates something of the problematics of exemplarity that Malory will continue to explore in the rest of his narrative.

CHAPTER 6

DISPLACED PERSONS:
READERS, LOVE, DEATH,
AND COMMEMORATION

The celebration of Arthurian chivalric cohesion through the healing of Sir Urry declares embodiment the site of chivalric value, and Urry's partial imitation of Gareth articulates a faith in Arthurian narrative, but the episode also suggests that the Arthurian tales, "rehearsed" *in parvo* in the roll call of the knights, find coherence, not (as in the French romances) by virtue of their juxtaposition in a fully authorized narrative, or through their replication of similar trajectories, but primarily through an unexplained act of grace. The Urry episode reassuringly remakes the chivalric and Arthurian body, but this ritual remaking is in tension with the suggestive image of the weeping Launcelot, which detail problematically constitutes the means to our apprehension of the hero's selfhood. The terms of our narrative engagement with this episode make it impossible, then, for us to recuperate it as a straightforward divine endorsement of the Arthurian world. Other sequences in the post-*Sankgreal* section of the *Morte* invite further examination in terms of displacement and defamiliarization, even as they urge engagement and commemoration. The May passage, as we saw in the preface, intimates that the very tropes and readerly training that supposedly allow us access to the narrative will frustrate our sympathies. I want to use Chaucer's *Prologue* to the *Legend of Good Women* as a specific reference point for examining Malory's conceptualization, in the May passage, of Arthurian legend as a means to recognizing the difficulties of understanding the past in ways that can change or shape our present. I want also to pursue the implications of this narratorial positioning for our readerly reception of Launcelot and Guinevere as lovers, which in turn will lead to an exploration of how the narrative displaces Guinevere from roles already "rehearsed" for her earlier in the *Morte*. Guinevere's displacement in relation to social and legal institutions expresses itself through evocations (and interruptions) of her bodily placement in spectacle and pageantry, that themselves pose questions about representation and meaning. The *Morte* also sustains a tension between commemoration and the notion of chivalric embodiment on which it has based its epistemology, in its presentation of death and burial rites. Although such rites accord in general terms with fifteenth-century practice, Launcelot's body is made central to funerary ceremony (sometimes with disregard to common practice), as if to test the reach of his signification. Ultimately, I want to suggest that Malory's mode of narration is not "historical," in that his disjunctions—in terms of rhetoric, institutions, characters, and readers—make it difficult to read the *Morte*'s events as historical commentary, or an allegory for his own times. Rather, his project of partial recuperation and commemoration raises important questions about the very possibility of historical and political language, about the limits of writing as a mode of knowing.

The May Passage

The May passage self-reflexively meditates on what it means to recuperate Arthurian legend, and Mark Lambert for one finds its tone predominantly nostalgic.[1] However, this passage also delegates to the reader a less than nostalgic responsibility for the text's making. Mention of a spring topos might bring to mind texts other than Chaucer's for a fifteenth-century reader making connections across writings.[2] The Prose *Merlin*, for example, includes a no-less literarily aware description of spring, which acts contextually to signal new hope for national stability, when Lot's sons go to join Arthur in his fight against the Saxons, at a time when "woods and gardens are in bloom and the meadows turn green again with new grass shoots and all kinds of sweet-smelling flowers among them [. . .] and newly-awakened love gladdens youths and maidens whose hearts are made merry and gay by the sweetness of this time of renewal" (*Merlin* 134; Lacy 1:240). And when Malory later reinvokes this first May passage with his note that the season sets the scene for "grete angur and unhappe" (3:1161.7), he is drawing on a well-established contrastive literary deployment of the spring topos. To compare Malory's exposition of Maytime with Chaucer's language in the *Prologue* to the *Legend of Good Women*, however, affords a sharper focus on how Malory, like Chaucer, concerns himself with the status of the book. Malory differs from Chaucer in that his interest lies more in the accountability of the reader (and the narrator as reader), than in the issue of authorial responsibility. But, as with Chaucer, there is also an interest in the possibilities and implications of society's mediation and specific literary articulations of true love and human experience. Chaucer's *Prologue,* like the May passage, is perplexing in terms of how the theorizing of the subject of love, and the consequences of certain modes of writing and interpretation, might interrelate. Malory takes over, and further complicates, through displacement and condensation, the problems of writing about love and, obliquely, male/female difference, that Chaucer's own *Prologue* sets up and explores. As part of a claim for Chaucer as integral to Malory's remaking of Arthurian tradition, I want to explore how the *Prologue* illuminates the May passage's particular use of the spring topos, the relation between author, reader, and text, and the notion of the exemplary.

The *Prologues* to the *Legend* (insofar as one can discuss them generally together though this comparison will concentrate on the F *Prologue*) present a theorizing framework for both literary recuperation and social behavior. The poet as maker begins with a meditation on the need for faith in "old bokes,"[3] which are the community's repository of memory and wisdom. Borrowing a rhetorical topos from his "appreved stories Of hooliness" and "love" (F 21–23), the narrator goes out to do observance to May, declares that no one loved "hotter" (F 59) in his life than he in his devotion to his daisy and, having done homage to his flower, he goes home and falls asleep, to meet the God of Love and Queen Alceste. The queen has several poetic functions; she personifies his daisy, she is exemplary of womanhood, she is a reader of his works and an intercessor on his behalf. The imperious God of Love, surrounded by ladies "trewe of love [. . .] echon" (F 290), upbraids the hapless, if self-declaredly passionate, dreamer for his "negligence" in transgressing his laws and not writing about "trew" women. The God of Love figures women's integrity through witness of the sexual fidelity of ladies located in a classical past and, at the instigation of Alceste, who devises a "penance" for the dreamer of the composition of a "glorious legende Of goode wymmen" (F 483–84), instructs the narrator to write about women accordingly.

The *Prologue*'s debate about the function and purpose of writing and interpretation involves a certain fluidity of roles. Sheila Delany suggests that the poem concerns the "making" of the poet in both an active and a passive sense.[4] Chaucer as maker, and Chaucerian writing, are both subject to various readings, favorable and unfavorable. Alceste, too, is both a "read," interpreted object and a reading subject, and the legends following the *Prologue* emerge as aesthetically and emotionally unsatisfying in their polarization of gender roles, where the "fact" of "true" women is predicated on the existence of "untrue" men. Chaucer is setting up a disjunction between the intention informing the exemplary, and imposed written modes of communicating it.[5] In his persona as maker and dreamer, Chaucer is also introducing a slippage between identification and interpretation, between the genuineness of feeling and literature as its apparently straightforward vehicle—evident, for example, in his assertion that love's practitioners can best articulate what love is (F 69–73)—and the ways in which his own writing is accommodated to different interpretations.

Malory does not reproduce exactly, but he reconfigures, some central aspects of Chaucer's poem, both situational and stylistic. He redeploys his material and maintains a Chaucerian fluidity of roles as of linguistic reference, which further complicates the debate. The play on literal and figurative, for example, in both the May passage and its broader narrative context, seems especially Chaucerian. For the F *Prologue* dreamer, the scattering of flowers on his bed (206–07) sympathetically prefigures his dream of pastoral landscape and of his Flower who is also queen, intercessor, and patron (although the transformations also confirm his anxiety about his flower "that I so love and drede" [F 211]). Malory appears to be undertaking two kinds of translation, in that details of Chaucer's *Prologue* resurface as elements in the *Morte*'s narrative, and imagery within the May passage finds literal replication in the story itself. So where the highly rhetoricized description of the May sun as zodiacally in the sign of Taurus alludes in Chaucer's poem to the rape of Europa (F 103–14), Maytime in the *Morte* becomes "naturally" the setting for Guinevere's abduction by Meleagaunt (3:1121.4–13), and Malory claims the authority of the book to assert the intensity of Meleagaunt's desire (3:1121.9), although there is no parallel episode at this point in the Vulgate cycle.[6] To give an example of "literalization," the "heat" of human passion finds expression in the fire that on three occasions threatens Guinevere in the latter part of the *Morte*.[7]

When we consider the configurations of the *Prologue*'s actants, we discover that the God of Love is an imperious reader,[8] the dreamer bemused and put-upon, and Alceste (among other things) a classical *exemplum*. Malory's May passage conflates, as does Chaucer, the spring topos, individual motivation and literary judgment, but switches the roles around, which has the effect of concentrating more on the function of the reader than the author. In the later text, it is the narratorial voice that echoes the God of Love in its uncompromising pronouncements, and this "controlling" voice upbraids a wavering and continually redefined readership (one that cannot answer back) rather than an author figure. As is the case with the *Prologue*'s maker, in the May passage the narrator presents the possibility of redemptive identification with the month as a season of renewal as "natural" for the addressed community: "For, lyke as trees and erbys burgenyth and florysshyth in May, in lyke wyse every lusty harte that ys ony maner of lover spryngith, burgenyth, buddyth, and florysshyth in lusty dedis" (3:1119.3–6). The narrator also shares with another mediator of common lore about love, Chaucer's Pandarus, the proverbial observation that "ther was never worshypfull man nor worshypfull woman but they loved one bettir than anothir" (3:1119.26–27).[9] Thus the narrator bolsters his argument with proverbial sayings common also to Chaucerian characters, as part of his diatribe against "untrue" lovers/readers (although the connection with Chaucer, once recognized, might warn wary readers). In the *Prologue,* meanwhile, it is the nature of Chaucer-the-poet's amorous allegiance that is subsequently probed, found lacking, and relocated in the context of another literary practice (that of exemplarity), which is itself then exposed as deficient, and alien to the "maker" himself.

The May passage offers a highly condensed and complex variation on the relation between author, reader, and rhetorical topos that animates Chaucer's *Prologue.* Chaucer the Maker affirms that books are authoritative, and seems to assume that they are accessible, although we are warned that, were they lost, we would lose with them the "(keye) of remembraunce" (F 26) of more than the individual memory can contain. The narrator describes how the joys of the summer season urge a temporary renunciation of bookish allegiance: "whan that the month of May Is comen [. . .] Farewel my bok and my devocioun!" (F 36–39). In like manner, the earth "forgets" the ravages of winter (F 125–29). But the very literariness of the narrator's experience within the spring topos means that he does not so much abandon as revisit the rhetorical sites of literary production. Forgetfulness is part of renewal. At the same time, the God of Love tells the narrator that he is guilty of "necligence," both in composition (F 537–43), and recuperating appropriate texts, the latter omission most marked in the G *Prologue,* when the God demands: "in alle thy bokes ne coudest thow nat fynde Som story of wemen that were goode and trewe?" (G 271–72). The reader response that prescribes the dreamer's writing task makes literary mappings seem rather less stable and straightforward at the end of the poem than at its inception.

Malory's May passage reworks the meaning of the topos rather more abruptly. No sooner has the Malorian narrator invoked a consonance between vernal renewal and human memory of love (3:1119.6–13) than he reverses his (and Chaucer's) exposition of love, as we noted in the preface, and glosses "wynter rasure"'s obliteration of summer as simile for human forgetfulness in love (3:1119.14–16), a forgetfulness for which he calls us to account. Chaucer uses the spring topos and the image of the daisy as part of a playful engagement with the pleasures and problems of interrelating the experience of books with the experiences of life. But if Chaucer's daisy and its transformations ultimately provide an ironic account of the narrator's relation to love, comparison with Malory illuminates how the narrator in the later text is both more anxious about the consequences of forgetfulness and more absolute in his idea that readers are culpable of a cultural "negligence," which is index of their immorality. Where Chaucer as maker produces images of womanhood that depend on untrue men, in Malory the reader is cast as untrue. Chaucer uses gender relations as a vehicle for considering the business of writing, and the impact reader response has on writing; Malory's invocation of love as primarily concerned with a readerly hermeneutic is the more marked when set against Chaucer.

A Chaucerian subtext to the May passage also offers a useful point of reference for its closing lines. The argument of Malory's text, although it assumes faithfulness for both male and female as indicative of general integrity, meets up with the *Prologue* in its final mention of Guinevere, which conflates female virtue and the process of "true loving." In the preface, I suggested that this reference reflects to us the text's own interpretive difficulties in the light of its cultural context. All those who are lovers ought to remember Guinevere because "whyle she lyved she was a trew lover, and therefor she had a good ende" (3:1120.12–13). Chaucer's God of Love's declaration that he will ensure no "trewe lover" goes to hell (F 553) provides a context for Guinevere's status as "trew lover," and at the same time draws attention to the difference between Arthur's queen and Alceste, who is, the God of Love explains, the perfect model "To any woman that wol lover bee" (F 543). Alceste possesses exemplary wifeliness, as well as an intercessory role:

> "For she taughte al the craft of fyn lovynge,
> And namely of wyfhod the lyvynge,
> And all the boundes that she oghte kepe." (F 544–46)

Guinevere, of course, severs the link that binds "wyfhod" to "fyn lovynge." The Chaucerian model offers a frame for recognizing how (as Chaucer himself later does with his own taxonomy of "good women") Malory's narrator problematizes his description of his exemplary woman even as he invokes her. The means by which Guinevere-as-character evades the terms that in the May passage ostensibly define her signals a particularly Chaucerian debt. Susan Crane has drawn on anthropology to discuss later medieval courtly Maying ritual in general, and to argue for ritual's legitimizing of the operation of metaphor in the *Legend,* which makes Alceste both queen and daisy; this metaphoric transformation, integral to the workings of ritual, in turn serves to define and regulate female sexuality.[10] If (as I suggested in the preface) the split between narrative event and its glossing here divides an Arthurian world of the imagination from this particular textual manifestation of Arthurian legend, the *Morte* also takes

Chaucerian poetics a stage further and puts the possibility of metaphor as
episteme into question. The memorializing of Guinevere as a true lover
who "therefore" has a good end, in a narrative context in which it is the
very renunciation of secular "true love" that leads to the good end, sets a
"knowledge" of Guinevere apart from a desire to represent her in a particular way. Such a formulation also obfuscates our access to the apparently
"historical," realist level of character that many modern commentators ad-
mire in Guinevere's representation, the sense of interiority her character
conveys by means of an apparent sexual autonomy.[11] It is not simply a
question of Guinevere's appearing to occupy an uneasy role between exemplarity and historical action, but of the difficulties of our recuperating a
logic for the linear narrative and the narrative gloss.

The May passage's complex stratagem of amorous engagement and distance feeds into narratorial and reader responses to Guinevere and
Launcelot as lovers. The story of Chaucer's most famous lovers, Troilus and
Criseyde, intimates that textual engagement (narratorial or readerly) is primarily sexual. A. C. Spearing, examining *Troilus and Criseyde*'s consummation scene, argues that the poem ultimately displaces onto us the moral
responsibility for the voyeuristic aspects of the episode (for example, the
extent and nature of Pandarus's participation), because we are left in part
to construct them.[12] The climax of the episode, of course, also involves the
narrator in voicing a sexual desire that is simultaneously a literary climax,
when he celebrates the lovers' union—"Why nad I swich oon with my
soule y-bought?" (3:1319)—and defers to those with "felyng [. . .] in
loues arte" (3:1333) to supplement (or even abbreviate) his poetry. The
Troilus narrator assures us that human needs and desires remain essentially
unchanged, and that historical difference in human mores is largely cos-
metic (2:22–42), but at the same time he worries that synchronic as well
as diachronic "diuersite In Englissh" will misrepresent his work, or even
make it unintelligible (5:1793–798). If we can grasp the past through his
poetry, of what kind of past do we lay hold: the "true" experiences of the
lovers, or a heightened awareness of a "mediated" Troilus and Criseyde,
whose very movements are literary constructs: "As writen clerkes in hire
bokes olde" (3:1199)?

Malory's narrator further develops this difficult relation between love
and its literary expression by making the very terms of our engagement
the terms of disavowal: "For, as the Freynshe booke seyth, the quene and
sir Launcelot were togydirs. And whether they were abed other at other
maner of disportis, me lyste nat thereof make no mencion, for love that
tyme was nat as love ys nowadayes" (3:1165.10–13). "Negligence" is, it
seems, now necessary to keep faith with a particular view of the past.
Robert Sturges, making a strong case for the nature of the distinct textual

practices on which Malory and his sources draw, suggests Malory chooses ignorance at this point as a way of confirming readerly power over the "truth"-asserting French texts, and of registering the uncertainty of human knowledge and narrative.[13] The inscribed narrative role of the flexibly defined readership, however, further complicates this arresting interpretation. In political matters, for example, the narrator, after the manner of contemporary chronicles, indicts the populace for their endemic wavering political allegiance and love of novelty, exemplified in their turning to Mordred's cause;[14] but he also equates "us now" with "people then" in this respect:

> Lo, ye all Englysshmen, see ye nat what a myschyff here was? [. . .] thus was the olde custom and usayges of thys londe, and men say that we of thys londe have nat yet loste that custom. Alas! thys ys a greate defaughte of us Englysshemen, for there may no thynge us please no terme. (3:1229.6–14)

How do we reconcile this straightforward moral responsibility on the level of historical action, with the earlier assurance that past customs and historical events are inscrutable? The refusal to "tell" about Launcelot and Guinevere's sexual relations marks more than the "unknowability" of event; it returns us to the precise question of our own abject situation as "modern" lovers, and to the general issue of how regarding Launcelot involves us in the complex institutional and sexual aspects (literary and historical) of our own reading, aspects to which the narrator gives voice, on our behalf, only selectively, but which are understood to trammel our interpretation. To some extent, the reader is perhaps object of a narratorial frustration with literary inevitability—the Arthurian legend cannot ultimately resist its own tradition, however much the narrator might seek to remake the terms of Launcelot as hero. Indeed, the reader is now implicitly asked to disengage from a sexualizing of Launcelot that the presentation of his earlier adventures (as we saw in chapter three) has paradoxically served tacitly to reinforce, in the very process of denying it. The diverse constitutions and "placings" of the reader themselves reflect the composite nature of the Arthurian literary legacy. We can recuperate the testamentary artifacts of a historical world; at Dover, "all men may se the skulle" of Gawain and the mark of the wound Launcelot dealt it (3:1232.18–20). Yet, our recuperation of the nature of that world is ultimately faulty. In the final episodes of the *Morte,* then, the Arthuriad's own methodology comes under scrutiny, and as the story draws to narrative closure, the narrator appears to insist on our continuing engagement with the action, and yet to suggest that we have no access to all-encompassing categories of understanding or of knowledge.

Launcelot and Guinevere's adultery sharply focuses this question of categories, as "our" unspoken "knowledge" is also now inevitably a plot function. Elizabeth Edwards has noted how, in narrative terms, "private"
adultery sustains "public" courtly life;[15] but Malory goes even further, in
having the representation of "adultery" involve the transcendence, revisiting, or reworking, of particular registers and spaces. When Agravain "discovers" the couple, Launcelot and Guinevere's language of martyrdom and
invocations of Christ's aid—"Jesu Cryste, be Thou my shylde and myne armoure!" (3:1167.5–6)—bespeaks their innocence and moral integrity.[16]
"Knowledge" of adultery destabilizes, and yet is intrinsic to, our position
as readers, and the loss of security about perspectives and categories
heightens awareness that moral and judicial problems are intractable. The
latter part of the *Morte* sees both a multiplying of factual matter and assurances of "meaning"—the narrator's reiterative "wyte yow well"s, and the
characters' increased use of this term, convey an anxiety over conveying accuracy of narrative and of individual feeling alike[17]—and yet also a lack of
reassuringly definitive readings. E. Kay Harris points out how the rhetorical presentation of Launcelot may invite his interpretation as both traitor
and as saint.[18] Malory's source has its own moral displacements and problems. Sarah Kay writes of how the *Mort Artu* does not directly comment
on adultery, but issues of sexual guilt are swiftly converted into accusations
over killings, for which the lovers are individually brought to account. The
reluctance to address adultery is of a piece with a universe in which love
and death are ultimately "resistant to moral judgement."[19] In general, the
Mort uncomfortably questions the feudal institution's capacity to adminis-
ter justice.[20] For Malory, meanwhile, Arthurian law is a disconcerting
blend of recognizable contemporary practice and less familiar legislation,
and the issue is perhaps less the law per se than how and what people come
to signify within institutions in these last books, and how closure also en-
tails destabilization.

Representing Guinevere

In representing Guinevere, Malory does not fully engage with those vexed
terms of medieval queenship familiar from recent research, whereby the
queen's "interstitial" position, as someone from "outside" who is nonetheless intimate with the king, concentrates anxieties about legitimacy, power,
and rule by women, especially in relation to wifehood and motherhood
(although Guinevere's lack of motherhood itself highlights and obviates
anxiety over legitimacy and succession).[21] Instead, Guinevere relates more
to the fellowship than to genealogy, and in this the text skews what we
might call the normative modes of representing queenship. The bride who

brings the Round Table and its knights as dowry to Arthur (1:98.18–25) is
also the subject of a stark unequivocal prophecy that she and Launcelot
will be lovers (1:97.29–32),[22] yet she can, like her husband, dispense ethical justice, as when she leads a judicial inquiry to decide Gawain's penalty
for killing a woman (1:108.25–109.3). In chapter three, I traced an implicit
reassuring symbolic function for Guinevere in the *Arthur and Lucius* section, where she (and her body's violability) represents the vulnerable land
Arthur successfully defends. The latter part of the *Morte* reconfigures and
repeats details already encountered in that earlier narrative, and Guinevere's
assumed symbolic function and framing of the action then, and even the
significance of the spaces she occupies, become open to reformulation and
redefinition, as Merlin's early prophecy about her is complexly realized.
The text revisits locations and replays situations to emphasize how much
more complex is the interrelation of action and judgment in contrast to
the earlier narrative. Both Meleagaunt and Launcelot "abduct" Guinevere,
for example, yet each adventure contrasts strongly with the narrative sequence of the abduction and rape of the Duchess of Brittany in the *Arthur
and Lucius* episode, and raises questions about the treatment of Guinevere's
person, and the nature of "treason." Guinevere takes on an active conciliatory role when she resolves the Meleagaunt episode pragmatically (to the
dismay of her lover, who seeks revenge), in her autonomous establishing of
terms with her abductor, frightened by Launcelot's imminent arrival to
rescue her: "bettir ys pees than evermore warre, and the lesse noyse the
more ys my worshyp" (3:1128.16–17). In the *Arthur and Lucius* episode,
safe custodianship of Guinevere is taken for granted, while at the end of
the *Morte,* Guinevere has to resist the claims of the man in whose care
Arthur entrusts her (3:1211.8–11). If the May passage indicates the difficulty of translating event into neat moral lessons, the *Morte* also allocates to
Guinevere a greater freedom of action, a freedom that itself cannot be
"read" against a conventional set of ritual coordinates for the queen.
Rather, the very nature and uses of ritual here come under scrutiny.

In *La Mort le roi Artu,* Guenièvre is more consistently and explicitly associated with the land and interpreted politically in relation to her husband; at the reported death of Arthur, the barons tell the queen that she
must marry his successor (174; Lacy 4:136).[23] In the *Mort,* as in the *Queste,*
Guenièvre may be read also against the familiar trope of women's wiles
that in the light of the experience of David, Solomon, and Samson, sees no
man safe from female perfidy (70–71; Lacy 4:109). In Malory, incidental
language around Guinevere makes instead for a fragmenting incongru-
ence, rather than an invitation to confirm her behavior from established
rhetorical coordinates. So the connection between Guinevere and the land
emerges disturbingly and allusively, as when Launcelot half-echoes the

Giant of Mont St. Michel's desire (1:201.10–13) in his wish that he might have saved Guinevere from Meleagaunt: "I had lever [. . .] than all Fraunce that I had bene there well armed" (3:1125.6–7). And prior to fighting his way out of Guinevere's chamber, Launcelot formally addresses her as "Most nobelest Crysten quene" (3:1166.13), an appellation apparently borrowed from the title that it is the prerogative of a pope to grant a king (Urry addresses Arthur as "moste noble crystynd kynge" [3:1147.14]).[24] But a few pages later, Launcelot uses the same collocation in his apostrophe to the England from which he is being exiled: "Most nobelyst Crysten realme, whom I have loved aboven all othir realmys!" (3:1201.9–10). Guinevere is now regal agent, now one whose function is that of representation or of exchange.

Just as the apparently incidental deployment of collocations can have complex echoes, so complications of meaning attend narrative repetitions of motif and circumstance. Details of preparations for Guinevere's immolation have been characterized as Malorian "melodrama,"[25] but repetition of this motif gains for it a quasi-symbolic resonance, an element of ritualization that asks us to ponder its function and meaning. Guinevere is three times threatened with burning. The first time she falls foul of the law, before a champion arrives to defend her against the charge of the murder of Patryse, the queen has already been "put in the Conestablis awarde and a grete fyre made aboute an iron stake" (2:1055.9–10). The narrative explains the treatment of Guinevere in terms of the "custom" of "tho dayes," which espouses social and judicial equality: "for favoure, love, other affinité there shold be none other but ryghtuous jugemente [. . .] as well uppon a quene as uppon another poure lady" (2:1055.11–15).[26] But this explanation obscures the preparations as precipitate near-anticipation of Mador's successful martial prosecution of his accusation that the queen is a poisoner. The claims of a spectacularly realizable punishment, "jugemente," threaten to overtake justice in relation to Guinevere, whose relation to due legal process is oblique. When, in the later "Knight of the Cart" episode, Launcelot arrives at the last moment to answer Meleagaunt's charge of treason against the queen, Guinevere has again been "brought tyll a fyre to be brente" (3:1137.6–7), in anticipation of the success of her opponent's claim. This iconicity of "judgment" for Guinevere, during the legal process itself, concretizes the "hasty jougement" characterizing these closing chapters, which Robert Kelly argues would have disturbed a contemporary audience and led them to condemn Arthur.[27] On this second occasion, Meleagaunt has demanded the King do him "justyse," and burn the queen, "othir ellys brynge forth sir Launcelot" (3:1137.10). The threatened violence against Guinevere in the context of her surrogacy for Launcelot also, however, raises the question of bodies' relation to the law. The ethos of

Launcelot's chivalric violence appears to put him beyond the law even as he declares he upholds it; he tells Arthur he is obliged to help the queen "in ryght othir in wronge" (2:1058.31–32), but while his successful physical defense of her is "proof" of her innocence, Arthur later articulates a gulf between what Launcelot's body registers and what constitutes "law," when he says Launcelot "trustyth so much uppon hys hondis and hys myght that he doutyth no man. And therefore for my quene he shall nevermore fyght, for she shall have the law" (3:1175.20–23). If Launcelot's case highlights the limits of social and moral institutional control of the body, the treatment of Guinevere's person as "treasonous" offers a different focus on sex and killing in relation to institutions.

When Guinevere is led to the stake for the third time (3:1177.10–14), judgment has already been passed on her. There is an element of ritualization in this process, understood in the terms offered by Catherine Bell, who suggests we might go beyond an Althusserian model of ritual practice as primarily concerned "to order, rectify, or transform a particular situation," to appreciate more keenly the dynamics of ritualization as a strategic play of power, domination, and resistance within the social body. Bell argues that where ritualization may suggest a straightforward demonstration of a community's traditional values, the very idea of consensus the ritual declares itself constitutes a "misrecognition" that is the basis for ritualization's success in maintaining particular power relations, and marks the limits of ritualization's own social power.[28] The punishment of Guinevere registers just such a point of uneasy consensus and limitation—the narrative asserts that the queen must be killed, but notes also the reluctance of many to participate fully in the event (3:1177.13–14)—and raises questions about the slippage between intention, event, and representation. The very nature of Guinevere's relation to the law appears to be at issue, and recent scholarly historicist readings of the text assess the evidence differently. For Robert Kelly, for example, the treason charge against the queen relates to her part in the killing of the knights who have sought to trap Launcelot, whereas, for E. Kay Harris, adultery is the central crime, and the *Morte* can be read as a protest against certain modes of interpretation in fifteenth-century legal procedure.[29]

The "displacement" of Guinevere in institutional terms contributes to these readings' divergent emphases. The difficulties over establishing her moral and criminal culpability in relation to adultery, and the consequent question of what to do with her body, belong to the general "problem" of woman's volition, and to the nature of her physical integrity in relation to the law, that the *Morte* shares ideologically with the blind spots of later medieval legislation over sexual violation. Guinevere's position seems anomalous, both in terms of the Arthurian treason law that condemns her

(3:1174.21–25) and in terms of historical legislation for high treason. Historically, the Statute of Treason of 1352 (25 Edward III, Statute 5) makes
rape treason when it concerns the bodies of women related to the king: "si
homme violast la compaigne le Roi, ou leisnesce fille le Roi nient marie,
ou la compaigne leisne filz et heir du Roi" [if a man violate the consort
of the king, or the eldest unmarried daughter of the king, or the consort
of the eldest son and heir of the king].[30] The statute makes no reference to
women's volition, so does not address consensual sexual acts, putting the
legal aspect of Guinevere's behavior, itself "unknowable," under debate in
historical terms (as will be the case with Anne Boleyn in the following
century[31]). Part of the problem in interpreting the *Morte,* however, lies in
its admixture of contemporaneous and fictive legal process, and Meleagaunt's earlier unequivocal equation of adultery with treason on finding
Guinevere's sheets bloodied may clarify her position: "now I have founde
you a false traytouras unto my lorde Arthur [. . .] Therefore I wille calle
you of treson afore my lorde kynge Arthure [. . .] for a wounded knyght
thys nyght hath layne by you" (3:1132.15–22).[32] But the syntax of the account of Guinevere's "hasty jougement" (3:1174.25) intimates that, whatever legal provision might exist to punish the consort's adultery, the queen
indeed stands accountable not for adultery, but for killings the legal status
of which the terms of her condemnation itself holds in suspension. She
must die: "bycause sir Mordred was ascaped sore wounded, and the dethe
of thirtene knygthes of the Rounde Table" (3:1174.26–27).[33] Guinevere,
with little legal language to account for her own situation, appears then as
displaced surrogate for Launcelot, whose own deeds here are at issue, yet
without legal articulation.[34] Her death sentence therefore also occludes the
unavailability of forms of legal jurisdiction to answer adequately to the
events that have taken place.

Kay Harris argues that the fissures between evidence and judgment are
paradigmatic of a text that in broader terms calls into question "the basis of
interpretive activity," even while it enacts a "rush to judgment."[35] This
analysis returns us to the issue of reader responsibility, but also by default reminds us that legal language is only one of the narrative registers that demands interpretation. The judgment against Guinevere represents a
breakdown in legal accountability, as Launcelot suggests to his men: "the
kyng woll in thys hete and malice jouge the quene unto brennyng"
(3:1171.14–15). But mention of heat also suggests the narrative is obeying
an "imperative" to literalize, as we saw above, and dilutes the emphasis on
the king's responsibility. The French source criticizes Arthur's manipulation
of the law by carefully locating Guenièvre within the normative representation of queenship. Malory erases many of these coordinates and so makes
more bewildering the social placing and accountability of individuals and

their actions. The *Mort,* making explicit that Guenièvre is being punished for adultery, explains her mode of death:

> Et li rois commande a ses sergenz qu'il feïssent en la praerie de Kamaalot un feu grant et merveillex, ou la reïne sera mise; car autrement ne doit reïne morir qui desloiauté fet, puis que ele est sacree.

> [The King ordered his servants to go to the field at Camelot and to prepare a great and wondrous fire, in which the queen would be burned, for a queen who commits treason, because she has been consecrated, should not die in any other way]. (121–22; Lacy 4:122, modified)

Guenièvre's journey to the place of execution directs us to read the queen in conventional terms; a fine set piece evokes the grief of the crowd and her progress, richly dressed, beautiful and weeping, through the streets to her death, accompanied by sympathetic onlookers who urge the king to relent, and also indict Arthur for "desloiauté" [disloyalty] and call his advisors "traïteur" [traitors] (122; Lacy 4:123). The crowd grieves as if for their own mother, and the people remember her compassion to the poor, in classical tropes of good queenship (122; Lacy 4:122–23).[36] The *Mort* spectacle here confirms the queen's regal identity and role; the *Morte* omits these details, and minimizes Guinevere's role, in what becomes the occasion for a commemorative roll call of the "full many a noble knyght" (3:1177.24) killed during the queen's rescue. The formal ritualistic markers of the queen's importance cede to the dynamics of action.

The *Morte* bypasses the opportunity to exploit Guinevere's ritual role as queen in her execution scene, and further dislocates her from this function when it describes the pageantry attendant on Launcelot's return of the queen to the king at Carlisle after the knight has saved her from the fire for a third time (3:1196.5–25). Launcelot organizes a hundred knights, dressed in green velvet and holding olive branches, and twenty-four ladies accompany the queen, while Launcelot himself is followed by twelve young riders dressed, like Launcelot and the queen, in white and gold. The scene elaborates the Stanzaic *Morte's* expansion of the French text at this point (2350–79; *Mort* 133; Lacy 4:132), and also asks to be read against the earlier instance of Guinevere's riding out, in May, with her knights, after the narratorial disquisition on the relation between love and arms. Read against that passage, Guinevere is here dislocated from an autonomous role. Her trajectory between Joyous Garde and Carlisle significantly places her between sites of power, for Launcelot and for Arthur respectively. The attendants' green clothing recalls the apparel of the Maytime revelers, but now has political resonance; the olive branches the attendants bear "in tokening of pees" (3:1196.11)[37] contrast with the Maytime knights "bedaysshed with erbis, mossis and floures in the freyssheste maner" (3:1122.3). Where Guinevere has earlier organized the Maytime festivities, here Launcelot stage manages the procession and even positions her body in response to Arthur's reactions (3:1196.25–1197.3). Launcelot also occupies more of the field of vision than does Guinevere, and the narrative gaze dwells more on the richness of the horses' harness (3:1196.16–18) than on the queen. The description also "frames" the queen, with Arthur and then with Launcelot, although attention to such details as the dress of the participants displaces her as the scene's focal point. Inarticulate tears provide the outermost frame of the spectacle: the tears that fall from the king's eyes (3:1196.7; 32–34), and the "wepyng ien" of the onlookers (3:1196.25).

Why does the *Morte,* which shows no great interest in royal pageantry,[38] here amplify description, although it does not make the queen central? The text highlights Launcelot's active role, and also foregrounds process rather than resolution. The scene "locates" Guinevere in relation to the men in a way that does not strictly define her, while that very positioning is cause for sorrow on all sides. The queen, while she is certainly being "handed over" from one man to another, is perhaps less an "object of exchange" than a locus of Launcelot's interpretive memorializing. Richly arrayed, respectfully treated, and lacking in autonomy, she "translates" in ritual terms insofar as her dress declares a purity of intention that requires glossing. As Launcelot tells Arthur: "she ys trew and clene to you" (3:1197.8–9). But Launcelot also uses this occasion to reaffirm the status of his chivalric body as "legal currency"—he will "make hit good" on the body of any other knight that Guinevere is "trew" to Arthur (3:1187.6–10)—and to justify his own role in recent events: "I had more cause to rescow her from the fyer whan she sholde have ben brente *for my sake*" (3:1197.18–19, emphasis added). The pageantry, rather than confirm Guinevere's identity, whether as lover or queen or "true" wife, here holds those functions in suspension in its declaration of an integrity that defies investigation. The *Morte,* by omission, conveys the lack of a language adequately to describe and account for Guinevere and her intentions. If Malory's Guinevere does not correspond to "normative" queenship and its representation, the *Morte* does not itself forge a new vocabulary for the queen but seems, rather, to use her to declare the limits of literary representation. In her last interview with Launcelot, a self-aware Guinevere declares complicity in the downfall of the Round Table: "Thorow the and me," she tells Launcelot, "ys the floure of kyngis and knyghtes destroyed" (3:1252.24–25). After this interview, Guinevere is borne sorrowing to her chamber, which last vision of her recalls, and asks us to measure the distance between, this scene and her distress in the book of *Arthur and Lucius* at Arthur's leaving the country

(1:195.11–13; 3:1253.32–33). This final scene, with its symbolic echo and its "moral" reading of Guinevere's actions, suggests a "definitive" rhetoric is substitutive for, rather than constitutive of, historical analysis. This concern with whether forms of closure are more apparent than real is evident also in the text's recording of death rites.

Death and Commemoration

When Launcelot arrives with his men at Dover, only to learn that the carnage of the Last Battle has already taken place, he organizes a requiem for Gawain, after which he declares: "we ar com to late, and that shall repente me whyle I lyve, but ayenste deth may no man rebell" (3:1251.12–14).[39] Launcelot here denies a relation between human behavior and death, between knighthood and killing, at the same time as the chivalric ideology that informs his metaphor declares death to be, after all, institutionalized by the social order.[40] Launcelot's language reflects how the last books unevenly articulate human agency and unfathomable external forces as constituents of the final tragedy. Anthropologically, death rites pointedly voice the social and cultural norms and attitudes of the living.[41] As part of this cultural mirroring death is, of course, imbricated with literature's self-reflexive aspect for, as Elisabeth Bronfen and Sarah Webster observe, we know death only through representation; no one is in a position to offer expert witness on the experience of death. Death functions as a metatrope; by means of it, art addresses problems of representation itself. And representation and corpse alike have no clear position, even as they elicit a desire for stability.[42] Death therefore, apparently "definitive," biologically at least, is nonetheless ambivalent: marginal yet central, anomalous yet powerful.[43] The *Mort* concentrates, in its accounts of burials, on the commemorative power of inscriptions. That subsequent knowledge or revised perspectives can rewrite these inscriptions acknowledges the contingency of what one can establish about event and agency,[44] yet also testifies to the Vulgate Cycle's faith in writing as forensic tool. The *Morte,* narratively allusive and metonymically referential by comparison with its French source, is nonetheless more systematic in its account of burial rites, the details of which invite comparison with fifteenth-century practice (although I will argue that the *Morte*'s intermittent lack of consonance with historical rite and commemoration serves an epistemological purpose).[45] The greater involvement with the process, rather than the finality, of death rituals, accords with English Arthurian romance's emphasis on the performative.

The requiem for Gawain is one of several episodes involving death rites in which the *Morte* reworks and supplements *La Mort le roi Artu* to play down those funeral arrangements that do not involve Launcelot, and to accord him the central role in commemorative processes. In chapter three, I argued that Hallewes's sinister imagining of Launcelot as corpse offers a nightmarish memorialization of knighthood that focuses the narrative's own confusions over the nature of Launcelot's heroism and its representation, and that also implicates us as readers, for we inevitably conceptualize the hero as sexual. If, in the Hallewes episode, death is displaced onto the feminine (as Bronfen and Goodwin argue is endemic to a male Western culture that envisages both death and the feminine as tropes for enigma),[46] this form of attention to Launcelot "feminizes" him only insofar as he is part of Malory's making both narrative and fifteenth-century referent newly uncanny, for Launcelot's privileging also involves some departures from conventional death practices. The incorporation of Launcelot into the principal commemorative mourning scenes[47] makes for a multifaceted exploration of representation as well as of mourning. Launcelot enacts all modes of participation in death rituals. He is mourner, penitent survivor making restitution, officiating priest, *memento mori* and, finally, the corpse itself. Bell writes of ritualization as the means to embodying relations of power, and notes the fluidity of ritualization as far as concerns its participants' involvement in a play of dominance and resistance; it may consolidate continuity between self and social body, or emphasize a subjectivity that polarizes a personal self and a social body.[48] The constitution of Launcelot's "public" self is certainly at issue here, especially with regard to his shifting status as perceived "representative" of a community's values; striking about Launcelot's function, however, is that ostensible closure balances carefully with the possibility of plural readings, as ritual asks to be read against experience as well as in confirmation of it. Malory avoids "definitive" aspects of commemoration in favor of positioning Launcelot as emotional center of mourning practices. These practices both depend on an established rhetoric of engagement with death and commemoration, and intermittently dislocate the relation between human feeling, the monumental, and rhetoric, to suggest the lack of an all-encompassing commemorative language.

In general, as noted above, the French account stresses the decorum of burial and the tombstone as locus for recording judgment, and the *Morte,* the physical processes of mourning. One forensic inscription in the *Morte,* however, that for Sir Patryse's tomb, compensates for an epitaph in the source that remains uncorrected; in the *Mort,* the tomb of Gaheris de Karaheu, the victim of the "poisoned apple" episode, records the queen has poisoned him (78; Lacy 4:112). When Lancelot successfully defends the queen, no memorial records her innocence (107; Lacy 4:118). In the *Morte,* Launcelot's condition for granting the defeated Mador life is that the tomb makes clear Guinevere had no part in the crime (2:1058.1–3). Nineyve finally resolves the mystery, and the dead knight's tomb explains his "misfortune," along with a detailed history of the case (2:1059.26–1060.2). In other instances in which *Mort* inscriptions document event and judgment, the *Morte* relies on the performative, and this exception perhaps expresses particular anxiety over documentation where supernatural knowledge has had to supplement judicial procedure. The *Mort's* "oversight," meanwhile, suggests technical knowledge of Guenièvre's legal position; even unawares, she *has* poisoned the knight, so the inscription does not declare "guilt," but fact.

The Maid of Escalot's tomb, meanwhile, implicates Lancelot; its inscription proclaims that she died for love of him (92; Lacy 4:114), which registers the court's response to her death. Lancelot is ignorant of the burial until after the event, and the episode primarily serves to foreground the relationship between Guenièvre and Lancelot. The Maid of Ascolat's letter, however, asks that Launcelot be chief mourner at her funeral (2:1096.31–35). This request conflicts with the practice, consolidated by the College of Heralds from the early 1460s onward, whereby the principal mourner was of the same sex as the deceased.[49] (Indeed, the only mourners identified at the Maid's burial are men: Launcelot and Round Table knights [2:1097.33–1098.2].) This burial rite, transgressive of custom, registers desire rather than past event; it "confirms" for Elaine a relationship that did not obtain in life, both with Launcelot and with the Round Table. It also leaves open to speculation the extent to which Launcelot's participation is an act of penance.

The element of the penitential is strongest in the aftermath of the accidental killing of Gareth and Gaheris, which witnesses a disjunction between spectacular modes of reparation, and the nature of human grief. In the *Mort*, Gawain finds his brother Gaheriet's bloody corpse in his uncle's arms; Guerrehet, Agravain, and Gaheriet are all prepared for burial in tombs at St. Stephen's Cathedral as befits their high status and their careers as "good knights," with Gaheriet accorded the most splendid memorial; the inscription baldly declares Lancelot Gaheriet's killer (132–33; Lacy 4:125). As he dies, Gawain asks to change Gaheriet's inscription, so as to register his own culpability in his and his brother's death (220, 224; Lacy 4:148, 149). Malory's Arthur, however, has the bodies of Gareth and his brothers buried with almost indecent haste, so as to spare Gawain grief (3:1185.22–25). Launcelot makes an extravagant offer of restitution to Gawain for his brothers' deaths; he will make a penitential journey, the length of the kingdom, from Sandwich to Carlisle, and will found chantries at every ten-mile interval in memory of Gareth and Gaheris (3:1199.29–1200.6). There is historical precedent for Launcelot's proposal; the Duke of York and his party were required in 1458 to endow a

perpetual chantry at St. Albans Abbey on behalf of the souls of the Earl of
Northumberland and others killed at the Battle of St. Albans.[50] While
Launcelot makes his offer in good faith, it unfortunately reminds Gawain
of what he has lost. Gawain rejects the offer—"I woll never forgyff the
my brothirs dethe" (3:1200.15–16)—and the *Morte*'s grandest, most fabu-
lously costly project of commemoration, and of what Kelly terms "penitence as a remedy for war," never finds material realization. There is
instead an echo of the original intention in Launcelot's taking on the organization of the commemorative service for Gawain, mentioned above
(3:1250.20–1251.7). The *Mort* recounts at length the lamentation over
Gawain's body, its enshrouding in fine cloths and precious stones, the vigil
kept over it, and its transferal to Camelot in chivalric procession, a ritual
broken by a savage sequence that distills the relation of love and arms that
has characterized the amorous Gawain's life; a former lover of his is
butchered by her husband and the mourners, having killed the husband,
have to fight off an attack on them by his people (221–25; Lacy
4:148–49). In Malory's account, Arthur buries the body quickly
(3:1232.16–20), and the funeral rite proper has to await Launcelot's arrival. Launcelot's involvement is authorized by Gawain's death-letter request to him: "I requyre the [. . .] that thou wolte se my tumbe"
(3:1232.8–10). Launcelot's feelings express themselves in the splendor of
the obsequies and the generosity of the offerings, as well as in his two-day
demonstration of inordinate grief. As Andrew Lynch notes, Launcelot's
body becomes, in these last episodes, "the register of emotion rather than
its practical arbiter."[51] And his emotion is part of a process of mourning
that eclipses any idea of lasting memorial. It is Gawain's skull that the narrator assures us we may still see, not his tomb.

Malory's funeral rites do not mention tombs and monuments that legitimize and confirm kingship or knighthood.[52] The tomb of Arthur and
Guinevere is an anomalous site of commemoration for both king and
queen. In the *Mort* account, Girflet, three days after the last battle, finds the
"marvelous and rich" tomb of Arthur, which commemorates how the king
conquered twelve kingdoms (251; Lacy 4:156). By contrast, Malory's Bedivere finds only "a tumbe was newe gravyn" (3:1241.9), and the narrator
says that the only witness to the burial does not know "in sertayne"
(3:1242.19) that the body in the grave is Arthur's. The mysterious Latin inscription—"rex quondam rexque futurus" (3:1242.29)—promises transcendence for the hero, yet its existence has the status of hearsay, just as
others "say" that Arthur will return for a crusade (3:1242.21–28). Derek
Brewer reads the report of Arthur's tomb as paradigmatic of death as a mystery resisting interpretation.[53] The question of Arthur's death is also central to the *Morte*'s conception of writing. Representation inevitably erases

and substitutes for what it seeks to represent; in Derrida's terms, writing is "testamentary," and "the original absence of the subject of writing is also the absence of the thing or the referent."[54] The narrator here plays on the subject of Arthurian legend as presence and absence, its historicity unknowable beyond its immediate articulation. With his refusal fully to endorse the inscription's promise—"I wolde sey: here in thys worlde he chaunged hys lyff" (3:1242.26–27)—an expression that holds mortality and immortality in balance,[55] the narrator makes the story a place of inquiry, uncertainty, and partiality, where the French text insists (finally) on death as a locus of closure.

Launcelot's body becomes the principal material aspect of Arthur and Guinevere's tomb, and the last pages reinforce his physicality as our means of connection to the Arthurian world. When Guinevere dies, the ceremony around her is in keeping with her ritual displacement at the end of the *Morte*. A vision charges her lover to undertake and organize the funeral: "in remyssyon of his synnes" (3:1255.15). Launcelot is officiating priest and chief mourner at Guinevere's funeral:

> And so he dyd al the observaunce of the servyce hymself, bothe the dyryge and on the morne he sange masse. And there was ordeyned an hors-bere, and so wyth an hondred torches ever brennyng aboute the cors of the quene and ever syr Launcelot with his eyght felowes wente aboute the hors-bere, syngyng and redyng many an holy oryson, and frankensens upon the corps encensed. (3:1256.4–10)

Guinevere's body, embalmed and wrapped in fine cloth and wax, and then sealed in lead before being placed in a marble coffin (3:1256.18–20), receives the treatment appropriate to a royal corpse.[56] There is, however, no description of Guinevere's tomb in accordance with English queens' funerary monuments, which would typically reflect the individual's living function, document her genealogy and lineage, and celebrate her role as intercessor.[57] It would perhaps not be unusual for an abbess, as a woman who has withdrawn from the world, to have a modest tomb, but Guinevere appears to be buried with the regalia of neither abbess nor queen.[58] This tomb appears to efface Guinevere's status as queen even as she is placed in her husband's grave. This anomalous "noncommemoration" is complicated by Launcelot's own body, as the narrative effectively translates Launcelot into funerary sculpture, a living substitution for stonework that subsumes both king and queen. In his abject positioning as mourner, he might be one of the "pore men and wemen [. . .] with their bedys In theire handes," whom Isabel, Countess of Warwick, projected as part of the sculpture for the sides of her tomb at Tewkesbury Abbey, a splendid affair that was to have included an image of her naked body and statues of her favorite saints.[59]

At the queen's burial, Launcelot, overcome with emotion, loses consciousness, for which his fellow religious rebukes him (3:1256.24–25). In response, Launcelot recreates in words the beauty and nobility of both king and queen that late-medieval sculpture would have rendered in stone; he reconstitutes their memories in words, all the while acknowledging the feelings of guilt and remorse the vision engenders for him. Although Launcelot speaks of beholding the bodies of the king and the queen, it is not clear what their relation is, at this point, in physical space: "whan I sawe his corps and hir corps so lye togyders, truly myn herte wold not serve to susteyne my careful body" (3:1256.31–32). If this seems to contradict the details of the marble-coffined queen and the unidentifiable body that may be Arthur's, Launcelot, like the narrator as late-medieval reader, and, like Derrida's author, recreates Arthur (and Guinevere) from absence and lack. Our mode of access to the king and queen is the physical person of Launcelot, which wastes away as he mourns "grovelyng" and inconsolable on the tomb (3:1257.1–11).

At this point, Wynkyn de Worde's 1498 edition interpolates a commemorative piece of its own, which implicitly reads Launcelot's body (and the undescribed tomb) as a *memento mori,* affording it the same interpretation as one might accord an effigy:

> O ye myghty and pompous lordes, shynynge in the glory transytory of thys unstable lyf [. . .] Ye also ye fyers and myghty chyualers so valyaunte in auenturous dedes of armes: Behold beholde: se how this mygh[t]y conquerour Arthour / whom in his humayne lyf / all the world doubted / ye also this noble quene Gueneuer / that som tyme sate in her chare a[d]ourned with golde. perle and precious stones: now lye ful lowe in obscure fosse or pytte coueryd with cloddes of erth and clay ¶ Behold also this myghty cha[m]pyon Launcelot / pyerles of knyghthode: se now how he lyeth grouelynge on the colde moulde. now beynge to feble and faynt that somtyme was so terrible: how and in what manere oughte ye to be so desyrous of the mondayne honour so daungerous. Therefor me thynketh this present boke callid La mort da[r]thur is ryght necessary often to be radde. For in it shal ye fynde the gracious kny3tly and virtuous werre of moost noble knyghtes of the worlde / wherby they gat praysyng contynuell [. . .] And the more that god hath geuen you the tryumfall honour / the meker ye oughte to be / euer feryng the unstablynesse of this dysceyuable worlde [. . .].[60]

Tsuyoshi Mukai reads this intervention as evidence of (possibly) de Worde's "personal disposition," and finds in it a sermonlike tone "incompatible with Malory's secular bias."[61] But the interpolation is consonant

with a late-fifteenth-century response to funeral sculpture, and makes
Launcelot himself the living object of meditation, and also mimics
Launcelot's own reaction to the "sight" of Arthur and his queen. The death
tableau moves the editor to a conventional musing on the instability of the
world. The dialogue poem, "A Disputation between the Body and the
Worms," for example, similarly invokes the Nine Worthies, kings, and em-
perors as models of earthly transience.[62] De Worde is reading the text in
the same way as Launcelot "reads" the scene before him, and draws on the
concept of death as process. Launcelot's shriveling body serves as embodiment of earthly decay on his king's tomb. Paul Binski observes the fifteenth-century popularity of the "transi" tombs, which represented the
body in decay as well as the incorrupt body; they confront notions of the
physical that funerary art had previously sought to conceal, and the con-
templation of such a representation, that plays on the integrity to person-
hood of the physical body, Binski suggests: "challenges our selfhood as well
as that of the dead. We mourn ourselves."[63] Launcelot both creates and
constitutes the object of mourning.

The most detailed postmortem treatment of a body is that of Launcelot
himself; his glorious saintly figurative translation into heaven, and his
sweet-smelling corpse, enact the "incorrupt" body of tomb sculpture
where his living mourning of Arthur has figured physical transience.[64] The
funeral rites stress his earthly valor, and the furniture of ritual offers
oblique, rather than explicit, connections between his body and his former
life. The same bier as served the queen, for example, serves Launcelot's
body (3:1258.20–23). The rites for Launcelot accord him the privileges of
late-medieval royalty, in that he is exposed to view before burial, although
the assurance that it is the practice of "tho dayes," that men of honor
should lie "with open vysage" (3:1258.32–33) resolves a potential ambiguity, as fifteenth-century practice affords such treatment to traitors as well
as to a king such as Edward IV.[65] The process of transporting Launcelot to
Joyous Garde for interment, and his lying-in-state, takes upward of a
month; these details suggest that, while the very existence of Arthur's
corpse is in question, the narrative seems reluctant to part with Launcelot's
incorrupt body.

There is no mention of Launcelot's tomb's having any of the accoutrements, such as armor or harness, that in the fifteenth century accompany chivalric monuments.[66] Ector's spoken eulogy, rather than a
monument, commemorates Launcelot as knight; Ector unites spiritual and
secular in celebrating Launcelot as: "hede of al Crysten knyghtes"
(3:1259.9–10), and hints at paradoxes and tensions in chivalric selfhood—
Launcelot is "the kyndest man that ever strake wyth swerde" (3:1259.16)—
that resolve themselves, in the course of performed narration, into familiar

literary commemoration. By the end of Ector's speech, Launcelot is "the mekest man [. . .] in halle" and the "sternest knyght to thy mortal foo" (3:1259.18–20), terms that recall Hardyng's celebration of Arthur.[67] Spoken witness is clearly more important to the narrator as memorial than is the nature of the tomb. The Post-Vulgate account of the final catastrophe of the Arthurian world, by contrast, articulates chaos by means of the destruction of relics and monuments. King Marc invades Arthur's territories and razes every religious foundation, in order to eradicate all trace of Arthur's empire's existence. Marc's ultimate act of desecration is to have Lancelot's tomb thrown into a lake, and his still incorrupt body burned to ashes. Marc himself is killed while trying to murder the remaining handful of Arthur's knights, and is buried outside hallowed ground (Lacy 5:311–12). For Malory, the engagement with memory, rather than with relic, is important.

Malory was buried in a prestigious location, in St. Francis's chapel in the Greyfriars Church at Newgate. The register of monuments simply describes his tomb as that of a knight ("miles valens"), giving notice of his name, origins, and date of death.[68] But his own valediction at the end of the book, where he asks, "whan I am deed, I praye you all praye for my soule" (3:1260.24), echoes the Maid of Ascolat's request to Launcelot (2:1096.34), as well as the formulae of contemporary and earlier epitaphs.[69] This inscribed appeal acknowledges the mortality of the author and casts the book itself not as a commemoration in a monumental sense but as a testimonial that urges a continuing and active engagement on the part of the living. Malory brings to the *Morte* an awareness of the fifteenth-century fashionings of death, but so translates them as not to account for or unproblematically to commemorate the mortality of his protagonists by unquestioningly asserting the legitimacy and efficacy of death rituals, as to provoke meditation on the expediency and contingency of the workings of ritual and whom they serve, and to ask what and how we commemorate. The text movingly solicits our engagement, while it also partially dismantles the means to our remembering. Above all, through Launcelot, Malory emphasizes the human body itself, in excess, beyond tractability and exemplarity, beyond precise articulation in language, as the primary site of literary and ethical interest. Ultimately, the exemplary is insufficient to account for the histories that we have experienced. The *Morte* is a book that addresses loss, and questions the very terms of our literary access and our memorializing; but, at the same time, in the integrity of its engagement, it urges as necessary the continual process of remaking Arthurian legend.

NOTES

Preface

1. *The Works of Sir Thomas Malory,* ed. Eugène Vinaver, rev. P. J. C. Field, 3rd edn., 3 vols. (Oxford: Clarendon Press, 1990), 3:1119.14–1120.3. All future citations are in the text, by volume, page and line number.

2. C. David Benson cites some typical responses, and suggests that Malory's lack of rhetorical training makes his prose "obscure" here: "The Ending of the *Morte Darthur,*" in *A Companion to Malory,* ed. Elizabeth Archibald and A. S. G. Edwards (Cambridge, UK: Brewer, 1996), pp. 221–38 (p. 227).

3. Uther's desire fits the pattern of erotic narrative Michael Hoey outlines, whereby an expression of desire for another "licenses" use of another's body and is accompanied by metaphors that suggest such desire is "uncontrollable": "The Organisation of Narratives of Desire," in *Language and Desire: Encoding Sex, Romance, and Intimacy,* ed. Keith Harvey and Celia Shalom (London: Routledge, 1997), pp. 85–105 (pp. 103–04).

4. See Kevin Grimm, "Knightly Love and the Narrative Structure of Malory's Tale Seven," *Arthurian Interpretations* 3 (1989): 76–95; and his "Editing Malory: What's at (the) Stake?" in "Special Issue on Editing Malory," ed. Michael N. Salda, *Arthuriana* 5.2 (1995): 5–14 (7–9). See also Carol M. Meale, "'The Hoole Book': Editing and the Creation of Meaning in Malory's Text," in ed. Archibald and Edwards, *Companion,* pp. 3–17 (p. 16).

5. I am indebted to Nick Davis, "Narrative Composition and the Spatial Memory," in *Narrative: From Malory to Motion Pictures,* ed. Jeremy Hawthorn (London: Edward Arnold, 1985), pp. 24–39, for initially drawing the meaning and significance of these terms to my attention.

6. The scribe initially writes "worshypfull man" twice, at fol. 435r of the Winchester Manuscript (London, British Library MS Additional 59678), as if unconsciously anticipating the occlusion of woman as subject. See *The Winchester Malory: A Facsimile,* intro. N. R. Ker, EETS s.s. 4 (London: Oxford University Press, 1976).

7. On the question of sexual and narrative dilation, see especially Patricia Parker, "Literary Fat Ladies and the Generation of the Text," chapter two of *Literary Fat Ladies: Rhetoric, Gender, Property* (London: Methuen, 1987), pp. 8–35.

8. See Felicity Riddy, *Sir Thomas Malory* (Leiden: Brill, 1987) and Jill Mann, whose important writings include: *The Narrative of Distance, the Distance of Narrative in Malory's* Morte Darthur, The William Matthews Lectures, 1991 (London: Birkbeck College, University of London, 1991); "Malory: Knightly Combat in *Le Morte D'Arthur,*" in *The New Pelican Guide to English Literature,* volume I, ed. Boris Ford (Harmondsworth, UK: Penguin, 1982), pp. 331–39; "'Taking the Adventure': Malory and the *Suite du Merlin,*" in *Aspects of Malory,* ed. Toshiyuki Takamiya and Derek Brewer (Cambridge, UK: Brewer, 1981), pp. 71–91.

9. This project also intercalates to some extent with the work of Elizabeth Edwards, *The Genesis of Narrative in Malory's* Morte Darthur (Cambridge, UK: Brewer, 2001), published when my own work was in its final stages of preparation.

10. Thomas J. Csordas, "Embodiment as a Paradigm for Anthropology," *Ethos* 18 (1990): 5–47 (5).

11. Thomas J. Csordas, "Introduction," in *Embodiment and Experience: The Existential Ground of Culture and Self,* ed. Thomas J. Csordas (Cambridge, UK: Cambridge University Press, 1994), pp. 1–24 (p. 12).

12. Homi K. Bhabha, *The Location of Culture* (London: Routledge, 1994).

13. See Carol Meale, "'The Hoole Book,'" pp. 13–14.

Chapter 1

1. Jean Froissart, *Chroniques,* ed. Kervyn de Lettenhove, 25 vols. (1867–77. Repr. Osnabrück: Biblio Verlag, 1967), 5:418–19.

2. Ronald Stewart-Brown, "The Scrope and Grosvenor Controversy, 1385–1391," *Transactions of the Historic Society of Lancashire and Cheshire* 89 (1937): 1–22.

3. "Là fu-il mors et occis en servant son signeur; et voelent bien maintenir et dire li aucun que ce fu pour les parolles que il avoit eu le journée devant à monsigneur Jehan Chandos." [He was dead and slain there serving his lord; and some would willingly hold and affirm that this was on account of the words that he had exchanged the day before with my lord John Chandos.] (*Chroniques,* 5:439)

4. Richard Firth Green, *Poets and Princepleasers: Literature and the English Court in the Late Middle Ages* (Toronto: University of Toronto Press, 1980), p. 10.

5. The *dame* may (from the details of sunbeam and garment color) be a Madonna, but a secular interpretation is also possible. Froissart notes the knights are "jone et amoureuse" [young and in love], *Chroniques,* 5:418. Thanks to Karen Watts of the Royal Armouries, Leeds, for discussing the *dame's* ambiguity. The arms of the John Chandos who died in 1370 are (according to English sources), *or, a pile gules* (gold with a red charge). Of the Clermonts, none has a "dame bleue." On Chandos, see Joseph Foster, *Some Feudal Coats of Arms* (Oxford and London: James Parker, 1902), p. 45, and Anthony Wagner, *Historic Heraldry of Britain* (Chichester: Phillimore, 1972),

p. 52. For Clermont, see S. M. Collins, *The French Rolls of Arms, An Ordinary and an Armory* (Unpublished TS, London: College of Arms, 1942). Thanks to Robert Yorke, archivist at the College of Arms, for generously supplying bibliography on this subject.

6. See Gerard J. Brault, *Early Blazon: Heraldic Terminology in the Twelfth and Thirteenth Centuries, with Special Reference to Arthurian Literature* (Oxford: Clarendon Press, 1972).

7. Helmut Nickel, "Heraldry," in *The New Arthurian Encyclopedia,* ed. Norris J. Lacy (New York: Garland, 1996), pp. 230–34 (p. 230). Arthur in Geoffrey of Monmouth's *Historia regum Britanniae* has a device of the Virgin on his shield at the Battle of Bath: Ed. Acton Griscom (London: Longmans, 1929), p. 438. In the 1464 *The Chronicle of Iohn Hardyng,* ed. Henry Ellis (London: Rivington, 1812), Arthur's "chiefe" banner has: "An ymage of our Lady of golde enthronde / Crowned of golde" (p. 122).

8. See Lesley Johnson and Jocelyn Wogan-Browne's comparison of manuscripts of Laȝamon's *Brut* in "National, World, and Women's History: Writers and Readers of English in Post-Conquest England," in *The Cambridge History of Medieval English Literature,* ed. David Wallace (Cambridge, UK: Cambridge University Press, 1999), pp. 92–121 (pp. 94–100).

9. W. R. J. Barron, "Arthurian Romance: Traces of an English Tradition," *English Studies* 61 (1980): 2–23.

10. Michelle R. Warren, *History on the Edge: Excalibur and the Borders of Britain, 1100–1300* (Minneapolis: University of Minnesota Press, 2000).

11. Julia C. Crick, *The* Historia regum Britannie *of Geoffrey of Monmouth: IV. Dissemination and Reception in the Later Middle Ages* (Cambridge, UK: Brewer, 1991). Some 215 manuscripts of the *Historia* proper survive (p. 9).

12. Robert W. Hanning, *The Vision of History in Early Britain: From Gildas to Geoffrey of Monmouth* (New York: Columbia University Press, 1966), pp. 152–54. See also Martin B. Shichtman and Laurie A. Finke, "Profiting from the Past: History as Symbolic Capital in the *Historia Regum Britanniae,*" *Arthurian Literature* 12 (1993): 1–35.

13. Michelle Warren, *History,* pp. 25–59; Lesley Johnson, "Etymologies, Genealogies, and Nationalities (Again)," in *Concepts of National Identity in the Middle Ages,* ed. Simon Forde, Lesley Johnson, and Alan V. Murray, Leeds Texts and Monographs n.s. 14 (Leeds: University of Leeds, 1995), pp. 125–36.

14. Ad Putter, "Finding Time for Romance: Medieval Arthurian Literary History," *Medium Ævum* 63 (1994): 1–16.

15. "Ne tut mençunge, ne tut veir"; *Le Roman de Brut,* ed. Ivor Arnold, 2 vols. (Paris: Société des anciens textes français, 1938–40), 2:515, l. 9793.

16. For a differently nuanced account of the following issues, see Catherine Batt and Rosalind Field, "The Romance Tradition," in *The Arthur of the English,* ed. W. R. J. Barron (Cardiff: University of Wales Press, 1999), pp. 59–70.

17. Michel Zink, "Une mutation de la conscience littéraire: Le langage romanesque à travers des exemples français du XIIe siècle," *Cahiers de Civilisation Médiévale, Xe-XIIe siècles* 24 (1981): 3–27; Rita Copeland, "Between

Romans and Romantics," *Texas Studies in Literature and Language* 33 (1991): 215–24 (216).

18. Renate Blumenfeld-Kosinski, "Old French Narrative Genres: Towards the Definition of the *Roman Antique,*" *Romance Philology* 34 (1980): 143–59; Barbara Nolan, *Chaucer and the Tradition of the* Roman Antique (Cambridge, UK: Cambridge University Press, 1992).

19. On the importance of the Trojan myth to historiographical writing in French, see Gabrielle M. Spiegel, *Romancing the Past: The Rise of Vernacular Prose Historiography in Thirteenth-Century France* (Berkeley: University of California Press, 1993). On the Trojan myth and the later-medieval production and promotion of French national identity, see Colette Beaune, *The Birth of an Ideology: Myths and Symbols of Nation in Late-Medieval France,* trans. Susan Ross Huston, ed. Fredric L. Cheyette (Berkeley: University of California Press, 1991).

20. Francis Ingledew, "The Book of Troy and the Genealogical Construction of History: The Case of Geoffrey of Monmouth's *Historia regum Britanniae,*" *Speculum* 69 (1994): 665–704.

21. James Carley, "Arthur in English History," in ed. Barron, *Arthur,* pp. 47–57.

22. Zink, "Une mutation," p. 26. Spiegel, *Romancing the Past,* p. 63, suggests Arthurian romance, not obligated to religious or historical truth, signals its literary autonomy through its presentation as "literary game."

23. Siân Echard, *Arthurian Narrative in the Latin Tradition* (Cambridge, UK: Cambridge University Press, 1998), pp. 32–33.

24. Over 160 manuscripts of parts of the Vulgate are extant, though only eight exemplars of the full cycle survive. See Richard Trachsler, *Clôtures du Cycle Arthurien: Étude et textes* (Geneva: Droz, 1996), pp. 557–64.

25. E. Jane Burns, "Vulgate Cycle," in Lacy, *Encyclopedia,* pp. 609–14.

26. For Nolan, *Chaucer,* p. 353, the Cycle self-consciously corrects the secular tendencies of the *roman antique.* E. Jane Burns, *Arthurian Fictions: Rereading the Vulgate Cycle* (Columbus: Ohio State University Press, 1985), argues for the Vulgate's more playful authorial attitude. For biblical echo, see M. Victoria Guerin, *The Fall of Kings and Princes: Structure and Destruction in Arthurian Tragedy* (Stanford: Stanford University Press, 1995), pp. 19–86.

27. Warren, *History,* chapter six, pp. 171–221 (pp. 171–72). On aristocratic investment in Chrétien's romances, see Beate Schmolke-Hasselmann, *The Evolution of Arthurian Romance: The Verse Tradition from Chrétien to Froissart,* trans. Margaret and Roger Middleton (Cambridge, UK: Cambridge University Press, 1998); Donald Maddox, *The Arthurian Romances of Chrétien de Troyes: Once and Future Fictions* (Cambridge, UK: Cambridge University Press, 1991). See also Peter Johanek, "König Arthur und die Plantagenets," *Frühmittelalterliche Studien* 21 (1987): 346–89.

28. *Les Prophecies de Merlin,* ed. Lucy Allen Paton, 2 vols. (New York: Modern Language Association of America, 1926–27).

29. *La Mort le roi Artu,* ed. Jean Frappier (Geneva: Droz, 1964), p. 263: "Gautiers Map [. . .] fenist ci son livre si outreement que aprés ce n'en porroit

nus riens conter qui n'en mentist de toutes choses" [Walter Map here finishes his book so completely that afterward no one can tell any more without lying on every count]. Translation, modified, from *Lancelot-Grail: The Old French Arthurian Vulgate and Post-Vulgate in Translation,* gen. ed. Norris J. Lacy, 5 vols. (New York: Garland, 1993–96), 4:160. Future translations from the Cycles are in the text, by general editor, volume, and page number. Ralph Hanna cites Deuteronomy 4.2; "Ye shall not add unto the word which I command you, neither shall ye diminish aught from it," as "the oldest statement of canonicity," in: *Pursuing History: Middle English Manuscripts and Their Texts* (Stanford: Stanford University Press, 1996), p. 177.

30. Elspeth Kennedy, "Études sur le *Lancelot* en prose. I: Les allusions au *Conte Lancelot* et à d'autres contes dans le *Lancelot* en prose. II: Le roi Arthur dans le *Lancelot* en prose," *Romania* 105 (1984): 34–62 (46), notes how the romances develop from a promised to an actual inclusiveness as they become part of larger cycles.

31. Fanni Bogdanow, *The Romance of the Grail: A Study of the Structure and Genesis of a Thirteenth-Century Arthurian Prose Romance* (Manchester: Manchester University Press, 1966), introduction. See also her introduction to and edition of the text, *La Version Post-Vulgate de la* Queste del Saint Graal *et de la* Mort Artu: *Troisième Partie du* Roman du Graal, vols. 1, 2, 4i (Paris: Société des anciens textes français, 1991-), 1.

32. Eilert Löseth collates the *Tristan* texts in *Le Roman en prose de Tristan: le roman de Palamède et la compilation de Rusticien de Pise: analyse critique d'après les manuscrits de Paris* (1891: repr. New York: Burt Franklin, 1970). See also further research by Emmanuèle Baumgartner, *Le* Tristan *en prose: Essai d'interprétation d'un roman médiéval* (Geneva: Droz, 1975), pp. 15–87.

33. Cedric E. Pickford provides a full overview of this manuscript and its French prose romance contexts, in *L'Évolution du roman arthurien en prose vers la fin du moyen âge d'après le manuscrit 112 du fonds français de la Bibliothèque Nationale* (Paris: Nizet, 1960).

34. Larry D. Benson argues against full availability of the Vulgate: *Malory's Morte Darthur* (Cambridge, MA: Harvard University Press, 1976), p. 8.

35. Emmanuèle Baumgartner, "Les Techniques narratives dans le roman en prose," in *The Legacy of Chrétien de Troyes,* ed. Norris J. Lacy, Douglas Kelly, and Keith Busby, 2 vols. (Amsterdam: Rodopi, 1987, 1988), 1:167–90, notes that the French Gawain is not central to narratives tending toward closure, such as the prose cycles: he can then function as an ever-available hero, in a delimited Arthurian space and time (p. 169). The self-contained episodic aspect of Gawain narratives may account as much for the hero's popularity in English as does the idea that he is a "local hero." On Gawain's lack of "coherent identity" in insular literature, see Thomas Hahn's edition of *Sir Gawain: Eleven Romances and Tales,* TEAMS Middle English Texts Series (Kalamazoo, MI: Medieval Institute Publications, 1995), pp. 1–35 (p. 3).

36. Felicity Riddy, "Reading for England: Arthurian Literature and National Consciousness," *BBIAS* 43 (1991): 314–32 (330–31). On the popularity of

the *Brut,* see Lister M. Matheson, "The Middle English Prose *Brut:* A Location List of the Manuscripts and Early Printed Editions," Analytical and Enumerative Bibliography 3 (1979): 254–66, and emendations in his "Historical Prose," in *Middle English Prose: A Critical Guide to Major Authors and Genres,* ed. A. S. G. Edwards (New Brunswick: Rutgers University Press, 1984), pp. 209–48 (pp. 232–33).

37. *Joseph of Arimathie,* ed. David Lawton (New York: Garland, 1983); see also V. M. Lagorio, "The *Joseph of Arimathie:* English Hagiography in Transition," *Medievalia et Humanistica* n.s. 6 (1975): 91–101.

38. Ed. Barron, *Arthur,* offers a comprehensive overview of Middle English Arthurian texts.

39. For London mercantile interest in French as in English romance, see P. R. Coss, "Aspects of Cultural Diffusion in Medieval England: The Early Romances, Local Society and Robin Hood," *Past and Present* 108 (1985): 35–79 (40). On mid-fourteenth-century mercantile and courtly audiences for romance, see John Simons, "Northern *Octavian* and the question of class," in *Romance in Medieval England,* ed. Maldwyn Mills, Jennifer Fellows, and Carol M. Meale (Cambridge, UK: Brewer, 1991), pp. 105–111 (p. 106). See also John J. Thompson, "Popular Reading Tastes in Middle English Religious and Didactic Literature," in *From Medieval to Medievalism,* ed. John Simons (Basingstoke: Macmillan, 1992): pp. 82–100, on the *Cursor Mundi* poet's assumption of audience knowledge of languages (pp. 85–86).

40. Lee C. Ramsey, *Chivalric Romances: Popular Literature in Medieval England* (Bloomington, Indiana, 1983), p. 10. Michael Chesnutt, "Minstrel Reciters and the Enigma of the Middle English Romance," *Culture & History* 2 (1987): 48–67, posits an interplay between the oral and the literary more complex than an "evolutionary" model (from "oral" to "written" mode) acknowledges.

41. M. T. Clanchy, *From Memory to Written Record. England 1066–1307* (Oxford: Blackwell, 1993), pp. 197–223.

42. Douglas Kibbee, *For to Speke Frenche Trewely: The French Language in England, 1000–1600: Its Status, Description, and Instruction* (Amsterdam: Benjamins, 1991); On Anglo-Norman as a *lingua franca,* see William Rothwell, "The Role of French in Thirteenth-Century England," *Bulletin of the John Rylands Library, University of Manchester* 58 (1975–76): 445–66.

43. Ian Short, "Patrons and Polyglots: French Literature in Twelfth-Century England," in *Anglo-Norman Studies 14. Proceedings of the Battle Conference, 1991.* Ed. Marjorie Chibnall (Woodbridge, UK: Brewer, 1992), pp. 229–49 (p. 230), finds a strong connection between "England's unique trilingual culture" and its "literary precocity."

44. Thomas H. Bestul, *Texts of the Passion: Latin Devotional Literature and Medieval Society* (Philadelphia: University of Pennsylvania Press, 1996), p. 12.

45. Thorlac Turville-Petre, *England the Nation: Language, Literature, and National Identity, 1290–1340* (Oxford: Clarendon Press, 1996), pp. 181–221.

46. *Robert Mannyng of Brunne: The Chronicle,* ed. Idelle Sullens (Binghamton, NY: Binghamton University, 1996), pp. 349–50, ll. 10769–72. Lesley Johnson, "Robert Mannyng of Brunne and the History of Arthurian Literature," in *Church and Chronicle in the Middle Ages: Essays Presented to John Taylor,* ed. Ian Wood and G. A. Loud (London: Hambledon Press, 1991): pp. 129–47, examines how Mannyng negotiates and intercalates English and French narrative traditions.

47. *Of Arthour and Of Merlin,* ed. O. D. Macrae-Gibson, 2 vols., EETS o.s. 268, 279 (Oxford: Oxford University Press, 1973, 1979), 1:5, ll. 25–26. Vol. 1 contains the edited text, 2 the commentary: future references are by line number.

48. French also provides a vocabulary of insult. Rion calls Bohort "Fiȝ a putain" (8998). The corresponding passages in the source for the examples cited do not specify Latin, and the other instances here of French usage in *Of Arthour* are not, in the main, direct translations from the source, at least as represented by the Vulgate *Estoire de Merlin,* ed. H. O. Sommer from British Library, Additional MS 10292, *The Vulgate Version of the Arthurian Romances,* 8 vols. (Washington, DC: Carnegie Institute, 1908–16), 2. All future references to the *Estoire de Merlin* will be to this edition, by page number.

49. "Þo schosen þai so Dieu me saut / A noble kniȝt lord of Nohaut" (7379–80).

50. William Rothwell, "The Trilingual England of Geoffrey Chaucer," *Studies in the Age of Chaucer* 16 (1994): 45–67 (56).

51. Carole Meale detects English interest in French romance into the sixteenth century: "Caxton, de Worde, and the Publication of Romance in Late Medieval England," *The Library* 6th series 14 (1992): 283–98.

52. On the relation of language to ethnic identity in premodern states, see John Armstrong, *Nations Before Nationalism* (Chapel Hill: University of North Carolina Press, 1982), Chapter 8, "Language: Code and Communication," pp. 241–82.

53. L. Delisle, *Recherches sur la librairie de Charles V,* 3 vols. (Paris: Champion, 1907), 2:177, 193–95. On the borrowing of romances, see Cedric E. Pickford, "Fiction and the Reading Public in the Fifteenth Century," *Bulletin of the John Rylands Library, Manchester* 45 (1962–63): 423–38 (426–27). Patrick M. de Winter, *La Bibliothèque de Philippe le Hardi, Duc de Bourgogne (1364–1404)* (Paris: Centre National de la Recherche Scientifique, 1985), p. 168, notes, inventoried in 1384, a "roumant de Merlin" either given or loaned by her aristocratic employer to "la demiselle qui garde lez enffans" [the young woman who looks after the children].

54. Susan H. Cavanaugh, "Royal Books: King John to Richard II," *The Library* 6th series 10 (1988): 304–16 (304).

55. Juliet Vale, *Edward III and Chivalry: Chivalric Society and Its Context 1270–1350* (Woodbridge, UK: Boydell, 1982), pp. 42–56.

56. Susan Cavanaugh, *A Study of Books Privately Owned in England, 1300–1450,* unpublished doctoral dissertation, University of Pennsylvania, 1980, p. 456.

Edith Rickert, "King Richard II's Books," *The Library* 4th series 13 (1933): 144–47 (145).

57. Jeanne Krochalis, "The Books and Reading of Henry V and His Circle," *The Chaucer Review,* 23.1 (1988): 50–77 (64). Mary de Bohun, Henry's mother, owned a copy of the Vulgate *Lancelot* (now BL Royal MSS 20.D. iii and iv)(54).

58. Margaret Kekewich, "Edward IV, William Caxton, and Literary Patronage in Yorkist England," *Modern Language Review* 66 (1971): 481–87. Janet Backhouse, "Founders of the Royal Library: Edward IV and Henry VII as Collectors of Illuminated Manuscripts," in *England in the Fifteenth Century: Proceedings of the 1986 Harlaxton Symposium,* ed. Daniel Williams (Woodbridge, UK: Boydell, 1987), pp. 23–41.

59. Madeleine Blaess, "L'Abbaye de Bordesley et les livres de Guy de Beauchamp," *Romania* 78 (1957): 511–18 (512, 513).

60. For Simon Burley, see V. J. Scattergood, "Two Medieval Book Lists," *The Library,* 5th series 23 (1968): 236–39 (237–38); For Gloucester, see Viscount Dillon and W. H. St. John Hope, "Inventory of the Goods and Chattels Belonging to Thomas, Duke of Gloucester," *Archaeological Review* 54 (1897): 275–308.

61. Madeleine Blaess, "Les Manuscrits français dans les monastères anglais au moyen âge," *Romania* 94 (1973): 321–58 (341, 355).

62. Ethel Seaton, *Sir Richard Roos* (London: Rupert Hart-Davis, 1961), pp. 547–48. H. L. D. Ward, *The Catalogue of Romances in the Department of Manuscripts in the British Museum,* 2 vols. (London: Longmans, 1883, 1893), 1:341–42; 354–55.

63. R. S. Loomis and Laura Hibbard Loomis, *Arthurian Legends in Medieval Art* (London: Oxford University Press, 1938), pp. 89–130.

64. Pickford, "Fiction," 424–25.

65. G. A. Lester, "The Books of a Fifteenth-Century English Gentleman, Sir John Paston," *Neuphilologische Mitteilungen* 88 (1987): 200–17. H. S. Bennett, "The Production and Dissemination of Vernacular Manuscripts in the Fifteenth Century," *The Library* 5th series 1 (1946–47): 167–78 (171–72). Bennett estimates that some sixty-five of the eighty-four extant romances are so preserved. Derek Pearsall's study concludes that sixty-five of ninety-five verse romances were extant in fifteenth-century manuscripts: "The English Romance in the Fifteenth Century," *Essays and Studies* 29 (1976): 56–83 (58).

66. *La Suite du Roman de Merlin,* ed. Gilles Roussineau, 2 vols. (Geneva: Droz, 1996), 1: XLIII–XLV.

67. Louis Malet, Sire de Graville, owned a (ca. 1475) *Tristan* on paper, now BL MS Egerton 989 (Ward, *Catalogue,* 1:362–64). A fifteenth-century *Tristan,* now BL MS Harley 49 (Ward, *Catalogue,* 1:358–59), although on vellum, has no ornamentation other than initials in blue, flourished in red, and bears the signatures of Richard, Duke of Gloucester, and of Elizabeth of York.

68. Carol M. Meale, "Manuscripts, Readers and Patrons in Fifteenth-Century England: Sir Thomas Malory and Arthurian Romance," *Arthurian Literature* 4 (1985): 93–126.

69. John M. Ganim, *Style and Consciousness in Middle English Narrative* (Princeton, NJ: Princeton University Press, 1983), pp. 16–54; Geraldine Barnes, *Counsel and Strategy in Middle English Romance* (Cambridge, UK: Brewer, 1993).

70. Elspeth Kennedy examines cyclic and noncyclic versions in "The Rewriting and Re-reading of a Text: the Evolution of the Prose *Lancelot,*" in *The Changing Face of Arthurian Romance: Essays on Arthurian Prose Romances in Memory of Cedric E. Pickford,* ed. Alison Adams, Armel H. Diverres, Karen Stern, and Kenneth Varty (Cambridge, UK: Brewer, 1986), pp. 1–9.

71. Baumgartner, "Les Techniques," p. 171, notes that where an individual romance from the Cycle exists in isolation, rubrics and other critical apparatus establish its Vulgate context.

72. For the context of *Lancelot of the Laik,* in Cambridge University Library MS Kk.I.5., parts vi-vii, see Gisela Guddat-Figge, *Catalogue of Manuscripts Containing Middle English Romances* (Munich: Fink, 1976), pp. 103–05. For the Thornton Miscellany, see pp. 135–42.

73. For the *Awntyrs'* possible connection with the Neville family, see Rosamund Allen, "*The Awntyrs off Arthure*: jests and jousts," in *Romance Reading on the Book: Essays on Medieval Narrative Presented to Maldwyn Mills,* ed. Jennifer Fellows, Rosalind Field, Gillian Rogers, and Judith Weiss (Cardiff: University of Wales Press, 1996), pp. 129–42.

74. R. Howard Bloch, *Etymologies and Genealogies: A Literary Anthropology of the French Middle Ages* (Chicago: University of Chicago Press, 1983); Alexandre Leupin, *Le Graal et la littérature: Étude sur la vulgate arthurienne en prose* (Lausanne: L'Âge d'Homme, 1982); Burns, *Arthurian Fictions.*

75. *Lancelot. Roman en prose du XIIIe siècle,* ed. Alexandre Micha, 9 vols. (Geneva: Droz, 1978–1983), 8:243 (Lacy 2:177). All future references are in the text, by editor and page number.

76. Baumgartner, "Les Techniques," p. 176.

77. Roberta Krueger, "The Author's Voice: Narrators, Audiences, and the Problem of Interpretation," in ed. Lacy, Kelly, Busby, *Legacy* 1:115–40 (p. 139).

78. David A. Fein, in "'Que vous en mentiroie?': The Problem of Authorial Reliability in Twelfth-Century French Narrative," *Philological Quarterly* 71 (1992): 1–14, argues that similar authorial intrusions in other texts acknowledge a failure to establish narrative authority, and so complicate the audience-narrator relation. For Baumgartner, the *Lancelot* passage ratifies the authority of the narrator over "li contes" ("Les Techniques narratives," pp. 176–77).

79. Ninienne herself knows "les forches des paroles" [the powers of words] and records Merlin's spells in writing (Micha 7:38, 42; Lacy 2: 11, 12).

80. Micha prints the "Robert de Boron" account of Merlin BN MS 110 substitutes for this passage, in an appendix, 7:459–62. Elspeth Kennedy also

discusses four manuscripts that omit these details in: "The Scribe as Editor," in *Mélanges de langue et de littérature du moyen âge et de la renaissance offerts à Jean Frappier par ses collègues, ses élèves et ses amis,* ed. J. C. Payen and C. Régnier, 2 vols. (Geneva: Droz, 1970), 1:523–31 (pp. 525–26). For Leupin, *Le Graal,* pp. 78–80, the Satanic element in Merlin's genealogy radically disrupts the narrative's orthodox lineage (p. 80).

81. *L'Estoire del Saint Graal,* ed. Jean-Paul Ponceau, 2 vols. (Paris: Champion, 1997), 1:4 (Lacy 1:4). Future references are by page number, in the text.

82. E. Jane Burns, *Arthurian Fictions,* p. 53, argues the romances question biblical written authentication, substituting for it an "ambiguous" and "fictive" truth.

83. The iconography of BL MS Additional 10292 stresses the importance of commemorative writing: fols. 80v, 137v, 163v, 188r, have miniatures showing Merlin dictating events to Blase.

84. Leupin, *Le Graal,* p. 36; Rupert T. Pickens, "Autobiography and History in the Vulgate *Estoire* and in the *Prose Merlin,*" in *The Lancelot-Grail Cycle: Text and Transformations,* ed. William W. Kibler (Austin: University of Texas Press, 1994), pp. 98–116 (p. 111).

85. Warren, *History,* pp. 177–81.

86. On the affair as "surplus," both in technical and social terms, see Leupin, *Le Graal,* p. 46: "l'écriture non localisible de l'interstice soutient [. . .] le dire subversif" [A nonlocatable interstitial writing underpins [. . .] the subversive spoken].

87. *La Queste del Saint Graal,* ed. Albert Pauphilet (Paris: Champion, 1980), pp. 279–80 (Lacy 4:87). Future references are by page number in the text.

88. On the vexed question of the historical Walter Map's attitude to vernacular literary production, see Clanchy, *From Memory,* pp. 203–05. For another reading, see Warren, *History,* pp. 180–81.

89. Löseth, *Tristan,* pp. 423–24. Juliet Vale discusses the historical possibilities of this claim in *Edward III and Chivalry,* pp. 19–20.

90. *Le Roman de Tristan en prose,* ed. Renée Curtis, 3 vols. Vol. 1 (Munich: Hueber, 1963); Vol. 2 (Leiden: Brill, 1976); Vol. 3 (Cambridge, UK: Brewer, 1985), 1:39–40 (p. 39).

91. R. Howard Bloch, *Medieval French Literature and Law* (Berkeley: University of California Press, 1977), pp. 44–45.

92. Joerg O. Fichte conflates what he calls English "historiographic fiction" and the Vulgate as "imaginative poetic elaborations" of "historical 'facts'" in "Grappling with Arthur or Is There an English Arthurian Verse Romance?" in *Poetics: Theory and Practice in Medieval English Literature,* ed. Piero Boitani and Anna Torti (Cambridge, UK: Brewer, 1991), 149–163 (p. 156). But for Fichte, in other Middle English texts, the Arthurian court's participation in historical process destroys its idyllic uniqueness and paves the way for "individual interpretations" of its meaning (p. 163).

93. Michèle Perret, "De l'espace romanesque à la matérialité du livre: L'espace énonciatif des premiers romans en prose." *Poétique* 50 (1982): 173–82.

94. *The Auchinleck Manuscript: National Library of Scotland, Advocates' MS 19.2.1.,* intro. Derek Pearsall and I. C. Cunningham (London: Scolar Press, 1977).

95. Laura Hibbard Loomis, "The Auchinleck Manuscript and a Possible London Bookshop of 1330–1340," *PMLA* 57 (1942): 595–627 (627).

96. *An Anonymous Short English Metrical Chronicle,* ed. Ewald Zettl, EETS o.s. 196 (London: Milford, 1935 [for 1934]). References are by line number in the text. The variants of this chronicle Zettl points out (pp. lxi-lxiv), in terms of "fact" and interpretation, attest to the flexibility of English treatments of the Arthurian legend.

97. *Receuil général et complet des fabliaux des XIIIe et XIVe siècles,* ed. Anatole de Montaiglon and Gaston Reynaud, 6 vols. (Paris: Librairie des bibliophiles, 1872–90), 3 (1878), 1–39. R. Howard Bloch discusses this in the context of Arthurian "chastity test" narratives, in *Medieval Misogyny and the Invention of Western Romantic Love* (Chicago: University of Chicago Press, 1991), pp. 94–97. Bloch describes the Arthurian fabliau as "a generic perversion," possessed of "scandalous indeterminacy" (p. 94); perhaps it is so recognized because the French prose texts ostensibly promote a firmer sense of the parameters and decorum of Arthurian legend than English treatments provide.

98. On "Englishness," see David Burnley, "Dynastic Romance," in ed. Barron, *Arthur,* pp. 83–90.

99. The author also refers to "Þe gest" (8679) and to "Þis romaunce" (626). It is uncertain what the audience would understand by these terms, although the author refers to a French source as "Þe romaunce" (8908).

100. See Macrae-Gibson, note to line 937, 2:88.

101. *England the Nation,* pp. 108–41 (p. 126).

102. Barnes, *Counsel and Strategy,* pp. 62–67.

103. In *Merlin* (206–07: Lacy 1:280) Merlin here foretells his own end, and mentions other events uniquely in the future of the narrative.

104. For tags as literary markers of English romance's "traditional quality," see Carol Fewster, *Traditionality and Genre in Middle English Romance* (Cambridge, UK: Brewer, 1987), pp. 22–38 (p. 30). Tim William Machan uses minstrel tags to consider the importance to English romance of orality and literacy's ostensible interrelation in "Editing, Orality, and Late Middle English Texts," in *Vox Intexta: Orality and Textuality in the Middle Ages,* ed. A. N. Doane and Carol Braun Pasternak (Madison: University of Wisconsin Press, 1991), pp. 229–45.

105. Burnley, "Dynastic Romance," p. 87.

106. G.V. Smithers, "The Style of *Hauelok,*" *Medium Ævum* 57 (1988): 190–218. Smithers, in his edition of *Kyng Alisaunder,* 2 vols., EETS o. s. 227, 237 (London: Oxford University Press, 1952, 1957), 2:30–40, finds Old French literary models for the romances' battle imagery and seasons topoi. (As only 410 lines of *Kyng Alisaunder* survive in Auchinleck, the text of the romance is from Bodleian Library, Laud MS Misc. 622).

107. Macrae-Gibson, *Of Arthour,* 2:65–75.

108. *Laʒamon's "Arthur": The Arthurian Section of Laʒamon's* Brut, ed. and trans. W. R. J. Barron and S. C. Weinberg (Harlow, UK: Longman, 1989), ll. 10636, 10644–10645:

> "[. . .] ligeð i þan straeme stelene fisces;
> mid sweorde bigeorede heore sund is awemmed;
> heore scalen wleoteð swulc gold-faʒe sceldes;
> þer fleoteð heore spiten swulc hit spæren weoren."(ll. 10640–43)

109. *Havelok,* in *Medieval English Romances, Part One,* ed. A. V. C. Schmidt and Nicholas Jacobs (London: Hodder & Stoughton, 1980), pp. 37–121: ll. 2689–92.

110. *Of Arthour,* 2:70–72.

111. The precedent for the softness of the season providing conditions suitable for warfare is probably biblical: cf. 2 Kings 11.1: "at the return of the year, at the time when kings go forth to war."

112. Joyce Coleman, *Public Reading and the Reading Public in Late Medieval England and France* (Cambridge, UK: Cambridge University Press, 1996), pp. 141–42.

113. *Le Morte Arthur,* ed. P. F. Hissiger (The Hague: Mouton, 1975), ll. 1–8. Future references are by line number in the text.

114. So adventures are recounted and recorded, and Gawain revises "chevalerie," prowess, as "pechié," sin, when he confesses to killing eighteen knights, Bademagu among them, on the quest of the Grail (1–3; Lacy 4:91).

115. See also Roger Dalrymple, "The Literary Use of Religious Formulae in Certain Middle English Romances," *Medium Ævum* 64 (1995): 250–63 (258).

116. The English poem does, however, have its own, less formulaic, political recourse to antifeminism when the Bishop appeals to Lancelot not to ruin England for the sake of a woman (2300–01).

117. *Lancelot of the Laik and Sir Tristrem,* ed. Alan Lupack, TEAMS Middle English Texts Series (Kalamazoo, MI: Medieval Institute Publications, 1994), ll. 299–313. Future references are by line number in the text.

118. For the texts in the same hand as *Lancelot,* see *Ratis Raving and Other Moral and Religious Pieces, in Prose and Verse,* ed. J. Rawson Lumby, EETS o.s. 43 (London: Trübner, 1870).

119. Bertram Vogel, "Secular Politics and the Date of *Lancelot of the Laik,*" *Studies in Philology* 40 (1943): 1–13. Walter Scheps, "The Thematic Unity of *Lancelot of the Laik,*" *Studies in Scottish Literature* 5 (1967–68): 167–75, reads the poem as a means to link Arthurian legend and Christian orthodoxy (p. 175). See also Douglas Wurtele, "A Reappraisal of the Scottish *Lancelot of the Laik,*" *University of Ottawa Quarterly* 46 (1976): 68–82.

120. Lupack, Introduction, pp. 7–8.

121. The *Lancelot* simply reports that Leodegan was in love with the woman (Micha 1:95; Lacy 2:262).The Vulgate *Merlin,* problematizing conceptions, recounts this same incident as rape (148–49; Lacy 1:248).

122. Judith Ferster, *Fictions of Advice: The Literature and Politics of Counsel in Late Medieval England* (Philadelphia: University of Pennsylvania Press, 1996), p. 9.

123. "Contextualizing *Le Morte Darthur:* Empire and Civil War," in ed. Archibald and Edwards, *Companion,* pp. 55–73 (p. 71).

124. On distinguishing between the "post-colonial" as political situation and the "postcolonial" as relation between cultures in process of continual change, see Vijay Mishra and Bob Hodge, "What is Post(-)colonialism?" in *Colonial Discourse and Post-Colonial Theory. A Reader,* ed. Patrick Williams and Laura Chrisman (Hemel Hempstead, UK: Harvester Wheatsheaf, 1993), pp. 276–90. On the "elasticity" of the concept of the postcolonial, and the range of critical practices postcolonial criticism and theory adumbrate, see further, Bart Moore-Gilbert, *Postcolonial Theory: Contexts, Practices, Politics* (London: Verso, 1997), pp. 5–21 (especially pp. 11–14).

125. Ruth Evans suggests the potential fruitfulness of exploring medieval translation practice in terms of postcolonial theory, as well as advising caution on employing such theory as a template for the medieval cultural condition: see "Translating Past Cultures?" in *The Medieval Translator 4,* ed. Roger Ellis and Ruth Evans (Exeter: University of Exeter Press, 1994), pp. 20–45, and "Historicizing Postcolonial Criticism: Cultural Difference and the Vernacular," in *The Idea of the Vernacular: An Anthology of Middle English Literary Theory 1280–1520,* ed. Jocelyn Wogan-Browne, Nicholas Watson, Andrew Taylor, and Ruth Evans (Exeter: University of Exeter Press, 1999), pp. 366–70. For translation as a "problematic," see Tejaswini Niranjana, *Siting Translation: History, Post-Structuralism, and the Colonial Context* (Berkeley: University of California Press, 1992), p. 8. Homi Bhabha, *The Location of Culture,* p. 5, sees the "translational" as a space of cultural productivity.

126. From the four ways of making a book, in *Commentary on Peter Lombard's Sentences,* in *Medieval Literary Theory and Criticism, c. 1100-c. 1375: The Commentary-Tradition,* ed. A. J. Minnis and A. B. Scott, with the assistance of David Wallace (Oxford: Clarendon Press, 1988), pp. 223–38 (p. 229). I do not claim for the term "compilation" any sense more technical than "anthologizing." For a caveat against confusing the English and Latin terms, and some account of the flexibility of the term "compilatio" in the Middle Ages, see R. H. Rouse and M. A. Rouse, "*Ordinatio* and *Compilatio* Revisited," in: *Ad litteram. Authoritative Texts and Their Medieval Readers,* ed. Mark D. Jordan and Kent Emery, Jr. (Notre Dame, IN: University of Notre Dame Press, 1992), pp. 113–34 (especially pp. 119–20). Pickford questions the literal truth of Gonnot's declaration that he has only followed "authorized" books (*L'Évolution,* p. 24), but see Fanni Bogdanow, "Part III of the Turin Version of *Guiron le Courtois:* A Hitherto Unknown Source of MS. B.N. 112," in *Medieval Miscellany Presented to Eugène Vinaver,* ed. F. Whitehead, A. H. Diverres, and F. E. Sutcliffe (Manchester: Manchester University Press,

1965), pp. 45–64). Gonnot's skill as a compiler is more at issue than his "originality."

127. The inscription at 4: fol. 233a was later altered, and now proclaims the author to be Micheau Gantelet, and his home town, Tournay. On identifying Gonnot as scribe of BN f.fr. 112, see Pickford, *L'Évolution*, pp. 19–24. Transcriptions of material from BN f.fr. 112 (unless explicitly from a printed source) are my own, and references are by volume, folio number, and column.

128. Susan Amato Blackman, *The Manuscripts and Patronage of Jacques d'Armagnac, Duke of Nemours (1433–1477)*, unpublished doctoral dissertation, University of Pittsburgh, 1993. On the Duke's political career, see Bernard de Mandrot, "Jacques d'Armagnac, duc de Nemours, 1433–1477," *Revue Historique* 43 (1890): 274–316; 44 (1890): 241–312.

129. Pickford, *L'Évolution*, Appendice I, pp. 279–319, provides a synopsis of the compilation, together with notes of its sources.

130. Gonnot copied several works for Jacques d'Armagnac's library, ranging from romance to pious literature. In 1463 he completed a copy of the Prose *Tristan* (now BN MS f.fr. 99). Jacques d'Armagnac owned several copies of the Vulgate Cycle and other Arthurian romance, some inherited, others commissioned. See Pickford, *L'Évolution*, pp. 272–90; "A Fifteenth-Century Copyist and His Patron," in ed. Whitehead, Diverres, Sutcliffe, *Medieval Miscellany*, pp. 245–62; "Fiction and the Reading Public in the Fifteenth Century."

131. A late-fifteenth-century copy of Jehan Vaillant's *Guiron le Courtois*, now BN MSS f.fr. 358–63, has Helye, its apparent translator, announce that his work will fill the gaps in extant accounts of the Arthurian legend: the long prologue at BN MS f.fr. 359, fols. 1a–3c, makes much of the entertainment value of the text, its "dis plaisans et delectables" [pleasing and delightful words], while stressing that it has much of moral worth to teach the wise and discriminating who wish to listen, for "des bons ne peut on trop de bien dire" [one can't speak too well of good people]: above all, this tale exemplifies the "courtoisie" of those at Arthur's court. Pickford, *L'Évolution*, pp. 265–70, notes the early printed editions of *Lancelot* and *Tristan* similarly proclaim the romances' didactic qualities.

132. A reference in his account of the good knight Brunor, for example, directs us to "la grant histoire de Tristan" [the great story of Tristan](2: fol. 182b). Brunor the younger avenges his father and performs deeds, as "messire luce du lac" (2:183c) reports them. Fanni Bogdanow, "Part III of the Turin Version," pp. 57–58, traces clear references to *Guiron le Courtois*. 2: fol. 182c mentions events "as told in the history of Lancelot." The compiler, if not exact in his references, is specific in the kinds of text with which the reader is to align his work.

133. Judson Boyce Allen, "The Medieval Unity of Malory's *Morte Darthur*," *Mediaevalia* 6 (1980): 279–309. For Allen, Malory's and Gonnot's writings have the same exemplary aims (285).

134. Pickford, "A Fifteenth-Century Copyist and His Patron," in ed. Whitehead, Diverres, Sutcliffe, *Medieval Miscellany*, pp. 245–62 (p. 260).

135. See Pickford's summary of 4: fols. 1–82 in *L'Évolution*, pp. 312–19.

136. Geoffrey Chaucer, *Troilus and Criseyde*, ed. B. A. Windeatt (Harlow, UK: Longman, 1984), Bk. 2, ll. 17–18. Future references are by book and line number, in the text.

137. Harry Berger, Jr., "Bodies and Texts," *Representations* 17 (1987): 144–66 (147).

138. This is not to endorse Bhabha's view of the Middle Ages, for example, in "DissemiNation: time, narrative, and the margins of the modern nation," in *Nation and Narration,* ed. Homi K. Bhabha (London: Routledge, 1990), pp. 291–322 (p. 308), which, as Carolyn Dinshaw observes, act as totalizing fall guy to his ideas about hybridity: *Getting Medieval: Sexualities and Communities, Pre- and Postmodern* (Durham, NC: Duke University Press, 1999), pp. 16–21 (p. 18).

139. Sherry Simon sees Bhabha's own privileged status as "transnational" academic as partly accounting for his positive position on translational culture: *Gender in Translation: Cultural Identity and the Politics of Transmission* (London: Routledge, 1996), p. 153.

140. Bhabha, *The Location of Culture*, p. 214.

Chapter 2

1. John Steinbeck, *The Acts of King Arthur and His Noble Knights, from the Winchester MSS. of Thomas Malory and Other Sources,* ed. Chase Horton (New York: Noonday Press, 1993), p. 299.

2. Elizabeth Kirk, "'Clerkes, Poetes and Historiographs': The *Morte Darthur* and Caxton's 'Poetics' of Fiction," in *Studies in Malory,* ed. James W. Spisak (Kalamazoo: Medieval Institute Publications, Western Michigan University, 1985), pp. 275–95 (pp. 286–92). Riddy argues Arthur's generally assumed fictionality allows Malory to rework Arthurian history (*Sir Thomas Malory,* p. 43).

3. William Caxton, *The Book of the Ordre of Chyualry,* ed. Alfred T. P. Byles, EETS o.s. 168 (London: Oxford University Press, 1926 [for 1925]), p. 122.

4. Benedict Anderson proposes capitalism and print technology together make possible "a new form of imagined community," one that lays the foundation for the "modern nation," in *Imagined Communities: Reflections on the Origin and Spread of Nationalism* (1983: rev. edn. London: Verso, 1991), p. 46. Yet Caxton clearly has actively to create his community rather than have print technology automatically constitute it.

5. Horst Schroeder, *Der Topos der Nine Worthies in Literatur und bildender Kunst* (Göttingen: Vandenhoeck and Ruprecht, 1971). See also Diana B. Tyson, "King Arthur as a Literary Device in French Vernacular History Writing of the Fourteenth Century," *BBIAS* 33 (1981): 237–57.

6. Russell Rutter, "William Caxton and Literary Patronage," *Studies in Philology* 84.4 (1987): 440–70.

7. Elizabeth Armstrong, "English Purchases of Printed Books from the Continent 1465–1526," *English Historical Review* 94 (1979): 268–90 (269).

8. N. F. Blake, *Caxton's Own Prose* (London: André Deutsch, 1973) p. 69. Kevin Brownlee discusses French examples of the flexible relation of crusading topos to nationalistic impulses: "Cultural Comparison: Crusade as Construct in Late Medieval France," *L'Esprit Créateur* 32.3 (1992): 13–24.

9. On the candidature of Anthony Wydville as chief patron for the *Morte* and related works, see J. R. Goodman, "Malory and Caxton's Chivalric Series, 1481–85," in ed. Spisak, *Studies,* pp. 257–74 (pp. 266–67).

10. Hayden White, "The Historical Text as Literary Artifact," in *The Writing of History: Literary Form and Historical Understanding,* ed. R. H. Canary and H. Kozicki (Madison: University of Wisconsin Press, 1978), pp. 41–62 (p. 50).

11. "Cradok's mantle" might suggest, to some English readers, not only the fabliau, but also the loyal knight who, in the Alliterative *Morte Arthure,* arrives in pilgrim guise, "A renke in a rownde cloke," to warn Arthur of Mordred's treachery: *Morte Arthure: A Critical Edition,* ed. Mary Hamel (New York: Garland, 1984), ll. 3456–556 (l. 3470). (All future references are to this edition, by line number.) In the latter poem, Arthur's ethical integrity, rather than the community's sexual propriety, is at issue.

12. Schroeder, *Der Topos,* p. 333.

13. Mannyng, *Chronicle,* pp. 340–41, ll. 10401–402: "þer is of him no þing said / þat ne it may to gode laid."

14. *Polychronicon Ranulphi Higden Monachi Cestrensis; Together with English Translations of John Trevisa and of an Unknown Writer of the Fifteenth Century,* ed. Churchill Babington and Joseph Rawson Lumby, 9 vols. (London: Longman, 1865–1886), 5:330–39. Higden observes as extraordinary the absence from the writings of so many historians of someone who has reputedly performed marvels such as to kill the Emperor Lucius and make subject the king of France (p. 336).

15. Boccaccio supplies a moral to the story, to the effect that "in this world only the humble things endure," but doubts Arthur's historicity (*The Fates of Illustrious Men,* trans. and abbr. Louis Brewer Hall [New York: Ungar, 1965], pp. 214–15, 218. Higden himself is skeptical of Geoffrey of Monmouth, while Higden's translator Trevisa, more sympathetic to Arthur, questions his source's objections and argues that extravagant accounts of Arthur's deeds do not necessarily invalidate his historicity (*Polychronicon Ranulphi Higden,* 5:339).

16. N. F. Blake, *Caxton's Own Prose,* pp. 128–33 (pp. 131, 129).

17. "Introduction: Caxton, Foucault, and the Pleasures of History," in *Premodern Sexualities,* ed. Louise Fradenburg and Carla Freccero (New York: Routledge, 1996), pp. xii–xxiv.

18. Robert S. Sturges, *Medieval Interpretation: Models of Reading in Literary Narrative, 1100–1500* (Carbondale: Southern Illinois University Press, 1991), p. 219.

19. This contrasts with the specific gendered reading practice outlined for the romance *Blanchardin and Eglantine* (1489), where constancy is the proper feminine response to men's acts of valor (Blake, *Caxton's Own Prose,* pp. 57–58).

20. Caxton, *The Lyf of the Noble and Crysten Prynce, Charles the Grete,* ed. Sidney J. H. Herrtage, 2 vols., EETS e.s. 36, 37 (London: Trübner, 1880, 1881), 1:1–3 (p. 2).

21. *Receuil des Chroniques,* ed. W. Hardy, Rolls Series 39, 5 vols. (London: Longman, Green, Longman, Roberts, and Green, 1864–91), 1:229–90.

22. *Laurence Minot: Poems,* ed. T. B. James and J. Simons (Exeter: University of Exeter Press, 1989). Poem 7, p. 43, on Edward III's French campaigns.

23. "The Figure of Merlin in Middle English Chronicles," in *Comparative Studies in Merlin from the Vedas to C. G. Jung,* ed. James Gollnick (Lewiston, UK: Edwin Mellen, 1991), pp. 21–39. Merlin says that the first king, the lamb, will appear in A.D. 1215 or 1216. *The Brut or The Chronicles of England,* ed. Friedrich W. D. Brie, 2 vols., EETS o.s. 131, 136 (London: Kegan Paul, Trench, Trübner, 1906, 1908), 1:72–76.

24. Bloch, *Etymologies,* p. 3.

25. On teleology, see Valerie Lagorio, "The Apocalyptic Mode in the Vulgate Cycle of Arthurian Romances," *Philological Quarterly* 57 (1978): 1–22.

26. John Johnston, "Translation as Simulacrum," in *Rethinking Translation: Discourse, Subjectivity, Ideology,* ed. Lawrence Venuti (London: Routledge, 1992), pp. 42–56.

27. Paul de Man, *The Resistance to Theory,* foreword Wlad Godzich (Minneapolis: University of Minnesota Press, 1986), p. 82.

28. *Merlin, or The Early History of King Arthur,* ed. H. B. Wheatley, intro. W. E. Mead, EETS o.s. 10, 21, 36, 112 (London: Kegan Paul, Trench, Trübner, 1865, 1866, 1869, 1889), printed in 2 vols., 1:1–3. The Vulgate and Post-Vulgate *Merlin* contain the same account of Merlin's origins, derived from Robert de Boron's *Merlin.*

29. On the text's similarities to Pseudo-Matthew, see Paul Zumthor, *Merlin le prophète: un thème de la littérature polémique de l'historiographie et des romans* (Lausanne: Payot, 1943), pp. 174–76.

30. Blase's book is a major source of our knowledge: see 1:166; 2:259; 2:303.

31. For a fifteenth-century readership, mention of Rome and Jerusalem hints at the subordination of the other Christian Worthies' *imperium* to that of Arthur.

32. Claude Lévi-Strauss notes that cooking is situated between nature and culture and so reflects both domains (*The Origin of Table Manners,* trans. J. Weightman and D. Weightman (London: Jonathan Cape, 1978), p. 489. Significantly, roast meat, which pertains to both raw and cooked states (pp. 479–89) and honey, which is "more than raw" (pp. 479, 256), belong to marked interstitial categories in the analysis.

33. Cf. Marbod of Rennes (ca. 1035–1123), *Liber decem capitulorum:* "Woman [. . .] dislodges kings and princes from the throne, makes nations clash, convulses towns, destroys cities, multiplies slaughters, brews deadly poisons." *Woman Defamed and Woman Defended,* ed. Alcuin Blamires, with Karen Pratt and C. W. Marx (Oxford: Clarendon Press, 1992), p. 100.

34. So in the *Estoire del Saint Graal,* Ypocras's fate as a wise man made foolish by love (*Estoire* 2:349–69; Lacy 1:101–06) is the model for Merlin's own,

and both stories reflect on women's being craftier than the devil (*Merlin* 280: Lacy 1:322). Even Merlin's beginning wryly reworks this antifeminist trope, for his mother's piety is the "art" by which he escapes the devil's control.

35. An example is the story of the knight who restores a princess to her kingdom, which the *moralitas* rewrites as Christ saving the human soul for God, whose kingdom is Paradise. *The Early English Versions of the* Gesta Romanorum, ed. Sidney J. H. Herrtage, EETS e.s. 33 (London: Trübner, 1879), pp. 42–44.

36. Spiegel, *Romancing the Past*, pp. 224–25.

37. *Merlin* (385: Lacy 1:380) does not have the (here italicized) English repetition of detail: "When the kynge herde Merlin so speke, *that in the same place the fader sholde sle the sone, and the sone sle the fader, and the londe of the grete breteigne a-bide with-outen heir and lordles,* he hym prayed [. . .] to telle a partye of that more clerly to his vndirstondinge" (2:579). The Prose *Brut* expresses similar regret that Arthur should leave "none childe of his body bigeten" (1:91).

38. Geoffrey of Monmouth blames the people's depravity for the civil war after Arthur's days, and for the plague, famine, and Saxon dominion with which the *Historia* closes (pp. 506–07, 530–31). The Lambeth MS 84 account of the *Brut* similarly ends with plague at home, and loss of men through venereal disease abroad (2:604).

39. Capgrave, *The Abbreuiacion of Cronicles,* ed. Peter J. Lucas, EETS o.s. 285 (Oxford: Oxford University Press, 1983), p. 97.

40. See Carol Meale, "The Manuscripts and Early Audience of the Middle English *Prose Merlin,*" in ed. Adams, Diverres, Stern, Varty, *The Changing Face,* pp. 92–111. Meale identifies as Elyanor Guldeford's the hand that on CUL MS Ff.3.11 marks passages such as Arthur's and Gonnore's respective conceptions, and the arrival of Ban at Agravadain's castle. See also Meale's later reservations about authorship: " . . . alle the bokes that I haue of latyn, englisch, and frensche": Laywomen and Their Books in Late Medieval England," in *Women & Literature in Britain 1100—1500,* ed. Carol M. Meale (Cambridge, UK: Cambridge University Press, 1993), pp. 128–58 (p. 154, n. 66).

41. No totem is made at this point in the French text, although Merlin explains the meaning of the dragon (*Merlin* 52; Lacy 1:195).

42. Arthur does not understand, without Merlin's gloss, that his later dream of a victorious dragon pertains to him (2:644–45).

43. See Warren's detailed exposition of the mythical histories attaching to Rion's sword Marmiadoise in the Vulgate *Merlin,* and the negative implications of Arthur's desire for it, *History,* pp. 202–210.

44. See also Warren on romance desire and history in the Vulgate, *History,* pp. 209–210.

45. Richard Firth Green, "Notes on Some Manuscripts of Hoccleve's *Regiment of Princes,*" *British Library Journal* 4 (1978): 37–41, points out that British Li-

brary MS Arundel 59 is in the hand of scribe who worked for a London stationer during the reign of Edward IV, and made the copy of the English Prose *Merlin* of which only a leaf is extant, Bodleian Rawlinson Miscellany MS D. 913 (fol. 43).

46. *The Regiment of Princes,* ed. Charles Blyth, TEAMS Middle English Texts Series (Kalamazoo, MI: Medieval Institute Publications, 1999).

47. In additions to the French text, Merlin tells Blase that Uther and Pendragon are young and "haue grete nede of counseile" (1:47), and Pendragon tells his brother they need Merlin "to be with vs of oure counseile" (1:48).

48. *The Active Policy of a Prince,* in *George Ashby's Poems,* ed. Mary Bateson, EETS e.s. 76 (London: Kegan Paul, Trench, and Trübner, 1899), pp. 12–41 (l. 283).

49. Arthur also declares, before the first Battle of Salisbury, "oure lorde foryeteth not his Synner" (2:578).

50. Andrew Lynch, *Malory's Book of Arms: The Narrative of Combat in* Le Morte Darthur (Cambridge, UK: Brewer, 1997), p. 4.

51. Helen Cooper, "M for Merlin: The Case of the Winchester Manuscript," in *Medieval Heritage: Essays in Honour of Tadahiro Ikegami,* ed. Masahiko Kanno, Hiroshi Yamashita, Masatoshi Kawasaki, Junko Asakawa, and Naoko Shirai (Tokyo: Yushodo, 1997), pp. 93–107 (pp. 96–97). My thanks to Professor Cooper for a copy of her article.

52. Kate Cooper, "Merlin Romancier: Paternity, Prophecy, and Poetics in the Huth *Merlin,*" *Romanic Review* 77 (1986): 1–24.

53. Balin recognizes Merlin, for example, simply from his offer of advice: "ye ar Merlion. We woll be ruled by youre counceyle" (1:73.21–26).

54. Elizabeth T. Pochoda's argument, *Arthurian Propaganda:* Le Morte Darthur *as an Historical Ideal of Life* (Chapel Hill: University of North Carolina Press, 1971), pp. 105–06, that Malory implicitly condemns Arthurian society for its refusal to see prophecy as imaginative moral engagement with event, is perhaps more apt a comment on the French texts, and on the *Suite* in particular, where the framework of sin and moral responsibility, and its control, is more explicit.

55. The phrase "out of measure," which occurs some fifty times in the *Morte,* can denote intensity of and/or moral judgment on excessive feeling. See *A Concordance to the Works of Sir Thomas Malory,* ed. Tomomi Kato (Tokyo: University of Tokyo Press, 1974), p. 816.

56. Merlin in the Vulgate uses disguise to test Ulfin's good faith, and Uther recognizes the stratagem as index of Merlin's superior control (*Merlin* 64–65; Lacy 1:202–03).

57. Jay Clayton reviews desire in narrative, and the term's historical contingencies, in: "Narrative and Theories of Desire," *Critical Inquiry* 16 (1989): 33–53.

58. Nicholas Doe, *Fundamental Authority in Late Medieval English Law* (Cambridge, UK: Cambridge University Press, 1990).

59. See Rosemary Morris, *The Character of King Arthur in Medieval Literature* (Cambridge, UK: Brewer, 1982), pp. 24–35.

60. Fortescue, *On the Laws and Governance of England,* ed. Shelley Lockwood (Cambridge, UK: Cambridge University Press, 1997), pp. 55–59 (p. 56).

61. *Brut* 1:66. On different versions of the encounter, see Rosemary Morris, "Uther and Igerne: A Study in Uncourtly Love," *Arthurian Literature* 4 (1985): 70–92.

62. On rape and the Arthurian, see Kathryn Gravdal, *Ravishing Maidens: Writing Rape in Medieval French Literature and Law* (Philadelphia: University of Pennsylvania Press, 1991), chapter six. See also my "Malory and Rape," *Arthuriana* 7.3 (1997): 78–99.

63. Only in Malory does Merlin ask Uther whether Arthur will reign after him (1:12.1–2). In the English Prose *Merlin,* Merlin tells Uther his son will be king, through Christ's power (1:95).

64. Malory appropriates for Merlin the English Prose *Merlin* Archbishop's words concerning Arthur's election and dominance of "logres" (for Malory, "Englond"). Compare 1:18.7–10 with the Prose *Merlin,* 1:112:"the archebisshop seide he sholde be kynge and haue the reame of logres, who-so-ever therto wolde contrarye, seth that it was godes will, for he wolde hym helpe."

65. Contrast with the *Suite,* in which Merlin, who has roundly denounced Arthur's incest, further stresses the moral culpability of seeking the death of one as yet innocent (1:10–13; Lacy 4:169–70).

66. Alliterative *Morte,* 4320–23. Field, "Malory's Mordred and the *Morte Arthure,*" in ed. Fellows, Field, Rogers, Weiss, *Romance Reading,* pp. 77–93.

67. Jill Mann, "'Taking the Adventure.'"

68. Chrétien de Troyes, *Le Roman de Perceval ou Le Conte du Graal,* ed. Keith Busby (Tübingen: Niemeyer, 1993), ll. 3581–95.

69. *The Continuations of the Old French* Perceval *of Chrétien de Troyes,* ed. William Roach, 5 vols. (Philadelphia: University of Pennsylvania Press, 1949–83), 1: ll. 12707–13602.

70. Jeanie R. Brink, "The Design of Malory's 'Tale of Balin': Narrative and Dialogue in Counterpoint," *Studies in Short Fiction* 17 (1980): 1–7.

71. The *Suite* is more explicit about Balain's infringement and Arthur's withdrawal of good will (1:72–73; Lacy 4:187).

72. Mann, "Taking the Adventure," pp. 82–83.

73. "Critique of Violence," in *One-Way Street and Other Writings,* trans. Edmund Jephcott and Kingsley Shorter (London: Verso, 1985), pp. 132–54 (pp. 150–51).

74. See Louise Olga Fradenburg, *City, Marriage, Tournament: Arts of Rule in Late Medieval Scotland* (Madison: University of Wisconsin Press, 1991), p. 207, on how violence dramatizes selfhood in late-medieval tournament by breaking and remaking boundaries "between friend and foe, same and other."

75. *Violence and the Sacred,* trans. Patrick Gregory (London: Athlone Press, 1988), pp. 143–68.

76. Sarah Kay, *The* Chansons de geste *in the Age of Romance: Political Fictions* (Oxford: Clarendon Press, 1995), pp. 52–76 (pp. 58–59).

77. Girard, *Violence,* p. 49.

78. Girard, *Violence,* p. 36.

79. "Balin, Mordred, and Malory's Idea of Treachery," *English Studies* 68 (1987): 66–74 (69): "the deaths of ladies assume an independent form of betrayal that underlies all Balin's misadventures."

80. Heng, "Enchanted Ground: The Feminine Subtext in Malory," (1990) repr. *Arthurian Women: A Casebook,* ed. Thelma S. Fenster (New York: Garland, 1996), pp. 97–113 (p. 101).

81. See my "'Hand for Hand' and Body for Body': Aspects of Malory's Vocabulary of Identity and Integrity with Regard to Gareth and Lancelot," *Modern Philology* 91 (1994): 269–87 (285).

82. Ulfin promises the lovesick Uther that Merlin "shalle do yow remedy" (1:8.14).

83. Bloch, "Merlin and the Modes of Medieval Legal Meaning," in *Medieval French Literature and Law,* traces the prophet's relation to legal institutions.

84. For an example from fourteenth-century law, see Batt, "Malory and Rape," 87.

85. Richard Helmholz documents the expectation that absent fathers would pay maintenance for their children, in *Marriage Litigation in Medieval England* (Cambridge, UK: Cambridge University Press, 1974), pp. 108–09.

86. Heng, "Enchanted Ground," pp. 290–91.

87. Lisa Jefferson, "Tournaments, Heraldry and the Knights of the Round Table: A Fifteenth-Century Armorial with Two Accompanying Texts," *Arthurian Literature* 14 (1996): 69–157 (141–44). The third rule specifies a knight must support "women, widows, orphans and maidens."

88. Richard Barber, "Malory's *Le Morte Darthur* and Court Culture under Edward IV," *Arthurian Literature* 12 (1993): 133–55 (149).

89. The Oath thus combines the two kinds of rules the anthropologist Meyer Fortes observes, drawing on Piaget; those society's members might experience as absolutely binding, imposed by some external force, and those possibly open to change by common agreement because arrived at by the authority of society: *Rules and the Emergence of Society* (London: Royal Anthropological Institute, 1983), pp. 8–9.

90. Ellis, "Balin," 69.

91. *The Black Book of the Admiralty,* ed. Sir Travers Twiss, 4 vols., Rolls Series 55 (London: Longman, 1871), 1:459–72 (p. 460). In contrast to the Pentecostal Oath, the law on the rape of women is here last in a series of prohibitions concerning desecration and violation, the first of which stipulates the death penalty for desecrating the Eucharist (p. 459). For a further note on BL MS Lansdowne 285, John Paston's "Grete Book," see 1:lxxxvi. In English civil law, the Westminster Statute of 1285 mandates the death penalty for rape, but this appears not to have been common legal practice.

John Marshall Carter, *Rape in Medieval England. An Historical and Sociological Study* (New York: University Press of America, 1985).

92. Brownmiller, *Against Our Will: Men, Women, and Rape* (New York: Fawcett Columbine, 1975), p. 16. For a counterargument, see Peggy Reeves Sanday's careful work on "The Socio-Cultural Context of Rape: A Cross-Cultural Study," in *Gender Violence: Interdisciplinary Perspectives,* ed. Laura L. O'Toole and Jessica R. Schiffman (New York: New York University Press, 1997), pp. 52–66.

93. Maddox, *The Arthurian Romances,* pp. 36–48.

94. "Felaw" argues that the individual's attainment of inner peace is a solution to civil war: *A Familiar Dialogue of the Friend and the Fellow,* ed. Margaret S. Blayney, EETS o.s. 295 (London: Oxford University Press, 1989), p. 16.

95. Jacques Derrida, *Of Grammatology,* trans. Gayatri Chakravorty Spivak (Baltimore, MD: Johns Hopkins University Press, 1976), pp. 141–64 (pp. 144–45).

96. See Niranjana, *Siting Translation,* pp. 8–9.

Chapter 3

1. *The Body in Pain: The Making and Unmaking of the World* (New York: Oxford University Press, 1985), p. 117.

2. Mark Breitenberg, *Anxious Masculinity in Early Modern England* (Cambridge, UK: Cambridge University Press, 1996). The link between Lacan and chivalric narrative can be productive, as Lacan draws on romance vocabulary to describe psychoanalytic processes. See Robert S. Sturges, on Chrétien's Lancelot, in *"La(ca)ncelot,"* *Arthurian Interpretations* 4.2 (1990): 12–23 (p. 12); Fradenburg, *City, Marriage, Tournament,* especially chapter eleven; Jeffrey Jerome Cohen and the members of Interscripta, "The Armour of an Alienating Identity," *Arthuriana* 6.4 (1996): 1–24; Kathleen Coyne Kelly, "Malory's Multiple Virgins," *Arthuriana* 9.2 (1999): 21–29.

3. Calvin Thomas, *Male Matters: Masculinity, Anxiety, and the Male Body on the Line* (Urbana: University of Illinois Press, 1996).

4. For the fantasy of physical integrity, see Kathleen Coyne Kelly, "Malory's Body Chivalric," *Arthuriana* 6.4 (1996): 52–71.

5. Benjamin, "Critique of Violence," p. 142.

6. Geoffrey of Monmouth, *Historia,* p. 501, recounts how Arthur passes his crown to his cousin Constantine.

7. Riddy, *Sir Thomas Malory,* pp. 43–47: "Its rampant patriotism [. . .] floats free" (p. 44).

8. Lee Patterson, *Negotiating the Past: The Historical Understanding of Medieval Literature* (Madison: University of Wisconsin Press, 1987), pp. 197–230; Elizabeth Porter, "Chaucer's Knight, the Alliterative *Morte Arthure,* and the Medieval Laws of War: a Reconsideration," *Nottingham Medieval Studies* 27 (1983): 56–78; Juliet Vale, "Law and Diplomacy in the Alliterative *Morte Arthure,"* *Nottingham Medieval Studies* 23 (1979): 31–46.

9. 1:195.14–16 resolves the potential ambiguity of 1:195.6–7: "the kynge resyned all the rule unto thes two lordis and quene Gwenyvere." In the Alliterative *Morte,* the extent of Waynour's power at this point is difficult to determine. Arthur at first simply asks that she be treated with respect: "in wyrchipe be holden" (652), although later Arthur tells her Mordred is answerable to her, "vndyre thy seluen" (710).

10. The Stanzaic *Morte Arthur* has the Archbishop promise the recuperation of political stability, and respectful treatment of Gaynour, by means of the queen's physical return "into hyr boure" (2314). For archaeological evidence of noblewomen's "enclosure," see Roberta Gilchrist, "Medieval Bodies in the Material World: Gender, Stigma, and the Body," in *Medieval Bodies,* ed. Sarah Kay and Miri Rubin (Manchester: Manchester University Press, 1994), pp. 43–61.

11. For London as "king's chamber" and the king's "bridal chamber," in the entry to celebrate Richard II's reconciliation with the City in 1392, and as "secret chambre of Englond," in the welcome of Katherine of Aragon as Prince Arthur's bride in 1501, see Gordon Kipling; respectively, *Enter the King: Theatre, Liturgy, and Ritual in the Medieval Civic Triumph* (Oxford: Clarendon Press, 1998), pp. 16–17; *The Receyt of the Ladie Kateryne,* EETS o.s. 296 (Oxford: Oxford University Press, 1990), p. 9.

12. The Caxton account instead stages citizens' welcomes to Arthur, who is "nobly receyued of alle his comyns in euery cite and burgh" (1:246.16–247.1).

13. Launcelot later sees history as inaccurate and partisan record (3:1203.4–6).

14. James Turner Johnson, *Ideology, Reason, and the Limitation of War* (Princeton, NJ: Princeton University Press, 1975), cites the thirteenth-century writer Guerrero, to the effect that "a prince may make war to free himself from unjust tribute" (p. 50). See also M. H. Keen, *The Laws of War in the Late Middle Ages* (London: Routledge and Kegan Paul, 1965), pp. 63–81.

15. Blake, *Caxton's Own Prose,* p. 131.

16. Malory sets the giant apart by omitting the source's reference to Roman violators. King Angwysshaunce complains the occupying Romans: "raunsomed oure elders and raffte us of oure lyves" (1:188.20); Aungers, in the alliterative poem, tells how the Romans: "rade in theire ryotte and rauyschett oure wyfes" (294).

17. For the pattern of shaming the poem achieves by this motif, see Hamel's notes to 998 ff. and 1023–24, pp. 291–92; Hamel notes the similarity between the submissive behavior the old woman recommends to Arthur, and the actions of the Roman senators defeated at Sessye, whose beards Arthur has shaved (2330–35). Malory's Arthur is earlier outraged at Royns's request for his beard (1:54.35–55.10).

18. Karen Pratt traces, in the *Mort,* this association with land, "the most important symbolic meaning of a woman's body" in the Middle Ages "The Image of the Queen in Old French Literature," in *Queens and Queenship in*

Medieval Europe, ed. Anne K. Duggan (Woodbridge, UK: Boydell, 1997), pp. 235–59 (pp. 255, 256).

19. On rape's association with the foundation of states, see Laurie A. Finke and Martin Shichtman, "The Mont St. Michel Giant: Sexual Violence and Imperialism in the Chronicles of Wace and Laȝamon," in *Violence against Women in Medieval Texts,* ed. Anna Roberts (Gainesville: University Press of Florida, 1998), pp. 56–74. E. Annie Proulx, *Postcards* (London: Harper Collins, 1994) offers a finely judged and resolutely antifoundational treatment of rape as narrative beginning and dynamic. On expansionism and Christendom, see Robert Warm, "Arthur and the Giant of Mont St Michel: The Politics of Empire Building in the Later Middle Ages," *Nottingham Medieval Studies* 41 (1997): 57–71.

20. Winchester has Arthur ask finally only for the cloak (fol. 78v): "So I have the curtyll I kepe no more." Cf. the Alliterative *Morte* (1191): "Haue I the kyrtyll and þe clubb, I coueite noghte ells."

21. Elizabeth Archibald observes fellowship as particular to Malory's Arthurian world: "Malory's Ideal of Fellowship," *Review of English Studies* n.s. 43 (1992): 311–28.

22. For critical response to this section as a journeyman piece, see Vinaver's introduction (1:li–lvi); P. J. C. Field, *Romance and Chronicle: A Study of Malory's Prose Style* (London: Barrie and Jenkins, 1971), p. 67. Sally Shaw argues for Caxton's reworking of an "unsophisticated" text in "Caxton and Malory," in *Essays on Malory,* ed. J. A. W. Bennett (Oxford: Clarendon Press, 1963), pp. 114–45 (p. 143). John Withrington, in "Caxton, Malory, and The Roman War in The *Morte Darthur,*" *Studies in Philology* 89 (1992): 350–66, offers further evidence for Caxton's hand in revision of the tale. A lively debate continues over Malory's putative authorship of the "Caxton" version; see the articles in "Special Issue," ed. Salda: Shunichi Noguchi, "The Winchester Malory," 15–23; Charles Moorman, "Desperately Defending Winchester: Arguments from the Edge," 24–30; P. J. C. Field, "Caxton's Roman War," 31–73.

23. Compare the heavily alliterative description of "Chastelayne, a chylde of kyng Arthurs chambir"'s valor against Cheldrake and his death in the subsequent skirmish (1:239.12–20), with Caxton's laconic "in that stoure was syr Chestelayne a chyld and ward of syre Gawayne slayne" (1:239.6–7).

24. David Lawton, ed., *Joseph of Arimathie,* p. xxvii.

25. *Merlin* (396): "si i peust on ueoir mainte merueille faire darmes & maint cheualier verser et trebucier & maint hauberc desrompre & desmaillier & hiaumes uoler des testes & escus des cols . . ." [great wonders of skilled fighting could be seen, with many knights tumbling and thrown down, many hauberks cut through and links undone, many helmets flying from heads and shields from necks] (Lacy 1:386).

26. See for example: "The gome and þe grette horse at þe grounde lyggez" (*Morte Arthure,* 1372), and:
    "Schaftes schedred wer sone & scheldes yþrelled,

And many schalke thurghe schotte withe þe scharpe ende," *The Siege of Je-rusalem*, ed. E. Kölbing and Mabel Day, EETS o.s. 188 (London: Milford, 1932), ll. 1117–18).

27. Cf. *Merlin* (171): "plora des iex de sa teste." Roberd the Robber "wepte faste water with hise eighen," William Langland, *The Vision of Piers Plow-man: A Critical Edition of the B-text*, ed. A. V. C. Schmidt (London: Dent, 1978), Passus V, l. 473.

28. "The water [. . .] brought down sheldes and speres fletynge grete foyson [. . .] and [he] saugh [. . .] vpon the watir fletynge the harneys of knyghtes and of horse that were deed and drowned" (1:248).

29. *The Riverside Chaucer*, ed. Larry D. Benson et al. (Oxford: Oxford University Press, 1988), I, 2603–10. Future references to *The Canterbury Tales* are by fragment and line number.

30. See also Jeremy Smith, "Language and Style in Malory," in ed. Archibald and Edwards, *Companion*, pp. 97–113 (p. 106).

31. This provides an exception to Jill Mann's observation, in *The Narrative of Distance*, p. 31, that "(Malory's) narrative never masquerades as a present event; it is always separated from us by a barrier of time that holds it at a distance."

32. The Emperor Lucius's band of "horryble peple" (1:194.3) includes "Saresyns" and giants "engendirde with fendis" (1:193.25), but is not as alien as the enemy in the poem, peculiar in the practice of war as in their accoutrements (2283–89). At 1:239.1–4, Priamus's men send word that they are leaving the Duke of Lorraine's service, "for the love of oure lyege lorde Arthure."

33. See Vinaver's comment (3:1388), and cf. Beverly Kennedy, *Knighthood in the Morte Darthur* (Cambridge, UK: Brewer, 1985), p. 107. Kennedy charac-terizes Arthur's view as "rational and pragmatic" where Launcelot is "irra-tional and impractical," yet concludes that Launcelot is "more noble."

34. On the episode as concerned with the gloomy recursiveness of history, see Patterson, *Negotiating the Past*, pp. 221–22. For a more optimistic reading of the heroes' homosocial and spiritual bonding, see Hamel's notes to 2587 ff, p. 340, and "The 'Christening' of Sir Priamus in the Alliterative *Morte Arthure*," *Viator* 13 (1982): 295–307. Hamel argues that as member of the Greek rather than the Western Church, Priamus would have been consid-ered a schismatic—hence the reference to "thy Cryste."

35. The text also forgets the rationale for Palomides's own behavior in its anx-iety for integration.

36. The narrative prays for "A verry final pees in al Cristen reames, þat þe In-fidelis & miscreantes may be withstanden & destroied, & our feith en-haunced, which in thise dayes is sore mynnshed by þe puissaunce of þe Turkes & hethen men; And þat after þis present & short life we may come to þe euer-lastyng life" (*Brut*, ed. Brie, 2:533).

37. The Winchester Manuscript itself supplements the poem where Arthur will not spare those who ally themselves with the Saracens (1:224.1–3), but

their enmity against Arthur defines them more than does their religion: "sle doune and save nother hethyn nothir Crystyn" (1:224.4). For Caxton, the enemy is heathen: Gawain counsels that with God's help they will over-throw the "sarasyns and mysbyleuyng men" (1:235.6). Caxton's version of Arthur's campaign replicates the partisan element in *Godeffroy of Boloyne,* ed. Mary Noyes Colvin, EETS e.s. 64 (London: Kegan Paul, Trench, Trüb-ner, 1893), p. 152, where "oure peple," the crusaders, fight "mescreauntes."

38. This has romance as well as chronicle precedent; the hero of *Sir Percyvell of Gales* also dies in the Holy Land: *Ywain and Gawain, Sir Percyvell of Gales, The Anturs of Arther,* ed. Maldwyn Mills (London: Dent, 1992), ll. 2280–283. Malory's account of Arthur's death conflates the *Brut's* report that it is "dotous," with the ending of the *Brut* itself.

39. Lesley Johnson, "King Arthur at the Crossroads to Rome," in *Noble and Joy-ous Histories: English Romances, 1375–1650,* ed. Eiléan Ní Cuilleanáin and J. D. Pheifer (Dublin: Blackrock, 1993), pp. 87–111, argues the *Morte* "ques-tions whether, and how far, the quest for an empire is compatible with that for salvation" (p. 111).

40. Hardyng apostrophizes Guinevere (and her beauty) and Fortune, as well as Mordred and his treachery, in his analysis of Arthur's fate, *Chronicle,* pp. 148–49.

41. "To King Henry the Fourth: In Praise of Peace," *The English Works of John Gower,* ed. G. C. Macaulay, 2 vols., EETS e.s. 81, 82 (London: Oxford Uni-versity Press, 1900, 1901), 2:481–92 (p. 489, ll. 283–84).

42. Malory does not recount this episode, although in the *Tristram* a damsel asks for "Launcelot that wan the Dolorous Garde" (1:388.25).

43. See *Suite* 1:85; Lacy 4:190. Malory has changed part of what in the *Suite* is an inscription, into an oral prophecy.

44. Bhabha suggests one can apply the terms of psychic anxiety to interstitially sited narratives: *The Location of Culture,* pp. 213–14.

45. See Beverly Kennedy, "Malory's Lancelot: 'Trewest lover, of a synful man,'" *Viator* 12 (1981): 409–56; Joerg O. Fichte, "From 'Shyvalere de Charyot' to 'The Knyght That Rode in the Charyot': Thoughts on Malory's Adapta-tion of the *Vulgate Lancelot,*" in: *Genres, Themes, and Images in English Liter-ature,* ed. Piero Boitani and Anna Torti (Tübingen: Narr, 1988), pp. 73–89, argues Lancelot is primary expositor of Malory's "ideal of active knight-hood" (p. 89). For more skeptical inquiries into Malorian masculinity, see Cohen, "The Armour"; Coyne Kelly, "Malory's Body Chivalric."

46. Thomas, *Male Matters,* pp. 2–3. Thomas is primarily interested in "*writing it-self as a bodily function*" (p. 3), but his remarks are suggestive for thinking through the *Morte's* anxieties of somatic representation.

47. Gary Ferguson, "Symbolic Sexual Inversion and the Construction of Courtly Manhood in Two French Romances," *The Arthurian Yearbook* 3 (1993): 203–13 (203).

48. Who koude telle yow the forme of daunces
So unkouthe, and swiche fresshe contenaunces,

Swich subtil lookyng and dissymulynges
For drede of jalouse mennes aperceyvynges?
No man but Launcelot, and he is deed. (V, 283–87)

49. For a woman's gift of a sword as Arthurian motif, see Jennifer R. Good-
    man, "The Lady with the Sword: Philippa of Lancaster and the chivalry of
    Prince Henry the Navigator," in *Chivalry and Exploration, 1298–1630*
    (Woodbridge, UK: Boydell, 1998), pp. 134–48 (pp. 144–47). John F. Plum-
    mer discusses the shield's emblematization of sexual consummation and
    loss of male psychic wholeness, in "Frenzy and Females: Subject Formation
    in Opposition to The Other in the Prose *Lancelot*," *Arthuriana* 6.4 (1996):
    45–51.
50. E. Jane Burns, "Which Queen? Guinevere's Transvestism in the French
    Prose *Lancelot*," in *Lancelot and Guinevere: A Casebook,* ed. Lori Walters
    (New York: Garland, 1996), pp. 247–65.   •
51. See Commentary (3:1408–13). 1:253.20–264.5 correspond to Micha
    4:165–95 (Lacy 3:153–60). 1:264.6–272.31 are analogous to Micha
    5:25–47 (Lacy 3:212–217). The rescue of Kay at 1:272–278 derives from
    Micha 5:281–93 (Lacy 3:272–77. The Melyot adventure (1:278–84) is
    based on *Li Haut Livre du Graal: Perlesvaus,* ed. William A. Nitze and T. A.
    Jenkins, 2 vols. (Chicago: University of Chicago Press, 1932–37), 1:340–45.
    Launcelot's encounter with Pedyvere, 1:284.15–286.18 finds analogue in
    Micha 4:317–25, 339–45 (Lacy 3: 189–90, 193–94). The conclusion to the
    tale (1:286.19–287.26) is based on Micha 4:393–99 (Lacy 3:205–06).
    P. J. C. Field demonstrates how the Paris text of the *Lancelot* Micha edits is
    rather closer to Malory's source than is the London version Sommer edited
    that Vinaver used for comparison, in: "Malory and the French prose
    Lancelot," *Bulletin of the John Rylands University Library of Manchester* 75
    (1993): 79–102. David R. Miller relates sources to the *Tale's* structure in:
    "Sir Thomas Malory's *A Noble Tale of Sir Launcelot du Lake* Reconsidered,"
    BBIAS 36(1984): 230–56; A. E. Hartung, "Narrative Technique, Character-
    ization, and the Sources in Malory's 'Tale of Sir Lancelot,'" *Studies in Philol-
    ogy* 70 (1973): 252–68.
52. Edward Donald Kennedy, "Malory's 'Noble Tale of Sir Launcelot du Lake',
    the Vulgate *Lancelot,* and the Post-Vulgate *Roman du Graal*," in *Arthurian
    and Other Studies Presented to Shunichi Noguchi,* ed. Takashi Suzuki and
    Tsuyoshi Mukai (Cambridge, UK: Brewer, 1993), pp. 107–29, sees the
    events of the Launcelot section as important primarily for their connective
    function (p. 108).
53. See 1:256.27, 260.26–28, 279.13–14. The Damsel of the White Palfrey
    asks Launcelot his name (1:264.17–21), but clearly knows of him
    (1:270.15–27). Tellingly, male characters earlier in the *Tale* do not rec-
    ognize Launcelot—cf. the words of Terquyn (1:266.14–19) and Gaheris
    (1:268.2–3)—although later, Phelot (1:283.7–8) and Pedyvere
    (1:284.28) both know him.

54. For example: "Now turne we unto sir Launcelot that had ryddyn longe in a grete foreste." (1:275.7–8): "Now leve we there and speke we of sir Launcelot that rode a grete whyle in a depe foreste." (1:278.18–19) Also, 1:269.17; 1:286.19.

55. In *Lancelot,* a damsel tells Hector how Tericam has abducted Lionel (Micha 4:168–69; Lacy 3:154), but Malory's Ector asks about "adventures" of "a man was lyke a foster" (1:254.30–34). In Micha 4:166–68 (Lacy 3:154), Lionel is captured while helping a damsel; in Malory's version, Lionel's adventure is wholly masculine (1:254.3–26).

56. Burns, "*La Voie de la Voix:* The Aesthetics of Indirection in the Vulgate Cycle," in: ed. Lacy, Kelly, and Busby, *The Legacy of Chrétien de Troyes,* 2:151–67.

57. Dante, *The Divine Comedy 1: Inferno,* ed. and trans. John D. Sinclair (New York: Oxford University Press, 1961), p. 78 (5.121–38).

58. Female agency in general disappears, for Pelles's Daughter has no name here, and emerges only as a negative; when a wrathful Lancelot wants to kill his lover, her request for mercy such as God showed to Mary Magdalene appears to acknowledge sexual guilt (Micha 4:212; Lacy 3:165).

59. A damsel who rescues Lancelot from a well only just escapes burning (Micha 4:304–30; Lacy 3:187–91). Lancelot reacts too slowly to save another damsel who cries for help (Micha 5:280; Lacy 3:273–74).

60. Even the dog that, in the *Perlesvaus,* guides Lancelot to the body of Sir Gylberd, is female in Malory's version (1:278.18–35).

61. In the source, Lancelot is lodging with a forester at the edge of a wood when the adventure begins (Micha 5:281; Lacy 3:274). In Malory, he stays with "an olde jantylwoman" (1:272.37).

62. D. A. Miller, *The Novel and the Police* (Berkeley: University of California Press, 1988), p. 195. Coyne Kelly also draws on Miller, to argue for the erasure of violence in this text as another "open secret," "Malory's Body Chivalric," p. 65, fn.2.

63. Miller, *Novel,* p. 207.

64. For moral readings, see: Derek Brewer, "Malory's 'Proving' of Sir Launcelot," in ed. Adams, Diverres, Stern, and Varty, *The Changing Face,* pp. 123–36; Andrew Welsh, "Lancelot at the Crossroads in Malory and Steinbeck" *Philological Quarterly* 70 (1991): 485–502, argues Launcelot's love is "admirable in its loyalty but sinful and destructive in its effects" (p. 498).

65. At Micha 1:315 (Lacy 2:315) for example, Lancelot tells Morgain that he would never reveal to her the name of one he loved.

66. The *Memoriale Credencium* warns that the adulterer will suffer "some myschef oþer schenschip in þis world" as well as in the next, and that lechery in general "makiþ a man to lese his strengþe and his gode loos and catel and grace in doyng of alle his dedis." *Memoriale Credencium: A late Middle English Manual of Theology for Lay People edited from Bodley MS Tanner 201,* ed. J. H. L. Kengen (Nijmegen: Catholic University of Nijmegen, 1979), pp. 139–41.

67. Janet Jesmok, "'A knyght wyveles': The Young Lancelot in Malory's *Morte Darthur,*" *Modern Language Quarterly* 42 (1981): 315–30. Felicity Riddy writes of the text's "painful ambivalence" toward women, *Sir Thomas Malory,* p. 58: "by virtue of their sex they should be protected, but by virtue of their sexuality they deserve to die."

68. Coyne Kelly, "Malory's Body Chivalric," 53.

69. "Malory's Body Chivalric," 60–61.

70. Cohen, "The Armour," 1.

71. See Thomas's opening chapter, *Male Matters.*

72. Julia Kristeva, *Powers of Horror: An Essay on Abjection,* trans. Leon S. Roudiez (New York: Columbia University Press, 1982), p. 4.

73. Confusion of the chivalric body with huntable meat is a leitmotif of the horrific in Malory; see Balin's apprehension of himself as game (1:88.11–12) and Launcelot's own abject condition as the recipient of the huntress's arrow, which he receives because she has lost the "veray parfit fewtre" of the deer she has been pursuing (3:1104.22).

74. Elisabeth Bronfen, *Over Her Dead Body: Death, Femininity, and the Aesthetic* (Manchester: Manchester University Press, 1992). See also, Elisabeth Bronfen and Sarah Webster Goodwin, "Death and Gender," pp. 13–15 of "Introduction" to *Death and Representation,* ed. Sarah Webster Goodwin and Elisabeth Bronfen (Baltimore, MD: Johns Hopkins University Press, 1993).

75. This line suggests that written authority can somehow contain or erase the problems of readerly identification. The "French book" also provides initial justification for telling stories of Launcelot (1:253.12–15), and towards the end, it reveals Pedyvere's fate (1:286.14).

76. See Calvin Thomas: "whereas masculine anxieties are largely phantasmatic, women's fears of being marginalized and silenced—indeed, of being raped and murdered—are anything but: men's fears *produce* women's fate" (*Male Matters,* pp. 16–17).

77. Bronfen remarks on how the spectator or reader is inevitably implicated by means of voyeuristic engagement in the narrative representation of death and how her/his own position is consequently destabilized (*Over Her Dead Body,* p. 54).

78. Riddy, *Sir Thomas Malory,* p. 49, sees the incident as "ambivalent." Kennedy, "Malory's 'Noble Tale of Sir Launcelot du Lake,'" pp. 127–28, sees Launcelot's qualified success as appropriate to his future Grail experiences.

79. Unlike Launcelot's fantasized corpse, Pedyvere's wife's body is evacuated of meaning but that Launcelot designates it her husband's punishment and penance.

80. Kennedy draws out the similarity between the fates of Pedivere and Lancelot in: "Malory's 'Noble Tale of Sir Launcelot du Lake,'" p. 128.

81. We "speke of" (1:329.18) and "turne to" (1:328.4) others than Gareth (1:319.27), for example.

82. On Gareth's "normalcy," and the idea that he belongs to a comedy embedded in a tragic narrative, see Donald L. Hoffman, "Perceval's Sister:

Malory's 'Rejected' Masculinities," *Arthuriana* 6.4 (1996): 72–83 (74–75). Hoffman's analysis assumes that Gareth's married state is the primary defining aspect of his masculinity.

83. Fradenburg, *City, Marriage, Tournament,* p. 171.

84. Kay's assumption that Gareth requests to serve in the kitchens because he has been "fosterde up in som abbey" (1:295.22) links Gareth ironically to Galahad (2:854.14–15), and shows the distance between the two.

85. For *Gareth* as family drama and maturation narrative, see Derek Brewer, *Symbolic Stories* (Cambridge, UK: Brewer, 1980), pp. 100–11. See also Thomas L. Wright, "On the Genesis of Malory's *Gareth,*" *Speculum* 57 (1982): 569–82. For the link with courtesy books, see Felicity Riddy, *Sir Thomas Malory,* pp. 60–83. Wheeler interprets Gareth's career in terms of alchemical processes in "'The Prowess of Hands': The Psychology of Alchemy in Malory's 'Tale of Sir Gareth,'" in *Culture and the King. The Social Implications of the Arthurian Legend,* ed. Martin B. Shichtman and James P. Carley (Albany: State University of New York Press, 1994), pp. 180–95.

86. Daniel Pigg, in Cohen, "The Armour of an Alienating Identity," p. 8, notes Malory attempts "to write (Gareth) more fully in one version of masculinity."

87. On the "bipartite form" as a conventional medieval structure, see William W. Ryding, *Structure in Medieval Narrative* (The Hague: Mouton, 1971). I do not endorse Ryding's opinion on the *Morte* itself as (p. 160): "a series of independent stories whose presentation as one continuous romance was due entirely to Caxton."

88. Davis, "Narrative Composition," p. 32.

89. Felicity Riddy pertinently observes how Bewmaynes tends to be indulged, as one would a child. *Sir Thomas Malory,* p. 67.

90. Jane Gallop, *Thinking Through the Body* (New York: Columbia University Press, 1988), p. 7.

91. See my "'Hand for Hand' and 'Body for Body': Aspects of Malory's Vocabulary of Identity and Integrity with Regard to Gareth and Lancelot," *Modern Philology* 91 (1994): 269–87 (276).

92. Pierre Bourdieu, *Language and Symbolic Power,* ed. and intro. John B. Thompson, trans. Gino Raymond and Matthew Adamson (Cambridge, UK: Polity Press, 1991), p. 118, notes how rites of institution "naturalize" social oppositions.

93. Commentary, 3:1435. See Micha 4:71–73 (Lacy 3:131–32). Vinaver's synopsis does not reveal that Brandeliz's "lady" is a damsel he desires, who sleeps with him after he kills her lover in a fight over her.

94. Olivier de La Marche, *Traités du duel judiciare. Relations de pas d'armes et tournois,* ed. Bernard Prost (Paris: Léon Willem, 1872), pp. 55–95. Fradenburg also mentions this briefly, *City, Marriage, Tournament,* p. 211.

95. In the combat with the Red Knight, Gareth's opponent reappropriates "the gaze" Gareth and Lyonesse share, for the furtherance of masculine combat: "Leve thy beholdyng and loke on me, I counsayle the, for [. . .] she is my lady, and for hir I have done many stronge batayles" (1:321.35–37).

96. Later mentions of Lynet as a "damesell Saveaige" (at 1:357.32, for instance), when she is fully socially accommodated and accommodating, suggest a continuing performativity.

97. *Lybeaus Desconus,* ed. M. Mills, EETS o.s. 261 (London: Oxford University Press, 1969), l. 1414; the narrator describes how:

Wyth fantasme and fayrye
Þus sche blerede hys yȝe,
Þat euell mot sche þryue. (ll. 1432–34)

98. Renaut de Beaujeu, *Le Bel Inconnu,* ed. G. Perrie Williams (Paris: Champion, 1929):

Mais por un biau sanblant mostrer
Vos feroit Guinglain retrover
S'amie, que il a perdue,
Qu'entre ses bras le tenroit nue. (ll. 6255–58)

[But for a fair look, he will ensure for you that Guinglain finds his love, whom he has lost, and will hold her naked in his arms.]

Simon Gaunt, *Gender and Genre in Medieval French Literature* (Cambridge, UK: Cambridge University Press, 1995), pp. 102–13, looks at the ending of the poem in the context of the ambivalence of romance constructs of masculine identity.

99. Miller, *The Novel and the Police,* p. 207.

100. Lynch, *Malory's Book of Arms,* p. 67.

101. Laurie A. Finke and Martin B. Shichtman, "No Pain, No Gain: Violence as Symbolic Capital in Malory's *Morte d'Arthur,*" *Arthuriana* 8.2 (1998): 115–34 (123–24).

102. Coyne Kelly, "Malory's Multiple Virgins," 26.

103. Bonnie Wheeler points out that if there is any educative process at work here, it is for Lynet rather than for Gareth: she learns not too heal him so quickly on the next occasion: "The Prowess of Hands," p. 186.

104. Maureen Fries, "How many Roads to Camelot? The Married Knight in Malory's *Morte Darthur,*" in ed. Carley and Shichtman, *Culture and The King,* pp. 196–207: "wedlock restrains knightly development" (p. 204).

105. *Malory's Book of Arms,* p. 74: "The discourse of blood contains a conflict between some of the text's major symbolic systems."

106. See also: 1:312.29–34; 1:315.19–20; 1:326.19–25.

107. Donald L. Hoffman comments on Gareth's success generally in contrast with Balin's failure, in: "Malory's 'Cinderella Knights' and the Notion of Adventure," *Philological Quarterly* 67 (1988): 145–56 (145–48).

108. The name is used when the Red Knight is identified, at the chivalric display of the healing of Sir Urry (3:1150.32)

109. "No Pain, No Gain," 125.

Chapter 4

1. This contrasts with the clearer focus of the notes for the *Sankgreal* section, which mention, for example, features of Galahad's career (fols. 349v; 351r; 351v), the death of Perceval's Sister (fol. 398v), and Launcelot's vision of the Grail at Corbenic (fol. 401v).

2. "'Gentyl Audiences' and 'Grete Bookes': Chivalric Manuals and the *Morte Darthur*," *Arthurian Literature* 15 (1997): 205–16 (215). James I. Wimsatt suggests the section "effectively supplements contemporary courtesy books," "The Idea of a Cycle: Malory, the Lancelot-Grail, and the *Prose Tristan*," in *The Lancelot-Grail Cycle*, ed. Kibler, pp. 206–18 (p. 216).

3. "A structure of memory has been substituted for specific memories. Since the responsibility for memory resides in the text, rather than in the reader, we must also forget what it forgets": "Amnesia and Remembrance in Malory's *Morte Darthur*," *Paragraph* 13.2 (1990): 132–46 (143).

4. Edwards, "Amnesia and Remembrance," 144.

5. Lynch, *Malory's Book of Arms*, pp. 79–133. Mann observes the intersection and pursuit of different narrative threads conveys the sense that the "real" narrative is always somehow taking place elsewhere, and remarks on the deferral and oblique reporting of deaths: *The Narrative of Distance*, pp. 23–26; 29–30.

6. Riddy, *Sir Thomas Malory*, pp. 83–84, notes that Merlin rescues Melyodas after (one assumes) the Roman wars, but Merlin disappears before Arthur's campaign.

7. Vinaver identifies Malory's source as a version of the narrative for which he cites several manuscripts as close cousins, among them BN fr. 103, 334, and 99 (*Commentary*, 3:1449), but Michael N. Salda, "Reconsidering Vinaver's Sources for Malory's 'Tristram,'" *Modern Philology* 88 (1991): 373–81, suggests a composite text, closer to the manuscript that would have served as a base text for the 1489 printed edition of *Tristan*. Renée Curtis's edition covers the story up to Tristan's period of madness in the forest, with MS Carpentras 404 as the base text. Vienna, Österreichische Nationalbibliothek MS 2542, continues and concludes the narrative; gen. ed. Philippe Ménard, 9 vols. (Geneva: Droz, 1987–1997). References to these editions will be by editor, volume, and page number. Neither of these manuscripts fully represents Malory's source. *Tristan 1489* is a facsimile edition of the printed text, with an introductory note by C. E. Pickford (London: Scolar Press, 1976).

8. Malory does not mention the sexual violence that awaits Iseut in the "lazar-cote" (1:432, 18; cf. Curtis 2:143–45), nor the intrigue surrounding the substitution of Brangain's virgin body for Iseut's on Iseut's wedding-night, and the plans to dispose of Brangain (Curtis 2:92–101.

9. See Riddy, *Sir Thomas Malory*, chapter four; Helen Cooper, "The Book of Sir Tristram de Lyones," in ed. Archibald and Edwards, *Companion*, pp. 183–201 (p. 198).

10. Gerald L. Bruns, "The Originality of Texts in a Manuscript Culture," *Comparative Literature* 32 (1980): 113–29, notes writing is "always mediated by the texts that provide access to the system. To write is to intervene in what has already been written" (123).

11. *Le* Tristan en prose, pp. 85–87.

12. Van Coolput, *Aventures quérant et le sens du monde: Aspects de la réception productive des premiers romans du Graal cycliques dans le* Tristan en prose (Leuven: Leuven University Press, 1986). See also Janina P. Traxler, "Ironic Juxtaposition as Intertextuality in the Prose *Tristan*," in *Text and Intertext in Medieval Arthurian Literature,* ed. Norris J. Lacy (New York: Garland, 1996), pp. 147–63.

13. Lyn Pemberton, "Authorial Interventions in the *Tristan en Prose*," *Neophilologus* 68 (1984): 481–97, notes how, when the narrator continually highlights his own narrative's structure, "the referential function almost becomes subsidiary to the artistic function" (p. 496).

14. For Van Coolput, the work makes no claims to possessing transcendent truths, but recognizes the limits of its own narration (*Aventures quérant,* p. 220). See also Baumgartner, *La Harpe et l'épée: tradition et renouvellement dans le* Tristan *en prose* (Paris: SEDES, 1990), pp. 43–61.

15. Those who want to know the "verite" [truth] are told to take up the story that "Luces dou Chastel de Gaut" made "assez bele et cointement" [very beautifully and artfully], Curtis 3:150.

16. Malory's note of the drink's permanent effect (1:412.21–25) is similar to the version in *Tristan 1489,* g.iii.a: "Haa dieu or sont en tribulacion que iamais ne leur fauldra iour de leur vie car ilz ont beu leur destruction et leur mort" [Ah God, now they have an affliction that will not leave them for all of their lives, for they have drunk their destruction and their death].

17. In Thomas's poem, the lines are Tristan's: "El beivre fud la nostre mort, / Nus n'en n'avrum ja mais confort" [The drink was our death: we will never have comfort from it]. *Thomas: Les Fragments du Roman de Tristan,* ed. Bartina H. Wind (Geneva: Droz, 1960), ll. 1223–24. Baumgartner, *La Harpe,* p. 55.

18. Emmanuèle Baumgartner, *La Harpe,* p. 115.

19. Arnold A. Sanders argues that the transitional formulae of "turning" to the text, and the folkloric "hit befelle" draw attention to episodes in the narrative concerning human volition and fate respectively: "Malory's Transition Formulae: Fate, Volition, and Narrative Structure," *Arthurian Interpretations* 2 (1987): 27–46. Sanders's taxonomy of transitional formulae differs from my interpretation of their nature and function in that he categorizes the "turning" of the tale and of the narrator/reader to new subject matter as belonging to the same group of formulae ("Type IV"), whereas I distinguish between book and human actant, and draw an analogy between the active engagement of the character in the text and the imagined reader.

20. The text may articulate the switch of attention between different knights alternately as the result of "our" desire—"Now woll we turne unto sir

Launcelot" (2:550.36)—and of the book's reclaiming of the initiative: "Now spekith thys tale of sir Trystram" (2:551.6).

21. Lynch, *Malory's Book of Arms,* p. 89, suggests proverbs express "a feeling for relativity of values and practical wisdom."

22. Anne Rooney, *Hunting in Middle English Literature* (Cambridge, UK: Brewer, 1993), pp. 85–93; Corinne J. Saunders, "Malory's *Book of Huntynge:* the Tristram section of the *Morte Darthur,*" *Medium Ævum* 62 (1993): 270–84.

23. Rooney, *Hunting,* p. 15, remarks on the hunting register as mode of social exclusion. Riddy, *Sir Thomas Malory,* p. 95, argues, however, that medieval handbooks enable the bourgeois to cross class barriers.

24. P. J. C. Field considers the accusation against Malory for breaking into the Duke of Buckingham's deer park, *The Life and Times of Sir Thomas Malory* (Cambridge, UK: Brewer, 1993), pp. 100–01. I. M. W. Harvey discusses late-medieval state suspicion of hunting as a cover for seditious practices, in: "Was There Popular Politics in Fifteenth-Century England?" in *The Mc-Farlane Legacy: Studies in Late Medieval Politics and Society,* ed. R. H. Britnell and A. J. Pollard (New York: St. Martin's Press, 1995), pp. 155–74 (p. 163).

25. Sylvia Huot, *From Song to Book: The Poetics of Writing in Old French Lyric and Lyrical Narrative Poetry* (Ithaca, NY: Cornell University Press, 1987). Emmanuèle Baumgartner, *Le* Tristan en prose, pp. 298–307, provides a list of the lyrics and their subject matter. See also Maureen Barry Mc-Cann Boulton, *The Song in the Story: Lyric Insertions in French Narrative Fiction, 1200–1400* (Philadelphia: University of Pennsylvania Press, 1993), pp. 42–51.

26. Tatiana Fotitch and R. Steiner, *Les Lais du* Roman de Tristan en prose, *d'après le manuscrit de Vienne 2542* (Munich: Fink, 1974).

27. Boulton, *The Song in the Story,* p. 135.

28. See Baumgartner, *La Harpe,* pp. 114–24, on the lais' emotive power.

29. See Maureen Boulton, "Tristan and his Doubles as Singers of *Lais:* Love and Music in the Prose *Roman de Tristan,*" in *Shifts and Transpositions in Medieval Narrative: A Festschrift for Dr Elspeth Kennedy,* ed. Karen Pratt (Cambridge, UK: Brewer, 1994), pp. 53–69 (p. 65).

30. *La Harpe,* p. 159.

31. See Lynch, *Malory's Book of Arms,* pp. 125–29.

32. *Trauma: Explorations in Memory,* ed. with intros. Cathy Caruth (Baltimore, MD: Johns Hopkins University Press, 1995), p. 8.

33. Freud, "Remembering, Repeating and Working-Through," *The Standard Edition of the Complete Psychological Works of Sigmund Freud,* gen. ed. James Strachey, 24 vols. (London: Hogarth Press, 1958), 12:145–56.

34. Extract edited in Patterson, *Negotiating the Past,* pp. 121–27 (p. 126).

35. See Françoise Le Saux, "*Pryvayly and secretely:* Personal Letters in Malory's 'Book of Sir Tristram de Lyones,'" *Études de Lettres* 3 (1993): 21–33 (21); Georgiana Donavin, "Locating a Public Forum for the Personal Letter in Malory's *Morte Darthur,*" *Disputatio* 1 (1996): 19–36.

36. See, for example, Iseut's elaborate eulogistic address to Arthur's queen, as surpassing all others "de bonté, de beauté, de valor, de sens, de cortoisies et de hautesce" [in goodness, beauty, worth, wisdom, courteous behavior and high station], while she identifies herself as "chetive" [wretched] (Curtis 2:165).

37. Vinaver's notes point out examples at 2:513.16–22; 627.12–14; 785.16–17.

38. See James I. Wimsatt on Dynadan as partaking in the fluidity of perspective that characterizes the *Tristram* in general: "Segwarydes' Wife and Competing Perspectives within Malory's *Tale of Sir Tristram* and Its Model, the Prose *Tristan*," in *Retelling Tales: Essays in Honor of Russell Peck*, ed. Thomas Hahn and Alan Lupack (Woodbridge, UK: Brewer, 1997), pp. 321–39 (pp. 333–39).

39. MS BN fr. 244000 (summarized in Löseth, pp. 407–09), recounts Dinadan's extravagant mourning for the dead Tristan, which also marks a peripety in the minor character's presentation, and absorbs Dinadan's dissenting voice in the larger narrative endorsement of Tristan's chivalry.

40. Joyce Coleman, *Public Reading,* p. 214. Coleman continues: "Malory's personal reading map [. . .] seems to regard private reading as suspect and public reading as socially restorative." See also Donavin, "Locating a Public Forum," 23.

41. *Tristan 1489* gives the letter's text when Tristan first reads it (ll.6.v), but does not repeat it as Malory does.

42. "Thomas Hardy, Jacques Derrida, and the 'Dislocation of Souls,'" in *Taking Chances: Derrida, Psychoanalysis, and Literature,* ed. Joseph H. Smith and William Kerrigan (Baltimore, MD: Johns Hopkins Press, 1984), pp. 135–45 (p. 136). Françoise Le Saux, "*Pryvaly and secretely*" (30), maintains that the iconography of Launcelot's holding Mark's letter reinforces its truth-value, which interestingly relativizes Launcelot's body.

43. Donavin, "Locating a Public Forum," 26.

44. By contrast, the source has the Maid address herself not to Launcelot and "all ladies" but to the members of the Round Table, for whom she characterizes Lancelot as noblest and most base of knights (*Mort* 89–90; Lacy 4:114).

45. Philippe Ménard, "Les Fous dans la société médiévale," *Romania* 98 (1977): 433–59, discusses, with literary examples, the multiple coexisting interpretations of the madman, from the demonically possessed, to the mentally ill, the one who may speak out with no fear of reprisal and the Holy Fool. Lillian Feder generalizes on madness and moral culpability in *Madness in Literature* (Princeton, NJ: Princeton University Press, 1980), p. 101: "English imaginative literature of the fourteenth and fifteenth centuries generally reflects the assumption that madness, a sign of inner corruption, is inspired sometimes by God and more commonly by the devil."

46. *On the Properties of Things: John Trevisa's Translation of Bartholomæus Anglicus, De Proprietatibus Rerum,* gen. ed. Malcolm Seymour, 3 vols. (Oxford: Clarendon Press, 1975–1988), 1:348–50 (p. 348).

47. Segwarydes accuses his wife in these terms (1:394.35–395.1). Launcelot calls Elaine "traytoures" after their night together (2:795.27–28).

48. *On the Properties of Things,* 1:350.

49. On Brewnys (Brehus) as violent knight *par excellence* in the French romances, see Richard Trachsler, "Brehus sans Pitié: portrait-robot du criminel arthurien," in *La Violence dans le monde médiéval, Sénéfiance* 36 (1994): 525–42.

50. Riddy, *Sir Thomas Malory,* p. 109. Andrew Lynch, *Malory's Book of Arms,* pp. 5–6, suggests the episode epitomizes the strength and resilience of Launcelot's "good name." Jill Mann, *The Narrative of Distance,* p. 25, detects a "deliberate alienation of actions from self, which leaves a note of distance counterpointing the scenes of joyous union that close the tale."

51. Cf. Micha 6:202; Lacy 3:162. In the French text, also, Lancelot does not make any explicit connection between his sexual experiences and this prophecy.

52. Georgianna Ziegler, "The Hunt as Structural Device in Malory's *Morte Darthur,*" *Tristania* 5 (1979): 15–22 (18).

53. Arthur Brittan, *Masculinity and Power* (Oxford: Blackwell, 1989), p. 141.

54. On this issue see Thomas Laqueur, *Making Sex: Body and Gender from the Greeks to Freud* (Cambridge, MA: Harvard University Press, 1990), pp. 161–62. For English law on this point, see Batt, "Malory and Rape," p. 87.

55. "Don't Ask, Don't Tell: Murderous Plots and Medieval Secrets," in ed. Fradenburg and Freccero, *Premodern Sexualities,* pp. 137–52 (p. 137).

56. Shoshana Felman, *Writing and Madness (Philosophy/Psychoanalysis/Literature),* trans. Martha Noel Evans and the author, with the assistance of Brian Massumi (Ithaca, NY: Cornell University Press, 1985), pp. 14, 254.

57. Trachsler, *Clôtures,* p. 246. Fanni Bogdanow edits parts of BN 112 in her edition of the Post-Vulgate *Queste* and *Mort.* References to her (incomplete) edition are by volume and page number.

58. The manuscript's iconographical program also conveys a sense of unease about Arthur's rape. The rubric draws attention to the fact that Arthur (4: fol. 115a) "jut avecques la demoiselle" [lay with the maiden], but the illustration, inappropriately, shows a couple in bed in a domestic setting.

59. Claude Roussel, "Le jeu des formes et des couleurs: observations sur 'la beste glatissant,'" *Romania* 104 (1983): 49–82, connects this creature's alterity with that of the later *beste glatissant.*

60. See the summaries in William A. Nitze, "The Beste Glatissant in Arthurian Romance," *Zeitschrift für romanische Philologie* 56 (1936): 409–18; Nitze argues, from a comparison of the beasts, for *Perlesvaus* as a source for the *Graal* continuation.

61. Janina P. Traxler, "Observations on the Beste Glatissant in the *Tristan en prose,*" *Neophilologus* 74 (1990): 499–509 (501).

62. Traxler, "Observations," 506–07.

63. See Löseth, pp. 463–64. Pickford, "L'Évolution," pp. 115–17.

64. See also Fanni Bogdanow, *The Romance of the Grail,* pp. 125–26. The illustration of the prince's death and the *Beste*'s birth, BN 112 4: fols. 152 a/b, is reproduced on plate 2, facing p. 125.

65. Batt, "Malory's Questing Beast and the Implications of Author as Translator," in *The Medieval Translator: The Theory and Practice of Translation in the Middle Ages*, ed. Roger Ellis (Cambridge, UK: Brewer, 1989), pp. 143–66 (p. 152).

66. *The Middle English Dictionary*, ed. Hans Kurath, S. M. Kuhn, and others (Ann Arbor: University of Michigan Press, 1954-), definitions 4 and 6.

Chapter 5

1. *Hoccleve's Works: The Minor Poems*, ed. Frederick J. Furnivall and I. Gollancz, EETS e.s. 61, 73 (1892, 1925). Rev. Jerome Mitchell and A. I. Doyle, in 1 vol. (London: Oxford University Press, 1970), pp. 8–24 (ll. 193–200).

2. On women in the Lollard community, see Margaret Aston, "Lollard Women Priests?" in *Lollards and Reformers: Images and Literacy in Late Medieval Religion* (London: Hambledon, 1984), pp. 49–70.

3. For historical evidence of the Lollard movement as in fact more attractive to men than to women, who were better served by the devotional practices (especially the cult of the saints) available to them through orthodox Catholicism, see Shannon McSheffrey, *Gender and Heresy: Women and Men in Lollard Communities* (Philadelphia: University of Pennsylvania Press, 1995); McSheffrey cites Eleanor McLaughlin on the tendency of hostile accounts to represent heresies as predominantly female, for political reasons, pp. 138–39.

4. See the *Middle English Dictionary*, "ransaken."

5. See James Gairdner, *Lollardy and the Reformation in England: An Historical Survey*, 4 vols. (London: Macmillan, 1908–13), 1:85, cited by Sarah Beckwith, *Christ's Body: Identity, Culture and Society in Late Medieval Writings* (London: Routledge, 1993), who notes, p. 75, the Eucharist's function here as "symbol() of political power." Gairdner, *Lollardy*, p. 85, raises the question of how far Oldcastle's images (other ensigns bore emblems of Christ's Passion) were compatible with Lollardy.

6. McSheffrey, *Gender and Heresy*, p. 146, points out that Wycliffite sermons themselves see women as credulous and susceptible to the seductive power of images.

7. Helen Cooper argues (in part from Hoccleve's poem) that English romance typically addresses a male audience, while women own French romances: "Romance after 1400," in ed. Wallace, *Cambridge History*, pp. 690–719 (p. 703). But if the extant evidence—that there are no "original" English Lancelot narratives, and that, with the exception of the Stanzaic *Morte*, which gives us only the end of Lancelot's career, there are no translations before Malory's time—reflects cultural conditions with any accuracy, this assessment makes Hoccleve's classification anomalous.

8. Nicholas Watson, "Censorship and Cultural Change in Late-Medieval England: Vernacular Theology, the Oxford Translation Debate, and Arundel's Constitutions of 1409," *Speculum* 70 (1995): 822–64 (848–49).

9. Transcript from the copy in the John Rylands University Library of Manchester, L.4.v.

10. From *The Scholemaster,* cited in *Malory: The Critical Heritage,* ed. Marylyn Jackson Parins (London: Routledge, 1988), pp. 56–57. Parins cites divergent views, from Tudor historians and Renaissance scholars, pp. 52–59.

11. Jill Mann briefly considers the question of Cistercian authorship, in "Malory and the Grail Legend," in ed. Archibald and Edwards, *Companion,* pp. 203–220 (pp. 207–08). For endorsement of Cistercian authorship of the *Queste,* see Martin B. Shichtman, "Politicizing the Ineffable: The *Queste del Saint Graal* and Malory's 'Tale of the Sankgreal,'" in ed. Shichtman and Carley, *Culture and the King,* pp. 163–79. Karen Pratt concludes from the *Queste's* glorification of chivalry that the author knew of Cistercian religious practice but was not in orders: "The Cistercians and the *Queste del Saint Graal,*" *Reading Medieval Studies* 21 (1995): 69–96 (88). On the Grail narrative's appropriative strategies, see Leupin, *Le Graal,* pp. 127–57.

12. "The Body and the Struggle for the Soul of Romance: *La Queste del Saint Graal,*" in *The Body and the Soul in Medieval Literature,* ed. Piero Boitani and Anna Torti (Cambridge, UK: Brewer, 1999), pp. 31–61 (p. 54).

13. Laurence N. de Looze, "A Story of Interpretations: The *Queste del Saint Graal* as Metaliterature," *Romanic Review* 76.2 (1985): 129–47.

14. On the importance of intertextual reference—to Chrétien as well as to the Vulgate—to the *Queste's* meaning and rewriting, see Andrea M. L. Williams, "The Enchanted Swords and the Quest for the Holy Grail: Metaphoric Structure in *La Queste del Saint Graal,*" *French Studies* 48 (1994): 385–401; Emmanuèle Baumgartner, "From Lancelot to Galahad: The Stakes of Filiation," trans. Arthur F. Crispin, in *The Lancelot-Grail Cycle,* ed. Kibler, pp. 14–30.

15. John W. Baldwin, "From the Ordeal to Confession: In Search of Lay Religion in Early Thirteenth-Century France," in *Handling Sin: Confession in the Middle Ages.* York Studies in Medieval Theology 2, ed. Peter Biller and A. J. Minnis (York: York Medieval Press, 1998), pp. 191–209 (pp. 206–08).

16. Riddy, *Sir Thomas Malory,* pp. 113–38.

17. Colin Richmond, "Religion and the Fifteenth-Century English Gentleman," in *The Church, Politics and Patronage in the Fifteenth Century,* ed. R. B. Dobson (Gloucester, UK: Sutton, 1984), pp. 193–208; Eamon Duffy, *The Stripping of the Altars: Traditional Religion in England c.1400-c.1580* (New Haven, CT: Yale University Press, 1992).

18. On trends in the "devotional," poised between public, liturgical, and private, contemplative, see Richard Kieckhefer, "Major Currents in Late Medieval Devotion," in *Christian Spirituality: High Middle Ages and Reformation,* ed. Jill Raitt (London: Routledge and Kegan Paul, 1987), pp. 75–108.

19. Mervyn James, *Society, Politics and Culture* (Cambridge, UK: Cambridge University Press, 1986), p. 317.

20. James, *Society,* p. 370.

21. See especially Miri Rubin, *Corpus Christi: The Sacrament in the Later Middle Ages* (Cambridge, UK: Cambridge University Press, 1991), and Beckwith, *Christ's Body*.

22. See Shichtman, "Politicizing the Ineffable," p. 173, on the breakdown in sign systems. John Plummer notes of Malory's editing of the source's explicatory material that "the text has become difficult of access": "The Quest for Significance in *La Queste del Saint Graal* and Malory's *Tale of the Sankgreal*," in *Continuations: Essays on Medieval French Literature and Language In Honor of John L. Grigsby,* ed. Norris J. Lacy and Gloria Torrini-Roblin (Birmingham, AL: Summa, 1989), pp. 107–19 (p. 117).

23. Riddy, *Sir Thomas Malory,* p. 123.

24. "Mes atant lesse ores li contes a parler de lui et retorne a Perceval. Or dit li contes que quant Perceval se fu partiz de Lancelot, qu'il retorna a la recluse [. . .]" [The story stops speaking about him here and returns to Perceval. Now the story says that when Perceval and Lancelot parted ways, Perceval returned to the recluse](*Queste* 71; Lacy 4:24).

25. The Winchester Manuscript strongly emphasizes the consonance of inscribed reader and textual determinism: "Now turne we to Sir Galahad and to Sir Percivall. Now turnyth the tale vnto *sir* galahad & *sir* percivall þat were in a chapell all nyght in hir prayers" (fol. 399r). Cf. *Queste* 244; Lacy 4:77: "Mes a tant se test ore li contes [. . .] et retorne as deus compaignons [. . .]. Or dit li contes que toute la nuit furent en la chapele entre Galaad et Perceval."

26. The Winchester Manuscript marks the distance between the two narratives spatially: the colophon is at fol. 346v, and the Grail story begins at fol. 349r.

27. Valerie M. Lagorio adduces fifteenth-century English political deployment of St. Joseph as part of ecclesiastical history: "The Evolving Legend of St Joseph of Glastonbury," *Speculum* 46 (1971): 209–31. Hardyng's *Chronicle* embeds this tale in a complex of cultural configurations of knighthood, religious, and political issues. See Edward Donald Kennedy, "John Hardyng and the Holy Grail," *Arthurian Literature* 8 (1989): 185–206; Felicity Riddy, "Chivalric Nationalism and the Holy Grail in John Hardyng's Chronicle," in *The Grail: A Casebook,* ed. Dhira B. Mahoney (New York: Garland, 2000), pp. 397–414.

28. Stephen Knight reads medieval Grail narratives as increasingly compensatory for the historical loss of land and power: "From Jerusalem to Camelot: King Arthur and the Crusades," in *Medieval Codicology, Iconography, Literature, and Translation: Studies for Keith Val Sinclair,* ed. Peter Rolfe Monks and D. D. R. Owen (Leiden: Brill, 1994), pp. 223–32.

29. The *Middle English Dictionary* lists definitions of "signification" as sign, the interpretation of sign, and prefiguring.

30. Caxton's colophon omits mention of Malory's authorship and his prayer for Christ's help (2:1037.13; Winchester MS, fol. 408v).

31. Martin B. Shichtman charts this fully in "Percival's Sister: Genealogy, Virginity, and Blood," *Arthuriana* 9.2 (1999): 11–20: see also Maureen Fries,

"Gender and the Grail," *Arthuriana* 8.1 (1998): 67–79, on the whirlpool the companions encounter as "suggestive of sexual turmoil" (75).

32. For Philippa Beckerling, "Perceval's Sister: Aspects of the Virgin in the *Quest of the Holy Grail* and Malory's *Sankgreal*," in *Constructing Gender: Feminism and Literary Studies,* ed. Hilary Fraser and R. S. White (Nedlands: University of Western Australia Press), pp. 39–54, she is in both texts merely an adjunct. For Maureen Fries, "Gender and the Grail," she is a "surrogate" for "male bonding" (77), an observation Martin Shichtman develops in "Percival's Sister." Ginger Thornton and Krista May, "Malory as Feminist? The Role of Perceval's Sister in the Grail Quest," in *Sir Thomas Malory: Views and Re-views,* ed. D. Thomas Hanks (New York: AMS Press, 1992), pp. 43–53, afford her a more positive role.

33. See also Hoffman, "Perceval's Sister," 73.

34. On the Marian associations of Perceval's Sister's castle in the *Queste,* see Beckerling, "Perceval's Sister," pp. 42–44.

35. *Aelred of Rievaulx's De Institutione Inclusarum: Two English Versions,* ed. John Ayto and Alexandra Barratt, EETS o.s. 287 (London: Oxford University Press, 1984), p. 9: "remembrith" here translates 1 Cor. 7, "cogitat," "is mindful of."

36. Robert W. Hanning, "Arthurian Evangelists: The Language of Truth in Thirteenth-Century French Prose Romances," *Philological Quarterly* 64 (1985): 347–65 (360–61).

37. Stephen G. Nichols, "Solomon's Wife: Deceit, Desire, and the Genealogy of Romance," in *Space, Time, Image, Sign: Essays on Literature and the Visual Arts,* ed. James A. W. Heffernan (New York: Peter Lang, 1987), pp. 19–40.

38. Susan Aronstein, "Rewriting Peceval's Sister: Eucharistic Vision and Typological Destiny in the *Queste del San Graal*," *Women's Studies* 21.2 (1992): 211–30. Jennifer E. Looper, "Gender, Genealogy, and the 'Story of the Three Spindles' in the *Queste del Saint Graal*," *Arthuriana* 8.1(1998): 49–66.

39. On spindle imagery, see Frances M. Biscoglio, "'Unspun' heroes: iconography of the spinning woman in the Middle Ages," *Journal of Medieval and Renaissance Studies* 25.2 (1995): 163–84. On the meaning of "fuissel," and on "spindles" as a marked translation (and part of a moral indictment of women) see James Dean, "Vestiges of Paradise: The Tree of Life in *Cursor Mundi* and Malory's *Morte Darthur*," *Mediaevalia et Humanistica* n.s. 13 (1985): 113–26 (118–21).

40. Looper, "Gender, Genealogy," 61.

41. Dean, "Vestiges of Paradise," 120.

42. Williams, "The Enchanted Swords," 396–97. Warren discusses Galahad's swords in the context of the Grail adventures as a "spiritual invasion" that condemns Arthurian history (*History,* pp. 213–16).

43. Malory inherits the Sword in the Stone's link between Launcelot and Galahad from the *Suite du Merlin.*

44. Williams, "The Enchanted Swords," 394.

45. Williams, "The Enchanted Swords," 395; Warren, *History*, p. 215; Shichtman, "Percival's Sister," 17.

46. *The Lanterne of Li3t*, ed. Lilian M. Swinburn, EETS o.s. 151 (London: Kegan Paul, Trench, Trübner, 1917 [for 1915]), p. 65. For the same gloss, see the Epistle Sermon 51 in *English Wycliffite Sermons*, ed. Pamela Gradon and Anne Hudson, 5 vols. (Oxford: Clarendon Press, 1983–1996), 1:685–89 (p. 687). The *Queste* and *Sankgreal* imagery complements Paul's combination of metaphoric armor and the appellation of the faithful as children of God in this passage.

47. The Post-Vulgate version establishes explicit continuity with Balin's story; Pellehan tells Galahad of his wound, "You see here the Dolorous Blow that the Knight with the Two Swords struck" (Lacy 5:279).

48. In the *Queste*, Galahad distinguishes between his "uncle" King Pelles, and the Fisher King, his grandfather (8; Lacy 4:5). See also Bloch's general observations on confusions and doubling through naming in the Vulgate, *Etymologies and Genealogies*, p. 211.

49. Beckerling, "Perceval's Sister," pp. 50–51.

50. See Caroline Walker Bynum, *Fragmentation and Redemption: Essays on Gender and the Human Body in Medieval Religion* (New York: Zone Books, 1991), p. 102. Bynum is commenting specifically on the phenomenon of the stigmata. Barbara Newman discusses the thirteenth-century Guglielmite context for Perceval's Sister's story, in *From Virile Woman to WomanChrist: Studies in Medieval Religion and Literature* (Philadelphia: University of Pennsylvania Press, 1995), pp. 214–15.

51. Richard Kieckhefer, "Holiness and the Culture of Devotion: Remarks on Some Late Medieval Male Saints," in *Images of Sainthood in Medieval Europe*, ed. Renate Blumenfeld-Kosinski and Timea Szell (Ithaca, NY: Cornell University Press, 1991), pp. 288–305.

52. See also Hoffman, "Perceval's Sister," 82.

53. Hoffman, "Perceval's Sister," 77.

54. Cf. *Queste*, 247 (Lacy 4:77); "Biau peres" [Dear Father].

55. Rosalyn Rossignol analyzes the *Queste* Grail as the masculine appropriation of metaphors of maternal nurture that shows the Grail knights to be at an arrested stage of development in their dependence on and submission to God the Father: "The Holiest Vessel: Maternal Aspects of the Grail," *Arthuriana* 5.1 (1995): 52–61.

56. Catherine Pickstock, "Thomas Aquinas and the Quest for the Eucharist," in *Catholicism and Catholicity: Eucharistic Communities in Historical And Contemporary Perspectives*, ed. Sarah Beckwith (Oxford: Blackwell, 1999), pp. 47–68 (p. 60).

57. *Feminine Sexuality: Jacques Lacan and the école freudienne*, ed. Juliet Mitchell and Jacqueline Rose (New York: Norton, 1982), p. 23.

58. "On a Question Preliminary to Any Possible Treatment of Psychosis," in Jacques Lacan, *Écrits: a Selection*, ed. and trans. Alan Sheridan (London: Tavistock, 1977).

59. Jane Flax, "Signifying the Father's Desire: Lacan in a Feminist's Gaze," in *Criticism and Lacan: Essays and Dialogue on Language, Structure, and the Unconscious,* ed. Patrick Colm Hogan and Lalita Pandit (Athens: University of Georgia Press, 1990), pp. 109–19 (pp. 115–16).

60. Flax, "Signifying the Father's Desire," p. 112.

61. Gilbert D. Chaitin, *Rhetoric and Culture in Lacan* (Cambridge, UK: Cambridge University Press, 1996).

62. Robert Con Davis, *The Paternal Romance: Reading God-the-Father in Early Western Culture* (Urbana: University of Illinois Press, 1993), p. 121.

63. Stacey L. Hahn, "Genealogy and Adventure in the Cyclic Prose *Lancelot,*" in *Conjunctures: Medieval Studies in Honor of Douglas Kelly,* ed. Keith Busby and Norris J. Lacy (Amsterdam: Rodopi, 1994), pp. 139–51.

64. The *Queste* has the court speculate that only God could have accorded Galahad the grace to sit at the siege perilous (9; Lacy 4:5).

65. The *Queste* does not give Lancelot this responsibility.

66. See also 2:1030.1–22, where the Grail knights see the suffering Christ "bledynge all opynly," yet are promised that they have not yet seen the Grail "so opynly" as they will. Launcelot speaks of the privilege of seeing the divine mysteries "opynly" (2:1017.8).

67. See, for example, *The Treatise of Perfection of the Sons of God,* in *The Chastising of God's Children and The Treatise of Perfection of the Sons of God,* ed. Joyce Bazire and Eric Colledge (Oxford: Blackwell, 1957), which affirms that those who work according to the spirit of God are His sons (p. 243).

68. Chaucer, *Boece,* Prosa 6, *Riverside Chaucer,* ed. Benson, p. 466.

69. Symeu tells Lancelot that, were it not for his father's adultery (Micha 2:37; Lacy 3:13), he would achieve all his son will accomplish.

70. See Deuteronomy 24.16: "The fathers shall not be put to death for the children, nor the children for the fathers: but everyone shall die for his own sin." The Old Testament appears to distinguish between human social law and law against God, in this respect: cf. Exodus 20.5: "I the Lord your God am a jealous God, visiting the iniquity of the fathers upon the children to the third and the fourth generation of those who hate me."

71. St. Thomas Aquinas, *Knowing and Naming God,* in *Summa Theologiæ,* Vol. 3, ed. and trans. Herbert McCabe (London: Eyre and Spottiswoode, 1964), pp. 47–79 (pp. 69–71).

72. *Dives and Pauper,* ed. Priscilla Heath Barnum, 2 vols., EETS o.s. 275, 280 (London: Oxford University Press, 1976, 1980), 1:304–59 (p. 313).

73. *Dives and Pauper,* pp. 358, 329.

74. The *Brut* account of Thomas of Lancaster's revolt against the evil rule of Edward II characterizes times of "vnkyndenesse" as lawless, involving disrespect for the Church and for family loyalties: "And in þat bataile was þe fader aȝeins þe sone, and þe vncle aȝeins his nevew." (*Brut* 1:220).

75. In the *Queste,* 271 (Lacy 4:85), the nonelect are to be divested of the "honor" they were earlier given.

76. This contrasts with the positive address in the *Queste,* 272 (Lacy 4:85): "Mi fil et ne mie fillastre" [My sons and not My stepsons].

77. *The Chastising of God's Children,* ed. Bazire and Colledge, pp. 98–99.

78. *The Minor Poems of John Lydgate,* Part 1, ed. Henry Noble MacCracken, EETS e.s. 107 (Oxford: Oxford University Press, 1911 [for 1910]), pp. 60–71 (ll. 123–36).

79. Lydgate, "Exposition," ll. 305–09.

80. Chaucer, F *Prologue* to the *Legend of Good Women,* in ed. Benson, *The Riverside Chaucer,* ll. 73–77.

81. Grace Armstrong Savage, "Father and Son in the *Queste del Saint Graal,*" *Romance Philology* 31 (1977): 1–16 (16).

82. The Post-Vulgate *Queste* enthusiastically elaborates on Guenièvre's role in Lancelot's vision of his lover consumed by the flames of hell, who warns him against his sin (Lacy 5: 171).

83. Malory is also here retelling the episode in the *Mort* (79–80; Lacy 4:111) in which a huntsman wounds Lancelot accidentally. On the significance of the episode for Launcelot, see Catherine La Farge, "The Hand of the Huntress: Repetition and Malory's *Morte Darthur,*" in *New Feminist Discourses: Critical Essays on Theories and Texts,* ed. Isobel Armstrong (London: Routledge, 1992), pp. 263–79.

84. See, for example, Lancelot's grandfather's tomb as locus of miraculous healing (*Estoire* 2:575; Lacy 1:162), and in the *Mort,* the veneration of Lancelot's shield at St. Stephen's (161–62; Lacy 4:133).

85. Batt, "'Hand for Hand,'" 284–86.

86. *The Sermons of Thomas Brinton, Bishop of Rochester (1373–1389),* ed. Sister Mary Aquinas Devlin, 2 vols. (London: Royal Historical Society, 1954), 1:87–94, cited in Kieckhefer, "Major Currents," pp. 87–88.

87. Reproduced in Duffy, *The Stripping of the Altars,* p. 244.

88. *Gertrude d'Helfta: Œuvres spirituelles,* ed. and trans. J. Hourlier, A. Schmitt, P. Doyère, and J.-M. Clément, 5 vols. (Paris: Éditions du Cerf, 1967–86), 2:246–47.

89. Douglas Gray, "The Five Wounds of Our Lord," *Notes and Queries* 208 (1963). 1:50–51; 2:82–89; 3:127–34; 4:163–68.

90. Lynch, *Malory's Book of Arms,* pp. 91–133.

91. Lynch, *Malory's Book of Arms,* also notes how "marvellous and unmotivated episodes" (p. 78) provide wholeness in the latter part of the *Morte.*

92. "Ful ofte paramours he gan deffie, And weep as dooth a child that is ybete" (A, 3758–59). Bartlett Jere Whiting, *Proverbs, Sentences, and Proverbial Phrases from English writings, mainly before 1500* (Cambridge, MA: Harvard University Press, 1968), entry C223.3.

93. *The Chastising of God's Children,* ed. Bazire and Colledge, pp. 113–15 (Revelations 3.19; see also Hebrews 12.6–9).

94. *Contemplations of the Dread and Love of God,* ed. Margaret Connolly, EETS o.s. 303 (Oxford: Oxford University Press, 1993), pp. 31–32.

95. Sigmund Freud, "'A Child is Being Beaten': A Contribution to the Study of the Origin of Sexual Perversions," in *The Standard Edition of the Complete Psychological Works,* gen. ed. James Strachey, 24 vols. (London: Hogarth Press, 1955), 17: 175–204.

96. Jeffrey Jerome Cohen, "Masoch / Lancelotism," *New Literary History* 28 (1997): 231–60 (231).

97. On guilt, see Lynch, *Malory's Book of Arms,* p. 7. For Stephen C. B. Atkinson, Launcelot interprets God's benevolence as "a stinging rebuke:" "Malory's 'Healing of Sir Urry': Lancelot, the Earthly Fellowship, and the World of the Grail," *Studies in Philology* 78 (1981): 341–52 (349). On nostalgia, see Mark Lambert, *Malory: Style and Vision in* Le Morte Darthur (New Haven, CT: Yale University Press, 1976), p. 65.

98. Kaja Silverman, *Male Subjectivity at the Margins* (New York: Routledge, 1992), pp. 185–213 (p. 205).

99. La Farge, "The Hand of the Huntress," p. 272.

Chapter 6

1. Lambert, *Malory: Style and Vision,* p. 146.

2. Someone of Malory's class would surely have had access to English court poetry as well as to French Arthurian romance; see M. C. Seymour's investigation of late-medieval ownership of court poetry in English: "manuscripts containing the *Legend of Good Women,* like most of the books of fifteenth-century courtly verse [. . .] were owned by the armigerous and the prosperous, socially aspirant, middle-classes:" *A Catalogue of Chaucer Manuscripts: Volume 1. Works Before the* Canterbury Tales (Aldershot, UK: Scolar Press, 1995) pp. 79–100 (p. 82).

3. F *Prologue, Legend of Good Women,* in *The Riverside Chaucer,* ed. Benson, l. 25. Future references are in the text, by line number.

4. Sheila Delany, *The Naked Text: Chaucer's* Legend of Good Women (Berkeley: University of California Press, 1994), p. 13.

5. Lisa J. Kiser, *Telling Classical Tales: Chaucer and the* Legend of Good Women (Ithaca, NY: Cornell University Press, 1983), p. 89, writes of the "distortion and oversimplification" that result from the task prescribed the narrator as symptomatic of "the moral exemplum in its worst, most limited form."

6. In the Prose *Lancelot,* Meleagant's abduction of the queen takes place much earlier (Micha 2:1–108; Lacy 3:3–32).

7. Nick Davis, "Narrative Composition," pp. 35–36, notes the "thematic force" of the alternation of heat and cold, which the Malorian narrator says is typical of modern love (3:1120.1–2), in the relationship between Launcelot and Guinevere as the *Morte* describes it.

8. On the God of Love as exemplifying the tyrannical wishes of the unsympathetic male reader, see James Simpson, "Ethics and Interpretation: Reading Wills in Chaucer's *Legend of Good Women,*" *Studies in the Age of Chaucer* 20 (1998): 73–100 (86–87).

9. Cf. *Troilus and Criseyde,* 1:977–79:

> Was neuere man or womman 3et bigete
> That was vnapt to suffren loues hete,
> Celestial, or elles loue of kynde.

Windeatt directs us to Whiting M224 for analogues on one's not being able to escape love.

10. Susan Crane, "Maytime in Late Medieval Courts," *New Medieval Literatures* 2 (1998): 159–79 (178–79).

11. See, for example, George Saintsbury's (admittedly curious) remark that Guinevere is "the first perfectly human woman in English literature" (on the strength, it appears, that her jealous loyalty to Launcelot cancels out her wifely infidelity), in *The Flourishing of Romance and the Rise of Allegory* (Edinburgh: Blackwood, 1897), p. 124; or C. David Benson's claim that Malory is emotionally engaged with his characters, with whom modern readers identify: "The Ending," p. 221.

12. A. C. Spearing, *The Medieval Poet as Voyeur: Looking and Listening in Medieval Love-Narratives* (Cambridge, UK: Cambridge University Press, 1993), pp. 120–39 (p. 136).

13. Sturges, "The Epistemology of the Bedchamber: Textuality, Knowledge, and the Representation of Adultery in Malory and the Prose *Lancelot,*" *Arthuriana* 7.4 (1997): 47–62 (60–61).

14. Compare 3:1228.30–1229.23 with John Warkworth's explanation, in his *Chronicle,* of popular ignorance and love of novelty as a reason for Henry VI's reversals: *Three Chronicles of the Reign of Edward IV,* intro. Keith Dockray (Gloucester, UK: Sutton, 1988), pp. 11–12.

15. Edwards, "The Place of Women in the *Morte Darthur,*" in ed. Archibald and Edwards, *Companion,* pp. 37–54 (p. 48).

16. See D. Thomas Hanks on the "sacramental" aspect of the language and gestures at this point, in "Malory, the *Mort[e]s,* and the Confrontation in Guinevere's Chamber," in ed. Hanks, *Sir Thomas Malory,* pp. 78–90 (pp. 83–85).

17. For example, at 3:1257.21–23; 3:1196.32–34. See Tomomi Kato, *Concordance,* pp. 1563–64.

18. E. Kay Harris, "Lancelot's Vocation: Traitor Saint," in ed. Kibler, *The Lancelot-Grail Cycle,* pp. 219–37.

19. Sarah Kay, "Adultery and Killing in *La Mort le roi Artu,*" in *Scarlet Letters: Fictions of Adultery from Antiquity to the 1990s,* ed. Nicholas White and Naomi Segal (Houndmills, UK: Macmillan, 1997), pp. 34–44 (p. 43). Kay perhaps overstates her case (p. 36) as, when Guenièvre is caught, Agravain and his brothers specifically declare that her adultery "par droit" ("in justice," "by law," though Lacy translates "proper"), demands a shameful death, "car trop avoit fet grant desloiauté, quant ele en leu del roi qui tant estoit preudom avoit lessié gesir un autre chevalier" [for she had committed a very disloyal act when she let a knight other than the most noble king

sleep with her](*Mort* 121; Lacy 4:122). The *Mort* makes clear, however, that coercion, rather than clear legal guidance, is involved; the barons agree to the sentence "a fine force," of necessity, because the king wants it.

20. R. Howard Bloch, "The Death of King Arthur and the Waning of the Feudal Age," *Orbis Litterarum* 29 (1974): 291–305 (292).

21. Louise Fradenburg, "Introduction: Rethinking Queenship," in *Women and Sovereignty*, ed. Louise Olga Fradenburg (Edinburgh: Edinburgh University Press, 1992), pp. 1–13 (pp. 4–5). On the barrenness of adulterous queens in literature as means to displace women's power, see Peggy McCracken, "The Body Politic and the Queen's Adulterous Body in French Romance," in *Feminist Approaches to the Body in Medieval Literature,* ed. Linda Lomperis and Sarah Stanbury (Philadelphia: University of Pennsylvania Press, 1994), pp. 38–64.

22. Edwards, "The Place of Women," p. 44, explores Guinevere's "profound and ambivalent role" in the male chivalric order.

23. Karen Pratt, "The Image of the Queen," p. 256.

24. See ed. Gordon Kipling, *The Receyt of the Ladie Kateryne,* note to Book 2, l. 621 (p. 138), where Henry VII is described as "Moost Cristen kyng and moost stedfast in the feithe." Beaune, chapter six of *The Birth of an Ideology,* "The Most Christian King and Nation," pp. 172–93, traces French kings' (supposedly unique) claim to this title.

25. See Vinaver, Commentary, 3:1598.

26. The origin of these lines is probably the *Mort* king's declaration to his wife that "ge ne feroie tort ne por vos ne por autre" [I would not act unjustly for you or anyone else] (*Mort* 86; Lacy 4:113). There is no fire in the *Mort Artu* at this point, although, in the Stanzaic *Morte,* 1420, the queen sees the fire being prepared.

27. Robert L. Kelly, "Malory and the Common Law: *Hasty jougement* in the 'Tale of the Death of King Arthur,'" *Medievalia et Humanistica* n.s. 22 (1995): 111–40.

28. Catherine Bell, *Ritual Theory, Ritual Practice* (New York: Oxford University Press, 1992), pp. 108, 210.

29. Kelly, "Malory and the Common Law"; E. Kay Harris, "Evidence against Lancelot and Guinevere in Malory's *Morte Darthur:* Treason by Imagination," *Exemplaria* 7.1 (1995): 179–208.

30. *The Statutes of the Realm,* 9 vols. (London: Record Commission, 1810–28), 1:319–20. Also cited in Kelly, "Malory and the Common Law," 123–24.

31. John Bellamy, *The Tudor Law of Treason: An Introduction* (London: Routledge and Kegan Paul), pp. 40–41, notes the confusion caused in Boleyn's case by the lack of precedent for equating the queen's adultery with treason. See also Kelly, "Malory and the Common Law," p. 124, who takes this to show that Guinevere's adultery cannot be treasonable.

32. In the Vulgate, Meleagant accuses the queen of "desloialté" [disloyalty] to Arthur (Micha 2:76; Lacy 3:24).

33. See also Harris, "Evidence," 204–05.

34. Harris, "Evidence," 206, fn. 55, sees Guinevere as "a sign" for Launcelot, and "an object of exchange between Lancelot and Arthur."

35. Harris, "Evidence," 208.

36. John Carmi Parsons, "Ritual and Symbol in the English Medieval Queenship to 1500," in ed. Fradenburg, *Women and Sovereignty,* pp. 60–77, gives examples of queens' intercessions for the underprivileged and sharing in the Marian imagery of motherhood.

37. Trevisa, *On the Properties of Things,* 2:1002, notes the political and diplomatic importance of the olive: "for wiþoute spray of olyue no messangeres were ysent fro Rome to gete pees noþer to profre pees to oþere men." See also Caxton's account of the emissaries in *Arthur and Lucius* (1:185).

38. Claire Vial, "Images of Kings and Kingship: Chaucer, Malory, and the Representation of Royal Entries," in *"Divers toyes mengled." Essays on Medieval and Renaissance Culture in honour of André Lascombes.* Ed. Michel Bitot, with Roberta Mullini and Peter Happé (Tours: Université François Rabelais, 1996), pp. 43–54, comments (p. 54) on the "relative absence of 'royal religion'" in the *Morte.* There is even an element of "antiritual," when Guinevere later evades Mordred by pretending to prepare for the practicalities of the public legitimization of the wedding she is resisting (3:1227.15–16).

39. Conversely, in the *Mort,* Death is an outsider; its "entering" the Maid of Escalot's body is seen as "vileinne," a wicked violation of courtliness (88; Lacy 4: 114). Arthur also calls Death "vileinne," base and dishonorable (221; Lacy 4:148).

40. On this last point, see Herbert Marcuse, "The Ideology of Death," in *The Meaning of Death* ed. Herman Feifel (New York: McGraw-Hill, 1959), pp. 64–76 (p. 74).

41. R. C. Finucane, "Sacred Corpse, Profane Carrion: Social Ideals and Death Rituals in the Later Middle Ages," in *Mirrors of Mortality: Studies in the Social History of Death,* ed. Joachim Whaley (London: Europa, 1981), pp. 40–60 (pp. 40–41).

42. Bronfen and Webster, "Introduction," in *Death and Representation,* pp. 3–25 (p. 13).

43. Bronfen and Webster, "Introduction," p. 19.

44. On the unfathomability of this world, see Karen Pratt, "*La Mort le roi Artu* as Tragedy," *Nottingham Medieval Studies* 30 (1991): 81–109 (92).

45. Christopher Daniell, *Death and Burial in Medieval England 1066–1550* (London: Routledge, 1997), p. 65, notes a fifteenth-century audience would have been familiar with the funeral rites and liturgy as Malory describes them.

46. Introduction, *Death and Representation,* pp. 13–15, 20.

47. The exception is Arthur's "burial," at which a group of ladies offers a generous "hondred tapers, and [. . .] a thousande besauntes" (3:1241.18–19), but Launcelot eventually visits this site when he buries Guinevere.

48. Bell, *Ritual Theory,* pp. 215–17.

49. Clare Gittings, *Death, Burial and the Individual in Early Modern England* (London: Routledge, 1984), p. 174. Malory shows little interest in the College of Heralds' forms of surveillance and organization of aristocratic funerals that were to become, as Gittings has claimed (p. 178), part of the machinery by which the crown controlled its subjects.

50. Robert L. Kelly, "Penitence as a Remedy for War in Malory's 'Tale of the Death of Arthur,'" *Studies in Philology* 91.2 (1994): 111–135 (111, 113).

51. Lynch, *Malory's Book of Arms*, p. 156.

52. The monument the young King Arthur erects to celebrate his victory over the rebel kings (1:78.1–8) seems now to belong to a different era.

53. Derek Brewer, "Death in Malory's *Le Morte Darthur*," in *Zeit, Tod und Ewigkeit in der Renaissance Literatur* 3, ed. James Hogg (Salzburg: Universität Salzburg, 1987), pp. 44–57 (p. 57).

54. Derrida, *Of Grammatology*, p. 69.

55. Alan J. Fletcher, "King Arthur's Passing in the *Morte D'Arthur*," *English Language Notes* 31.4 (1994): 19–24 (23).

56. Jane Seymour's body was treated in a similar fashion: Daniell, *Death and Burial*, p. 44.

57. John Carmi Parsons, "'Never was a body buried in England with such solemnity and honour': The Burials and Posthumous Commemorations of English Queens to 1500," in ed. Duggan, *Queens and Queenship*, pp. 317–37.

58. Roberta Gilchrist provides some notes on nuns' tombs, in *Gender and Material Culture: The Archaeology of Religious Women* (London: Routledge, 1994), pp. 56–61.

59. Frederick J. Furnivall, *The Fifty Earliest English Wills in the Court of Probate*, EETS o.s. 78 (London: Trübner, 1882), pp. 116–19 (p. 117).

60. Transcript from the 1498 Wynkyn de Worde, *Le morte da[r]thur*, John Rylands University Library of Manchester, fol. E.3.v. See also Parins, *Malory: The Critical Heritage*, pp. 51–52.

61. Tsuyoshi Mukai, "De Worde's Displacement of Malory's Secularization," in *Arthurian and Other Studies*, ed. Suzuki and Mukai, pp. 179–87 (pp. 185–86).

62. "A Disputation," in *Middle English Debate Poetry: A Critical Anthology*, ed. John W. Conlee (East Lansing, MI: Colleagues Press, 1991), pp. 50–62 (ll. 86–97).

63. Paul Binski, *Medieval Death: Ritual and Representation* (London: British Museum, 1996), p. 150.

64. Karen Cherewatuk traces hagiographic associations for Launcelot's representation in: "The Saint's Life of Sir Launcelot: Hagiography and the Conclusion of Malory's *Morte Darthur*." *Arthuriana* 5.1 (1995): 62–78.

65. Daniell, *Death and Burial*, pp. 42, 44; College of Arms MS I.7.f.7, in *Letters and Papers Illustrative of the Reigns of Richard III and Henry VII*, ed. James Gairdner, 2 vols. (London: Longman, Green, Longman and Roberts, 1861), 1:1–8 (2).

66. For examples, see F. H. Cripps-Day, *On Armour Preserved in English Churches* (London: privately printed, Chiswick Press, 1922); F. H. Cripps-Day and A. R. Duffy, *Fragmenta Armamentaria,* 5 vols. Vol. 5, *Church Armour* (Frome, UK: privately printed, Butler and Tanner, 1939).

67. John Hardyng's *Chronicle* "commendacion" calls the king "a lyon in felde" and "In house a lambe" (p. 148).

68. C. L. Kingsford, *The Grey Friars of London.* British Society of Franciscan Studies 6 (Aberdeen: University Press, 1915), pp. 70–133 (p. 93).

69. See Gilchrist, *Gender and Material Culture,* p. 60, for illustrations of late-fifteenth-century brasses carrying the same pious wish, in Latin.

BIBLIOGRAPHY

Abbreviations

BBIAS	*Bibliographical Bulletin of the International Arthurian Society*
EETS	Early English Text Society
e.s.	extra series
n.s.	new series
o.s.	original series
s.s.	supplementary series

Manuscripts

London, British Library Additional 10292.
London, British Library Additional 59678.
Paris, Bibliothèque Nationale fonds français 112.
Paris, Bibliothèque Nationale fonds français 358–63.

Primary Sources

Aelred of Rievaulx. *Aelred of Rievaulx's De Institutione Inclusarum: Two English Versions.* Ed. John Ayto and Alexandra Barratt. EETS o.s. 287. London: Oxford University Press, 1984.

An Anonymous Short English Metrical Chronicle. Ed. Edward Zettl. EETS o.s. 196. London: Milford, 1935 [for 1934].

Aquinas, St. Thomas. *Knowing and Naming God.* In *Summa Theologiæ* Vol. 3, ed. and trans. Herbert McCabe. London: Eyre and Spottiswoode, 1964.

Ashby, George. *The Active Policy of a Prince.* In *George Ashby's Poems.* Ed. Mary Bateson. EETS e.s. 76. London: Kegan Paul, Trench, Trübner, 1899.

The Auchinleck Manuscript: National Library of Scotland, Advocates' MS 19.2.1. Intro. Derek Pearsall and I. C. Cunningham. London: Scolar Press, 1977

The Black Book of the Admiralty. Ed. Sir Travers Twiss. 4 vols. Rolls Series 55. London: Longman, 1871.

Boccaccio, G. *The Fates of Illustrious Men.* Trans. and abbr. Louis Brewer Hall. New York: Ungar, 1965.

Brinton, Thomas. *The Sermons of Thomas Brinton, Bishop of Rochester (1372–1389)*. Ed. Sister Mary Aquinas Devlin. 2 vols. London: Royal Historical Society, 1954.

The Brut or The Chronicles of England. Ed. Friedrich W. D. Brie. 2 vols. EETS o.s. 131, 136. London: Kegan Paul, Trench, Trübner, 1906, 1908.

Capgrave, John. *The Abbreuiacion of Cronicles*. Ed. Peter J. Lucas. EETS o.s. 285. Oxford: Oxford University Press, 1983.

Caxton, William. *The Book of the Ordre of Chyualry*. Ed. Alfred T.P. Byles. EETS o.s. 168. London: Oxford University Press, 1926 [for 1925].

———. *Caxton's Own Prose*. Ed. N. F. Blake. London: André Deutsch, 1973.

———. *Goddefroy of Boloyne*. Ed. Mary Noyes Colvin. EETS e.s. 64. London: Kegan Paul, Trench, Trübner, 1893.

———. *The Lyf of the Noble and Crysten Prynce, Charles the Grete*. Ed. Sidney J. H. Herrtage. EETS e.s. 36, 37. London: Trübner, 1880, 1881.

Chartier, Alain. *A Familiar Dialogue of the Friend and the Fellow*. Ed. Margaret S. Blayney. EETS o.s. 295. London: Oxford University Press, 1989.

The Chastising of God's Children and *The Treatise of Perfection of the Sons of God*. Ed. Joyce Bazire and Eric Colledge. Oxford: Blackwell, 1957.

Chaucer, Geoffrey. *The Riverside Chaucer*. Gen. Ed. Larry D. Benson. Oxford: Oxford University Press, 1988.

———. *Troilus and Criseyde*. Ed. B. A. Windeatt. Harlow, UK: Longman, 1984.

Chrétien de Troyes. *Le Roman de Perceval ou Le Conte du Graal*. Ed. Keith Busby. Tübingen: Niemeyer, 1993.

Collins, S. M. *The French Rolls of Arms, An Ordinary and an Armory*. Unpublished TS. London: College of Arms, 1942.

Conlee, John W., ed. *Middle English Debate Poetry: A Critical Anthology*. East Lansing, MI: Colleagues Press, 1991.

Contemplations of the Dread and Love of God. Ed. Margaret Connolly. EETS o.s. 303. Oxford: Oxford University Press, 1993.

The Continuations of the Old French Perceval of Chrétien de Troyes. Ed. William Roach. 5 vols. Philadelphia: University of Pennsylvania Press, 1949–83.

Dante. *The Divine Comedy. 1: Inferno*. Ed. and trans. John D. Sinclair. New York: Oxford University Press, 1961.

de Montaiglon, Raymond, and Gaston Reynaud, eds. *Receuil général et complet des fabliaux des XIIIe et XIVe siècles*. 6 vols. Paris: Librairie des Bibliophiles, 1872–90. 3.

Dives and Pauper. Ed. Priscilla Heath Barnum. EETS o.s. 275, 280. London: Oxford University Press, 1976, 1980.

The Early English Versions of the Gesta Romanorum. Ed. Sidney J. H. Herrtage. EETS e.s. 33. London: Trübner, 1879.

L'Estoire del Saint Graal. Ed. Jean-Paul Ponceau. 2 vols. Paris: Champion, 1997.

Estoire de Merlin. The Vulgate Version of the Arthurian Romances. Ed. H. Oskar Sommer. 8 vols. Washington, DC: Carnegie Institute, 1908–16. 2.

A Familiar Dialogue of the Friend and the Fellow. Ed. Margaret S. Blayney. EETS o.s. 295. London: Oxford University Press, 1989.

Fortescue, John. *On the Laws and Governance of England*. Ed. Shelley Lockwood. Cambridge, UK: Cambridge University Press, 1997.

Fotitch, Tatiana and R. Steiner. *Les Lais du Roman de Tristan en prose, d'après le manuscrit de Vienne 2542*. Munich: Fink, 1974.

Froissart, Jean. *Chroniques*. Ed. Kervyn de Lettenhove. 25 vols. 1867–77. Repr. Osnabrück: Biblio Verlag, 1967.

Furnivall, Frederick J. *The Fifty Earliest English Wills in the Court of Probate*. EETS o.s. 78. London: Trübner, 1882.

Gairdner, James, ed. *Letters and Papers Illustrative of the Reigns of Richard III and Henry VII*. 2 vols. London: Longman, Green, Longman and Roberts, 1861.

Geoffrey of Monmouth. *The Historia Regum Britanniæ of Geoffrey of Monmouth*. Ed. Acton Griscom. London: Longmans, 1929.

Gertrude, St. *Legatus Divinae Pietates*. In *Gertrude d'Helfta: Œuvres spirituelles*. Ed. and trans. J. Hourlier, A. Schmitt, P. Doyère, J.-M. Clément. 5 vols. Paris: Éditions du Cerf. 1967–86. 2.

Gower, John. *The English Works of John Gower*. Ed. G. C. Macaulay. EETS e.s. 81, 82. London: Oxford University Press, 1900, 1901.

Gradon, Pamela, and Anne Hudson, eds. *English Wycliffite Sermons*. 5 vols. Oxford: Clarendon Press, 1983–1996. 1.

Hahn, Thomas, ed. *Sir Gawain: Eleven Romances and Tales*. TEAMS Middle English Texts Series. Kalamazoo, MI: Medieval Institute Publications, 1995.

Hardyng, John. *The Chronicle of Iohn Hardyng*. Ed. Henry Ellis. London: Rivington, 1812.

Havelok. In *Medieval English Romances. Part One*. Ed. A. V. C. Schmidt and Nicholas Jacobs. London: Hodder & Stoughton 1980.

Higden, Ranulph. *Polychronicon Ranulphi Higden Monachi Cestrensis; Together with English Translations of John Trevisa and of an Unknown Writer of the Fifteenth Century*. Ed. Churchill Babington and Joseph Rawson Lumby. 9 vols. London: Longman, 1865–1886. 5.

Hoccleve, Thomas. *Hoccleve's Works: The Minor Poems*. Ed. Frederick J. Furnivall and I. Gollancz. EETS e.s. 61, 73 (1892, 1925). Rev. Jerome Mitchell and A. I. Doyle, in 1 vol. London: Oxford University Press, 1970.

———. *The Regiment of Princes*. Ed. Charles Blyth. TEAMS Middle English Texts Series. Kalamazoo, MI: Medieval Institute Publications, 1999.

The Holy Bible: Douay Version. London: The Catholic Truth Society, 1956.

Jehan de Waurin. *Receuil des Chroniques*. Ed. W. Hardy. Rolls Series 39. 5 vols. London: Longman, Green, Longman, Roberts, and Green, 1864–91.

Joseph of Arimathie. Ed. David Lawton. New York: Garland, 1983.

Kyng Alisaunder. Ed. G. V. Smithers. EETS o.s. 227, 237. London: Oxford University Press, 1952–57.

Laȝamon. *Laȝamon's Arthur: The Arthurian Section of Laȝamon's Brut L*. Ed. and trans. W. R. J. Barron and S. C. Weinberg. Harlow, UK: Longman, 1989.

Lancelot: Roman en prose du XIIIe siècle. Ed. Alexandre Micha. 9 vols. Geneva: Droz, 1978–83.

Lancelot of the Laik and *Sir Tristrem*. Ed. Alan Lupack. TEAMS Middle English Texts Series. Kalamazoo, MI: Medieval Institute Publications, 1994.

Lancelot-Grail: The Old French Arthurian Vulgate and Post-Vulgate in Translation. Gen. ed. Norris J. Lacy. 5 vols. New York: Garland, 1993–96.

Langland, William. *The Vision of Piers Plowman: A Critical Edition of the B-text*. Ed. A. V. C. Schmidt. London: Dent, 1978.

The Lanterne of Liȝt. Ed. Lilian M. Swinburn. EETS o.s. 151. London: Kegan Paul, Trench Trübner, 1917 (for 1915).

Löseth, Eilert. *Le Roman en prose de Tristan: Le roman de Palamède et la compilation de Rusticien de Pise: analyse critique d'après les manuscrits de Paris*. 1891. Repr. New York: Burt Franklin, 1970.

Lybeaus Desconus. Ed. Maldwyn Mills. EETS o.s. 261. London: Oxford University Press, 1969.

Lydgate, John. *The Minor Poems of John Lydgate*. Part 1. Ed. Henry Noble Mac-Cracken. EETS e.s. 107. Oxford: Oxford University Press, 1911 (for 1910).

Malory, Thomas. *Le morte da[r]thur*, ed. Wynkyn de Worde, 1498. John Rylands University Library of Manchester.

———. *The Winchester Malory: A Facsimile*. Intro. N. R. Ker. EETS s.s. 4. London: Oxford University Press, 1976.

———. *The Works of Sir Thomas Malory*. Ed. Eugène Vinaver, rev. P. J. C. Field, 3rd edn., 3 vols. Oxford: Clarendon Press, 1990.

Mannyng, Robert, of Brunne. *Robert Mannyng of Brunne: The Chronicle*. Ed. Idelle Sullens. Binghamton, NY: Binghamton University, 1996.

Marbod of Rennes. *Liber decem capitulorum*. In *Woman Defamed and Woman Defended*. Ed. Alcuin Blamires, with Karen Pratt and C. W. Marx. Oxford: Clarendon Press, 1992.

Memoriale Credencium: A late Middle English Manual of Theology for Lay People edited from Bodley MS Tanner 201. Ed. J. H. L. Kengen. Nijmegen: Catholic University of Nijmegen, 1979.

Merlin, English Prose. *Merlin, or The Early History of King Arthur*. Ed. H. B. Wheatley. Intro. W. E. Mead. EETS o.s. 10, 21, 36, 112. London: Kegan Paul, Trench, Trübner, 1866, 1869, 1865, 1889.

Minnis, A. J., and A. B. Scott, with David Wallace, eds., *Medieval Literary Theory and Criticism c. 1100–c. 1375: The Commentary Tradition*. Oxford: Clarendon Press, 1988.

Minot, Laurence. *Laurence Minot: Poems*. Ed. T. B. James and J. Simons. Exeter: University of Exeter Press, 1989.

La Mort le roi Artu. Ed. Jean Frappier. Geneva: Droz, 1964.

Le Morte Arthur, Stanzaic: *Le Morte Arthur*. Ed. P. F. Hissiger. The Hague: Mouton, 1975.

Morte Arthure, Alliterative. *Morte Arthure*. Ed. Mary Hamel. New York: Garland, 1984.

Of Arthour and Of Merlin. Ed. O. D. Macrae-Gibson. EETS o.s. 268, 279. London: Oxford University Press, 1973, 1979.

Olivier de la Marche. *Traités du duel judiciaire: Relations de pas d'armes et tournois*. Ed. Bernard Prost. Paris: Léon Willem, 1872.

Perlesvaus. Li Haut Livre du Graal: Perlesvaus. Ed. William A. Nitze and T. A. Jenkins. 2 vols. Chicago: University of Chicago Press, 1932–37.

Les Prophecies de Merlin. Ed. Lucy Allen Paton. 2 vols. New York: Modern Language Association of America, 1926–27.

Proulx, E. Annie. *Postcards.* London: Harper Collins, 1994.

La Queste del Saint Graal. Ed. Albert Pauphilet. Paris: Champion, 1980.

Ratis Raving and Other Moral and Religious Pieces, in Prose and Verse. Ed. J. Rawson Lumby. EETS o.s. 43. London: Trübner, 1870.

The Receyt of the Ladie Kateryne. Ed. Gordon Kipling. EETS o.s. 296. Oxford: Oxford University Press, 1998.

Renaud de Beaujeu. *Le Bel Inconnu.* Ed. G. Perrie Williams. Paris: Champion, 1929.

Le Roman de Tristan en prose. Ed. Renée Curtis. 3 vols. 1. Munich: Hueber, 1963. 2. Leiden: Brill, 1976. 3. Cambridge: Brewer, 1985.

Le Roman de Tristan en prose. Gen. ed. Philippe Ménard. 9 vols. Geneva: Droz, 1987–1997.

The Siege of Jerusalem. Ed. E. Kölbing and Mabel Day. EETS o.s. 188. London: Milford, 1932.

Sir Percyvell of Gales. In *Ywain and Gawain, Sir Percyvell of Gales, The Anturs of Arther.* Ed. Maldwyn Mills. London: Dent, 1992.

The Statutes of the Realm. 9 vols. London: Record Commission, 1810–28.

Steinbeck, John. *The Acts of King Arthur and His Noble Knights, from the Winchester MSS. of Thomas Malory and Other Sources.* Ed. Chase Horton. New York: Noonday Press, 1993.

La Suite du roman de Merlin. Ed. Gilles Roussineau. 2 vols. Geneva: Droz, 1996.

Thomas. *Thomas: Les Fragments du Roman de Tristan.* Ed. Bartina H. Wind. Geneva: Droz, 1960.

Trevisa, John. *On the Properties of Things: John Trevisa's Translation of Bartholomæus Anglicus, De Proprietatibus Rerum.* Gen. ed. Malcolm Seymour. 3 vols. Oxford: Clarendon Press, 1975–88.

———. *Polychronicon.* See Higden, Ranulph.

Tristan 1489. Facsimile with introductory note by C. E. Pickford. London: Scolar Press, 1976.

La Version Post-Vulgate de la Queste del Saint Graal *et de la* Mort Artu: *Troisième Partie du Roman du Graal.* Ed. Fanni Bogdanow. Vols. 1, 2, 4i. Paris: Société des anciens textes français, 1991.

Wace. *Le Roman de Brut.* Ed. Ivor Arnold. 2 vols. Paris: Société des anciens textes français, 1938–40.

Warkworth, John. *Chronicle of John Warkworth.* In *Three Chronicles of the Reign of Edward IV.* Intro. Keith Dockray. Gloucester, UK: Sutton, 1988.

Secondary Sources

Adams, Alison, Armel H. Diverres, Karen Stern, Kenneth Varty, eds. *The Changing Face of Arthurian Romance: Essays on Arthurian Prose Romances in Memory of Cedric E. Pickford.* Cambridge, UK: Brewer, 1986.

Allen, Judson Boyce. "The Medieval Unity of Malory's *Morte Darthur.*" *Mediaevalia* 6 (1980): 279–309.

Allen, Rosamund. "*The Awntyrs off Arthure:* jests and jousts." In Fellows, Field, Rogers, Weiss. 129–42.

Anderson, Benedict. *Imagined Communities: Reflections on the Origin and Spread of Nationalism.* 1983. Rev. edn. London: Verso, 1991.

Archibald, Elizabeth. "Malory's Ideal of Fellowship." *Review of English Studies* n.s. 43 (1992): 311–28.

Archibald, Elizabeth, and A. S. G. Edwards, eds. *A Companion to Malory.* Cambridge, UK: Brewer, 1996.

Armstrong, Elizabeth. "English Purchases of Printed Books from the Continent 1465–1526." *English Historical Review* 94 (1979): 268–90.

Armstrong, John. *Nations Before Nationalism.* Chapel Hill: University of North Carolina Press, 1982.

Aronstein, Susan. "Rewriting Perceval's Sister: Eucharistic Vision and Typological Destiny in the *Queste del San Graal.*" *Women's Studies* 21.2 (1992): 211–30.

Aston, Margaret. *Lollards and Reformers: Images and Literacy in Late Medieval Religion.* London: Hambledon, 1984.

Atkinson, Stephen C. B. "Malory's 'Healing of Sir Urry': Lancelot, the Earthly Fellowship, and the World of the Grail." *Studies in Philology* 78 (1981): 341–52.

Backhouse, Janet. "Founders of the Royal Library: Edward IV and Henry VII as Collectors of Illuminated Manuscripts." In *England in the Fifteenth Century: Proceedings of the 1986 Harlaxton Symposium.* Ed. Daniel Williams. Woodbridge: Brewer, 1987. 23–41.

Baldwin, John W. "From the Ordeal to Confession: In Search of Lay Religion in Early Thirteenth-Century France." In *Handling Sin: Confession in the Middle Ages.* York Studies in Medieval Theology 2. Ed. Peter Biller and A.J. Minnis. York: York Medieval Press, 1998. 191–209.

Barber, Richard. "Malory's *Le Morte Darthur* and Court Culture under Edward IV." *Arthurian Literature* 12 (1993): 133–55.

Barnes, Geraldine. *Counsel and Strategy in Middle English Romance.* Cambridge, UK: Brewer, 1993.

Barron, W. R. J. "Arthurian Romance: Traces of an English Tradition." *English Studies* 61 (1980): 2–23.

———. Ed. *The Arthur of the English.* Cardiff: University of Wales Press, 1999.

Batt, Catherine. "Malory's Questing Beast and the Implications of Author as Translator." In *The Medieval Translator: The Theory and Practice of Translation in the Middle Ages.* Ed. Roger Ellis (Cambridge, UK: Brewer, 1989). 143–66.

———. "'Hand for Hand' and 'Body for Body': Aspects of Malory's Vocabulary of Identity and Integrity with Regard to Gareth and Lancelot." *Modern Philology* 91 (1994): 269–87.

———. "Malory and Rape." *Arthuriana* 7.3 (1997): 78–99.

———. and Rosalind Field. "The Romance Tradition." In Barron. 59–70.

Baumgartner, Emmanuèle. *Le Tristan en prose: Essai d'interprétation d'un roman médiéval.* Geneva: Droz, 1975.

———. "Les Techniques narratives dans le roman en prose." In Lacy, Kelly, Busby. 1: 167–90.

————. *La Harpe et l'Épée: Tradition et renouvellement dans le* Tristan *en prose*. Paris: SEDES, 1990.

————. "From Lancelot to Galahad: The Stakes of Filiation." Trans. Arthur F. Crispin. In Kibler. 14–30.

Beaune, Colette. *The Birth of an Ideology: Myths and Symbols of Nation in Late-Medieval France*. Trans. Susan Ross Huston. Ed. Fredric L. Cheyette. Berkeley: University of California Press, 1991.

Beckerling, Philippa. "Perceval's Sister: Aspects of the Virgin in the *Quest of the Holy Grail* and Malory's *Sankgreal*." In *Constructing Gender: Feminism and Literary Studies*. Ed. Hilary Fraser and R. S. White, with a preface by Penny Boumelha. Nedlands: University of Western Australia Press, 1994. 39–54.

Beckwith, Sarah. *Christ's Body: Identity, Culture and Society in Late Medieval Writings*. London: Routledge, 1993.

Bell, Catherine. *Ritual Theory, Ritual Practice*. New York: Oxford University Press, 1992.

Bellamy, John. *The Tudor Law of Treason: An Introduction*. London: Routledge and Kegan Paul, 1979.

Benjamin, Walter. "Critique of Violence." In *One-Way Street and Other Writings*, trans. Edmund Jephcott and Kingsley Shorter. London: Verso, 1985.

Bennett, H. S. "The Production and Dissemination of Vernacular Manuscripts in the Fifteenth Century." *The Library* 5th series 1 (1946–47): 167–78.

Benson, C. David. "The Ending of the *Morte Darthur*." In Archibald and Edwards. 221–38.

Benson, Larry D. *Malory's "Morte Darthur."* Cambridge, MA: Harvard University Press, 1976.

Berger, Jr., Harry. "Bodies and Texts." *Representations* 17 (1987): 144–66.

Bestul, Thomas H. *Texts of the Passion: Latin Devotional Literature and Medieval Society*. Philadelphia: University of Pennsylvania Press, 1996.

Bhabha, Homi K. "DissemiNation." In his ed. *Nation and Narration*. London: Routledge, 1990. 291–322.

————. *The Location of Culture*. London: Routledge, 1994.

Binski, Paul. *Medieval Death: Ritual and Representation*. London: British Museum, 1996.

Biscoglio, Frances M. "'Unspun' heroes: iconography of the spinning woman in the Middle Ages." *Journal of Medieval and Renaissance Studies* 25.2 (1995): 163–84.

Blackman, Susan Amato. *The Manuscripts and Patronage of Jacques d'Armagnac, Duke of Nemours (1433–1477)*. Unpublished doctoral dissertation, University of Pittsburgh, 1993.

Blaess, Madeleine. "L'Abbaye de Bordesley et les livres de Guy de Beauchamp." *Romania* 78 (1957): 511–18.

————. "Les Manuscrits français dans les monastères anglais au moyen âge." *Romania* 94 (1973): 321–58.

Bloch, R. Howard. "The Death of King Arthur and the Waning of the Feudal Age." *Orbis Litterarum* 29 (1974): 291–305.

————. *Medieval French Literature and Law*. Berkeley: University of California Press, 1977.

————. *Etymologies and Genealogies: A Literary Anthropology of the French Middle Ages.* Chicago: University of Chicago Press, 1983.

————. *Medieval Misogyny and the Invention of Western Romantic Love.* Chicago: University of Chicago Press, 1991.

Blumenfeld-Kosinski, Renate. "Old French Narrative Genres: Towards the Definition of the *Roman Antique.*" *Romance Philology* 34 (1980): 143–59.

Bogdanow, Fanni. "Part III of the Turin Version of *Guiron le Courtois:* A Hitherto Unknown source of MS. B.N. 112." In Whitehead, Diverres, Sutcliffe. 45–64.

————. *The Romance of the Grail: A Study of the Structure and Genesis of a Thirteenth-Century Arthurian Prose Romance.* Manchester: Manchester University Press, 1966.

Boulton, Maureen Barry McCann. *The Song in the Story: Lyric Insertions in French Narrative Fiction, 1200–1400.* Philadelphia: University of Pennsylvania Press, 1993.

————. "Tristan and his Doubles as Singers of Lais: Love and Music in the Prose *Roman de Tristan.*" In *Shifts and Transpositions in Medieval Narrative: A Festschrift for Dr Elspeth Kennedy.* Ed. Karen Pratt. Cambridge, UK: Brewer, 1994. 53–69.

Bourdieu, Pierre. *Language and Symbolic Power.* Ed. and intro. John B. Thompson. Trans. Gino Raymond and Matthew Adamson. Cambridge, UK: Polity Press, 1991.

Brault, Gerard J. *Early Blazon: Heraldic Terminology in the Twelfth and Thirteenth Centuries, with Special Reference to Arthurian Literature.* Oxford: Clarendon Press, 1972.

Breitenberg, Mark. *Anxious Masculinity in Early Modern England.* Cambridge, UK: Cambridge University Press, 1996.

Brewer, Derek. *Symbolic Stories.* Cambridge, UK: Brewer, 1980.

————"Malory's 'Proving' of Sir Launcelot." In Adams, Diverres, Stern, Varty. 123–36.

————. "Death in Malory's *Le Morte Darthur.*" In *Zeit, Tod und Ewigkeit in der Renaissance Literatur,* 3. Ed. James Hogg. Salzburg: Institut für Anglistik und Amerikanistik, Universität Salzburg, 1987. 44–57.

Brink, Jeanie. "The Design of Malory's 'Tale of Balin': Narrative and Dialogue in Counterpoint." *Studies in Short Fiction* 17 (1980): 1–7.

Brittan, Arthur. *Masculinity and Power.* Oxford: Blackwell, 1989.

Bronfen, Elisabeth. *Over Her Dead Body: Death, Femininity and the Aesthetic.* Manchester: Manchester University Press, 1992.

————. and Sarah Webster Goodwin. "Introduction." In Goodwin and Bronfen. 3–25.

Brownlee, Kevin. "Cultural Comparison: Crusade as Construct in Late Medieval France." *L'Esprit Créateur* 32.3 (1992): 13–24.

Brownmiller, Susan. *Against Our Will: Men, Women and Rape.* New York: Fawcett Columbine, 1975.

Bruns, Gerald L. "The Originality of Texts in a Manuscript Culture." *Comparative Literature* 32 (1980): 113–29.

Burnley, David. "Dynastic Romance." In Barron. 83–90.

Burns, E. Jane. *Arthurian Fictions: Rereading the Vulgate Cycle.* Columbus: Ohio State University Press, 1985.

———. "*La Voie de la Voix:* The Aesthetics of Indirection in the Vulgate Cycle." In Lacy, Kelly, Busby. 2: 151–67.

———. "Vulgate Cycle." In Lacy, *Encyclopedia.* 609–14.

———. "Which Queen? Guinevere's Transvestism in the French Prose *Lancelot.*" In *Lancelot and Guinevere: A Casebook.* Ed. Lori Walters. New York: Garland, 1996. 247–65.

Bynum, Caroline Walker. *Fragmentation and Redemption: Essays on Gender and the Human Body in Medieval Religion.* New York: Zone Books, 1991.

Carley, James. "Arthur in English History." In Barron. 47–57.

Carter, John Marshall. *Rape in Medieval England: An Historical and Sociological Study.* New York: University Press of America, 1985.

Caruth, Cathy, ed. and intros. *Trauma: Explorations in Memory.* Baltimore, MD: Johns Hopkins University Press, 1995.

Cavanaugh, Susan H. *A Study of Books Privately Owned in England, 1300–1450.* Unpublished doctoral dissertation, University of Pennsylvania, 1980.

———. "Royal Books: King John to Richard II." *The Library* 6th Series 10 (1988): 304–16.

Chaitin, Gilbert D. *Rhetoric and Culture in Lacan.* Cambridge, UK: Cambridge University Press, 1996.

Cherewatuk, Karen. "The Saint's Life of Sir Launcelot: Hagiography and the Conclusion of Malory's *Morte Darthur.*" *Arthuriana* 5.1 (1995): 62–78.

———. "'Gentyl Audiences' and 'Grete Bookes': Chivalric Manuals and the *Morte Darthur.*" *Arthurian Literature* 15 (1997): 205–16.

Chesnutt, Michael. "Minstrel Reciters and the Enigma of the Middle English Romance." *Culture & History* 2 (1987): 48–67.

Clanchy, M. T. *From Memory to Written Record. England 1066–1307.* Oxford: Blackwell, 1993.

Clayton, Jay. "Narrative and Theories of Desire." *Critical Inquiry* 16 (1989): 33–53.

Cohen, Jeffrey Jerome. "Masoch/Lancelotism." *New Literary History* 28 (1997): 231–60.

———, and the members of Interscripta, "The Armour of an Alienating Identity." *Arthuriana* 6.4 (1996): 1–24.

Coleman, Joyce. *Public Reading and the Reading Public in Late Medieval England and France.* Cambridge, UK: Cambridge University Press, 1996.

Cooper, Helen. "*The Book of Sir Tristram de Lyones.*" In Archibald and Edwards. 183–201.

———. "M for Merlin: The Case of the Winchester Manuscript." In *Medieval Heritage: Essays in Honour of Tadahiro Ikegami.* Ed. Masahiko Kanno, Hiroshi Yamashita, Masatoshi Kawasaki, Junko Asakawa, and Naoko Shirai. Tokyo: Yushodo, 1997. 93–107.

———. "Romance after 1400." in Wallace. 690–719.

Cooper, Kate. "Merlin Romancier: Paternity, Prophecy, and Poetics in the Huth *Merlin.*" *Romanic Review* 77 (1986): 1–24.

Copeland, Rita. "Between Romans and Romantics." *Texas Studies in Literature and Language* 33 (1991): 215–24.

Coss, P. R. "Aspects of Cultural Diffusion in Medieval England: the Early Romances, Local Society and Robin Hood." *Past and Present* 108 (1985): 35–79.

Crane, Susan. "Maytime in Late Medieval Courts." *New Medieval Literatures* 2 (1998): 159–79.

Crick, Julia C. *The* Historia regum Britannie *of Geoffrey of Monmouth: IV. Dissemination and Reception in the Later Middle Ages.* Cambridge, UK: Brewer, 1991.

Cripps-Day, F. H. *On Armour Preserved in English Churches.* London: privately printed, Chiswick Press, 1922.

———, and A. R. Duffy. *Fragmenta Armamentaria.* 5 vols. Vol. 5: *Church Armour.* Frome UK: privately printed, 1939.

Csordas, Thomas J. "Embodiment as a Paradigm for Anthropology." *Ethos* 18 (1990): 5–47.

———., ed. *Embodiment and Experience: The Existential Ground of Culture and Self.* Cambridge, UK: Cambridge University Press, 1994.

Dalrymple, Roger. "The Literary Use of Religious Formulae in Certain Middle English Romances." *Medium Ævum* 64 (1995): 250–63.

Daniell, Christopher. *Death and Burial in Medieval England 1066–1550.* London: Routledge, 1997.

Davis, Nick. "Narrative Composition and the Spatial Memory." In *Narrative: From Malory to Motion Pictures.* Ed. Jeremy Hawthorn. London: Edward Arnold, 1985. 24–39.

Davis, Robert Con. *The Paternal Romance: Reading God-the-Father in Early Western Culture.* Urbana: University of Illinois Press, 1993.

Dean, James. "Vestiges of Paradise: The Tree of Life in *Cursor Mundi* and Malory's *Morte Darthur.*" *Mediaevalia et Humanistica* n.s. 13 (1985): 113–26.

Delany, Sheila. *The Naked Text: Chaucer's "Legend of Good Women."* Berkeley: University of California Press, 1994.

Delisle, L. *Recherches sur la librairie de Charles V.* 3 vols. Paris: Champion, 1907.

de Looze, Laurence N. "A Story of Interpretations: The *Queste del Saint Graal* as Metaliterature." *Romanic Review* 76.2 (1985): 129–47.

de Man, Paul. *The Resistance to Theory.* Foreword Wlad Godzich. Minneapolis: University of Minnesota Press, 1986.

de Mandrot, Bernard. "Jacques d'Armagnac, duc de Nemours, 1433–1477." *Revue Historique* 43 (1890): 274–316; 44 (1890): 241–312.

Derrida, Jacques. *Of Grammatology.* Trans. Gayatri Chakravorty Spivak. Baltimore, MD: Johns Hopkins University Press, 1976.

de Winter, Patrick M. *La Bibliothèque de Philippe le Hardi, Duc de Bourgogne (1364–1404).* Paris: Centre National de la Recherche Scientifique, 1985.

Dillon, Viscount, and W. H. St. John Hope, "Inventory of the Goods and Chattels Belonging to Thomas, Duke of Gloucester." *Archaeological Review* 54 (1897): 275–308.

Dinshaw, Carolyn. *Getting Medieval: Sexualities and Communities, Pre- and Postmodern.* Durham, NC: Duke University Press, 1999.

Doe, Nicholas. *Fundamental Authority in Late Medieval English Law.* Cambridge, UK: Cambridge University Press, 1990.

Donavin, Georgiana. "Locating a Public Forum for the Personal Letter in Malory's *Morte Darthur.*" *Disputatio* 1 (1996): 19–36.

Duffy, Eamon. *The Stripping of the Altars: Traditional Religion in England c.1400-c.1580.* New Haven, CT: Yale University Press, 1992.

Duggan, Anne J., ed. *Queens and Queenship in Medieval Europe.* Woodbridge, UK: Boydell, 1997.

Echard, Siân. *Arthurian Narrative in the Latin Tradition.* Cambridge, UK: Cambridge University Press, 1998.

Eckhardt, Caroline. "The Figure of Merlin in Middle English Chronicles." In *Comparative Studies in Merlin from the Vedas to C. G. Jung.* Ed. James Gollnick. Lewiston, UK: Edwin Mellen, 1991. 21–39.

Edwards, Elizabeth. "Amnesia and Remembrance in Malory's *Morte Darthur.*" *Paragraph* 13.2 (1990): 132–46.

———. "The Place of Women in the *Morte Darthur.*" In Archibald and Edwards. 37–54.

———. *The Genesis of Narrative in Malory's* Morte Darthur. Cambridge, UK: Brewer, 2001.

Ellis, Deborah S. "Balin, Mordred, and Malory's Idea of Treachery." *English Studies* 68 (1987): 66–74.

Evans, Ruth. "Translating Past Cultures?" In *The Medieval Translator 4.* Ed. Roger Ellis and Ruth Evans. Exeter: University of Exeter Press, 1994. 20–45.

———. "Historicizing Postcolonial Criticism: Cultural Difference and the Vernacular." In *The Idea of the Vernacular: An Anthology of Middle English Literary Theory 1280–1520.* Ed. Jocelyn Wogan-Browne, Nicholas Watson, Andrew Taylor, and Ruth Evans. Exeter: University of Exeter Press, 1999. 366–70.

Feder, Lillian. *Madness in Literature.* Princeton, NJ: Princeton University Press, 1980.

Fein, David A. "'Que vous en mentiroie?': The Problem of Authorial Reliability in Twelfth-Century French Narrative." *Philological Quarterly* 71 (1992): 1–14.

Fellows, Jennifer, Rosalind Field, Gillian Rogers, and Judith Weiss, eds. *Romance Reading on the Book: Essays on Medieval Narrative Presented to Maldwyn Mills.* Cardiff: University of Wales Press, 1996.

Felman, Shoshana. *Writing and Madness (Philosophy/Psychoanalysis/Literature).* Trans. Martha Evans and the author, with the assistance of Brian Massumi. Ithaca, NY: Cornell University Press, 1985.

Ferguson, Gary. "Symbolic Sexual Inversion and the Construction of Courtly Manhood in Two French Romances." *The Arthurian Yearbook* 3 (1993): 203–13.

Ferster, Judith. *Fictions of Advice: The Literature and Politics of Counsel in Late Medieval England.* Philadelphia: University of Pennsylvania Press, 1996.

Fewster, Carol. *Traditionality and Genre in Middle English Romance.* Cambridge, UK: Brewer, 1987.

Fichte, Joerg O. "From 'Shyvalere de Charyot' to 'The Knyght That Rode in the Charyot': Thoughts on Malory's Adaptation of the *Vulgate Lancelot.*" In *Genres, Themes, and Images in English Literature.* Ed. Piero Boitani and Anna Torti. Tübingen: Narr, 1988. 73–89.

————. "Grappling with Arthur or Is There an Arthurian Verse Romance?" In *Poetics: Theory and Practice in Medieval English Literature*. Ed. Piero Boitani and Anna Torti. Cambridge, UK: Brewer, 1991. 149–63.

Field, P. J. C. *Romance and Chronicle: A Study of Malory's Prose Style*. London: Barrie and Jenkins, 1971.

————. "Malory and the French prose *Lancelot*." *Bulletin of the John Rylands University Library of Manchester* 75 (1993): 79–102.

————. *The Life and Times of Sir Thomas Malory*. Cambridge, UK: Brewer, 1993.

————. "Caxton's Roman War." In ed. Salda. 31–73.

————. "Malory's Mordred and the *Morte Arthure*." In Fellows, Field, Rogers, Weiss. 77–93.

Finke, Laurie A., and Martin Shichtman. "The Mont St. Michel Giant: Sexual Violence and Imperialism in the Chronicles of Wace and Laȝamon." In *Violence against Women in Medieval Texts,* ed. Anna Roberts. Gainesville: University Press of Florida, 1998. 56–74.

————."No Pain, No Gain: Violence as Symbolic Capital in Malory's *Morte d'Arthur*." *Arthuriana* 8.2 (1998): 115–34.

Finucane, R. C. "Sacred Corpse, Profane Carrion: Social Ideals and Death Rituals in the Later Middle Ages." In *Mirrors of Mortality: Studies in the Social History of Death*. Ed. Joachim Whaley. London: Europa, 1981. 40–60.

Flax, Jane. "Signifying the Father's Desire: Lacan in a Feminist's Gaze." In *Criticism and Lacan: Essays and Dialogue on Language, Structure, and the Unconscious*. Ed. Patrick Colm Hogan and Lalita Pandit. Athens: University of Georgia Press, 1990. 109–19.

Fletcher, Alan J. "King Arthur's Passing in the *Morte D'Arthur*." *English Language Notes* 31.4 (1994): 19–24.

Fortes, Meyer. *Rules and the Emergence of Society*. London: Royal Anthropological Institute, 1983.

Foster, Joseph. *Some Feudal Coats of Arms*. Oxford and London: James Parker, 1902.

Fradenburg, Louise Olga. *City, Marriage, Tournament: Arts of Rule in Late Medieval Scotland*. Madison: University of Wisconsin Press, 1991.

————, ed. and intro. *Women and Sovereignty*. Edinburgh: Edinburgh University Press, 1992.

————. "Introduction: Rethinking Queenship." In ed. Fradenburg. 1–13.

————, and Carla Freccero. "Introduction: Caxton, Foucault, and the Pleasures of History." In their *Premodern Sexualities*. New York: Routledge, 1996. xiii–xxiv.

Freud, Sigmund. "Remembering, Repeating and Working-Through." In Strachey. 12:145–56.

————"'A Child is Being Beaten: A Contribution to the Study of the Origin of Sexual Perversions." In Strachey. 17:175–204.

Fries, Maureen. "How Many Roads to Camelot? The Married Knight in Malory's *Morte Darthur*." In Shichtman and Carley. 196–207.

————. "Gender and the Grail." *Arthuriana* 8.1 (1998): 67–79.

Gairdner, James. *Lollardy and the Reformation in England: An Historical Survey*. 4 vols. London: Macmillan, 1908–13.

Gallop, Jane. *Thinking Through the Body.* New York: Columbia University Press, 1988.

Ganim, John M. *Style and Consciousness in Middle English Narrative.* Princeton, N. J.: Princeton University Press, 1983.

Gaunt, Simon. *Gender and Genre in Medieval French Literature.* Cambridge, UK: Cambridge University Press, 1995.

Gilchrist, Roberta. *Gender and Material Culture: The Archaeology of Religious Women.* London: Routledge, 1994.

———. "Medieval Bodies in the Material World: Gender, Stigma, and the Body." In *Medieval Bodies.* Ed. Sarah Kay and Miri Rubin. Manchester: Manchester University Press, 1994. 43–61.

Girard, René. *Violence and the Sacred.* Trans. Patrick Gregory. London: Athlone Press, 1988.

Gittings, Clare. *Death, Burial and the Individual in Early Modern England.* London: Routlege, 1984.

Goodman, Jennifer R. "Malory and Caxton's Chivalric Series, 1481–85." In Spisak. 257–74.

———. *Chivalry and Exploration, 1298–1630.* Woodbridge, UK: Boydell, 1998.

Goodwin, Sarah Webster, and Elisabeth Bronfen, eds. *Death and Representation.* Baltimore, MD: Johns Hopkins University Press, 1993.

Gravdal, Kathryn. *Ravishing Maidens: Writing Rape in Medieval French Literature and Law.* Philadelphia: University of Pennsylvania Press, 1991.

Gray, Douglas. "The Five Wounds of Our Lord." *Notes and Queries* 208 (1963), 1: 50–51; 2: 82–89; 3: 127–34; 4: 163–68.

Green, Richard Firth. "Notes on Some Manuscripts of Hoccleve's *Regiment of Princes,*" *British Library Journal* 4 (1978): 37–41.

———. *Poets and Princepleasers: Literature and the English Court in the Late Middle Ages.* Toronto: University of Toronto Press, 1980.

Grimm, Kevin. "Knightly Love and the Narrative Structure of Malory's Tale Seven." *Arthurian Interpretations* 3 (1989): 76–95.

———. "Editing Malory: What's at (the) Stake?" In ed. Salda. 5–14.

Guddat-Figge, Gisela. *Catalogue of Manuscripts Containing Middle English Romances.* Munich: Fink, 1976.

Guerin, M. Victoria. *The Fall of Kings and Princes: Structure and Destruction in Arthurian Tragedy.* Stanford: Stanford University Press, 1995.

Hahn, Stacey L. "Genealogy and Adventure in the Cyclic Prose *Lancelot.*" In *Conjunctures: Medieval Studies in Honor of Douglas Kelly.* Ed. Keith Busby and Norris J. Lacy. Amsterdam: Rodopi, 1994. 139–51.

Hamel, Mary. "The 'Christening' of Sir Priamus in the Alliterative *Morte Arthure.*" *Viator* 13 (1982): 295–307.

Hanks, D. Thomas, Jr., ed. *Sir Thomas Malory: Views and Re-Views.* New York: AMS Press, 1992.

———. "Malory, the *Mort[e]s,* and the Confrontation in Guinevere's Chamber." In Hanks. 78–90.

Hanna, Ralph. *Pursuing History: Middle English Manuscripts and Their Texts.* Stanford: Stanford University Press, 1996.

Hanning, Robert W. *The Vision of History in Early Britain: From Gildas to Geoffrey of Monmouth.* New York: Columbia University Press, 1966.

———. "Arthurian Evangelists: The Language of Truth in Thirteenth-Century French Prose Romances." *Philological Quarterly* 64 (1985): 347–65.

Harris, E. Kay. "Lancelot's Vocation: Traitor Saint." In Kibler. 219–37.

———. "Evidence against Lancelot and Guinevere in Malory's *Morte Darthur:* Treason by Imagination." *Exemplaria* 7 (1995): 179–208.

Hartung, A. E. "Narrative Technique, Characterization, and the Sources in Malory's 'Tale of Sir Lancelot.'" *Studies in Philology* 70 (1973): 252–68.

Harvey, I. M. W. "Was There Popular Politics in Fifteenth-Century England?" In *The McFarlane Legacy: Studies in Late Medieval Politics and Society.* Ed. R. H. Britnell and A. J. Pollard. New York: St. Martin's Press, 1995. 155–74.

Helmholz, Richard. *Marriage Litigation in Medieval England.* Cambridge, UK: Cambridge University Press, 1974.

Heng, Geraldine. "Enchanted Ground: The Feminine Subtext in Malory." (1990) repr. in *Arthurian Women: A Casebook.* Ed. Thelma S. Fenster. New York: Garland, 1996. 97–113.

Hoey, Michael. "The Organisation of Narratives of Desire." In *Language and Desire: Encoding Sex, Romance, and Intimacy.* Ed. Keith Harvey and Celia Shalom. London: Routledge, 1997. 85–105.

Hoffman, Donald L. "Malory's 'Cinderella Knights' and the Notion of Adventure." *Philological Quarterly* 67 (1988): 145–56.

———. "Perceval's Sister: Malory's 'Rejected' Masculinities." *Arthuriana* 6.4 (1996): 72–83.

Huot, Sylvia. *From Song to Book: The Poetics of Writing in Old French Lyric and Lyrical Narrative Poetry.* Ithaca, NY: Cornell University Press, 1987.

Ihle, Sandra Ness. *Malory's Grail Quest: Invention and Adaptation in Medieval Prose Romance.* Madison: University of Wisconsin Press, 1983.

Ingledew, Francis. "The Book of Troy and the Genealogical Construction of History: The Case of Geoffrey of Monmouth's *Historia regum Britanniae,*" *Speculum* 69 (1994): 665–704.

James, Mervyn. *Society, Politics and Culture.* Cambridge, UK: Cambridge University Press, 1986.

Jefferson, Lisa. "Tournaments, Heraldry and the Knights of the Round Table: A Fifteenth-Century Armorial with Two Accompanying Texts." *Arthurian Literature* 14 (1996): 69–157.

Jesmok, Janet. "'A knyght wyveles': The Young Lancelot in Malory's *Morte Darthur.*" *Modern Language Quarterly* 42 (1981): 315–30.

Johanek, Peter. "König Arthur und die Plantagenets." *Frühmittelalterliche Studien* 21 (1987): 346–89.

Johnson, James Turner. *Ideology, Reason, and the Limitation of War: Religious and Secular Concepts 1200–1740.* Princeton, NJ: Princeton University Press, 1975.

Johnson, Lesley. "Robert Mannyng of Brunne and the History of Arthurian Literature." In *Church and Chronicle in the Middle Ages: Essays Presented to John Taylor.* Ed. Ian Wood and G. A. Loud. London: Hambledon Press, 1991. 129–47.

————. "King Arthur at the Crossroads to Rome." *Noble and Joyous Histories: English Romances, 1375–1650*. Ed. Eiléan Ní Cuilleanáin and J. D. Pheifer. Dublin: Blackrock, 1993. 87–111.

————. "Etymologies, Genealogies, and Nationalities (Again)." In *Concepts of National Identity in the Middle Ages*. Ed. Simon Forde, Lesley Johnson, and Alan V. Murray. Leeds Texts and Monographs n.s. 14. Leeds: University of Leeds, 1995. 125–36.

————, and Jocelyn Wogan-Browne. "National, World, and Women's History: Writers and Readers of English in Post-Conquest England." In Wallace. 92–121.

Johnston, John. "Translation as Simulacrum." In *Rethinking Translation: Discourse, Subjectivity, Ideology*. Ed. Lawrence Venuti. London: Routledge, 1992. 42–56.

Kato, Tomomi. *A Concordance to the Works of Sir Thomas Malory*. Tokyo: University of Tokyo Press, 1974.

Kay, Sarah. *The Chansons de geste in the Age of Romance: Political Fictions* Oxford: Clarendon Press, 1995.

————. "Adultery and Killing in *La Mort le roi Artu*." In *Scarlet Letters: Fictions of Adultery from Antiquity to the 1990s*. Ed. Nicholas White and Naomi Segal. New York: St. Martin's Press, 1997. 34–44.

Keen, M. H. *The Laws of War in the Late Middle Ages*. London: Routledge and Kegan Paul, 1965.

Kekewich, Margaret. "Edward IV, William Caxton, and Literary Patronage in Yorkist England." *Modern Language Review* 66 (1971): 481–87.

Kelly, Kathleen Coyne. "Malory's Body Chivalric." *Arthuriana* 6.4 (1996): 52–71.

————. "Malory's Multiple Virgins." *Arthuriana* 9.2 (1999): 21–29.

Kelly, Robert L. "Penitence as a Remedy for War in Malory's 'Tale of the Death of Arthur.'" *Studies in Philology* 91.2 (1994): 111–35.

————. "Malory and the Common Law: *Hasty jougement* in the 'Tale of the Death of King Arthur,'" *Medievalia et Humanistica* n.s. 22 (1995): 111–40.

Kennedy, Beverly. "Malory's Lancelot: 'Trewest lover, of a synful man.'" *Viator* 12 (1981): 409–56.

————. *Knighthood in the "Morte Darthur."* Cambridge, UK: Brewer, 1985.

Kennedy, Edward Donald. "John Hardyng and the Holy Grail." *Arthurian Literature* 8 (1989): 185–206.

————. "Malory's 'Noble Tale of Sir Launcelot du Lake,' the Vulgate *Lancelot*, and the Post-Vulgate *Roman du Graal*." In Suzuki and Mukai. 107–29.

Kennedy, Elspeth. "The Scribe as Editor." In *Mélanges de langue et de littérature du moyen âge offerts à Jean Frappier par ses collègues, ses élèves et ses amis*. Ed. J. C. Payen and C. Régnier. 2 vols. Geneva: Droz, 1970. 1:523–31.

————. "Études sur le *Lancelot* en prose. I: Les allusions au conte Lancelot et à d'autres contes dans le *Lancelot* en prose;" II: "Le roi Arthur dans le *Lancelot* en prose." *Romania* 105 (1984): 34–62.

————. "The Re-writing and Re-reading of a Text: The Evolution of the Prose *Lancelot*." In Adams, Diverres, Stern, Varty. 1–9.

Kibbee, Douglas. *For to Speke Frenche Trewely: The French Language in England, 1000–1600: Its Status, Description and Instruction*. Amsterdam: Benjamins, 1991.

Kibler, William W., ed. *The Lancelot-Grail Cycle: Text and Transformations.* Austin: University of Texas Press, 1994.

Kieckhefer, Richard. "Major Currents in Late Medieval Devotion." In *Christian Spirituality: High Middle Ages and Reformation.* Ed. Jill Raitt. London: Routledge and Kegan Paul, 1987. 75–108.

———. "Holiness and the Culture of Devotion: Remarks on Some Late Medieval Male Saints." In *Images of Sainthood in Medieval Europe.* Ed. Renate Blumenfeld-Kosinski and Timea Szell. Ithaca, NY: Cornell University Press. 288–305.

Kingsford, C. L. *The Grey Friars of London.* British Society of Franciscan Studies 6. Aberdeen: University Press, 1915.

Kipling, Gordon. *Enter the King. Theatre, Liturgy, and Ritual in the Medieval Civic Triumph.* Oxford: Clarendon Press, 1998.

Kirk, Elizabeth. "'Clerkes, Poetes and Historiographs': The *Morte Darthur* and Caxton's 'Poetics' of Fiction." In Spisak. 275–95.

Kiser, Lisa J. *Telling Classical Tales: Chaucer and the "Legend of Good Women."* Ithaca, NY: Cornell University Press, 1983.

Knight, Stephen. "From Jerusalem to Camelot: King Arthur and the Crusades." In *Medieval Codicology, Iconography, Literature, and Translation: Studies for Keith Val Sinclair.* Ed. Peter Rolfe Monks and D. D. R. Owen. Leiden: Brill, 1994. 223–32.

Kristeva, Julia. *Powers of Horror: An Essay on Abjection.* Trans. Leon S. Roudiez. New York: Columbia University Press, 1982.

Krochalis, Jeanne. "The Books and Reading of Henry V and His Circle." *The Chaucer Review* 23.1 (1988): 50–77.

Krueger, Roberta. "The Author's Voice: Narrators, Audiences, and the Problem of Interpretation." In Lacy, Kelly, Busby. 1: 115–40.

Kurath, Hans, S. M. Kuhn, and others. *The Middle English Dictionary.* Ann Arbor: University of Michigan Press, 1954–.

Lacan, Jacques. *Écrits: a Selection.* Ed. and trans. Alan Sheridan. London: Tavistock, 1977.

Lacy, Norris J., ed. *The New Arthurian Encyclopedia.* New York: Garland, 1996.

———, Douglas Kelly, and Keith Busby, eds. *The Legacy of Chrétien de Troyes.* 2 vols. Amsterdam: Rodopi, 1987, 1988.

La Farge, Catherine. "The Hand of the Huntress: Repetition and Malory's *Morte Darthur.*" In *New Feminist Discourses: Critical Essays on Theories and Texts.* Ed. Isobel Armstrong. London: Routledge, 1992. 263–79.

Lagorio, Valerie M. "The Evolving Legend of St Joseph of Glastonbury." *Speculum* 46 (1971): 209–31.

———. "The *Joseph of Arimathie*: English Hagiography in Transition." *Medievalia et Humanistica* n.s. 6 (1975): 91–101.

———. "The Apocalyptic Mode in the Vulgate Cycle of Arthurian Romances." *Philological Quarterly* 57 (1978): 1–22.

Lambert, Mark. *Malory: Style and Vision in Le Morte Darthur.* New Haven, CT: Yale University Press, 1976.

Laqueur, Thomas. *Making Sex: Body and Gender from the Greeks to Freud.* Cambridge, MA: Harvard University Press, 1990.

Le Saux, Françoise. "*Pryvayly and secretely:* Personal Letters in Malory's 'Book of Sir Tristram de Lyones.'" *Études de lettres* 3 (1993): 21–33.

Lester, G. A. "The Books of a Fifteenth-Century English Gentleman, Sir John Paston." *Neuphilologische Mitteilungen* 88 (1987): 200–17.

Leupin, Alexandre. *Le Graal et la littérature: Étude sur la vulgate arthurienne en prose.* Lausanne: L'Âge d'Homme, 1982.

Lévi-Strauss, Claude. *The Origin of Table Manners.* Trans. J. Weightman and D. Weightman. London: Jonathan Cape, 1978.

Lochrie, Karma. "Don't Ask, Don't Tell: Murderous Plots and Medieval Secrets." In Fradenburg and Freccero. 137–52.

Loomis, Laura Hibbard. "The Auchinleck Manuscript and a Possible London Bookshop of 1330–1340." *PMLA* 57 (1942): 595–627.

Loomis, R. S., and Laura Hibbard Loomis. *Arthurian Legends in Medieval Art.* London: Oxford University Press, 1938.

Looper, Jennifer E. "Gender, Genealogy, and the 'Story of the Three Spindles' in the *Queste del Saint Graal.*" *Arthuriana* 8.1 (1998): 49–66.

Lynch, Andrew. *Malory's Book of Arms: The Narrative of Combat in* Le Morte Darthur. Cambridge, UK: Brewer, 1997.

Machan, Tim William. "Editing, Orality, and Late Middle English Texts." In *Vox Intexta: Orality and Textuality in the Middle Ages.* Ed. A. N. Doane and Carol Braun Pasternak. Madison: University of Wisconsin Press, 1991. 229–45.

Maddox, Donald. *The Arthurian Romances of Chrétien de Troyes: Once and Future Fictions.* Cambridge, UK: Cambridge University Press, 1991.

Mann, Jill. "Malory: Knightly Combat in *Le Morte d'Arthur.*" In *The New Pelican Guide to English Literature,* Vol. 1. Ed. Boris Ford. Harmondsworth, UK: Penguin, 1982. 331–39.

———. "'Taking the Adventure': Malory and the *Suite du Merlin.*" In Takamiya and Brewer. 71–91.

———. *The Narrative of Distance, the Distance of Narrative in Malory's* Morte Darthur. The William Matthews Lectures, 1991. London: Birkbeck College, 1991.

———. "Malory and the Grail Legend." In Archibald and Edwards. 203–220.

Marcuse, Herbert. "The Ideology of Death." In *The Meaning of Death.* Ed. Herman Feifel. New York: McGraw-Hill, 1959. 64–76.

Matheson, Lister M. "The Middle English Prose *Brut:* A Location List of the Manuscripts and Early Printed Editions." *Analytical and Enumerative Bibliography* 3 (1979): 254–66.

———. "Historical Prose." In *Middle English Prose: A Critical Guide to Major Authors and Genres.* Ed. A. S. G. Edwards. New Brunswick, NJ: Rutgers University Press, 1984. 209–48.

McCracken, Peggy. "The Body Politic and the Queen's Adulterous Body in French Romance." *Feminist Approaches to the Body in Medieval Literature.* Ed. Linda Lomperis and Sarah Stanbury. Philadelphia: University of Pennsylvania Press, 1993. 38–64.

McSheffrey, Shannon. *Gender and Heresy: Women and Men in Lollard Communities.* Philadelphia: University of Pennsylvania Press, 1995.

Meale, Carol M. "The Manuscripts and Early Audience of the Middle English *Prose Merlin*." In Adams, Diverres, Stern, Varty. 92–111.

———. "Manuscripts, Readers, and Patrons in Fifteenth-Century England: Sir Thomas Malory and Arthurian Romance." *Arthurian Literature* 4 (1985): 93–126.

———. "Caxton, de Worde, and the Publication of Romance in Late Medieval England." *The Library* 6th Series 14 (1992): 283–98.

———." . . . alle the bokes that I haue of latyn, englisch, and frensche": Laywomen and their Books in Late Medieval England." In *Women & Literature in Britain 1100–1500*. Ed. Carol M. Meale. Cambridge, UK: Cambridge University Press, 1993. 128–58.

———. "'The Hoole Book': Editing and the Creation of Meaning in Malory's Text." In Archibald and Edwards. 3–17.

Ménard, Philippe. "Les Fous dans la société médiévale." *Romania* 98 (1977): 433–59.

Miller, David A. *The Novel and the Police*. Berkeley: University of California Press, 1988.

Miller, David R. "Sir Thomas Malory's *A Noble Tale of Sir Launcelot du Lake* reconsidered." *BBIAS* 36 (1984): 230–56.

Miller, J. Hillis. "Thomas Hardy, Jacques Derrida, and the 'Dislocation of Souls.'" In *Taking Chances: Derrida, Psychoanalysis, and Literature*. Ed. Joseph H. Smith and William Kerrigan. Baltimore, MD: Johns Hopkins Press, 1984. 135–45.

Mishra, Vijay, and Bob Hodge. "What is Post(-)colonialism?" In *Colonial Discourse and Post-Colonial Theory: A Reader*. Ed. Patrick Willaims and Laura Chrisman. Hemel Hempstead, UK: Harvester Wheatsheaf, 1993. 276–90.

Mitchell, Juliet, and Jacqueline Rose, eds. *Feminine Sexuality: Jacques Lacan and the école freudienne*. New York: Norton, 1982.

Moore-Gilbert, Bart. *Postcolonial Theory: Contexts, Practices, Politics*. London: Verso, 1997.

Moorman, Charles. "Desperately Defending Winchester: Arguments from the Edge." *Arthuriana* 5.2 (1995): 24–30.

Morris, Rosemary. *The Character of King Arthur in Medieval Literature*. Cambridge, UK: Brewer, 1982.

———. "Uther and Igerne: A Study in Uncourtly Love." *Arthurian Literature* 4 (1985): 70–92.

Mukai, Tsuyoshi. "De Worde's Displacement of Malory's Secularization." In Suzuki and Mukai. 179–87.

Newman, Barbara. *From Virile Woman to WomanChrist: Studies in Medieval Religion and Literature*. Philadelphia: University of Pennsylvania Press, 1995.

Nichols, Stephen G. "Solomon's Wife: Deceit, Desire, and the Genealogy of Romance." In *Space, Time, Image, Sign: Essays on Literature and the Visual Arts*. Ed. James Heffernan. New York: Peter Lang, 1987. 19–40.

Nickel, Helmut. "Heraldry." In Lacy, *Encyclopedia*. 230–34.

Niranjana, Tejaswini. *Siting Translation: History, Post-Structuralism, and the Colonial Context*. Berkeley: University of California Press, 1992.

Nitze, William A. "The Beste Glatissant in Arthurian Romance." *Zeitschrift für romanische Philologie* 56 (1936): 409–18.

Noguchi, Shunichi. "The Winchester Malory." *Arthuriana* 5.2 (1995): 15–23.

Nolan, Barbara. *Chaucer and the Tradition of the Roman Antique.* Cambridge, UK: Cambridge University Press, 1992.

Parins, Marylyn Jackson, ed. *Malory: The Critical Heritage.* London: Routledge, 1988.

Parker, Patricia. *Literary Fat Ladies: Rhetoric, Gender, Property.* London: Methuen, 1987.

Parsons, John Carmi. "Ritual and Symbol in the English Medieval Queenship to 1500." In Fradenburg. 60–77.

———. "'Never was a body buried in England with such solemnity and honour': The Burials and Posthumous Commemorations of English Queens to 1500." In Duggan. 317–37.

Patterson, Lee. *Negotiating the Past: The Historical Understanding of Medieval Literature.* Madison: University of Wisconsin Press. 1987.

Pearsall, Derek. "The English Romance in the Fifteenth Century." *Essays and Studies* 29 (1976): 56–83.

Pemberton, Lyn. "Authorial Interventions in the *Tristan en Prose.*" *Neophilologus* 68 (1984): 481–97.

Perret, Michèle. "De l'espace romanceque à la matérialité du livre: L'espace énonciatif des premiers romans en prose." *Poétique* 50 (1982): 173–82.

Pickens, Rupert T. "Autobiography and History in the Vulgate *Estoire* and in the *Prose Merlin.*" In Kibler. 98–116.

Pickford, Cedric E. *L'Évolution du roman arthurien en prose vers la fin du moyen âge d'après le manuscrit 112 du fonds français de la Bibliothèque Nationale.* Paris: Nizet, 1960.

———. "Fiction and the Reading Public in the Fifteenth Century." *Bulletin of the John Rylands Library, Manchester* 45 (1962–63): 423–38.

———. "A Fifteenth-Century Copyist and His Patron." In Whitehead, Diverres, Sutcliffe. 245–62.

Pickstock, Catherine. "Thomas Aquinas and the Quest for the Eucharist." In *Catholicism and Catholicity: Eucharistic Communities in Historical and Contemporary Perspectives.* Ed. Sarah Beckwith. Oxford: Blackwell, 1999. 47–68.

Plummer, John F. "The Quest for Significance in *La Queste del Saint Graal* and Malory's *Tale of the Sankgreal.*" In *Continuations: Essays on Medieval French Literature and Language In Honor of John L. Grigsby.* Ed. Norris J. Lacy and Gloria Torrini-Roblin. Birmingham, AL: Summa, 1989. 107–19.

———. "Frenzy and Females: Subject Formation in Opposition to The Other in the Prose *Lancelot.*" *Arthuriana* 6.4 (1996): 45–51.

Pochoda, Elizabeth T. *Arthurian Propaganda:* Le Morte Darthur *as an Historical Ideal of Life.* Chapel Hill: University of North Carolina Press, 1971.

Porter, Elizabeth. "Chaucer's Knight, the Alliterative *Morte Arthure,* and Medieval Laws of War: a Reconsideration." *Nottingham Medieval Studies* 27 (1983): 56–78.

Pratt, Karen. "*La Mort le roi Artu* as Tragedy." *Nottingham Medieval Studies* 30 (1991): 81–109.

———. "The Cistercians and the *Queste del Saint Graal.*" *Reading Medieval Studies* 21 (1995): 69–96.

———. "The Image of the Queen in Old French Literature." In Duggan. 235–59.

Putter, Ad. "Finding Time for Romance: Medieval Arthurian Literary History." *Medium Ævum* 63 (1994): 1–16.

Ramsey, Lee C. *Chivalric Romances: Popular Literature in Medieval England.* Bloomington: Indiana University Press, 1983.

Richmond, Colin. "Religion and the Fifteenth-Century Gentleman." In *The Church, Politics and Patronage in the Fifteenth Century.* Ed. R. B. Dobson. Gloucester, UK: Sutton, 1984. 193–208.

Rickert, Edith. "King Richard II's Books." *The Library.* 4th Series 13 (1933): 144–47.

Riddy, Felicity. *Sir Thomas Malory.* Leiden: Brill, 1987.

———. "Reading for England: Arthurian Literature and National Consciousness." *BBIAS* 43 (1991): 314–32.

———. "Contextualizing *Le Morte Darthur:* Empire and Civil War." In Archibald and Edwards. 55–73.

———. "Chivalric Nationalism and the Holy Grail in John Hardyng's Chronicle." In *The Grail: A Casebook.* Ed. Dhira B. Mahoney. New York: Garland, 2000. 397–414.

Rooney, Anne. *Hunting in Middle English Literature.* Cambridge, UK: Brewer, 1993.

Rossignol, Rosalyn. "The Holiest Vessel: Maternal Aspects of the Grail." *Arthuriana* 5.1 (1995): 52–61.

Rothwell, William. "The Role of French in Thirteenth-Century England." *Bulletin of the John Rylands Library, University of Manchester* 58 (1975–76): 445–66.

———. "The Trilingual England of Geoffrey Chaucer." *Studies in the Age of Chaucer* 16 (1994): 47–67.

Rouse, R. H., and M. A. Rouse. "*Ordinatio* and *Compilatio* Revisited." In *Ad Litteram: Authoritative Texts and Their Medieval Readers.* Ed. Mark D. Jordan and Kent Emery, Jr. Notre Dame, IN: University of Notre Dame Press, 1992. 113–34.

Roussel, Claude. "Le Jeu des formes et des couleurs: observations sur 'la beste glatissant.'" *Romania* 104 (1983): 49–82.

Rubin, Miri. *Corpus Christi: The Sacrament in the Later Middle Ages.* Cambridge, UK: Cambridge University Press, 1991.

Rutter, Russell. "William Caxton and Literary Patronage." *Studies in Philology* 84.4 (1987): 440–70.

Ryding, William W. *Structure in Medieval Narrative.* The Hague: Mouton, 1971.

Saintsbury, George. *The Flourishing of Romance and the Rise of Allegory.* Edinburgh: Blackwood, 1897.

Salda, Michael N. "Reconsidering Vinaver's Sources for Malory's 'Tristram.'" *Modern Philology* 88 (1991): 373–81.

———, ed. *Arthuriana* 5.2 (1995).

Sanday, Peggy Reeves. "The Socio-Cultural Context of Rape: A Cross-Cultural Study." In *Gender Violence: Interdisciplinary Perspectives.* Ed. Laura L. O'Toole and Jessica R. Schiffman. New York: New York University Press, 1997. 52–66.

Sanders, Arnold A. "Malory's Transitional Formulae: Fate, Volition, and Narrative Structure." *Arthurian Interpretations* 2 (1987): 27–46.

Saunders, Corinne J. "Malory's *Book of Huntynge*: the *Tristram* section of the *Morte Darthur.*" *Medium Ævum* 62 (1993): 270–84.

Savage, Grace Armstrong. "Father and Son in the *Queste del Saint Graal.*" *Romance Philology* 31 (1977): 1–16.

Scarry, Elaine. *The Body in Pain: The Making and Unmaking of the World.* New York: Oxford University Press, 1985.

Scattergood, V. J. "Two Medieval Book Lists." *The Library* 5th series 23 (1968): 236–39.

Scheps, Walter. "The Thematic Unity of *Lancelot of the Laik.*" *Studies in Scottish Literature* 5 (1967–68): 167–75.

Schmolke-Hasselmann, Beate. *The Evolution of Arthurian Romance: The Verse Tradition from Chrétien to Froissart.* Trans. Margaret and Roger Middleton. Cambridge, UK: Cambridge University Press, 1998.

Schroeder, Horst. *Der Topos der Nine Worthies in Literatur und bildender Kunst.* Göttingen: Vandenhoeck and Ruprecht, 1971.

Seaton, Ethel, *Sir Richard Roos.* London: Rupert Hart-Davis, 1961.

Seymour, M. C. *A Catalogue of Chaucer Manuscripts: Volume I. Works Before the Canterbury Tales.* Aldershot, UK: Scolar Press, 1995.

Shaw, Sally. "Caxton and Malory." In *Essays on Malory.* Ed. J. A. W. Bennett. Oxford: Clarendon Press, 1863. 114–45.

Shichtman, Martin B. "Politicizing the Ineffable: The *Queste del Saint Graal* and Malory's "Tale of the Sankgreal." In Shichtman and Carley. 163–79.

———. "Perceval's Sister: Genealogy, Virginity, and Blood." *Arthuriana* 9.2 (1999): 11–20.

———, and James P. Carley, eds. *Culture and the King: The Social Implications of the Arthurian Legend: Essays in Honor of Valerie M. Lagorio.* Albany: State University of New York Press, 1994.

———, and Laurie A. Finke. "Profiting From the Past: History as Symbolic Capital in the *Historia Regum Britanniae.*" *Arthurian Literature* 12 (1993): 1–35.

Short, Ian. "Patrons and Polyglots: French Literature in Twelfth-Century England." In *Anglo-Norman Studies 14: Proceedings of the Battle Conference, 1991.* Ed. Marjorie Chibnall. Woodbridge, UK: Brewer, 1992. 229–49.

Silverman, Kaja. *Male Subjectivity at the Margins.* New York: Routledge, 1992.

Simon, Sherry. *Gender in Translation: Cultural Identity and the Politics of Transmission.* London: Routledge, 1996.

Simons, John. "Northern *Octavian* and the question of class." In *Romance in Medieval England.* Ed. Maldwyn Mills, Jennifer Fellows, and Carol M. Meale. Cambridge, UK: Brewer, 1991. 105–111.

Simpson, James. "Ethics and Interpretation: Reading Wills in Chaucer's *Legend of Good Women.*" *Studies in the Age of Chaucer* 20 (1998): 73–100.

Smith, Jeremy. "Language and Style in Malory." In Archibald and Edwards, 97–113.

Smithers, G. V. "The Style of *Hauelok.*" *Medium Ævum* 57 (1988): 190–218.

Spearing, A. C. *The Medieval Poet as Voyeur: Looking and Listening in Medieval Love-Narratives.* Cambridge, UK: Cambridge University Press, 1993.

Spiegel, Gabrielle M. *Romancing the Past: The Rise of Vernacular Prose Historiography in Thirteenth-Century France.* Berkeley: University of California Press, 1993.

Spisak, James W., ed. *Studies in Malory.* Kalamazoo: Medieval Institute Publications, Western Michigan University, 1985.

Stewart-Brown, Ronald. "The Scrope and Grosvenor Controversy, 1385–1391." *Transactions of the Historic Society of Lancashire and Cheshire* 89 (1937): 1–22.

Strachey, James, gen. ed. *The Standard Edition of the Complete Psychological Works of Sigmund Freud.* 24 vols. London: Hogarth Press, 1955–75.

Sturges, Robert S. *Medieval Interpretation: Models of Reading in Literary Narrative, 1100–1500.* Carbondale: Southern Illinois University Press, 1991.

———. "La(ca)ncelot." *Arthurian Interpretations* 4 (1990): 12–23.

———. "The Epistemology of the Bedchamber: Textuality, Knowledge, and the Representation of Adultery in Malory and the Prose *Lancelot.*" *Arthuriana* 7.4 (1997): 47–62.

Suzuki, Takashi, and Tsuyoshi Mukai, eds. *Arthurian and Other Studies Presented to Shunichi Noguchi.* Cambridge, UK: Brewer, 1993.

Takamiya, Toshiyuki, and Derek Brewer, eds. *Aspects of Malory.* Cambridge, UK: Brewer, 1981.

Thomas, Calvin. *Male Matters: Masculinity, Anxiety, and the Male Body on the Line.* Urbana: University of Illinois Press, 1996.

Thompson, John J. "Popular Reading Tastes in Middle English Religious and Didactic Literature." in *From Medieval To Medievalisem.* Ed. John Simons. Basingstoke: Macmillan, 1992. 82–100.

Thornton, Ginger, and Krista May. "Malory as Feminist?" In Hanks. 43–53.

Trachsler, Richard. "Brehus sans Pitié: portrait-robot du criminel arthurien." In *La Violence dans le monde médiéval, Sénéfiance* 36 (1994): 525–42.

———. *Clôtures du Cycle Arthurien: Etude et textes.* Geneva: Droz, 1996.

Traxler, Janina P. "Observations on the Beste Glatissant in the *Tristan en prose.*" *Neophilologus* 74 (1990): 499–509.

———. "Ironic Juxtaposition as Intertextuality in the Prose *Tristan.*" In *Text and Intertext in Medieval Arthurian Literature.* Ed. Norris J. Lacy. New York: Garland, 1996. 147–63.

Turville-Petre, Thorlac. *England the Nation: Language, Literature, and National Identity, 1290–1340.* Oxford: Clarendon Press, 1996.

Tyson, Diana. "King Arthur as a Literary Device in French Vernacular History Writing of the Fourteenth Century." *BBIAS* 33 (1981): 237–57.

Vale, Juliet. "Law and Diplomacy in the Alliterative *Morte Arthure.*" *Nottingham Medieval Studies* 23 (1979): 31–46.

———. *Edward III and Chivalry: Chivalric Society and Its Context 1270–1350.* Woodbridge, UK: Boydell, 1982.

Van Coolput, Colette-Anne. *Aventures quérant et le sens du monde: Aspects de la réception productive des premiers romans du Graal cycliques dans le Tristan en prose.* Leuven: Leuven University Press, 1986.

Vial, Claire. "Images of Kings and Kingship: Chaucer, Malory, and the Representation of Royal Entries." In *"Divers toyes mengled": Essays on Medieval and*

Renaissance Culture in honour of André Lascombes. Ed. Michel Bitot, with Roberta Mullini and Peter Happé. Tours: Université François Rabelais, 1996. 43–54.

Vogel, Bertram. "Secular Politics and the Date of *Lancelot of the Laik*." *Studies in Philology* 40 (1943): 1–13.

Wagner, Anthony. *Historic Heraldry of Britain*. Chichester, UK: Phillimore, 1972.

Wallace, David, ed. *The Cambridge History of Medieval English Literature*. Cambridge, UK: Cambridge University Press, 1999.

Ward, H. L. D. *The Catalogue of Romances in the Department of Manuscripts in the British Museum*. 2 vols. London: Longmans, 1883, 1893, repr. 1961.

Warm, Robert. "Arthur and the Giant of Mont St Michel: The Politics of Empire Building in the Later Middle Ages." *Nottingham Medieval Studies* 41 (1997): 57–71.

Warren, Michelle. *History on the Edge: Excalibur and the Borders of Britain, 1100–1300*. Minneapolis: University of Minnesota Press, 2000.

Watson, Nicholas. "Censorship and Cultural Change in Late-Medieval England: Vernacular Theology, the Oxford Translation Debate, and Arundel's Constitutions of 1409." *Speculum* 70 (1995): 822–64.

Welsh, Andrew. "Lancelot at the Crossroads in Malory and Steinbeck." *Philological Quarterly* 70 (1991): 485–502.

Wheeler, Bonnie. "'The Prowess of Hands': The Psychology of Alchemy in Malory's 'Tale of Sir Gareth'." In Shichtman and Carley. 180–95.

White, Hayden. "The Historical Text as Literary Artifact." In *The Writing of History: Literary Form and Historical Understanding*. Ed. R. H. Canary and H. Kozicki. Madison: University of Wisconsin Press, 1978. 41–62.

Whitehead, F. A. H. Diverres, and F. E. Sutcliffe, eds. *Medieval Miscellany Presented to Eugène Vinaver*. Manchester: Manchester University Press, 1965.

Whiting, Bartlett Jere. *Proverbs, Sentences, and Proverbial Phrases from English writings, mainly before 1500*. Cambridge, MA: Harvard University Press, 1968.

Whitman, Jon. "The Body and the Struggle for the Soul of Romance." In *The Body and the Soul in Medieval Literature*. Ed. Piero Boitani and Anna Torti. Cambridge, UK: Brewer, 1999. 31–61.

Williams, Andrea M. L. "The Enchanted Swords and the Quest for the Holy Grail: Metaphoric Structure in *La Queste del Saint Graal*." *French Studies* 48 (1994): 385–401.

Wimsatt, James I. "The Idea of a Cycle: Malory, the Lancelot-Grail, and the *Prose Tristan*." In Kibler. 206–18.

———. "Segwarydes' Wife and Competing Perspectives within Malory's *Tale of Sir Tristram* and Its Model, the Prose *Tristan*. In *Retelling Tales: Essays in Honor of Russell Peck*. Ed. Thomas Hahn and Alan Lupack. Woodbridge, UK: Brewer, 1997. 321–39.

Withrington, John. "Caxton, Malory, and The Roman War in The *Morte Darthur*." *Studies in Philology* (1992): 350–66.

Wright, Thomas L. "On the Genesis of Malory's Gareth." *Speculum* 57 (1982): 569–82.

Wurtele, Douglas. "A Reappraisal of the Scottish *Lancelot of the Laik.*" *University of Ottawa Quarterly* 46 (1976): 68–82.

Ziegler, Georgianna. "The Hunt as Structural Device in Malory's *Morte Darthur.*" *Tristania* 5 (1979): 15–22.

Zink, Michel. "Une mutation de la conscience littéraire: Le langage romanesque à travers des exemples français du XIIe siècle." *Cahiers de Civilisation Médiévale, Xe-XIIe siècles* 24 (1981): 3–27.

Zumthor, Paul. *Merlin le prophète: un thème de la littérature polémique de l'historiographie et des romans.* Lausanne: Payot, 1943.

INDEX

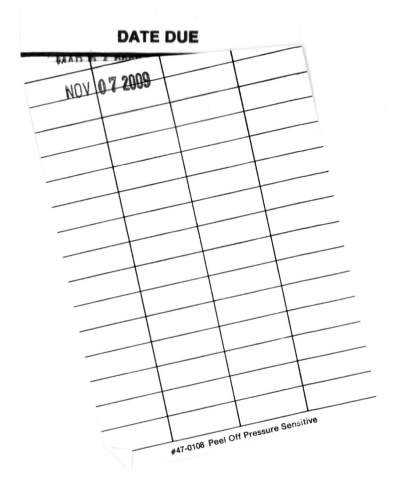